Come Love
a Stranger

Come Love
a Stranger

Kathleen E. Woodiwiss

RHAPSODY ROMANCE CLASSICS

Garden City, New York

To my Aunt Elizabeth,
whose dignity has and shall always remain.

With love,
K.E.W.

Whither will I wander,
Thither will I roam
'Round the world, and back again,
This way will I go,
Marching down the street hill,
Tramping up again.
Ever will I ramble,
'Til I'm home again

- *Prologue* -

The quiet peace of the moonlit river was broken by the hushed murmur of voices and the steady pulsing of pistons in a powerful engine.
The rushing burble of water beneath a stout hull softly harmonized
with the long sighs of these monster steam pistons and the chugging
splash of water under the paddle wheel as the huge floating palace
came around the bend and left in its wake a luminescent path
beneath the chasing moon. Lanterns shone from every deck, seeming to set the stern-wheeler ablaze with lights, but inside the pilothouse, which commanded a position well forward and high on the
uppermost deck, only a binnacle lamp was lighted, giving off a dim
glow as the helmsman grasped the wheel and scanned the oil-black
surface of the river far ahead. The captain stood close beside the
helmsman and, in a low voice, warned of approaching landmarks or
shoals. Under his direction, the steamer slid with firm, square-
shouldered ease around a sandbar and, further up the river, a floating tangle that had attached itself to a small uprooted tree.

A tall, broad-shouldered man leaned against a window jamb at
the rear of the pilothouse and smiled to himself as he felt the sure,
unfaltering pulse of the ship vibrate through the deck beneath his
feet. In the curve of his arm he held a young woman, and she nestled
close against his lean, muscular frame, savoring the relaxed pride of
her husband as his *River Witch* made her virgin voyage up the river.

Removing the pipe from his mouth, the captain turned his head
aside slightly and spoke over his shoulder: "She handles well for a
new one, sir." There was also a gruff pride in his voice. "A wee bit
tight, but as light on her feet as a frightened doe."

"That she is, Captain." Absently the tall man stroked his thumb
across the back of his wife's arm. "That she is."

The captain puffed again on his pipe before he remarked, "The boilers are well seasoned, and the pistons stroke with barely a whisper. Why, we must have made a good eight knots during the daylight hours, and that was against a healthy current. The river is a little higher than usual this year."

He leaned forward to speak with the helmsman as he pointed with his pipe to a large mass that floated far ahead of them near a turn in the river. "You'd better take her close to shore as you go around the bend. Otherwise, we might get tangled up in that."

The tall man hardly heard his captain's comments as he glanced down at the woman at his side and met the smiling green eyes. His arm tightened about her briefly, and her fingertips caressed his vested chest in answer. The man dragged his gaze away from her. "We'll leave you to your duties, Captain. Should you have a need, I'll be in my cabin."

"Good night, sir." He tipped his hat to the lady. "Missus."

Leaving the pilothouse, the couple made their way out along the narrow walkway to the stairs. They paused on the lower deck, and their two shadows merged as one as she leaned back against his chest. Together they admired the idyllic scene of silver-plated river and frothy white path stretching out behind.

"She's beautiful, Ashton," she murmured softly.

"So are you, my love," he whispered in her ear.

She turned within the circle of his arms and tenderly caressed the strong, manly line of his jaw. "I can hardly believe we're married. It seems like only yesterday I was resolving to be a spinster."

Ashton chuckled as he found humor in her statement. "Wasn't it only yesterday?"

Her soft laughter joined his as she shrugged. "Well, it must have been at least a month or so ago." She raised her arms, laying them around his neck, and pressed the length of her body against his. "Do you always sweep a lady off her feet in such haste?"

"Only when a lady captures my heart as fiercely as you have done." He peered down at her with a questioning brow raised. "Any regrets for not waiting for your father's approval?"

"None!" she assured him fervently before she returned an inquiry to him. "And you? Are you sorry you're no longer a bachelor?"

"My darling Lierin," he sighed as his lips lowered to hers. "I never knew what living was until you came into my life."

From somewhere below a sudden soft "pop" made Ashton pause and lift his head to listen. The sound was followed by a loud "clank" and then a louder "bang!" A shattering screech began and grew in volume until the couple's ears fairly ached. A billowing cloud of steam, roiling up from the boilers, engulfed the rear of the *River Witch*, and slowly the paddle wheel shuddered to a stop. The once graceful boat became an ungainly raft as she lost way and began to swing broadside to the current. Shouts of alarm came from below, and in the pilothouse the captain snatched for the whistle lanyard only to be rewarded with a bellicose wheeze as the last of the steam pressure faded. He snatched for the bell chain and kept yanking it to broadcast a warning to all who could hear.

The large mass of floating debris drifted nearer and, though it seemed impossible, took on more of a rectangle shape. It slammed into the side of the stern-wheeler with enough force to send a shudder through it. Almost immediately a swarm of men sprang from the piles of brush that had been used to disguise the now discernible barge and threw out grappling hooks to snare the wounded *River Witch*.

"Pirates!" Ashton shouted the single, dreaded word. Almost immediately a shot rang out, and a sound like an angry bee whizzed past his ear. He ducked, pulling his wife down with him, and barked out several more warnings to the crew as the brigands leaped across to the lower deck of the steamer. Brandishing various weapons, they sprinted along the gallery toward the stairs and climbed to the upper decks. Other shots began to swell as passengers and crew alike realized their peril and snatched whatever weapons they could lay hold of. The decks erupted in bedlam as the thirty or more river pirates scrambled to engage them, and there were bellows of challenge and rage as fighting broke out on every quarter.

Ashton tore off his dark coat and threw it over his wife's shoulders, making her pale-hued gown less of a target. Crouching low, they began to work their way toward the stairs. More shots zinged past, and he pressed her against the outer wall of a cabin as he shielded her body with his own. The sound of running feet drew Ashton's attention to the deck behind him, and he spun about to meet the vicious charge of a knife-wielding brigand. With a startled scream Lierin stumbled across to the railing as the force of the man's attack drove Ashton back against the wall. A frantic struggle ensued as the pirate tried to bury his blade in his opponent's flesh.

Similar battles had spread throughout the *River Witch* while the captain and helmsman struggled to regain some control of their clumsy vessel. The bow scraped across a bar they had previously passed, and the boat tilted to port as the currents lifted her up and over. She struck the main shoal and lurched hard to starboard, sending those in the pilothouse ricocheting off the walls of its narrow confines. The helmsman fell, blood streaming from a wound in his head, while the captain sank to his knees in stunned confusion.

The violence of the starboard lurch flung Lierin over the railing and far out into the black night. Her scream dwindled as she fell, and it ended abruptly in a loud splash. The sound cauterized Ashton's mind, and fear gave him the strength of a raging bull. Throwing off his assailant, he sprang to his feet and drove a booted heel into the other's face. The man went limp, and Ashton flung himself against the rail. His wife's name exploded from his lips as his eyes searched the flickering dark water for some trace of her. A gleam of something pale rose from the depths, and she broke the surface. Yanking off his boots, he grabbed the rail, intending to climb atop it and dive into the black void for below, but a crushing jolt took him in the side, spinning him halfway around as the roar of a pistol shot reverberated within his head.

"Lierin! Lierin!" his mind screamed as his legs slowly crumpled beneath him. He had to save her! He had to! She was his life, and without her, naught else mattered. He collapsed upon the deck, and the night seemed darker than before as he labored to lift his head. Through a haze, he saw a snarling, bearded face with a mop of curly black hair hanging about it. The thief came forward with a long-bladed knife held ready, but somewhere a rifle discharged, and the brigand halted in sudden shock and gaped in disbelief as a ragged, bloody hole appeared in the side of his chest. His right arm fell limp, and as he stared, the knife slid out of his numb fingers. The darkness closed in around Ashton, and he never knew when the pirate staggered back down the stairs.

Lierin was not as fragile as she looked, and her determination to survive had flared strong in her mind. The thought had flashed through her consciousness that she had not found love so recently just to let it be rudely snatched from her grasp. She struggled valiantly to stay afloat as her once buoyant skirts threatened to drag her down again into the murky depths. But fight she did . . . until she saw the flash of the pirate's pistol and her husband's fall. The thief ran forward to ensure his work was finished, and her spirit died. Only a gnawing emptiness remained where joy and hope had been only a few moments before. The current caught her skirts and whirled her about as it dragged her into the shadows. The cold dark waters closed over her head a second time, and the struggle to rise above the surface became too much for her. She sank into the stygian void, and slowly her arms ceased their labor.

– Chapter One –

March 9, 1833, Mississippi

A circling, confused wind had pelted the earth with a slashing rain for most of the day, but as night settled its ebon shroud upon the land, the driving storm and the erratic breezes abated. The countryside grew quiet in hushed relief. The very air seemed to hang in breathless suspense as an eerie white mist formed close upon the ground. The wraithlike vapors twined in aimless questing through the marshes and black-shadowed thickets, spreading ever onward, filling low hollows and rills and curling about massive trunks. High above the invading tendrils, gnarled branches waggled their mossy beards and sent small droplets plummeting into the roiling mass. Now and again the pale moon pierced the broken, scudding clouds and, with its silvered light, created an unearthly landscape of dark shapes rising from a luminous haze. A decrepit brick mansion, hugged by a cluster of trees in an overgrown yard and bounded on four sides by a tall, sharply spiked iron fence, seemed to merge with the small cookhouse in the rear. Together they drifted in the sea of fog as time slowed its passing. For a fleeting moment nothing moved and nothing stirred.

A squeak of hinges intruded into the silence, but the sound ended almost as quickly as it began. A bush twitched unnaturally by the back door, and a shadowy form cautiously emerged from behind the shrub. A waiting hush prevailed as the phantom carefully surveyed the enclosed yard; then like a large, winged bat the darkly cloaked figure flitted through the swirling vapors to the side of the house and settled beneath billowing folds at its base. There, the latticework between a pair of stone supports had been pulled away, and gloved hands hastily struck flint to steel over a small, sheltered mound of gunpowder. Sparks splashed outward until a sudden blaze flared up and became a cloud of dense gray smoke which mingled with the mists. Three slow fuses came to life in the flash and continued to glow after the powder was spent. Burning steadily, they trailed off in different directions beneath the house, meandering ever so slowly toward shallow, gunpowder-filled gullies that led to separate piles of oil-soaked rags and dry kindling. A nervous chittering and squealing grew as the fuses shortened, and as if sensing the approaching disaster, the furred denizens of the dank crawl space fled their burrows and nests to scatter abroad in the night.

The stealthy shadow retreated from the house and quickly crossed to the iron gate. A broken chain was lifted from it, and the earth-bound specter slipped through the opening and dashed toward the edge of the woods where a horse was tethered. It was a fine, tall gelding with a white star blazoned upon his forehead, an animal made for swiftness. Once astride, the rider held him in check, keeping him on the sodden turf to muffle the sound of their passage. When the need for caution was behind them, the quirt lifted and came slashing down, setting the steed to flight. Of a common hue with the night, the pair were quickly swallowed by darkness.

A deathlike stillness followed their passing, and the lonely house seemed to moan in sorrow for its impending doom. While jewel-bright raindrops fell like tears from its rotting eaves, a low, confused murmur began to drift from the house. Soft cries, distressed whimpers, and the mad, muted laugh of some demented soul shredded the night with haunting, mindless sounds. The distant moon hid its face behind a thick cloud and continued on its arc across the sky, heedless of time and these earthly things.

The triad of hissing serpents slithered with blind obedience along their prelaid paths until bright flashes marked their arrival at their goals; then larger heaps of gunpowder sputtered alight, suffusing the nearby mists with a pale, flickering yellow light. The fires jumped and spread as they feasted on the oiled rags and dry timbers, and soon the fresh-born flames licked hungrily at wooden floors. One of the front rooms began to show a dim light in the windows, and it brightened apace until the room was filled with a growing inferno and the black bars that covered the windows stood out in gaunt relief. The heat intensified, and the crystal panes burst, spraying shards of glass outward and allowing the flaming tongues to escape and lick upward over the brick walls.

The low, disconcerted moans that had come from the upper level became high-pitched shrieks of fear and deep-chested cries of outrage. Gnarled fingers clawed frantically at the bars, while bloodied fists smashed panes of glass. A heavy pounding sounded on the locked front door, and a moment later it crashed open, spilling forth a huge hulk of a man. He shielded his bald pate with both hands as if expecting to be struck down and scurried far out into the yard before he turned and stared in awe, much like a small child viewing some great spectacular event. An attendant escaped from the rear of the house and fled into the darkness, leaving the others to fumble in haste with reluctant keys and stubborn locks. Wailing cries and sobbing pleas came from those imprisoned behind locked doors, piercing even the loudening roar of the flames. One hefty hireling sought the release of those he could easily reach, while another of a slighter build was spurred to herculean effort by the sure knowledge that no one else would free the trapped inmates of the madhouse.

Soon a living stream of straggly, pitifully confused humans began to emerge from the burning house. They were garbed in various stages of dress; some had snatched shirts and gowns before being dragged or hustled from their cells. A few had seized their precious blankets and fared better for their foresight. Attaining safety, they huddled together in scattered groups like bewildered children, unable to comprehend what had befallen them.

Time and again the dauntless attendant braved the inferno to bring the helpless to safety until timbers began falling, blocking his way. Stumbling from the burning asylum for the last time, he carried a frail, elderly man out and dropped to his knees in the yard, where he gasped air into his aching lungs. Spent and exhausted, the attendant took no notice of the creaking gate or the several forms flitting through it. The escaping inmates fled into the brush, and the shadowy blur of their garments was quickly lost in the oblivion of darkness.

A reddish aura rose from the growing core of heat and flame and spread into the night sky, while a heavy, rolling mass of choking gray billowed above it. The constant roar deadened the ears to any other sound, and the hoofbeats came unnoticed as the long-legged gelding returned to that same hill where he had earlier trod. He was reined to a halt by the darkly cloaked figure on his back. Within the deep folds of the cowl, translucent eyes shone with the reflected light of the fire as they searched the clustered groups inside the yard. For a moment the gaze was steadfast and intense; then the rider turned, as if startled, to scan the crest of the hill behind. Slim hands jerked the reins, pulling the mount's head aside, and a thump of a heel urged him on again, this time into the dark, mottled shadow of the woods. The steed's flaring nostrils gave evidence of their rapid flight, but the one on his back allowed him no pause. It was a reckless, zigzagging dash through the wooded coppice, but one that seemed capably directed by the rider. The gelding soared over a fallen tree that lay across their path and came to earth again, flinging damp clods of leaf and mud helter-skelter while it scattered a chilling breath of fear before its flashing hooves.

The rushing wind snatched the woolen hood away, freeing long, curling tresses from its confines and whipping them out like a waving gonfalon. Spiteful twigs plucked at the silken strands and clawed at the flapping cloak as the girl rode past. Oblivious to these minor attacks, she raced on, throwing a hurried glance over her shoulder. Her eyes swept back along the trail as if she expected to find some fearsome beast following in slavering pursuit. The sudden movement of a deer darting through the trees brought a startled gasp from her, and she urged the gelding on, not caring how swiftly they flew along the untried path.

An open field, well lighted by the moon and raggedly cloaked with drifting shreds of fog, beckoned through the thinning trees. A shallow sense of relief surged within her throbbing breast. The rolling mead held a promise of an easier path where the horse could be pressed to its fastest gait. Almost eagerly she struck her bare heel against the steed's side, and the gelding responded with a surging bound, lifting his hooves and springing forward to clear the low spot where the mists had gathered.

Suddenly a bellowed, wordless warning, joined by the squeal of brake shoes dragging against turning wheels, broke into the rider's consciousness. The gelding's forefeet had not yet come to earth when she realized that she had plunged her mount directly into the path of an oncoming team and carriage. Cold, congealing horror seized her as the charging steeds bore down upon her, and for the barest instant she thought she could feel their snorting breath and see their blazing eyes. The black driver fought frantically to turn the racing team aside or stop the skidding carriage, but it was too late. A scream sprang from her throat, but it was quickly silenced by a jarring impact that struck the breath from her.

The wild gyrations of the closed landau had torn Ashton Wingate from his dozing and nearly turned him out of his seat, giving him cause to doubt his driver's sanity, but when the conveyance careened sideways through the slippery mire, he had a clear view of the collision and its result. A flailing form catapulted away from the tumbling mount and soared through the air like an injured bird, then fell, striking the road embankment, and rolled down into the ditch. Before the carriage slid to a halt, Ashton had flung off his cloak and was out the door, swinging down. As he raced along the slippery road, his anxious gaze reached beyond the wildly thrashing horse to where the motionless figure lay partially submerged in the water at the bottom of the gully. The mists swirled about him as he slid down the slick bank. He splashed through the frigid water, heedless of the mud that sucked at his boots, and braced a knee against the embankment as he pulled the unconscious girl from the murky riverlet and propped her against the sodden, overgrown bank. Her face was half covered by a snarled mass of wet hair, and leaning close, he could not detect any stirring of breath from her lips. He freed her arm and experienced a sudden trepidation as it hung limp in his grasp. He failed to find a pulse in the finely tapered wrist, and almost in dread he pressed his fingers against the slim column of her throat. There, beneath the chilled skin, he found what he sought . . . the assurance that she was alive, at least for the moment.

Ashton glanced up to find his driver standing on the shoulder of the roadway above him. It was the coachman's wont in the colder months, what with being exposed on the open seat, to secure his prized beaver hat atop his head by wrapping a long woolen scarf over its crown and knotting it snugly beneath his chin. Now in fretful worry, he was twisting the loose ends of the scarf in his huge gentle hands, unwittingly pulling his headgear down upon his ears.

"Calm yourself, Hiram. She's still breathing," Ashton assured the frightened man. The horse screamed again in pure anguish, nearly drowning his words, and lunged about as it tried to rise. Ashton indicated the maimed steed with a jerk of his hand. "Hiram! Fetch that old horse pistol you have in the boot and put that animal out of its misery!"

"Yassuh! Ah do it right now!" Though the task was hardly a pleasant one, Hiram was relieved to have something to occupy him.

Ashton bent over the girl again. She showed no sign of regaining consciousness, but lay inert against the bank where he had placed her. The chilly water was already making his legs ache, and her thoroughly soaked cloak was tangled about her like a frigid cocoon. He searched out the silken frogs that held the garment in place and plucked them free. His brows rose sharply in surprise when he peeled the sodden cloth away. Even in the unsteady light of the carriage lanterns he could see she was no fledgling lass as he had first supposed. The clinging wetness of the thin nightgown readily displayed the fact that she was a woman, still quite young but certainly mature enough to cause him to adjust his thinking.

A gunshot cracked sharply through the stillness, bringing Ashton's head up with a jerk. The thrashing died away with a gurgling moan, and the horse slowly collapsed, to slide into the water at the bottom of the ditch. Against the glow of the moonlit mists, Hiram was darkly etched with sagging shoulders. Ashton knew the servant had a sympathy for animals beyond other men, but the events of the moment left no time for such mourning when a more precious life was at stake.

"Hiram! Come on! We've got to get this girl home!"

"Yassuh!"

Spurred to action, the black came running back as Ashton extracted the injured woman from the bonds of her soggy cloak and lifted her in his arms. He raised her high, letting her head loll over his shoulder, then began the scrambling struggle up the slippery embankment to the roadway. Hiram was there to lend a hand the last step or two and sprinted on ahead to open the carriage door. As Ashton climbed inside, the servant mumbled a fervent prayer that all would be well. Death had been a cruel visitor to the Wingate man in the last ten years, first plucking the lives of his parents during a storm which swept away their home in the Carolinas; then three years ago it had come in the guise of a gang of river pirates who had disabled his stern-wheeler and caused the drowning of his new bride. Hiram was sure that if there was a choice, neither of them would elect to see the dreaded dark avenger for some time to come.

"Give me a moment to get settled," Ashton tossed over his shoulder as he placed the woman on his cloak and gathered it about her.

"Is she . . . is she gonna be all right, massa?" Hiram asked anxiously, craning his neck to see past the other's back.

"I just don't know, Hiram. I'm sorry," Ashton replied. He lifted his unconscious charge onto his lap where his own body would cushion hers and she could be held safe from further bruising during the rough ride ahead. As he cradled the seemingly fragile form close against him, a scent of jasmine wafted through his senses. A pang of sweet recall tugged at his memory, giving him pause, but he thrust the sensation away with a fierce determination. It could not be, and he would not let his mind torture him with impossible yearnings.

He reached up a hand to brush the tangled web of red tresses from her face. The begrimed mass resisted his effort, but with gentle persistance he separated the strands and swept a portion behind her ear. As he leaned back and the light caught the pale visage, he drew in his breath sharply. His mind tumbled to a halt, and he was held frozen by what he saw.

"Lierin?" he breathed as a piercing pain of longing went through him.

Like an avalanche, memories of that time in New Orleans when he had met and married his young bride came crushing down upon him. Though he had been assured that Lierin was dead, he was now struck with the thought that a horrible mistake had been made and it was she who was with him now. If not, the resemblance this young woman bore to his late wife was, to say the least, most startling.

Hiram failed to find reassurance in the wide range of expressions that crossed his master's face. "Massa, what's wrong? Yo look like yo just seen a ghost."

"Maybe I have," Ashton murmured in stunned amazement. An overriding hope began to build within him, mingling with an odd mixture of elation and fear. If this was Lierin . . .

The urgency of the moment pressed upon him, and his tone conveyed his growing anxiety as he commanded, "Hiram! Get up there, and lay the leather to those horses! Hurry!"

The startled man slammed the door and quickly climbed up to his place. Ashton braced his legs against the far seat as the brakes creaked loose and Hiram's shout echoed through the still night. "Yeeeaah! G'yap dere!"

The well-matched team lunged forward, taking their duties to heart, and in the cool evening air the steam rolled from their backs as Hiram drove them at a breakneck pace around a bend, not even checking their stride when the wheels caught a rut and the closed landau lurched sharply sideways. Ashton swayed with the careening motion and cradled his precious charge as if it were his own heart he carried. As he bent over her, his spirits soared with unaccustomed joy, and he closed his eyes as a prayer filled his soul: "Oh, God, let it be Lierin . . . and let her live!"

The shifting light of the carriage lanterns lent her pale skin a golden hue that belied the chilling touch of it while it teased him with haunting views of the delicate features. His fingers trembled and his brow creased in a pained frown as he tenderly touched the discolored swelling on her forehead, that same which once he might have kissed with loving affection. His emotions were unmercifully churned. While his hopes climbed to lofty heights with the hope that this was his own beloved Lierin, his fears at the same time ran as deep as a bottomless cavern, for he could not guess the extent of her injuries. It would be cruel fate if, after finding his wife alive, she was again taken from him. Indeed, he might find himself incapable of coping with the tragedy all over again.

Letting out his breath slowly, Ashton attempted to gather his scattered thoughts into some semblance of logical order. Was he just being plagued by memories of his dead wife? Was he going mad? Did he see a dearly remembered visage on another because of some trick of his mind? Was it only the rising hope of an aborted dream that made him think that it was she? After all, he had known Lierin less than a month before exchanging vows with her. Several of his friends in New Orleans had teased him about marrying her in an anxious fever while barely knowing her name. Then the black hand of tragedy had struck, and he had seen his love swirled away from him in currents dark and foul. Since that time he had counted the days until they had aged into three years, a month, and a week short a day. Now here she was again . . . or some young woman incredibly like his memories of Lierin. He had to allow that there was room for error, and yet he resisted his doubts, though he knew he could be leaving himself open to more pain and grief.

Gently he traced his lean fingers along her cheek, pausing at her temple until he felt the faint throbbing of a pulse. A sigh of relief slipped from him, but he could not ease the pounding of his heart.

A shout from Hiram announced their approach to the plantation house, and Ashton peered through the darkness toward the distant glow of lanterns that marked the mansion's presence among the huge towering oaks. Beyond sweeping grounds Belle Chêne stood with the magnificence of a French château, buttressed on either side by wide wings and tall trees. The thought flickered through his consciousness that he was at last bringing home his love.

As the landau neared the structure, Ashton became aware of the carriages crowding the lane and a number of horses tied to the hitching posts. He could only surmise that his grandmother had seized upon the excuse of his homecoming to have a party. His eyes passed gently over his companion. The elder lady would hardly be expecting this latest turn of events. His entrance with an unconscious and improperly garbed woman would likely give her a turn. After his brief courtship and marriage in New Orleans, Amanda Wingate had become leery of her grandson's jaunts downriver, and here he was returning from another such trip. It mattered naught to him that the incident would add grist to the grinding mill of gossip, but he had to consider that his grandmother was getting on in years.

Hiram stood on the brake, and in the lane the tethered horses stamped their feet in sudden distrust of this apparition that careened wildly through their midst. The landau was brought to a skidding stop in front of the verandah. There, the black man scrambled down and hurried to snatch open the carriage door. Ashton bundled his cloak carefully about his treasured burden and pressed her head upon his shoulder to protect her face from the crisp air. As he did so, the illusive scent tore through his senses once again, unlocking all the yearnings he had held in check these past three years. Their time together might have been brief, but he knew without a doubt that it had not been lacking in quality and worth.

"Send a fast rider for Dr. Page," Ashton barked over his shoulder as he bore her up the steps.

"Yassuh!" Hiram was quick to respond. "Ah send Latham ridin' out lickety-split."

Ashton's long, swift strides took him across the porch to the door. He fumbled with the knob until the catch clicked free; then he braced himself to kick the portal wide. The butler had almost accomplished the same duty, having heard the carriage arrive, and was there in the front foyer when the door burst open. As Ashton shouldered his way through with his burden, the usually imperturbable Willis stumbled back with sagging jaw. It was certainly not a moment for which his training in decorum had prepared him.

"Massa Ash—" His voice broke on a high note, and he had to clear his throat to start again. "Massa Ashton, it sho' good to see yo, suh. . . ." His speech fled completely as a snarled strand of red hair tumbled from the folds of the black woolen cloak. His prepared greeting somehow failed to fit the occasion, and he could only gape in stunned awe as the master of the house strode past.

Amanda Wingate shared the servant's dismay when she led her sister and several guests from the parlor into the wide hall, halting Ashton's progress to the stairs. Her attention was snared by the slimly curving bundle he carried and the telltale red tress, and her mind and heart gathered speed as she closed the space between them.

"Good heavens, Ashton!" She pressed a trembling hand to her bosom. "Have you stolen a march on us again and taken yourself another bride?"

Ashton felt the urgent need to take the girl upstairs, but he knew he should give his grandmother some sort of explanation for his entry. "It's not often anyone steals a march on you, Grand-mere," he murmured, using the form of address his own mother had affectionately reserved for the older woman. "However, in this case . . ."

"Amanda," Aunt Jennifer cautiously whispered, laying her hand upon her sister's arm, "perhaps we'd better not discuss what Ashton has done this time. At least, not while we have guests."

Amanda suppressed the questions that burned in her, but she was still worried and confused. From the stillness of the one being borne, she inferred a state of oblivion, and she could think of no logical explanation for what she was seeing except what she had immediately assumed, that Ashton was carrying his sleeping bride to his chambers. She could sense his impatience to be on his way as he kept edging toward the stairs. She was about to remove herself from his path when the cloak slipped slightly, allowing a glimpse of the shadowed face beneath the satin-lined garment. "Quite lovely . . ." she mused, not at all surprised that he should choose such a beautiful wife. Then her eyes widened as the wrap continued its sliding descent, revealing thinly clad limbs, and she finished the initial thought in an unplanned gasp as she grabbed the wayward garment. "And quite unsuitably garbed!"

Amanda glanced around to see who else had viewed the display and was dismayed by the proximity of several elderly matrons whose mouths hung slack in shock. Whispers began as a small, murmuring ripple and quickly became waves of conjectures that surged rapidly through the guests, with the words *nightgown* and *girl* being tossed along the crest.

"Grand-mere, it's not what it seems," Ashton whispered urgently, seeking to allay her fears.

Amanda moaned softly. "I don't know if I can bear the truth."

Aunt Jennifer leaned near to bolster her sister's courage. "Remember, Amanda. Papa always said to keep an even mind in the face of adversity."

A man jostled his way near, and, having heard only part of the exchange, urged in a friendly manner, "Come on, Ashton. Let's see what your new bride looks like. It's about time you took yourself another wife."

"Bride!" a strident feminine voice screeched from the adjoining room. "Wife!" There was a bustle in the crowd as the woman began to push her way through. "What is going on here? Let me by!"

Aunt Jennifer's own composure crumpled a bit as she mumbled beneath her breath, "I do believe this is just the time Papa was talking about."

A tall slender brunette stumbled forth and brought herself up with badly frayed dignity to view the newcomers. Marelda Rousse's dark eyes followed the long fall of damply tangled red hair and widened as they dropped to Ashton's wet trousers, then flew in questioning horror to his face. Breathless with worry, she struggled for composure. "Ashton, what is the meaning of this? You look as if you've been rolling in the swamp with this girl! Have you really gone and taken yourself another wife?"

Ashton chafed at this unexpected turn of questioning, but he had no intention of spilling his heart and his hopes before so many. His only concession would be to make them aware of the injured state of the one he carried. "There was an accident with the carriage, Marelda, and the girl was hurt when she was knocked from her horse."

"She was out riding in her nightgown? At this hour?" Marelda cried. "Really, Ashton, how can you expect us to believe a story like that?"

Ashton's jaw tensed with his growing irritation. Marelda Rousse had dared many things, but never had gone so far as to question his word, especially in his own home and before so many. "I don't have time to explain now, Marelda," he answered curtly. "The girl needs attention. Please, just let me by."

Marelda opened her mouth to complain, but her words were squelched by his piqued frown, and she could only move aside as she sensed a growing current of anger in his manner. There were times when Ashton Wingate seemed almost cruel in his reticence, and she knew it would do her little good to insist.

Amanda was embarrassed that she had allowed her own suspicions to leap out of control and saw the need for urgency. "The pink room in the east wing is empty, Ashton. I'll fetch Willabelle and send her up immediately." As her grandson strode toward the stairs, she gestured to the young black girl who had been watching the proceedings from the upper balustrade. "Luella May, run ahead and make the room ready."

"Yas'm, Miz Amanda!" the girl answered and promptly darted off.

Leaving behind a rising murmur of voices, Ashton swiftly climbed the winding staircase that swept upward against a curving wall to the second level. Three years ago he had dreamed of carrying his young bride up these same stairs and whisking her away to his own bedchamber. Now here he was, holding close to his heart a woman he believed was Lierin. Were she conscious, he might have settled the matter of bedrooms with a quick inquiry, and he would no more know the loneliness that had haunted him since that tragic night on the river.

He arrived at the guest room to find Luella May folding down the covers on the canopied bed. The girl quickly smoothed a narrow hand over the sun-whitened sheets, readying the place for the injured one before moving out of his way. "Dere ain't no need to worry yose'f, Massa Ashton," she assured him. "Mama be here directly, and she know what to do fo de lady. She knows all dere is to know 'bout doctahing. . . ."

Ashton hardly heard the girl's chatter as he lowered his charge to the bed. Reaching to the bedside table, he wet a cloth in the washbasin and began to gently wipe away the mud from the colorless cheeks. His task complete, he held the lamp close and carefully studied the oval face, seeking out whatever truth was to be found there. His eyes followed the slim, straight line of her nose downward to the soft, pale lips. The darkening bruise temporarily marred the perfection of her brow, but the creamy skin was otherwise unflawed. Soft brown brows swept upward in a delicate arc above thickly fringed black lashes, and he knew, if this was indeed his wife, the eyes were a deep emerald green and as lively as new leaves dancing before the wind. Her thick hair was matted with broken twigs, dried mud, and dead leaves, but the debris could not hide the bright hue. She was the very image of the one he had held so tenaciously in his memory. It had to be his wife!

"Lierin," he breathed in a yearning whisper. How long had he kept that name from his lips? Was he wrong in letting it escape for a second time this evening?

A tall woman of generous proportions entered the room and made a brief analysis of the situation before she gave hurried instructions to the girl: "Go fetch dat nightgown Miz Amanda was lookin' for, an' bring some hot water so's Ah can give dis lady a bath."

Luella May took off like a shot, and her mother hastened to the bedside to examine the bruise on the cool brow. Ashton watched from the end of the bed, where he gripped a post with white-knuckled tension.

"What do you think, Willabelle?" he asked anxiously. "Is she going to be all right?"

The housekeeper heard the concern in his voice, but did not pause as she lifted the girl's eyelid. "Now don' go frettin' like dat, massa. God willin', dis li'l gal gonna be fine and dandy in a few days."

"Can you be sure of that?"

Willabelle wagged her white kerchiefed head sorrowfully. "Massa, Ah ain't no doctah. Yo jes' gonna have to wait an' see."

"Damn!" Ashton growled and, turning from her, began to prowl about the room in restless agitation.

Surprised by his manner, the housekeeper considered him with increasing concern. There was more here than just what appeared on the surface. When the waters were troubled, one could bet that beneath the roiling turbulence there was a cause. She was even more certain of this when he returned to the foot of the bed.

"Isn't there something we can do until Dr. Page arrives?" he pressed.

"Yassuh," the black woman answered solemnly. "Ah can bathe her an' make her fresh an' comfor'ble, whilst yo go an' do de same fo' yo'se'f." She met his piqued frown, knowing she had offered him what wisdom she could.

Reluctantly Ashton relented, finding no argument to put forth. Laying his coat over his shoulder, he strode to the door and from there gazed back at the one in the bed. She lay deathly still, and it filled him with a cold, expanding dread. "Take good care of her, Willabelle."

"Ah aims to, massa," she vowed. "Don't yo worry 'bout dat."

Ashton swung the portal closed behind him and slowly made his way down the corridor. Pausing a moment beside the upper balustrade, he rested his hand on the polished rail and bowed his head in thought, trying to find answers for the many questions that plagued him. He knew it would have taken a miracle for Lierin to reach the far shore after she fell into the river, but if she had accomplished such a feat, why had she not let them know she was there? The *River Witch* had remained on the sandbar until the repairs were made, giving his men enough time to search several miles up and down the river, but they had failed to find any trace. If she had not drowned, why in the three years following the incident had he not received some word from her?

Finding no plausible explanations to encourage his hopes, he rolled his head back along his shoulders in an attempt to ease the ache that had formed behind his neck. As he tried to push the troubling doubts to the back of his mind, he deliberately focused his attention on his surroundings. He had built the mansion after accumulating some wealth, and now he wondered how Lierin would accept his home, if she would find it a delight as so many had before her, or if it would compare unfavorably with her father's estate in England.

His gaze wandered over the pale marble floor of the lower hall and the delicately hued mural that swept around the curving wall. He saw things he had taken for granted for many months, while he remembered facts he had let slip from his mind. High above the circling balustrade, a large crystal chandelier hung from an elaborately plastered ceiling where dancing prisms of light frolicked and played and chased each other across the raised scrolls and flowers that formed the intricate pattern. No evidence now remained of the damage suffered when a drunken, fun-loving river rat from Under-the-Hill broke into the house and, encouraged by Ashton's absence, threatened the servants by using the fixture for target practice. It was Amanda who had set the miscreant to flight when she had leveled a loaded gun at him. Later Ashton had demanded that painstaking care be taken by the craftsmen he hired to restore the hall to its former beauty; then he had sought out the brutish fellow who had caused the destruction and presented the bill to him. Just to even the odds in that rat hole by the river, he had taken a man with him, and between the two of them, they had taught the foolish buffoon and a full half-dozen of his cohorts a good lesson: keep their penchant for mayhem confined to the river's edge and pay their bills when due, especially when the one doing the asking was Ashton Wingate, ably assisted by his huge black overseer, Judd Barnum.

Ashton continued on to his suite, but he could find no relief from the fears that beset him. Moving automatically, he doffed his muddied clothes and went through the process of washing, shaving, and dressing before he returned to the door of the guest room. Willabelle gently shooed him away, saying she was still attending the girl, and reluctantly he made his way down the stairs. When he entered the parlor, he was met by a veritable wall of eager male faces.

"Tell us about her, Ashton," they urged.

"Who is she?"

"Where did you find her?"

"Is she from around these parts?"

"What was she doing out at night and all alone?"

"Is it true she was only wearing a nightgown?"

The questions flew at him with ever-increasing fervor, like a flock of disturbed bats. He held up a hand to plead for mercy and gave them a wry smile. "Gentlemen, please. I'm not a soothsayer. I can put no name to her at the moment. She's not from this area and, as far as I can tell, no one that any of you know. To explain why she was out there in a nightgown would be difficult, except that there's been a fire of some sort in the area, and she might have escaped from a burning house. The only thing I can say with any certainty is that she caught us completely by surprise when she came charging out of Morton's Woods."

"I hear she's a real beauty, Ashton. How do you manage to be so lucky?"

Lucky! His mind screamed the word. How could they even suggest such a thing when he had lost his love and then perhaps . . . in the very act of finding her again . . . had nearly killed her? "I won't consider myself lucky until I know she's all right."

"Aye, that's true," an elderly gentleman agreed. "If she's seriously hurt, I think all this caterwauling about Ashton bringing her home will bear heavily upon our conscience."

Marelda eyed Ashton from across the room, pricked that he had not seen fit to join her immediately. She contemplated several courses of action to convey her displeasure with him. Remaining distant for a noticeable period of time was one option, but when he seemed oblivious to her now, she could guess that such a ruse would be wasted. Had it been some other man, she might have fetched her wrap and left, but Ashton was an exceptionally handsome man. Indeed, a most magnificent specimen. Even in something less than the carefully tailored garments he now wore, he cut a figure to be admired, and she certainly had no wish to jeopardize her tenuous relationship with him. Perhaps a more direct maneuver would be advantageous. After all, she had gained much already by her boldness.

Marelda approached her host with as much determination as a full brigade of charging horsemen. She had spent many an hour perfecting a pretty pout and gave Ashton what she considered a best effort as she slipped an arm through his.

"I should scold you, Ashton, for making such a startling entry tonight."

Ashton accepted the hurried excuses of the other men and watched them scatter. They no doubt assumed Marelda's confrontation would lead into a lover's spat, and it was amazing to him how she had managed to establish herself as his chosen one. Still, he had to admit that as a widower he had been rather lax and blasé about her warming attentions and frequent visits. His indulgence had probably given encouragement to many unwarrented assumptions. "I apologize, Marelda. I didn't plan ahead to create a scene."

Marelda turned her head slightly to allow him an unhindered view of her profile. She knew she was pretty and was quite fond of her own silky black eyes and raven curls. "I suppose you couldn't help the little dear throwing herself into your path, but you do seem to have that effect on women . . ." A sudden thought struck her, and she asked hopefully, "Or is she a child? She seemed so small. . . ."

Ashton shook his head slowly. "Definitely more than a child!"

"And of course you would know that"—her pique was clearly audible—"having seen her in her gown. She certainly knew what to wear to catch your eye."

For her comment she received a casual regard with a hint of bland humor hiding somewhere in it. She had the distinct impression that he was laughing at her in the back of his mind, but jealousy had already sunk its sharp claws into her and would not free her from its grasp. Finally he deigned to give her a lazy shrug. "Actually she was wearing a cloak over her nightgown."

"She was still undressed underneath it!"

"Whatever your preference, Marelda," Ashton rejoined with light sarcasm. "It doesn't change the fact that it was an accident."

"Of course it was," Marelda scoffed. "She only waited to see if it was your carriage before driving her horse into it."

"I'm sure Dr. Page will soon be here to disclaim any doubts about her condition."

A high-pitched giggle came from behind them, and they turned, realizing they had gained an audience in the person of M. Horace Titch, a squat little man whose dark, liquid eyes seemed always on the brink of tears. Now he plainly relished his ability to deliver some news: "Doc Page can't come."

Ashton knew the fellow as a tiresome individual who made a point of minding everybody's business but his own. Amanda only invited him out of friendship for his sister, a woman who had, by good common sense, saved a sizable inheritance and the family plantation from the bungling efforts of her brother. Horace apparently had not been gifted with the same talent for management or astuteness as the older sibling had inherited and was definitely the last person Ashton wanted to see tonight.

"The doc's gone out to the Wilkins' place," Horace announced bluntly. "They've got another brat coming, and with the trouble the missus had the last time, Doc Page didn't want to take any chances. Seems to me they'd be a sight better off if they were to lose it, considering the mouths they have to feed."

Ashton smiled without humor. "Too bad there wasn't someone as selective as you when you were born, Titch. They might have brightened the whole outlook of Natchez."

Horace reddened profusely, and with his straight, dark hair standing out from his head, he gave a good impression of an enraged porcupine. "I . . . I'd advise you, Ashton, to keep a civil tongue in your h-head," he stuttered. "Re-remember some of that cotton you haul on your boat belongs to me."

Ashton laughed sharply. "I do business with your sister, Horace, and provide for her a larger profit than any vessel on the river. If she is ever of a mind to take her trade elsewhere, there'll be another planter to fill the space."

"Don't even speak of it, Ashton," Corissa Titch said as she joined the gathering. Somewhat brassy and unfeminine, she was not one to remain silent when there were matters to be set straight. "I know where I get the better value for our crops"—she stared hard into her brother's reddening face—"even if Horace doesn't."

Horace met the hazel eyes of his host and recognized the mockery gleaming in their smoky depths. Unable to deliver the threats he wanted to, he stumped away, chafing and silently vowing revenge upon his host. Corissa shrugged a mute apology to Ashton and followed her brother, knowing how his moods were wont to wallow in self-pity. Sometimes she wondered what his fits of depression would lead to someday.

A servant paused beside Ashton to offer champagne, and he used the respite to cool his irritation. Taking two goblets from the tray, he handed one to Marelda. She lifted hers in silent toast, and her heart tripped a time or two as she looked into the handsome visage. His features were crisp and classic, lightly bronzed by the wind and sun. His lips were sometimes warmly expressive, other moments stern and forbidding. Discounting the heavily lashed appeal of those smoky green-brown eyes flecked with gray, she sometimes thought his cheeks were the most expressive and fascinating feature about him. Beneath well-sculptured cheekbones the flesh was taut over muscles that were wont to tense and flex when he became angry.

Smiling up at him with glowing warmth, she reached out and caressed his lean, brown knuckles. "Welcome home, darling. I missed you. I missed you terribly."

Thick lashes were lowered over cool, hazel eyes as he stared into the pale amber wine. His thoughts were on Lierin, and it was a long moment before he responded: "It's always good to come home."

Marelda ran her fingers beneath his lapel, and the feel of the firmly muscled chest against the back of her hand brought a curious stirring in her own breast. "You worry me when you go off to New Orleans on one of your ventures, Ashton," she murmured. "It does something to you, makes you reckless. Why can't you just stay home and take care of your plantation like any normal planter?"

"Judd is more than adequate as an overseer, Marelda," he stated, "and I have no qualms about leaving the management of this plantation in his hands while I search out potential customers for my steamboat trade."

"You set a lot of store by Judd Barnum, don't you? Indeed, you're the only planter in these parts who has a black man for an overseer."

"May I remind you, Marelda, that I am also thought of as one of the most successful. Judd has proved that he and his judgment are to be trusted."

Marelda was never one to give up easily. "It just seems like you'd get more work out of your blacks with a white man taking over Judd's position."

"Make no mistake, Marelda. Judd expects them to work and work hard, but they're given enough food and rest to compensate for the hours they spend in the field. Considering Belle Chêne's prosperity, there's absolutely no reason for me to change the way I run the plantation. Now"—Ashton stepped back with a shallow bow of apology—"if you will excuse me. I thought I heard Latham returning, and I'd like to hear what he has to report."

Marelda held up a hand to delay him, intending to invite herself, but he quickly turned on a heel and was gone. She sighed and watched him leave the parlor. At times she was awed by his ability to bring life into a room with his mere presence and even more sure that, when he left, he took the joy with him.

Ashton made his way into the kitchen just as the boy came running in from the stables. Between gasps the lad announced that the doctor would not be coming until morning, but it was for a much different reason than they had supposed.

"De madhouse burnt, Massa Ashton," the youth explained. "Right down to ashes an' cinders, all 'ceptin' de cookhouse. Ah seen it all mahse'f when Ah tracked down de doctah dere."

"The madhouse!" Amanda gasped in horror, having entered a moment earlier with her sister. "Oh, how dreadful!"

"De doctah say he gotta tend de ones what's hurt, and dat's why he cain't come," Latham explained. "Dere's some been burned, but mostly dey got out alive."

"Mostly?" Ashton made the singular word a question.

Latham shrugged. "Some o' dem madfolk, dey either 'scaped or dey died in de fire. Dey ain't all been counted fo' yet, Massa Ashton."

"Did you make it known to Dr. Page that we will need his services as soon as possible?" Ashton pressed.

"Yassuh!" the young black readily affirmed.

Ashton drew the cook's attention from the hearth as he asked, "Do you think you can find this boy something to eat, Bertha?"

The old woman chortled and swept her hand to indicate the food-laden table. "Dere's plenty fo' dat chil', massa."

"You heard her, Latham." Ashton inclined his head toward the feast. "Help yourself."

"Thank yo, suh!" Latham responded with enthusiasm. Eager to sample his reward, he found it difficult to restrain himself as he fetched a plate and went around the table selecting from the vast assortment of delectables.

Ashton went to stand near the hearth and frowned into the flickering flames. He was troubled by the news the boy had reported and equally confused by Lierin's meager attire. The location of the madhouse was a good jaunt from town and yet only a short distance beyond the woods where she had emerged. If she had not escaped from the house and had been on her way out to Belle Chêne instead, why would she have come dressed in such a manner and riding so recklessly?

"Those poor, confused souls," Aunt Jennifer lamented, shaking her head sadly.

"We must take a wagonload of food and blankets over tomorrow," Amanda proposed. "Perhaps some of the guests will want to help, too. I'm sure there'll be a need for lots of clothing and quilts. . . ."

Aunt Jennifer frowned suddenly in thought. "Ashton, do you suppose the injured girl could have been from the madhouse?"

His head snapped up in surprise, and as he stared at his great-aunt, he could find no reply to give her. It was his grandmother who came to his aid.

"What would make you think such a thing, Jennifer?"

"Because there was some speculation about her escaping from a burning house, and now we hear the asylum has burned down."

"Probably only a coincidence," Amanda suggested, "and nothing to fret about. I'm sure the child will be able to explain it all when she wakes."

Ashton savored the word *coincidence*. The two events could not really be related, he told himself, nor could he give serious credence to the idea of Lierin being in such a place. It seemed foolish to muse on the possibility and to let his imagination race far ahead of his logic.

He returned to the guest bedroom and, pushing open the door, paused on the threshold for a moment, letting his eyes adjust to the meager light. A low fire burned in the hearth, softly illumining the room, while a chimneyed candle on the bedside commode cast a yellow glow across the tall, tester bed and its occupant. The fragile features remained still and undisturbed, and for a moment his heart halted in sudden trepidation; then he detected the slight rise and fall of her chest, and he was able to breathe again.

Across the room Willabelle pushed herself from a rocking chair, making him aware of her presence. "Ah been 'spectin' yo back."

"How is she?" he asked, approaching the bed.

The black woman joined him there. "She ain't woke up yet, Massa Ashton, but it seems like she be restin' easier now. She sho' been bruised, an' she gots a funny welt on her back dat Ah cain't quite figger out, almost like somebody done hit her." Willabelle rubbed the slender hand lying on top of the covers. "Luella May he'ped me wash her hair, an' we dried it, den Ah give her a bath an' put a fresh gown on her. Jes' bein' warm an' clean might he'p."

"I'd like to be alone with her for a while," Ashton murmured.

Willabelle looked up at him in surprise. His distant expression did not invite inquiry, but she delayed a moment out of her concern for him. He had grieved so deeply after the loss of his wife, she could not help but worry what effect this accident was having on him. "Miz Amanda was up here a li'l while ago, an' she'd reckon it mighty strange yo bein' up here alone wid a stranger."

"I'll have to talk to her."

His laconic reply prevented any glimpse of his inner emotions, and she made no further attempt to draw him out. She went to the door with a comment. "Ah reckon yo be wantin' to know: Miz Marelda, she done made plans to spend de night again."

Ashton sighed heavily, accepting the news with disappointment. One night could be dealt with, but Marelda was wont to extend her visits until it served her purpose to leave.

"Call if yo needs me, massa," Willabelle murmured gently and closed the door behind her.

As the sounds of the woman's footsteps faded in the hall, Ashton turned to the bed. He could feel the ache of loneliness building in his chest as his eyes slowly traced the softly curving form. She lay on her back with her long, red hair tumbling over the pillow. He reached out to touch her hand and found the skin soft and smooth beneath his fingers. The nails were long and carefully tended just as Lierin had always kept hers. They brought to mind a night aboard the *River Witch* when she had leaned over his shoulder as he worked at his ledgers and playfully raked her fingernails across his bare chest. Continuing to tease him, she had nibbled at his ear and rubbed her lightly clad bosom against his shirtless back. After such sweet temptations, recording figures in a stodgy accounting book had seemed far less important.

His mind flowed easily into the natural channel of remembering Lierin, and he relaxed his tightly held restraint, allowing his thoughts to wander where they would. He lowered his weight to the edge of the bed, recalling an afternoon in a hotel room when the sunlight had filtered in through louvered shutters and, with its radiance, had set the sheer white hangings of the bed aglow, wherein he and his young wife had lain entwined. Her jasmine fragrance had drifted with heady effect through his senses while he reveled in their shared intimacy. The pale-hued breasts, sleek limbs, and creamy-skin nakedness had whet his appetite until he had been driven to touch, taste, and possess, and in their brief time together they had savored their newly wedded bliss full measure. If it were possible to enrich such a deep and consuming love, then they had done just that. The intimate moments they had shared had made him marvel, for though he had experienced similar ventures with other light-o'-loves, he had never taken hold of the real treasures of true love until Lierin.

The shadow of the door, elongated by the well-lighted hall, moved across the ceiling, jarring Ashton back to reality. He looked around as Marelda cautiously entered the room.

"Ashton? Ashton . . . are you here?" she called softly, then glanced toward the bed as he rose to his feet. "Oh, there you are. I was begin-ning to wonder if I had the right room. I saw no one. . . ." She paused and looked about as her words dawned with full realization; then she stared with hardening eyes at the woman in the bed before lifting a rather skeptical gaze to him. "I thought at least there'd be someone else in the room, Ashton. This is hardly proper."

"No need to fear, Marelda," he said with a trace of sarcasm. "I haven't ravished the girl in her helpless state."

Marelda was nettled by his mockery. "Really, Ashton, you know how the gossips are. Your character would be lambasted from here to Vicksburg if this were known."

"If what were known?" A mildly tolerant smile lifted a corner of his lips. "That I was here alone with an unconscious woman who is my—" He bit off the word that would have staked his claim to the girl. How could he issue such a statement when there were so many questions yet to be answered? Still, too much had already been said, and he knew that Marelda would not give him rest until he finished with what he had started.

"*Your what?*" Marelda barked out. "What is that little trollop to you?" She grew more enraged by his coolly tolerant stare. "Dammit, Ashton, I want to know!"

Crossing to the door, he pushed it closed to prevent her voice from carrying through the house, then faced her with a suggestion. "I think you'd better sit down, Marelda," he said calmly. "You're not going to like what I have to say."

"Tell me!" she cried.

"I believe the lady is"—he smiled apologetically—"my wife."

For the second time that evening Marelda was thrust into a state of near panic. "Your *wife*?" She seemed to reel from the blow of his revelation and had to grasp hold of a nearby chair for support. She continued in a less volatile tone, though her voice was ragged with emotion: "I thought you said you hadn't taken another wife."

"I haven't."

She frowned at him, totally confused. "What are you trying to tell me?"

Casually he indicated the one in the bed. "I'm saying that I believe this woman is my first wife, Lierin."

"But . . . but I thought you said she had drowned," Marelda stammered in bewilderment.

"And that was what I also believed until I saw this woman's face."

Marelda considered him a long moment in deepening suspicion; then, setting her jaw, she went to the bed, lifted the candle, and held it close to the pillow where she could have a better look at the one lying there. Her eyes flared as she viewed the fairness of her rival, then narrowed with jealous hatred. Had she been alone, she might have added a few more bruises to that pale visage, for this was the woman who had already caused her so much pain and anguish. Or was she?

Realizing Ashton had spoken in an attitude of conjecture rather than fact, she faced him, taking hold of whatever uncertainty he might be harboring and using it as a battering ram against him. "Surely you're mistaken, Ashton. Your wife has been dead for three years now. You said yourself that she fell overboard, and you were unable to save her because someone shot you. Have you considered how farfetched the coincidence would be if this woman were truly your wife? You must admit that the likelihood of Lierin arriving in Natchez and then colliding with your carriage merely by chance is much too preposterous to accept. Somehow someone planned this whole thing as a scheme to make you think Lierin is alive, so you'd be tricked into giving her everything she asked for. Why, I bet right now the little darling, whoever she is, is hearing every word I say." Marelda gazed contemptuously at the still form. "But then, she'd have to be a very talented actress, or you'd have seen through her ploy from the beginning."

"Marelda," he said flatly, "it is Lierin."

"*No!*" she railed, slashing a fist downward through the air. "She is just some slut who is trying to get your money!"

"Marelda!" His voice had hardened. "Lierin has no need of my wealth. Her father is a rich merchant in England, and she has properties of her own in New Orleans and Biloxi, left to her by her kin."

"Oh, Ashton, please look at this objectively," Marelda implored, deciding a change of tactics might influence him. She went to him and tried to slip her arms about him, but he set her from him impatiently. A small sob caught in her throat, and tears began to spill down her cheeks. "As sure as you are, Ashton, that this is Lierin, I am just as convinced that it's not. If it were, what kept her away from you these past three years? Would you call her absence wifely devotion?"

"There's really no need to discuss any of this," he stated bluntly. "The matter will be settled when she wakes."

"No, it won't be settled, Ashton, for she will surely claim you are her husband, but it will be a lie, contrived by some money-hungry mind."

"I would know Lierin anywhere."

Dramatically Marelda straightened herself in the manner of one who faced the world alone. He was growing stubborn, and she needed time to think. "I'll leave you now . . . with her . . . I shall go to my room, but I will not sleep. Remember, Ashton, how much I love you."

A heroic martyr going gallantly to her doom could not have held her head as high as Marelda managed to do as she glided from the room. There was a brief but significant moment of suspense as she halted beyond the threshold, allowing Ashton to brace himself. Then the door slammed with a loud crash that was undoubtedly heard throughout the whole house. Ashton envisioned her flowing gracefully down the hall to her room, and he waited for the second thunderous closing of the door in the distance. He was not to be disappointed. The event sent a wave of noise echoing through the mansion and finally receded to be replaced by the rapid clatter of heels and the confused chatter of feminine voices in the hall. Ashton glanced up as the door was thrust open and could not subdue a smile as the startled pair of ancient siblings entered, gasping for breath.

"Good heavens, Ashton!" his grandmother exclaimed breathlessly. "What has taken hold of you? Why are you going about the house slamming all the doors?"

"Now, Amanda, don't be harsh with him," Aunt Jennifer coaxed. "With Dr. Page not coming until morning and with Ashton worried about the girl, you know he must be upset." She looked to her nephew for affirmation. "Isn't that true, dear?"

Amanda's apprehensions were not to be set aside so easily. "I should have begged him not to take another trip downriver," she fretted. "Something always happens when he goes to New Orleans. It's almost like a bad omen."

"Grand-mere, please calm yourself," Ashton cajoled gently, taking her hands and drawing her to the hearth. "I have something to tell you that's very important."

She studied him with a dubious gaze. "First tell me why you were slamming the doors; then if your explanation seems reasonable, I'll listen to the rest of what you have to say."

Ashton chuckled and laid his arm about her narrow shoulders in an affectionate manner. "Would you believe me if I told you that it was Marelda who slammed the doors?"

"Marelda?" Amanda was astonished by his claim. "Whatever for, Ashton?"

"Because I told her that the injured girl is Lierin. . . ."

"Lierin? Your wife Lierin?" Amanda questioned uncertainly. "But, Ashton . . . she's dead."

"She drowned, dear." Aunt Jennifer patted his arm consolingly, sure that he had taken leave of his senses.

"No, she's here. Alive! I cannot explain how she escaped from being drowned, but she's here," he insisted. "In this very room!"

Both women seemed stunned as they turned and went to the bed. Aunt Jennifer took the candle from the bedside table and held it where its tiny flame shone softly on the object of their perusal.

"She is pretty," Aunt Jennifer observed.

"Exquisite," Amanda corrected worriedly. She took a firm grip on herself, knowing that she must remain calm in the face of this latest event. Ashton had held to his grief so long, he might have unwittingly mistaken another of comparable looks for the woman he had loved so dearly. How could she be sure that he was not just fantasizing about his lost Lierin?

She glanced up as a thought struck her. There was a painting of Lierin hanging in Ashton's chambers. Perhaps it would serve to confirm his claim or help present a denial. "Ashton, dear, I think the girl does bear a resemblance to Lierin's portrait. Why don't you get it and let's make the comparison."

Ashton complied with his grandmother's wishes and returned at once to the guest room with the requested portrait in hand. One glimpse of the painting had reassured him there was cause to hope the girl and Lierin were one and the same.

In his short absence the two sisters had brought several lamps together around the bed and turned up the wicks to provide an abundance of light for a close study of their subject. Aunt Jennifer propped the painting against the headboard, then stood with her sister contemplating the comparison. The girl in the portrait wore a gown of yellow and had ribbons of the same hue coiled through her light auburn locks. Even on the flat surface of the canvas, the emerald eyes appeared to sparkle with a zest for life, yet for all of the similarity it bore to the one in the bed, there was still something lacking.

"The artist seems to have captured a certain warmth in his subject," Amanda murmured, "but if this girl is Lierin, then the painting has failed to do her justice. The features in the portrait are not as refined and delicate."

Ashton gave further study to the portrait, but the flaws seemed so small that he could only lay it to the inadequacy of the artist. Aunt Jennifer seemed to second his thoughts as she stated, "We can't expect perfection in portraits, Amanda. Most of the time the best we can hope for is to have the right color eyes and hair."

"You received the portrait after Lierin drowned?" Amanda made an inquiry of the statement and waited until she had received Ashton's verifying nod before continuing her query. "But where did it come from?"

"Her grandfather left instructions in his will for it to be delivered to me. I never saw it until after his death, but I understand it was one of a pair and that the other was a likeness of her sister, Lenore. Both of them were given to Judge Cassidy when the Somerton family came to visit him from England shortly before I met Lierin."

"It was really too bad you never had a chance to meet the rest of the family, Ashton," Aunt Jennifer commented sadly.

"I thought it was terrible that I never got to meet Lierin," Amanda declared. "How often did I stress to him that it was his duty to beget heirs for the continuance of the family name, and for so many years it seemed that Ashton wanted his liberty more than a family. When he finally did marry, he nearly caused my heart to fail by the suddenness of it, and then . . . poof!" Amanda snapped her fingers in the air. "He came home, wounded and . . . a widower."

"You must be patient, Amanda," Aunt Jennifer gently chided. "Ashton isn't getting any younger, true, but at four and thirty he's not exactly past his prime."

"He might as well be," Amanda quipped. "His mind seems set more toward building an empire than a family."

"Ladies, you are picking me apart like a pair of hens squabbling over a cricket," Ashton protested with a chuckle. "Have mercy!"

"Mercy, he says!" His grandmother gave him a sidelong stare, which was softened by a smile. "I should be the one begging for it."

Ashton secured the house after the last guest had departed, or at least gone to bed, and made his way to his own chambers. A glowing lamp aided his passage through his study and sitting room, and a warming fire greeted him in his bedchamber. Willis had anticipated his need and prepared a hot bath in the adjoining room, a small space that had been set aside specifically for his grooming needs. He doffed his clothes and, lowering himself into the steaming liquid, leaned back to soak and think. The ash of a long, black cheroot grew lengthy as he mulled over the happenings of the day, and absently he flicked the gray flakes into a porcelain dish that resided, alongside a crystal decanter and various jars, on a table near the tub. Leaning his head back against the high rim, he watched the smoke drift lazily toward the ceiling, while a train of long-suppressed impressions flitted through his mind. It seemed almost strange to savor and enjoy them without the tormenting feeling of loss.

He vividly remembered the morning when he first saw Lierin. She had been with an older woman on a street in New Orleans where shops for frilly, feminine things abounded. So completely did she take his eye, he had ignored a pressing appointment and followed them at a distance for six blocks or more. She had seemed unaware of him until she paused in front of a millinery shop and, from beneath a silk parasol, gave him stare for stare with a coquettishly raised brow of question. Much to his disappointment, a barouche had stopped alongside, giving him no time to press for an introduction, and the two women were whisked from sight, leaving him without even the tiniest prospect of ever seeing her again.

His hopes dashed, he had finally turned to the issue of his appointment and hailed a livery to convey him to the man's address. It had not promised to be a cordial meeting, and he had prepared himself for a heated debate, determined to protest the seizure of his steamboat and the arrest of its crew until he achieved satisfactory results. A charge of piracy had been brought against them, and the action was purportedly substantiated by proof, although a short time later the evidence was found to be falsified.

Arriving at Judge Cassidy's residence, he was shown into the man's chambers and was in the process of giving the honorable magistrate a piece of his mind when, from an adjoining room, an enraged and decidedly feminine shriek had brought him to an abrupt halt. No one had forewarned him that the aging magistrate was entertaining his granddaughter from England and that she was the very same one he had eyed so closely that afternoon. His anger had dissipated when she stormed into the room, and he had marveled at his good fortune at finding the young lady again. As for Lierin, she had suffered a momentary twinge of surprise when she saw him, but having a proper credit of Irish blood from her mother's side and being well fired with indignation, she had soundly berated him on his undisciplined conduct before an official of the law.

Ashton had been more than happy to accept the chastening. From the first moment he had found himself staring into the darkly lashed, blazing green eyes of Lierin Somerton, he had known that his life would be lacking a most important substance without her in it. With the opportunity to evaluate her at closer range, he had quickly concluded that she was an exceptionally beauteous young woman. The flashing eyes, the slim, pert nose, and the soft, expressive mouth had been structured with a delicate stroke of perfection that had captured his total interest. Thoroughly intrigued, he had stared so long that Lierin had finally become flustered beneath his openly admiring stare. She had later confided that she had never seen such a bold light come into a man's eyes, for they had fairly gleamed with warmth.

In a more decorous manner Ashton had offered a polite apology to her grandfather and went on to explain in careful detail the reason for his visit. Judge Cassidy had been amused by his infatuation with Lierin and extended an invitation for dinner on the premise that he wanted to review the case in more detail. Actually he had had more devious motives in mind, which he admitted to later, and they were to see one of his granddaughters settle down in close proximity to him so he could enjoy the companionship of his kin more freely than if they were wed to one of those English foreigners such as their mother had married. With the judge's favor bestowed upon him, Ashton had courted Lierin with a carefully controlled zeal.

Ashton rose from his bath and rubbed a towel over his matted chest and muscular ribs as his mind continued to flit through his memories of Lierin. He donned a long velvet robe, poured a drink, and, taking the cheroot, went out onto the balcony. The cool night air was laced with the fresh, pungent smell of a nearby pine, and he inhaled its fragrance as one of the pleasures of being home. He rested a thigh on the rail and leaned back against a post as he lost himself again in his memories.

Lierin had changed many things in his life. Once upon a time he had avoided marriage as if it were a deadly disease, but when he had to face the prospect of leaving New Orleans without her, he had been loath even to consider it. He could not name the exact moment when he started to think of her as a prospective wife, but it was a hope that had quickly risen to the forefront of his mind. Then, for all of his experience in entertaining women and potential customers, when it came to asking for her hand, he had done so rather haltingly, afraid she would insist upon a long and normal courtship and the questionable blessings of her father, but to his surprise she had been as eager as he. He had felt strangely humbled when he saw her eyes light up with joy, and quite unabashedly she had thrown her arms about his neck and cried in sheer happiness, "Oh, yes! Yes! Oh, yes!"

Despite their mutual eagerness, there were still problems to be faced. Her father's absence meant the marriage could not be sanctioned by him, and it had seemed doubtful that Robert Somerton would give his permission even if he were there. Lierin had sweetly suggested that her grandfather might be approachable on the matter of her hand. The strong possibility they were all inviting the wrath of the father did not escape their attention. Ashton had laughingly threatened to seduce her and get her with child, just in case her sire had to be convinced that she needed a husband.

Ashton had seen his own character go through other alterations during the abbreviated time he had been with Lierin. He had never really noticed flowers before, but while on a walk through a park, when Lierin had pointed out the beauty of them, he had become appreciative of their delicacy and fragrance. Throughout his years he had watched many a sun lower in the west and casually admired the hues, but when the two of them had shared a sunset from the window of their hotel suite, the event had become a glorious ending to an almost idyllic day wherein her face, her laughter, her soft voice had filled his heart with bliss.

Ashton placed his glass on the rail, and though the cigar stayed firmly clenched in his teeth, the coal died slowly as he perused the dark night beyond the balcony.

After a week of unparalleled rapture, the newly wedded couple had boarded the *River Witch* with the intention of journeying to Natchez to make the necessary introductions to his kin and to apologize for the haste of their marriage. They were also making arrangements to return to New Orleans when those plans were concluded, hopefully in time to meet the sojourning parent and sister. Lierin had warned him about her father. Robert Somerton was an Englishman who held no great love for the brash Americans. His one concession to this had been her mother, Dierdre, whom he had deeply loved. Because of Dierdre's reluctance to leave her father and her home, Robert had chosen to reside in New Orleans until her unexpected death, then he had taken his two small children and returned to England, where he had remained until his daughter Lenore became betrothed to a young aristocrat from the Caribbean. Since a voyage was to be made to visit the prospective groom in his island paradise, Robert had relented to Lierin's pleas and escorted her to New Orleans, giving her permission to stay with her grandfather while her sister and he departed to arrange the nuptials.

Ashton had guessed from the outset of his courtship that the more difficult task lay in telling Robert Somerton that, while he was away planning the wedding of one daughter, the other had fallen in love with a total stranger and married him. The trip to Natchez, however, had ended in tragedy, and subsequently the meeting between Ashton and Lierin's father never materialized. Word of her death had reached New Orleans before Ashton had recovered enough from his wound to make the voyage. By the time he could journey to the port city, the judge was ailing and on his deathbed. Ashton was informed that the Somertons, estranging themselves from the grandfather, had set sail for England without delay, not even bothering to inquire whether the husband had survived the pirate attack or not.

A cool breeze stirred in the night, drawing Ashton's mind back to the present. He turned his face into the fitful breeze and could feel the tingle of misty droplets on his face. A frigid puff of air billowed his robe and touched his naked body. The freshness of it brought back the memory of a similar night on the river, when the last moment of happiness in his life, up until now, had turned into one of pain. Though his own boat and many others had scoured the river for miles upstream and down, more than a week had passed before he finally conceded the inevitable. The moldering bodies of several pirates had been found, but there was no trace of Lierin, not even a shred of cloth or a muddied rag. He had finally had to face the tragic fact that the river had taken another victim to its bosom as it had so many times before and swept his love from the face of the earth while it continued to meander along in its lazy, unfeeling arrogance. The loss of his wife had haunted him for three long years. Now there was hope. Come the morrow, life would begin anew. Lierin was home.

– Chapter Two –

She became conscious of herself as one slowly stirring to life from a total void, knowing of no previous existence beyond the present indeterminate moment. Reason and memory played no part in the timeless vacuum. She was an embryo floating in darkness, living and breathing but somehow set apart from the world by a distant hazy film that existed beyond the sphere of her being. There, an aura of light glowed, tempting her to draw near. With a natural buoyancy her mind rose slowly upward to the surface of awareness, but as she neared the indistinct border where the first weak rays of reality penetrated, twin talons of pain began to pierce her temples. She recoiled from the harrowing torment and hovered just below the elusive level, not willing to break her bonds to an uncaring, painless oblivion and accept in its stead the sharp pangs of full consciousness.

A voice drifted to her as if through a long tunnel, reaching her with words that were blurred and muted, entreating her to make an effort to respond. "Can you hear me?" The murmured inquiry increased in volume as it was repeated. "Madam, can you hear me?"

Her distress mounted as she was drawn upward against her will into the realm of acute discomfort, and she moaned softly in feeble protest. A rack of torture might have produced a comparable agony, for her whole body ached as if it had been cruelly pummeled and abused. A great weariness weighed down her limbs, and when she tried to move, she had to fight against an almost unsurmountable rigidity. She opened her eyes, but quickly cried out and shaded them with a hand as she turned away from the windows where the rays of the dawning sun streamed in.

"Someone close the drapes." The request came from the man who sat at her bedside. "The light hurts her eyes."

The painful shards of brightness were shut off, and the room was comfortably shaded. Sinking back into the pillows, she dragged a shaking hand across her brow, but winced as her fingers touched a tender spot on her forehead. The bruise was perplexing, for she could not remember what had caused it. She blinked her eyes until the indistinct shadow that hovered near gradually resolved into the form of an older man with a grizzled beard. The winged whiskers were heavily frosted with white and his face was wrinkled with age. The passage of years, however, had not dulled the lively sparkle in his gray eyes. They twinkled at her through wire-rimmed spectacles.

"I was beginning to think you disliked our company, young lady. If you have any misgivings about me, I'm Dr. Page. I was summoned here to attend you."

She opened her mouth to speak, but a hoarse croak was all that issued forth. She ran a dry tongue over parched lips, and the doctor, recognizing her need, reached behind him to receive a glass of water from the black woman. He slipped an arm beneath his patient's shoulders and, lifting her up, pressed the rim of the glass to her lips. When her thirst had been quenched, he lowered her to the pillow again and placed a cool, wet cloth across her brow. The pulsing waves of pain ebbed slightly, and she managed to hold her eyes open without squinting.

"How do you feel?" he asked kindly.

A frown served as a reply before her gaze moved searchingly about the room. She lay in a large tester bed with a wealth of pillows at her back. Above her head a pleated sunburst of pale pink silk radiated from an oval tapestry of stitched roses, filling the dimensions of the canopy frame. The walls of the room were covered in a fresh floral pattern that combined the colors of pink, pale yellow, and fresh green with light wisps of brown. The overdrapes were of pale pink silk, trimmed with tassels and braided cords of pink and green. Several chairs had been placed about the huge room and were covered in complementary shades of the various colors.

It was a fresh and beautifully furnished room, but a growing sense of disorientation began to undermine her brief comfort as she found herself in a totally foreign world. Nothing she saw was familiar to her. No piece of furniture. No tiniest bit of glassware. No frame or painting. Not even the warm flannel nightgown that she wore or the people who stood watching her from different parts of the room.

Two elderly women had moved to a place in front of the richly draped windows, while a large black woman in starched white apron and neatly tied head kerchief waited just behind the doctor's chair. Beyond them, another man stood facing the fireplace. Unless she chanced a movement that might strain her painfully stiff muscles, he remained recognizable only by the back of his dark head, the white silk shirt, and muted-gray-striped trousers that he wore. A mild curiosity grew in her about this one who, in the face of the others' curiosity, kept his back to her, as if he wished to hold himself detached from her and her audience.

A young black girl entered the room carrying a tray laden with a cup of broth and a china tea service. Receiving the soup, Dr. Page offered it to his patient. "Drink this if you can," he cajoled. "It will give you strength."

The pillows were fluffed around her until they braced her in a half sitting position, and as she sipped the hot brew, her gaze lifted above the edge of the cup to peruse the room again. "Why am I here?"

"There was an accident with the carriage," Dr. Page replied, "and you were brought here after you were knocked from your horse."

"My horse?"

Again the doctor supplied the information, but taking care as he watched her face: "I'm sorry, madam. He had to be destroyed."

"Destroyed?" She searched her mind for some recollection of the event, but the probing inquiry only abetted the throbbing in her head until it became impossible to think. She pressed trembling fingers to her aching temples. "I can't seem to remember."

"You had a nasty fall, young lady. Just relax and rest. It will come to you."

Her gaze flew about the room again in a desperate pursuit of something familiar. "Where am I?"

"This is Belle Chêne. . . ." Dr. Page studied her closely as he continued. "Ashton Wingate's plantation home."

"Ashton Wingate?" She stared at him, her eyes wide and searching. She sensed the alert attention given her by those in the room, as if they were awaiting her reaction.

The man in the gray trousers slid the fireplace poker into the stand, gaining her full attention. Inexplicably, a sharp pang of anxiety ran through her even before she saw his face. Disconcerted, she pressed back against the pillows and eyed him warily as he crossed the room. Though she probed her memory, she could not fathom the cause of this sudden dismay. The crisp, handsome profile should have stirred feelings of warmth and admiration in her woman's breast. Yet there was something about the moment that made her heart lurch and grow cold within her chest. When he halted at the foot of the bed, the strength of his gaze held hers immobile, and staring into those smoky eyes, she put aside the broth as one dazed.

A strange smile played upon his lips. "I don't quite understand the miracle that has brought you back to me, my love, but I am extremely grateful."

She stared at him in a panic, wondering which one of them was mad. She rejected the idea of placing the blame on strong drink, for he seemed sober enough and his appearance was not that of a slovenly sot. Indeed, he carried himself with a proud, erect bearing that hinted of a man well in control of his faculties. So why was he speaking to her as if he knew her?

If the tiniest doubt had nibbled at the edges of Ashton's mind, the uncertainty dissipated abruptly when he looked into the dark green eyes. He knew those eyes, and they belonged to his wife. "I suffered quite a shock when I saw you last night. I thought you were dead, and now, after three long years, you have suddenly appeared, and I find to my joy that I'm not a widower after all."

It was she who was mad! It had to be! Why would the others tolerate his ravings if he were voicing only insanities? A sudden quickening of trepidation seized her, and she withdrew into her own mind to seek some secure haven wherein she could find succor from her distress. Disquieted by the fear that some insanity had seized her, she began to shake uncontrollably. The pressure at her temples increased until the pain became excruciating, and she writhed on the bed, holding her head and keeping her eyes tightly shut to bar the alien world from her sight.

"Lierin!" The name echoed hollowly through the haze, and the tone was somewhere between plea and command. Still, it struck no chord of recall and only confused her more. She could find no anchor for her thoughts, no grappling hook that would snare her from the bleak, murky blackness of the unknown and bring her to a firm footing with memory intact. There was only this moment and the few brief ones since she had awakened. What she had seen and heard only set her at odds with herself. The room whirled about her in a dizzying gyre, and she braced her arms widespread against the bed to steady her careening world, but her effort was useless as she was hurtled through a dark and bottomless eddy.

"Quickly!" Dr. Page gestured to Willabelle. "Fetch the smelling salts from my case." He thrust up a hand to halt Ashton as he tried to step near. "She's suffered a shock, Ashton. Give her time."

The younger man drew back and frowned in concern as he helplessly witnessed her ordeal. The doctor slipped a hand behind her head while his other brought a vial of powders beneath her nose. The sudden shock of searing fumes drove away the clinging cobwebs. Her eyes shot open, and she saw the room again with bright, clear, achingly intense vision. Each detail was etched in bold relief, and she saw her tormentor gripping the bedpost with white-knuckled strength, as if he were the one troubled and vexed.

Weak and exhausted, she fell back upon the bed, unmindful of the fact that she had swept off the satin quilt and lace-edged sheet. Her skin was moist with perspiration, and she welcomed the stabling touch of coolness that seeped through her cotton gown, but beneath the man's closely attentive gaze, she realized her gown provided no modesty beyond the thickness of the cloth. It clung to her clammy skin, boldly revealing the womanly curves of her body. Her cheeks flamed. Not only would this knave harass her, but it seemed that he would molest her with his eyes as well. Seeking the protection of the quilt, she rolled her head on the pillow and asked in a rasping whisper, "Could I have some more water, please?"

"Indeed, child," Dr. Page replied and reached for a glass.

Politely rejecting his help, she took the goblet into her shaky grasp and sipped from it slowly as her eyes flicked back to the figure at the end of the bed. He was quite a tall man with wide shoulders and a lean waist. A finely tailored silk shirt showed the expanse of a hard, tapering chest, while the slim trousers displayed the narrowness of his hips and the long, muscular length of his thighs. He was neither thin nor massive, but appeared to be in superb physical form. Obviously he had much to be conceited about.

She gave the glass back to the doctor, and feeling a need to set matters straight in her own mind, she inquired rather timidly, "Am I supposed to know anyone here?"

Dr. Page's jaw sagged in astonishment, and when he looked up at

Ashton, he found his surprise shared by the one who had claimed her as his wife. Ashton was totally confused. He had been so sure that this was Lierin, the one whom he had loved and wed. Indeed, he would have staked his life on it. "Are you not Lierin?"

Her brows came together in a slight frown. Disconcerted and yet reluctant to make an appeal for his sympathies, she responded with a confused shrug. "I . . . I . . . really don't know who I am."

Tormented by uncertainty, she awaited his reaction, afraid he would judge her mad by her confession. She saw the first wave of shock register on his face as he stared at her. His companions seemed no less startled.

Aunt Jennifer approached the bed and took the girl's slender hand to pat it comfortingly. "There, there, dear. I'm sure it will come to you in a moment."

"Jenny, no one forgets her name," Amanda chided. "The girl just needs some rest."

"Perhaps it's something more than that, Amanda," Dr. Page commented thoughtfully. "There've actually been several cases of memory loss recorded. Amnesia, I believe. From what I've read of it, it can either deal with a partial memory loss, where the patients forget a short phase of their lives or some event. Other times it's more extended, and those affected forget their names, where they live, the entire history of their lives, only retaining their abilities to read and write and so on. A few have experienced a total loss, and these have no recollection of having even existed before the moment they awake." The doctor spread his hands in a gesture of helplessness. "I must confess I'm at a loss. I've never known one who suffered from it."

"If you're at a loss, Franklin, think of this poor child," Amanda declared, somewhat beside herself. She had thought the matter of identity would be quickly solved when the young woman woke and could only worry how this would affect Ashton.

"Now, Amanda, you can hardly expect me to know everything," the elderly man replied.

"Don't make excuses, Franklin," Amanda admonished, patting his shoulder in the manner of one reproving an irresponsible student. "Just find out what the girl's problem is and cure it."

"I fear it will not be as simple as that, Amanda," he acknowledged. "There are several things that cause it. Shock. Illness. In this case I would venture to say it was brought about by the accident, but to my knowledge there are no determinate cures."

"But surely it will pass," Ashton pressed.

Dr. Page shrugged. "I'm sorry, Ashton. I really can't say what will happen. Perhaps after a few days when she's had a chance to rest, her memory will come back to her. Then again, it might take a while . . . or it may never return. Only time will tell. We'll just have to wait and see."

The patient stared at the bearded doctor. It all seemed like some terrible nightmare from which she could not escape. "Do you mean I could really be Lierin and not be aware of it?"

"Ashton insists that you are Lierin Wingate," Dr. Page informed her gently. "None of the rest of us can say because we never met her."

She cast an uncertain glance toward the younger man as she directed her question to the elder. "Is he supposed to be Ashton?"

"He *is* Ashton," Amanda stated. "Of that I'm sure."

The young woman turned to Ashton, and her consternation was evident as she asked, "But are you sure about who I am?"

The hazel eyes were soft as he made his reply. "Can a man forget his own wife?"

"Wife!" The word came out in a startled rush. She experienced a rising panic as she realized precisely the predicament that position placed her in. If what he said was true, she was married to a total stranger. She raised a shaking hand to cover her face and, accepting the darkness behind her lowered lashes, banished him from sight. "But I don't even know you!"

"Madam, may I introduce myself?" His warm reply won her attention. A long moment passed as his gaze probed the dark, translucent depths; then abruptly he grinned and gave her a brief bow. "Ashton Wingate, at your service, my lady, and this is"—he swept a hand to the two women—"my grandmother, Amanda Wingate, her sister, Jennifer Tate. And this is the housekeeper"—he indicated the black woman—"Willabelle." He assumed a more serious mien as he continued: "I believe Aunt Jenny and Willabelle will vouch for my identity as my grandmother as already done. They can also tell you that three years ago they were informed of my marriage to Lierin Somerton."

Her bewilderment deepened. What he related seemed inconsistent, and she gave voice to her doubt: "But if we've been married for three years and your relatives live here in the same house with you . . . then why can't they identify me?"

" 'Tis simple really. They never had the opportunity to meet you."

She raised a delicate brow, then reconsidered as the action intensified her discomfort. As she waited for him to continue, she wondered what kind of game he played with her. After all, he was the only one who said he could identify her.

Ashton recognized her skepticism and tried to soothe whatever fears she had. He did not fully understand her condition, but he was confident she was the same woman he had cherished enough to wed. "We were traveling up here when the steamboat was attacked by pirates. During the fight you were swept overboard, and I was shot. My men didn't realize you were gone until I regained consciousness. They searched the river and along the banks for more than a week, but you were not to be found. We presumed you had drowned."

"For three years you say you were under that assumption?" she queried.

"It was only last night that I realized otherwise."

She had no wish to be blindly obstinate, but there were other views to consider. "Perhaps your wife did die, sir, and I am someone else who bears a likeness to her. Three years is a long time to remember exactly how a person looks."

"Ashton, dear, show her the portrait of Lierin," Aunt Jennifer suggested. "Perhaps it will help convince her."

He complied, taking the painting from the table and holding it for the young woman's perusal. He was not greatly heartened by her look of perplexity.

"Is that what I look like?" she asked, raising a bemused expression to his.

"Dear child!" Amanda's amazement was complete. "Do you mean you have no idea what you look like?" She took a small hand mirror from the dressing table and gave it to the girl. "Here you are, my dear," she said, smiling with pleasure. "As you will no doubt see, you're somewhat bruised from the accident, but quite lovely nevertheless."

The younger woman stared into the silvered glass, seeing there the countenance of a stranger. Though the bruises that marked the brow and cheek were familiar to her, at least by feel, the visage was not recognizable. Critically she perused the pale, oval face with its high delicate cheekbones and fine features. The light auburn hair, highlighted with gold, tumbled over her shoulders in wildly tossed disarray. The darkly translucent eyes were wide with curious wonder as they turned to consider the portrait. The painting offered substantial evidence that she was among people who had known her before the accident, for she saw a definite likeness in the thickly lashed green eyes, the slender nose, and the gently curving mouth. The resemblance was there, and although not perfected, it presented her with bold, irrefutable evidence of the man's claim.

"This is going too quickly," she complained in a frail whisper. A deep fatigue seized her, and she leaned back into the feathery softness of the pillows, heaving a trembling sigh.

"Rest yourself, my dear," Dr. Page bade. "You are safe here and will be well cared for."

A cool, moist cloth was laid again upon her brow, half covering her hot and aching eyes, then the doctor pushed himself to his feet.

"And now, Amanda, I believe you offered me some breakfast." The three women followed as he made his way to the door. There he paused to look back at Ashton and, seeing the worry in the younger man's face, had no heart to bid him leave. "Don't be too long, Ashton."

The door closed behind them, and in the ensuing silence the two who remained stared at each other. There was more than a shade of uncertainty in the woman's wary gaze. As he drew near, Ashton looked into the face that had haunted his dreams for so long and was struck by a strong desire to take her in his arms and crush her close against him. With remarkable restraint he lowered his weight to the edge of the bed and only took her hand.

"My darling Lierin, I will await your recovery with a most eager heart. I know you are the one I have loved, and God willing, you will soon know it too."

Slowly, as if fearful of disturbing him, she withdrew her hand from his and pulled the bedcovers up close beneath her chin. "You call me Lierin, but the name stirs no memory. I do not recall beyond a few moments ago when I heard a voice calling to me. I must think on this. . . ." Her finely arched brows came together. "But I have nothing to think about. I'm tired . . . my head hurts. The doctor said I should rest . . . and so I shall." She could not interpret his fleeting frown and lightly touched the back of his hand with her fingertips. "I don't know you, Ashton." An unsteady smile wavered on her lips. "Perhaps this is my home"—her voice rose slightly to make the sentence a question as she glanced about—". . . and what you say may be the truth. In my present state I cannot protest overmuch. If it would satisfy you, I will accept the name Lierin . . . until such a moment when I might realize it is not my own." Deliberately she lowered her eyelids until the detail faded to a muted, indistinct background against which only his face could be seen. "I shall rest now, Ashton."

His hungering gaze fed upon her beauty and eased the yearnings of the past years when he had thought he would never look upon her again. Bending low, he brushed the lightest of kisses across her lips, then took himself across the room. He did not see the emerald eyes slip open and follow his departing back. When the chamber door was safely closed behind him, he braced an elbow high upon the passage wall and, pressing his brow against his forearm, struggled to subdue the triphammer beating of his heart. After a long moment he could breathe evenly again, and with slow and thoughtful tread he went to join the others in the dining room below.

His grandmother glanced up as he entered the room, but waited until he had settled at the head of the table before broaching the subject that plagued her: "I've seen the portrait for myself and agree that you have good reason to believe the girl is Lierin, but do you have any misgivings whatsoever about her? Is there the slightest doubt in your mind that she is not Lierin?"

"I cannot imagine how she can be another," he sighed. "When I look at her, I see Lierin."

"Dear, what do you know about Lierin's sister?" Aunt Jennifer asked.

Ashton paused as Willis presented a silver platter filled with ham and selected a slice. "Lenore is probably living on a plantation in the Caribbean by now. She was making plans for her wedding when I met Lierin, but I really can't say what happened to her after they went back to England. I never heard of them again."

Amanda took a sip of coffee from her porcelain cup. "You must recognize that your haste to marry Lierin caused us all some distress, Ashton. I'm sure that it was a terrible shock for Robert Somerton to receive news of his daughter's marriage and death in the very same moment."

"Proper amends were intended, Grand-mere," Ashton replied, "but as you know disaster struck before they could be carried through."

"That leads me to a puzzling matter, Ashton: Lierin's death. Why has it taken you so long to learn that she is alive? Why didn't she try to find you? Where has she been all this time?"

"Marelda has asked me those same questions."

"Well, you must admit they should be cleared up," his grandmother replied. "Is this amnesia a recurring illness? Is that why she made no attempt to find you?" She turned to Dr. Page for an answer. "What do you say, Franklin?"

"It seems doubtful." The aging man dropped a lump of sugar into his coffee, then cleared his throat, as if embarrassed by what he was about to say. "All of you know that the madhouse burned, but are you aware that the authorities have yet to find some of the inmates?"

Ashton lifted his gaze to the older man. "Latham mentioned that last night. What has that to do with Lierin?"

The doctor leaned his arms on the edge of the table and pressed his hands together almost in a prayerful pose. He knew how deeply Ashton had mourned the loss of his young wife and hoped he could express himself without causing resentment. "When you consider the facts surrounding the accident, such as where it happened, the proximity to the madhouse, and Lierin's state of undress, have you given thought to the possibility that she might have been fleeing from the asylum?"

Ashton's manner turned crisp. "Are you suggesting that my wife is mad?"

Franklin felt helpless as he met the stony gaze of his host. "Who knows what happened three years ago, Ashton? Lierin might have suffered severely from shock." Dr. Page saw the tensing muscles in Ashton's jaw and knew he trod on treacherous ground. He rushed on, hoping to allay the storm. "Ashton, listen to me. Sometimes people are condemned to a madhouse for the simplest cause or even when they shouldn't be. It's very much like being buried alive. They can rot in that hellish place without relatives knowing they're even there."

The click of heels sounded in the hall, and Ashton waved a hand, cautioning the doctor to silence. "It's Marelda. I don't want her to hear of this."

"You needn't worry, Ashton," Dr. Page assured him. "I brought that girl into the world, and I know her well enough to be cautious of what weapons I lay in her hands."

"Then we understand each other," Ashton responded.

The dark-haired woman swept into the room with a rustle of silk and paused in the doorway to allow the others to admire the results of her careful toilette. When all eyes came to rest upon her, she went around the table and placed a light kiss on the cheeks of the older women, then greeted her host with a smile as she slid into a chair close on his right.

"How are you this morning, Ashton?" She rushed on, giving him no time to answer: "I assume, since Dr. Page is here, that you've been with your guest upstairs." She bestowed her consideration on the doctor. "How is your patient anyway, Dr. Page? Has she come to her senses yet?"

Franklin was slow to reply. "She is still suffering some trauma."

"Not anything too serious, I'd wager," Marelda remarked with as much sarcasm as she dared.

"Only time will tell."

Marelda was not appeased by the physician's taciturn reply and glanced about the table at her companions, playing her longest stares on the women.

Aunt Jennifer grew uncomfortable with the silence and attempted to explain. "What Franklin means is that Lierin is having some trouble remembering right now, and it might be a while before she regains her memory."

Marelda's eyes grew cold and hard. "Lierin?" She managed a hint of a smile, but it held no more warmth than the frozen jet orbs. "I suppose she remembers just enough to identify herself as Ashton's wife, but has conveniently forgotten everything else."

Ashton lifted his cup to the waiting servant and pointedly ignored Marelda until Willis had filled it with the steaming black brew; then he reluctantly lent his attention to the woman. "Lierin couldn't even remember that much," he stated. "I had to tell her what her name was."

The green monster of jealousy stabbed Marelda to the quick, and it was difficult for her to feign any kind of caring reply. "You mean she can't even remember her name? Why, I've never heard of such a thing."

Amanda's thin lips curved into a smile. "Don't feel bad, Marelda. Franklin never had a patient with those particular symptoms before today."

"They're so farfetched I can understand why. The idea of forgetting one's own name. Why, the very thought is ridiculous."

"Not as farfetched as you might think, Marelda," Dr. Page said. "At least we have a name for it in the medical field. Amnesia may not be very common, but we do know that the condition exists."

"How can you be sure she has this . . . this . . . amnesia?" Marelda argued. "I mean, she could just be pretending."

The elderly man responded with a slow shrug. "I guess I can't really be certain of anything, but I see no reason as yet for the pretense."

"And you may never see a cause if she's clever." Marelda noticed the tensing of Ashton's features and had to yield herself to a more subtle approach to ease his irritation. "But then, the woman's plight could be very real."

"No need to doubt the girl at this point," Dr. Page said and, placing his hands flat on the table, gave a nod to Ashton and to the two older women. "I must beg to be excused. After such fine fare, I am reminded of my lack of sleep last night. I'll be nodding off in the buggy before I reach home." He got to his feet. "I'll come back later to check on Lierin. See that she gets plenty of sleep and as much nourishment as she can take. That is the best advice I can give at the moment."

Ashton rose from his chair. "I'll think about that matter we were discussing. I have to go into Natchez anyway, and I might as well make some inquiries, although I see no point in it."

"I hope it comes out well, Ashton," the doctor said sincerely.

Marelda was piqued that Ashton had not seen fit to inform her of his intentions and could not resist a snide inquiry: "Are you going to leave your precious little flower all alone?"

Ashton half turned and gave her a lightly mocking smile. "My dear Marelda, I was sure you'd be adequately entertained here at Belle Chêne while I'm away, but if you insist . . ."

The thrust of his mockery did not miss its mark, and feeling its light sting, Marelda corrected him haughtily: "I was referring to the one upstairs, Ashton dahling."

"My apologies, Marelda." He gave her an abbreviated bow, then left the room with Dr. Page.

In their absence Marelda petulantly picked at her food and sighed. "I do wish Ashton would listen to reason."

"Listen to reason?" Aunt Jennifer was clearly bemused. "How so, my dear?"

Marelda waved her hand toward the upper floor. "Ashton brings that strange little tramp into his house." She ignored the startled gasps of the women as she forged ahead with her diatribe. "He puts her in a fine bed, treats her like an honored guest." Her distress was apparent as her voice raised in pitch and fervor: "And then actually claims that she is his long lost wife."

Aunt Jennifer rose quickly to her nephew's defense: "My dear, you know Ashton would never insist that she's his wife unless he's totally convinced that it's true."

"I say the girl is an opportunist who looks like his wife," Marelda charged.

"Whatever she is," Amanda replied, "she has been badly hurt and deserves at least a few days' rest."

Dramatically Marelda lifted her hands and face to the ceiling and made her plea to some mystical force. "Oh, wicked fate, how oft must I be pierced by your cruel barbs? Is it not enough that I've been cast aside once? Must you punish me twice, or even thrice? How much am I to bear?" Her voice quivered with a barely restrained sob, and closing her eyes, she leaned her brow against her knuckles, missing the dismayed look Jennifer directed toward her sister, who responded by raising her hands to mime a soundless round of applause.

"Marelda dear, have you considered going on the stage?" Amanda asked. "You have such a flair for expressing yourself."

Somewhat deflated, Marelda sank back into her chair and pouted. "I can clearly see that I'm the only one who hasn't been taken in by that little tramp."

A brittle light flickered in Amanda's eyes as she raised her gaze to the woman, and her hand shook with suppressed anger as she dabbed a napkin to her lips. "Please refrain from applying such names to the girl. From all indications I would say that you are quite possibly defaming the character of my grandson's wife, and you should know by now that my loyalty to this family overrides everything else, even our friendship, Marelda."

Even in her zeal to set aright an injustice only she could see, Marelda recognized that she was in danger of losing a valuable ally. She was not so unwise as that. She put a hand to her brow and began to weep. "I am beside myself with the thought of losing Ashton again, and I have let my fears goad me into foolishness."

Amanda silently agreed, but considered that it was best to change the subject, lest they have another display of dramatics.

The woman who had taken on the name Lierin held up her hands in front of her face and stared at the thin fingers. On the third finger of her left hand she wore a thin, golden band, giving proof of her status as a married woman. It gave her no peace of mind, and she wondered how she could ever accept the man's declaration when she did not feel at all like a wife.

The drapes were still drawn over the windows, preventing the intrusion of the morning light and making the room seem cold and gloomy. She had a sudden desire to feel the warm sunshine on her skin, to bask in its light and let her anxieties be washed in its soothing rays. Ever so carefully she edged her way to the side of the bed. The pain of moving did much to convince her that she was being torn asunder, but she tightened her jaw in stubborn resolve and pressed on. She struggled to a sitting position, then rested a moment, pressing shaking fingers against her temples until the pounding in her head ebbed to a dull ache. Cautiously she eased her weight to her legs and leaned against the bed as her reeling senses threatened to overwhelm her. When the room stopped its insane writhing, she moved toward the end of the bed. Her progress was an unsteady shuffle as she walked her hands along the mattress to abet the hesitant gait of her feet. Once there, she wrapped both arms tightly around the heavy post while she rubbed her aching brow against the cool, smooth carving and waited for her strength to return. When it did, she plucked up her courage and boldly slid her foot outward and away from the four-poster. Her knees were inclined to wobble, and it took a true test of will to keep them firmly beneath her. Refusing to be daunted, she set progressively distant goals to encourage a cautious advance across the room.

Once at her goal she pushed the double layer of drapes aside and shielded her eyes against the glare as light poured through the crystal panes. The sun touched her like a warm, caring friend, and she felt its heat within her breast, momentarily putting her fears to flight. She rested her head against the shaded sill and let her gaze wander outward to the vast, neat lawn. High above the grounds, lofty branches formed huge airy canopies through which the warming sun penetrated. Though winter had stripped the limbs bare and sapped the verdant color from the lawn, it was immediately evident that great care went into maintaining the grounds. Neatly manicured brick walks meandered through a maze of trimmed shrubs and trailed around ivy-covered beds that had been formed around massive tree trunks. Only the upper part of an ornately roofed gazebo was visible behind carefully shaped evergreen foliage. Well protected from prying eyes, it was a place suited for lovers.

Carefully Lierin turned and braced a hand on the back of a nearby chair as she moved toward the bed. As she stepped free of the furnishing, a movement to her left caught her eye. Somewhat startled, she turned her head quickly, forgetting the sharp harrows that were ready to rake her brain. The piercing barbs of pain stabbed into her skull, making her pay dearly for her reckless movement. She grabbed for the chair with one hand and clasped the other tightly over her eyes until the tormenting spikes retreated and coherent thought was once more a possibility. When she could open her eyes again, she found herself staring at her own image reflected in a tall, standing mirror. Curiosity drew her toward the cheval glass, but the effort of further activity demanded more than she could cede. She relented to her growing fatigue and paused some distance away to consider her image, hoping she might glean some knowledge about herself that would encourage a return of her memory. She was not greatly impressed by what she saw. Indeed, she came to the conclusion that she looked as bad as she felt. What color there was in her cheeks was only on one side and that a light purplish blue. Her brow bore the same discoloration, only heavier, contrasting sharply with her fair skin. With her hair wildly tossed and her deep green eyes wide with worry, she looked very much like a bewildered waif. Although her mind gave her no hint of age, the body beneath the clinging flannel nightgown bore the curving shape and the upthrusting fullness of attained womanhood, while it also boasted of a slender firmness that bespoke of an active life.

Several languages came quickly to her tongue, and numbers flowed with ease through her thoughts, but the origins of both seemed almost mystical. She knew the proper setting of a table, the correct utensil to use, the form of a graceful curtsey, and the intricate steps of several dances, but it was beyond the capacity of her battered brain to identify the source from which she had received this knowledge.

"Lierin Wingate?" she breathed. "Are you truly the one I see?"

Her mind gave her no answer, but her dilemma ended when she became distracted by footsteps in the hall. When a light rap came upon the door, Lierin searched about for the nearest haven, having no wish to receive guests in her nightwear. Her throat was too constricted to issue more than a weak and raspy croak, making her attempt to call out ineffective. It was not enough to forestall intrusion, for the portal swung open without further ado. She came around with a gasp of surprise, but her sudden movement played havoc with her tenuous stability. The room dipped and through a hazy, swirling motion she saw Ashton halt in the doorway, no doubt surprised to see her up and about. She closed her eyes against the sickening erosion of balance, feeling as if she were teetering on the edge of a dark, bottomless crater that was drawing her down into its gaping maw. She stumbled, and the room swooped into a new, confusing orbit; then she became overpoweringly aware of strong arms closing about her and drawing her against a broad chest. They were alone in the room, and she realized her weakened condition made her extremely vulnerable to his whims. She tried to twist free, acutely conscious of the brush of his hardened thighs against her own and the manly feel of his body branding her through the light layer of her clothing, but he held her in a unrelenting vise of steel-thewed arms. His gentle but tenacious grasp put roots to her fear. She no longer questioned her sanity, but his! He was surely mad to accost her beneath the noses of his kin!

She pushed at his chest with one hand and, straining away, feebly pummeled him with a fist. "No! Please! You cannot!"

Her puny resistance was as naught against his strength. Her feet swung free as she was lifted clear of the floor. The bed swam before her heavily lidded eyes, and she envisioned the struggles that would soon take place there and surely result in her rape. Roweling fear assailed her as she was lowered to the mattress. She clenched her eyes tightly and, catching her hands in the edge of the blanket, clutched them beneath her chin in desperation.

"If you take me, it will only be by dent of strength," she ground out through clenched teeth. "I shall not yield myself to you, monster."

She heard a distant chuckle and felt a cool hand brush the hair from her brow. Her eyes flew open, and she found herself gazing up into laughing hazel eyes. He smiled down at her and sat beside her on the bed.

"My dearest Lierin, 'tis my fondest fantasy that we might once more share the cup of passion. When it happens, it will not be a matter of taking. Until then, madam, I urge you to take better care of yourself. Your strength has not yet returned, and should you persist in this activity, you will at the very least delay your recovery."

Sensing she had nothing to fear, she breathed a trembling sigh of relief. Ashton considered the pale features, noting the dark shadows around her eyes and the slight frown that hinted of a persistent ache. He dampened a cloth in the washbasin, waved it through the air to cool it, and placed it across her forehead. She sighed pleasurably as the pain abated, and for a long moment she enjoyed the comfort; then a thought came to her, and she opened her eyes to find him looking down at her with an expression so intensely loving and caring that she felt a softening in her heart toward him.

"When you spoke, you said, *when* it happens," she murmured in wary questing. "Don't you mean *if?*"

He raised the cloth and flipped a wet curl from her brow, then pointedly delayed his answer as his finger lazily traced her cheek and moved along her chin. He braced an arm on the other side of her and leaned slightly forward. Though his tone was light, she could see no humor in his face as he drawled a belated reply: "My dear madam, I am not given to a loose tongue, and I usually manage to say what I mean."

Of a sudden her pallor became a crimson blush, and with an effort she took her eyes away from his steady gaze and made a valiant attempt to change the subject. "You were the one who brought me here?"

He nodded. "And laid you here as I did this moment past."

She struggled to avoid making contact with that unrelenting

regard. "What was I wearing when you brought me here?" Lamely she waved a hand about the room. "I see no other clothes."

"Your gown was badly torn and muddy, so I bade them wash and fold it away, should you later want or have a need of it."

She raised her brow prettily, then winced at the effort it cost her. "Gown?"

He reached his hand out and plucked at the sleeve of the flannel nightgown she wore, drawing her surprised attention.

"A nightgown?" she gasped in amazement. She pressed a hand over the simple yoke as she asked, "Like this one?"

His head moved from side to side, and a slow smile curved the corners of his mouth upward. "More...ah...shall we say, wifely...or rather...bridely...such as on the first night."

Her consternation grew until it plowed a small furrow between her brows. "Bridely?"

With obvious relish, he went on to describe the garment in detail. "Much thinner. No sleeves and cut low here . . . and here. . . ."

Her face darkened perceptively as her gaze followed the stroke of his finger. Though he did not touch her, the single digit came close enough to halt her breath.

". . . With just a bit of lace here . . . and down on the sides here."

She started to speak, but was forced to clear her throat before she was able to. "You . . . ah . . . bathed me?"

He stepped away from the bed and stood staring dreamily into the distance a moment before he answered with tongue in cheek. "No, sadly enough Willabelle came in and bade me leave before she performed the task."

Lierin let out a long, slow breath to keep from sighing in loud relief. At least, she had kept some shred of dignity before this intrusive stranger.

He spoke over his shoulder as he crossed to the fireplace. "I'll be away for several hours, but Willabelle will be here to see to things while I'm gone." He took up the poker iron and began turning the logs in the fireplace. "If you need anything, just tell her."

Lierin's world turned suddenly sour. A bitter bile of fear rose in her throat as something dark and slender ripped through the back of her memory. Her mind was suddenly filled with chaotic visions, and rising to the fore of these was a face twisted by terror and forever frozen by a soundless scream. She mewled and cringed away, wanting to escape the nightmare that pressed down upon her.

Hearing the whimpering sounds, Ashton glanced around in wonder and found his wife braced against the headboard with fear-glazed eyes.

"Lierin?" He took a step toward her, but she shook her head frantically, unable to extract herself from the apparition.

"Go away!" she cried. "Please!"

"Lierin . . . what is it?" Completely confused, he advanced several more steps, but halted when he saw her scramble across the bed.

"Go away! Leave me alone!" she sobbed pleadingly. "Please go away. . . ."

"It's all right, Lierin." Ashton retreated. "I'm leaving now." He replaced the poker iron in its stand and, as she collapsed in exhausted relief upon the bed, made his way to the door. He was completely undone by her abrupt change of mood, for he could find no plausible explanation for it. Stepping into the hall, he closed the door behind him softly and let his breath out in a long, wavering sigh. Only then did he become aware of his wildly thumping heart and the feeling of cold dread in the pit of his stomach.

The house took on a midafternoon tranquillity as the ladies retired to their respective rooms for a nap. It was an excuse Marelda used to be alone so she could think through her dilemma. Her mind was left to its own devices for the seeking of a solution, for the small, leather-bound volume of poems that lay open on the bedside commode had given her no special insight. Indeed, at the moment her thoughts pawed through the lyric love notes like a raging bull through a flower bed. Gathering the shawl tightly about her shoulders, she paced the length of the thick, soft rug that accommodated the generous dimensions of the room and pivoted with mounting vexation at the limit of each circuit. Pausing by the bedside stand, she snatched up the book and riffled through the pages, reading a phrase or two here and there. Her ire peaked, and with gnashing teeth, she hurled the offending tome from her, flinging it to the far side of the room.

"A hoarded trump to cast upon thy queen of hearts," she ground out through snarling lips. "What foolishness do poets thus impart!" She made another circuit of the room again as she fretted. "I placed too much store in the simperings of love-lost swains. Now I am forced to see reality for the cold and bitter vetch it is." Her face became a harsh mask of hatred. "That little trollop has played her helpless scene so well she's beguiled my Ashton into believing that she is his wife! If only I could design a scheme that brilliantly so he would see *me* as his one and only love."

She paused and glared into the hissing fire that licked lazily at the remains of the oaken logs. The dwindling flames seemed to portray her hopes, once bright and burning strong, now failing and unnourished.

"Damn!" She resumed her agitated pacing. "That tart will have it all her way . . . unless . . . unless I can make them see the fallacy of her claim. How could the little snippet befuddle Ashton's senses so quickly and so cleverly? Did she know Lierin and plan this from the moment of her death?"

Chewing her lip, she stared thoughtfully at the door of her room. It was just down the hall from the guest room where the other woman rested.

"Perhaps if I confronted her outright . . ." Her dark eyes harbored a gleam as the idea took deeper root. "It certainly can do no harm. I have nothing to lose, and it may be my only chance."

Marelda eased the door open and listened for a moment. The house was quiet except for the distant sounds coming from the kitchen. She slipped from her room and hurried down the hall toward the far door. It stood slightly ajar, and when she pushed it open, Luella May rose from a chair near the window.

"What are you doing here?" Marelda demanded.

The girl was confused by the woman's angry tone, and blinked several times before she found her voice. "Ah . . . Massa Ashton told me jes' 'fore he left to come stay wid Miz Lierin whilst he was gone . . . jes' in case she got scared or somepin."

"I'll watch for a while." Marelda jerked her head sharply toward the door. "Go get something to drink. I'll ring the bell if I need you." The young servant nodded warily and crossed the room as the woman further bade her, "And close the door behind you."

Marelda made herself comfortable in a chair across from the one Luella May had vacated and, propping her chin upon her knuckles, considered her adversary. Snidely she wondered if the other wove her schemes in her sleep, for the girl looked quite innocent amid the lace-edged pillows and satin quilt. A distant thought pushed to the fore of Marelda's mind, and before she brushed it off as entirely insane she savored the idea of taking one of those fine pillows and smothering the life from the little fraud. No one would know, and even if it was really Lierin slumbering there, Marelda enjoyed the idea of being free of her forevermore.

"Forevermore . . ." she breathed in delicious revelry.

The soft chimes of the mantel clock intruded into Lierin's dreams and reminded her that she had not yet found her niche in life. She raised a hand to her aching head and gingerly explored the sore and swollen lump on her brow, wondering if another cooling compress would ease the pain. The pitcher had been left on the bed-side table, and struggling up against the pillows, she reached for the cloth that lay beside it.

"Well, it's about time you roused." Marelda's voice cut through the silence, startling a gasp from the other. "It's obvious you're not used to any kind of regulated life."

Lierin raised up on an elbow, but had to close her eyes as the room lurched, and a crushing pressure came against her temples. After a moment the throbbing diminished slightly, and she cautiously lifted her eyelids to look at the woman. "You have me at a loss, madam."

Marelda sneered derisively. "I doubt that."

Lierin was bemused by the other's sarcasm. She had no recollection of ever having known her and certainly could not remember a cause for her animosity. "I'm afraid I don't understand. Who are you, and what do you want of me?"

"I am Marelda Rousse, and I want you to tell everyone who you are and why you really came here."

Lierin pressed the heel of her hand against her forehead as she attempted to absorb the other's words. "Madam, I fear I don't know what my name should be, and even if it meant my life, I could not tell you why I'm here."

Marelda laughed coldly and when she spoke, her tone was honed to a knife-edge sharpness. "My dear . . . whatever your name is . . . your little act has already convinced an anguished man that you are his wife . . . when in actuality Lierin Wingate has been dead and gone these past three years."

"My act?" The emerald eyes opened wide in confused wonder,

then slowly closed as Lierin sank back into the pillows. "Oh, madam," she sighed, "were this an act, I pray it be the last and the play be done. Then I would be free of this mummery. I am so addled by my plight, sleep is my sole escape."

"And of course no one in the family would dream of interrupting your slumber to ask any pertinent questions," Marelda replied with rancor.

The green eyes opened again, this time a darker hue beneath a sharper frown, and fixed the other with a questioning stare. "Do you honestly think I purchased these bruises, and then, as they said, foolishly charged my mount into a running team?"

"I've known many," Marelda snapped, "who would do as much for what you stand to gain." She contemplated her long, carefully tended nails. "Though you whine of your injured wits, they seem sharp enough when your lies are confronted."

Lierin rolled her head listlessly on the pillows, and her frown deepened as she sought to find the key to this illusive puzzle. "I don't know why you come upon me with so much hatred. Though I cannot swear to it, I would say I never saw you before this moment, and I certainly mean you no ill."

Marelda could no longer bear the sight of the other's bruised but classic beauty, and rose to stare out the windows. "No ill, you say?" Her voice bore an unmistakable sneer. "If you are indeed the one you say . . ."

Lierin was growing tired and protested weakly. " 'Twas not I, but the Ashton man who put the name to me. I cannot say for sure if it's that or anoth—"

Marelda turned angrily, slashing her hands sideways with a gesture that cut off Lierin's words. "If you are in truth his wife . . . then you have already stabbed me once, twice, thrice. It was I, his intended bride, who was betrayed those years ago when he journeyed south to New Orleans and found one he fancied so much that he wed her and left me weeping on my lonely pillow. Then he returned the widower, and months passed before my hopes could rise again." Marelda paced back and forth beyond the foot of the bed. "He was so bereaved and anguished that he could see nothing outside his memories. Though I sought to comfort him and was ever at his side, he saw me not. I was less to him than the simplest kitchen charmaid. Finally he began to be a man again, and once more my hopes took flight. Last night we gathered to welcome his return, and I yearned for his sturdy arms to hold me in fondest welcome. He came . . . with *you* where I should have been. So in your innocence . . . if you are truly Lierin and I say not . . . I have still been wronged."

"I'm sorry," Lierin murmured quietly.

"You're sorry!" Marelda railed, then calmed slightly and, with curling lips, sneered, "How sweetly you mewl your apologies, but I'm not one you can cajole with your simpering innocence. Have your moment of delight, dear girl, but I will see the truth come out, and I will turn every stone to see it done. When your lies fly back into your face, I will laugh with delight. Good afternoon, my dear. Rest well . . . if you can."

She swept around in a swirl of skirts and, snatching open the door, departed, leaving the room still and quiet, much like a spring day after a passing thunderstorm.

Lierin was left shaken by the woman's venomous hatred. She had no way of discerning the truth of the matter, whether the judgment against her was fair or false, but at the present moment it was difficult to imagine herself being the cause of such furor.

– Chapter Three –

The Wingate carriage splashed through the water-filled ruts that pockmarked the road and turned in at the short, circular drive. Wide, rusty gates prevented further passage on the lane that circled close to the smoldering ruins of the madhouse. The porch roof hung in precarious suspension from the front of the gutted building, posing a threat to any who drew near. The smoke-blackened walls offered a similar danger. Huge sections of brickwork had been torn out when the roof collapsed, leaving a jagged silhouette against the sky and an undefinable second story. The openings of the darkly gaping windows were blurred with heat-curled strips of wooden framing and seemed to stare in bleary-eyed agony. Trees that had closely hugged the brick structure were oddly truncated and stood like giant, black-bodied mourners around a crypt. Thick trails of smoke still gathered and swirled in confused indecision, as if reluctant to make their departure from the besooted shell.

Tents had been pitched in the yard to provide temporary shelter for the outcasts, and a pair of attendants were struggling to rig up support for a large tarpaulin that was being raised in the back yard near the small cookhouse. A campfire had been built in close proximity to the remaining structure, which was barely large enough to accommodate the attendants, much less the inmates. A few demented souls displayed a fixed fascination with the flames and were discouraged from going too near by the stout, grim-faced matron who exerted her authority by means of a long, heavy switch, which she wielded with impartial fervor, sometimes catching those who had found bowls and gathered to await the distribution of food. The confusion of these innocents was closely comparable to the bewilderment of the ones who milled about in a dazed stupor, oblivious to everything around them. Others of a more violent nature had been chained to heavy stakes pounded into the ground.

The sight in the yard did not cheer Ashton's heart, for he saw the inmates as a pitiful bunch, whose treatment apparently depended on the whims of the staff. In good conscience he could never condemn anyone he loved to such a fate. Indeed, he was already forming an aversion for the switch-wielding matron, and he wondered if he would find himself embroiled in an argument before he concluded his business here.

He descended from the carriage and stepped with Hiram to the rear boot where they began unloading baskets of food, clothing, and wares. One of the attendants called a greeting and came at a run to open the small gate as they approached with their burdens. Following belatedly at a slower, halting pace were a few childlike wards. As Ashton pushed through the gate, they clapped him on the back and welcomed him as if he were a long-lost friend. He gave them each a basket, and the caretaker directed them to take the goods to the cookhouse. They hurried off, happy to do his bidding.

"There'll be more of the same coming in a few days," Ashton informed the gray-haired orderly. The man wore a perpetual harried look and seemed to be unaware of the raw blisters on his forearms and hands until Ashton gestured to them. "You should see to yourself."

The man raised his arms and stared at the burns as if seeing them for the first time, but he dismissed the sores with a shrug. "They give me no pain, sir. Most o' these poor folk canna look after themselves."

There was a hint of a Gaelic burr in the way he rolled his r's. "When they've had a bite to eat an' a place to sleep, I'll see to meself."

Ashton almost flinched as he heard the switch hit its mark again, and he could not resist a sardonic comment. "By that time, your charges will have no hide left to worry about."

Bemused, the man followed Ashton's directed stare and saw an example of the woman's treatment for himself as she lashed another with her willowly whip. "Miss Gunther!" he barked sharply. "Have ye no ken what these folk might do to ye should they take a notion? An' seein' as how ye've ignored me, I'd be inclined to turn me head."

The matron seemed taken aback by his threat and reluctantly dropped the switch. Satisfied, the gray-haired man faced Ashton again and held out a hand in introduction. "Name's Peter Logan, sir. I've been workin' here at the asylum for the last year or so, an' now with two o' the staff gone, I'm in charge now, much to Miss Gunther's displeasure." He lifted his shoulders and let them drop in dismay. "Before this happened, I was thinkin' I was doin' a wee bit o' good at improvin' the plight o' these poor wretches."

"Do you know what happened?"

Peter Logan stuffed the tail of his overlarge wrinkled shirt into his trousers, hesitating a moment before he answered. "I canna say for sure, sir. We were all asleep save for ol' Nick, who was makin' the night rounds, an' I'd guess he's off somewhere runnin' in the woods."

"Were any killed?" Ashton questioned, watching the trails of smoke drifting from the blackened shell.

"After takin' count we figured there's a full half-dozen o' the wards missing. We canna find a trace o' old Nick . . . and another ran off this mornin'. I guess he couldna endure the lot o' madfolk loose in the yard an' himself fenced in with the best." His mouth turned grim. "O' course, we canna know for sure till we stir through the ashes just how many we should have."

Ashton gave a wry smile of distaste. "I'd just as soon learn they escaped."

"Ye durna share a common view, sir, an' it warms me heart to see that there's a kind soul or two left in this world."

"Has someone been out here complaining?" Ashton asked.

The man laughed shortly and shook his head. "About anyone ye'd care to mention, sir. A Mr. Titch was out here pokin' around this mornin'. He was wonderin' about the possibility o' me wards escapin' into Natchez and neighborin' towns, an' what dangers the good citizens o' the area were in."

"I fear Horace Titch has nothing better to do than make matters worse and cause whatever trouble he can."

The attendant gazed furtively about, then lowering his voice, leaned close and spoke out of the corner of his mouth. "Seein' as yer heart's in the right place, sir, I'll tell ye a thing or two what will straighten yer hackles an' maybe the sheriff's when he comes out." He tapped Ashton's silk-vested chest with a hairy knuckle. "I've got me suspicions, all right. I found where some fuses were set over there by the part that isna completely burned. I'm thinkin' t'weren't no accident, sir, but a deliberate act against these poor people here. An' another thing . . . I scrubbed the floor in the cookshack meself yesterday, an' when I come in there this morn'n, there was blood on the floor in front o' the hearth an' marks like somethin' had been dragged through it. The poker had fallen into the fireplace, an' a large knife was missin' from the table. I'd be guessin' there was some mischief done in there, but I canna be sure, an' 'tis only yerself, sir, that I've talked with about it."

"The sheriff is a friend of mine. He'll be interested in what you have to say. If the fire was started, then the man responsible should be caught and made to pay."

"Aye, whoever the begger was, he should've set another fagot over his handiwork to destroy it. There be enough proof to show the sheriff an' make him believe."

Ashton's eyes flitted over the bedraggled figures gathered around the campfire, taking note of the mixed gender. "I see you have women here, too."

"Madness an' misfortune are not confined to men, sir," Peter responded laconically. "It attacks where it wills . . . even children."

Ashton had promised Dr. Page he would make an inquiry, but he did so with distaste, feeling as if he were being disloyal to Lierin by allowing the question to come into his mind. "Are there any women missing?"

"As a matter o' fact, sir, there is one. I'm thinkin' she escaped from the house, but I canna be sure. Who's to say? She might've gotten scared an' run back in." He paused again and thoughtfully chewed on his lip. "She was a strange one . . . She didn't seem that bad off generally . . . then there were times when I thought she was a ravin' lunatic. Somethin' would set her off, an' then I think she could've killed a mon."

An icy rivulet trickled along Ashton's spine. He could not say what had caused Lierin to react in such a panic before he left her. He kept telling himself it could be explained with a plausible reason, but even so, he was half afraid of making further inquiries.

"The attendant who's missin' watched after her a bit," Peter continued, taking the decision from him. "Every now an' then, he'd bring her a pretty or two, maybe somethin' to wear or a wee comb or whatnot. She wasna too hard to look at when she was in her right mind."

"Was she young...?" Ashton awaited the man's reply with bated breath, not knowing why he should even feel the least bit unsettled or anxious about the woman. Surely it couldn't be Lierin they were discussing.

"Fairly young, I'd be sayin', but this kind o' place has a way o' agin' a body. Who knows her age? At least she was still young enough to have her natural hair color. . . ."

"And that would be?"

"A reddish hue, if I recall aright."

Ashton stared at the man as the churning of dread began anew in his stomach. By dint of will, he forced himself on to another topic, not wishing to arouse the man's curiosity by his interest. "What will you do now?"

"I canna say, sir. There's a place in Memphis where we can go, but I've no way o' gettin' them there."

"I have a way," Ashton stated after a thoughtful pause and, at the man's look of surprise, explained: "I can arrange for a steamer to take you there. In fact, there's one at the docks now."

Peter was truly astounded by his generosity. "And ye'd do this for"—he waved his hand to indicate the ragged misfortunates who made up his camp—"these people?"

"Their plight seemed very distant to me . . . until today. I would like to do something more than donate a few baskets of clothing and food."

A sudden smile broke upon Peter's countenance. "If ye be really serious about the offer, sir, then I'll be more'n willin' to accept. Whene'er ye tell us, we'll be ready to move."

"I'll make the arrangements and notify you when you're to leave. It shouldn't be too long, only a few days or so. The steamer has to unload and take on supplies."

Peter glanced about at the facilities that had been erected only that morning. "I managed to borrow these tents from the railroad, but the men there told me I'd be havin' to bring everything back 'fore the month was out. I was wonderin' how we were goin' to manage after that. Now it seems me prayers have been answered. I canna thank ye enough, sir."

Ashton shook the man's hand in farewell and returned to the carriage. As he leaned back in the seat, he released a long sigh. It would probably work out well for all concerned if Peter Logan took his band of misfits to Memphis. Then he could be assured that Lierin and Peter would never meet.

The sun played out the day and had settled behind a billowing froth of vivid hues on the western horizon before Ashton concluded his business in Natchez and his carriage was seen coming up the drive. The house rang with Luella May's strident announcement, prompting Marelda to check her appearance quickly in the silvered glass and apply a fresh touch of her favorite perfume to her temples and behind each earlobe. She was determined to dominate as much of Ashton's attention as she could and planned to extend her visit to the plantation in order to fight for what she considered was hers. Once her adversary sank her hooks into Ashton and he became totally convinced that she was his wife, the game would be lost. Invitations to Belle Chêne would be limited. Ashton would become the doting husband again, and if the last time could be used as an example, no other woman would command his notice for more than a nominal length of time.

Leaving her guest room, Marelda moved down the hall, but paused in the shadows beyond the upper balustrade as she heard the low murmur of exchanged greetings in the front foyer. Ashton came into the main hall, and was followed by Willis and Luella May, who bore several elaborately tied boxes. Marelda's envy seethed anew as she took note of the fancy dressmaker's boxes. Anyone could tell the contents had not been procured at the general store, but had been purchased from the most successful and expensive couturier's shop in Natchez. It seemed that Ashton was eager to outfit his so-called wife in the finest apparel.

"Miz Lierin's asleep, Massa Ashton," Luella May informed him. "She ain't woke up hardly none at all since yo been gone. Doctah Page come, an' he say she jes' plum tuckered out."

"I won't disturb her then," Ashton replied and gestured for the pair to leave the boxes on the sideboard. "Willabelle can take these things up later."

Luella May set her parcels down and could not resist caressing the silken bows. "Yo musta bought somepin real pretty fo' Miz Lierin."

"Only a few essentials to tide her over until Miss Gertrude can

send out some of the rest. They should be delivered later this week."
He lifted the corner of a smaller box with a finger and grimaced ruefully. "At least, it seemed like only a few when I left the shop."

The servants left the hall, and Marelda smoothed her gown and
hair in anticipation of meeting Ashton, preparing herself to flow into
view when he reached the upper level. He had ascended only three
steps when a booming bass voice sounded from the back of the
house. Much to Marelda's disappointment, Ashton turned and
promptly descended the stairs again. A huge black strode into view,
meeting Ashton in the middle of the lower hall where they clasped
hands in a hearty greeting that bespoke of a close friendship.

"Judd! It's good to see you."

"Welcome home, suh."

Marelda's lip curled in repugnance as she observed the two from
her lofty niche. She could not understand their bond, and vowed if
she ever became mistress of Belle Chêne, she would see the black dis-
placed as overseer and his friendship with Ashton terminated. Such
familiarity with a servant was most degrading.

"I'm anxious about the spring planting," Ashton said to the
black, "and I have a few ideas I'd like to discuss."

"Yo wants to see Miz Lierin now, suh. Ah come back later," Judd
offered.

"Luella May said she was sleeping, so I won't disturb her. Come
to my study, and we'll talk about the planting now. I suppose you
heard about the accident. . . ."

The two men turned away from the stairs, leaving Marelda to
fume in outraged frustration. It was apparent she would have to wait
if she wanted a private moment with the master of the house.

Wait indeed! Ashton devoted himself to making arrangements
for the steamboat's journey to Memphis, sometimes coming home
too late to take the evening meal with the family. While the cargo
from the trip downriver was being unloaded, Ashton spread the
word abroad that the stern-wheeler would be making the short jaunt
upriver, and there would be room enough for some cargo if any of
the planters or merchants had a need for shipment to or from the
other city. Contracts were hurriedly drawn up, and merchandise and
goods began to arrive even before the old was gone. From all indications the trip would not be one of loss.

Lierin could hardly do more than sleep. It was her only escape from the unrelenting pain that savaged her waking moments. The slightest effort to accommodate necessities brought her back to the bed in blinding agony. The pain sapped her strength and plagued her every waking moment. Still, in the morning after a basin bath, she would don a fresh gown and allow her hair to be brushed by the black woman who gently tended her. Though it was not readily made use of, a green velvet robe was left within easy reach at the end of the bed, and satin slippers were placed nearby for her convenience. She was distantly aware that these articles were new and well fitting, but she had neither the will nor the strength to inquire as to their ownership. Slowly, almost imperceptively, her strength returned. With each new dawning of a day she could spend a few more minutes on her feet before the intolerable ache drove her back to bed. When the pain did relent and she found some ease from its intensity, she would sometimes prop herself up against the pillows and read or chat with Willabelle or Luella May as they cleaned the room.

She saw little of Ashton. He came to her room after her morning toilettes to exchange a few inconsequential words with her, but he seemed almost stilted and unsure of himself as he watched her. He stood beside her bed, tall, lean, handsome, well dressed and well mannered, with almost a hungry look in those soft, hazel eyes which hinted of his restrained emotions. She could only surmise that her outburst of fear had caused his reticence, but she failed to find a way to intrude into their polite exchanges and ask him what he was really thinking.

When she roused from slumber during the day, he would either be in Natchez or busy someplace else on the plantation. Sometimes she sensed his presence in the night, but could not break her bonds with slumber to rouse and speak. On one of her brief ventures from bed, she passed a window and glanced out to see him riding one of his stallions around on the lawn. The sight drew her admiration, for the dark, glistening steed pranced in high-stepping cadence while he arched his long neck and flagged his sweeping trail. The man on his back seemed in total control of the animal's movements, yet he did it with such ease, the pair flowed together as one.

The days of the week accumulated in number and were without success for Marelda. She despaired that she would ever have any time alone with Ashton. Her failure to seize the advantage made her increasingly anxious, for she realized the time wherein she could carry out her campaign without interference were quickly dwindling. At the onset of her maneuver she had been confident that Lierin would not jeopardize her injured demeanor to run after Ashton, thereby leaving the course open. But as the week aged, her panic increased, for it seemed that her plans went awry even before they were launched, giving them no chance for fruition.

The excuses were varied. On the second and third night after the mishap, houseguests from the Carolinas had to be entertained. Marelda breathed a sigh of relief when they left the next morning, but when the family gathered in the parlor that night to await the call for dinner, Latham came running in to inform his master that one of his blooded mares was showing signs of foaling. It was not enough that Ashton had been gone all day; he finished his brandy in a single gulp, excused himself, and hastily departed to change clothes, leaving Marelda in all her finery, with nothing more to look forward to than a chatty meal with the two older women. Her smile and temper were sorely tested even before Luella May announced the evening meal was ready for consumption.

On the fifth night Ashton failed to come home for dinner, and though Marelda waited up and carefully listened for the sound of his footsteps in the upper hall, she fell asleep, not realizing he had already passed with silent tread and closeted himself in his own suite. She might have consoled herself with the fact that Lierin was seeing less of him than she, but it was a hard reality to face that the twit would have free run at him after she left.

The house grew quite and subdued, and the last flickering flame was snuffed. Ashton went to his lonely bed and finally found the sleep he sought after much tossing and turning. It was later when he woke with a start. Staring into the darkness, he wondered what had snatched him so abruptly from a sound sleep. His naked body was clammy beneath the sheet, and he tossed away the covering to allow the cool air to dry the light mist of sweat. He rubbed his hand across his furred chest, feeling restless and uneasy, as if he had been plucked from a horrible nightmare. What had he found in his dreams that had been so distasteful to him?

He followed the path that his mind had taken through his slumber, and dark green eyes came in a vision before him and taunted him with their seductive gleam. Soft lips parted in a wanton smile, and wildly tossed red hair swirled around a temptingly curvaceous form that knelt amid a bed of rumpled sheets. His imagination was free to roam over the silken body, and though he realized he was becoming aroused by his thoughts, he let them wander on unhindered. Slender arms swept heavy tresses from off her neck, while she gave him a coy look that invited him to draw near and caress the full, delicately hued bosom and the slender hips and lithe thighs. In his mind he reached out and pulled her close, but in the next instant sharp talons cruelly raked him, and in his imagination he jerked back to see a hissing witch glaring at him with hatred-filled eyes. This was not *his* Lierin! This was some madwoman of his dreams! A witch with red hair!

Of a sudden he knew the reason for his abrupt awakening. His dreams of Lierin had turned to ones of tormenting doubt. A familiar sense of despair returned as fragmented memories flitted through his mind. He had seen Lierin taken from him by the strong, dark currents of the river, a river he had known for a good part of his life, one that refused to yield its prey even under the best of conditions. The question rose to haunt him. How could a slender young woman have found her way safely to shore in the dead of night when, even with the best of circumstances, it would have been impossible to discern the river's edge?

Deep within his reasoning there came a brief trembling of trepidation that there remained some remote chance that he was wrong. After all, many questions were as yet unanswered, and those answers might not be in tune with his desire.

The uncertainties attacked him unmercifully, raking him over the glowing coals of logic. He swung his long legs over the side of the bed and braced his elbows against his knees as he hung his head in a moment of roweling fear.

"What is the truth?" His mind would not let him rest on the matter. "Is she my Lierin or some wayward wench who wears only the outer shell?"

He rose to light the lamp beside his bed, then drew on a pair of trousers. He touched the wick of a candle to the glowing flame, then left his chamber to move barefoot down the hall until he was at Lierin's door. The nightmare left his mind half drowned in doubt. Would he find the beloved face he sought, or would it be only a cruel trick of his eye that awaited him?

Carefully he turned the knob and, without a sound, pushed the portal open. The room was dark, lighted only by the dying flames in the fireplace. He moved with soundless tread to the bed and placed the candle on the nightstand where it would spread its glow over the one he had come to see. He stared down at the face thus portrayed, and relief flooded through him.

A century or so ago he had also wandered in the dead of night and paused beside a bed in a hotel suite in New Orleans, where he had gazed down upon these same fine features. He had been amazed that her beauty could both burn his mind and, in the very same instant, freeze it with stunned awe. This was surely his Lierin, once lost, but now found by some unfathomable fall of chance.

Lierin sighed softly in her sleep, and her arm moved slowly aside, taking the sheet and quilt with it and leaving only her gown to cover her. The thin garment pulled into a taut shroud over her body, drawing Ashton's eyes downward to the full swell of her rising and falling bosom and the narrow curve of her waist. A flaming lust took hold of his body, starting the blood pounding in his veins and nearly overwhelming him with his hunger as his gaze wandered on across the flatness of her belly to where the garment had crept up to reveal her naked thighs and an arching hip.

Suddenly Ashton caught himself, realizing he had stepped forward with a hand outstretched and ready to caress a long, sleek limb. As he struggled with his craving lusts, a horror congealed within him that if he pressed her, such an act might thrust her deeper into her plight and forever destroy the path to reconciliation.

With some disgust for his own lack of self-control, Ashton kneaded his sweating palms together and moved several paces away from the bed. A trickle of sweat traced a cool path down his temple as he fought the raging desires that tore at him, leaving him trembling and tense. It was a laborious battle, and a short eternity passed before he managed to claim a small measure of victory. A long sigh slipped from him, and he shook his head, thinking of how close he had come to using force. He had always been repulsed by men who bragged of their forceful dominance or sniggered because of their lack of self-restraint. He had thought himself above that, but now he was catching a glimpse of a totally different profile.

His head lifted slowly as he forced his mind to take control, and he found himself staring at an image reflected in the cheval glass which stood a short arm's length from him. In the ebon mirror he saw his beloved floating behind the fragile barrier, haloed by the candlelight and surrounded by a sea of darkness while she nestled deeply in slumber, unaware of the battle that raged a few short paces from her. A pang of anguish stabbed him. He felt like smashing the mirror to destroy the barriers, but it was a foolish desire, for the obstacles were not really there, and he'd only lose the vision of her.

Gradually a calm deliberation overtook him. He had a strong will, and he would not let himself be governed by his lusts, no matter how they tormented him. In quiet resolve he returned to the bed and, bending low, pressed a light kiss upon her softly parted lips. It may have been his imagination, but it seemed that she responded for a moment, yet when he drew back a vague frown troubled her brow and her lips moved briefly in an unintelligible murmur.

A certain sadness tore at his spirit as he left the room. It was not a comforting thought to know that he would have to endure this aching, gnawing hunger. All too aware of the pain in the lower pit of his belly, he heaved a sigh. Time would have to be his ally. Time and patience. Or at least as much patience as he could muster.

A new dawn came stealing through the half-closed drapes of Lierin's room, touching her with its light and gently rousing her from the depths of morpheus. At first she felt exhilarated and greatly refreshed; then as she tried to stretch her arms above her head, everything came flooding back and she was reminded of her aching muscles and her lack of memory. Her enthusiasm for the new day dwindled, but only briefly. A light, airy spirit rose from somewhere deep within her, giving her a new vigor and a solid fortitude that her limited recall could not fathom. She knew not from where it came, but it had a familiar essence. She felt herself responding to its urging, growing stronger and more determined. Once again she stretched, this time deliberately seeking out each ache or pain and testing them as she moved this way and that. Whatever the source was of this new-found energy, it also gave her the sure knowledge that she had never avoided problems, and it was an inescapable fact that none of hers would depart until they were met and dealt with summarily. Sifting through the multitude that came to mind, she selected the first and most obvious. She could hardly spend the rest of her life in bed, and the sooner she dispensed with her immobility, the sooner she would regain some semblance of control of her life. A long soak in a hot tub would help loosen her stiff muscles, but making such a request might seem a trifle presumptuous in a strange household. Still, Ashton Wingate had insisted that she was his wife. Perhaps they would not deem it too much amiss if she asked for such a service.

Pushing herself out of the bed, she stood to her feet and, seeing no sign of her robe, cautiously made her way to the hearth. The fire had burned low, and a definite chill had settled in the room. A small store of split logs had been laid up in the brass woodbox, and she tossed several on the glowing coals, then reached back to take up the poker. As her fingers closed over the handle of the piece, an image of an upraised poker flashed through her mind. The vision was brief, but it left her feeling strangely weak. Trembling, she sank into a nearby chair and rubbed her temple with fingers that were now as cold as ice. She could find no reason for her reaction and tried to force it from her mind, but in its stead came a cold, clammy, distasteful void.

Lierin straightened, steeling herself against the disturbing sensation. The flames were cheerfully cavorting along the logs, and she knelt before the hearth, letting the radiating warmth drive away the frigid fingers of apprehension. A light knock came upon the door, and without pause, as if no answer were expected, the portal was pushed open. Willabelle entered and took a step or two toward the bed before noticing it was empty. She halted in consternation and searched about with her eyes until Lierin came to her feet with a polite clearing of her throat; then the housekeeper turned her massive bulk about.

"Lawsy, Miz Lierin. Ah di'n know yo was up an' about," the woman apologized in an elated tone.

"Yes, I'm feeling much better now."

Willabelle gave a little cackle of glee. "De massa be happy to hear dat. He been nearly 'side hisse'f, wantin' yo to be all right." She began smoothing the sheets on the bed. "Would yo be wantin' somepin to eat now, missus?"

Lierin replied with a tentative smile: "Actually, I was wondering if it might be possible for me to have a bath . . . I mean, a real one that I can soak in . . ."

Willabelle grinned broadly. "Yas'm, dat sho' is pos'ble." She retrieved the velvet robe that had fallen from the end of the bed and held it while the girl slipped into it. "Yo jes' rest yose'f right here, missus, whilst Ah goes downstairs an' fetches some things."

When the woman returned, it seemed a whole procession of servants accompanied her. Some carried boxes tied with fancy bows, other toted buckets of hot water, and the last servant entered bearing a brass tub in his arms. A bath was prepared, and as the servants left, Willabelle laid out fresh linens and placed vials of perfumed oils and a porcelain dish of scented soaps on a small table within easy reach of the tub.

Lierin thoughtfully sampled the fragrances of the vials until she found one of a pleasing flowery essence, then dribbled it into the bath. A scent of jasmine filled the room as she flicked her fingers through the steaming liquid, and she closed her eyes in pleasure as she savored the smell. Rolling up her hair into a massive knot upon her head, she eyed the boxes over her shoulder with a good measure of curiosity. "What are those?"

"Dem's from de dressmaker, missus. De massa ordered yo some mo' clothes a few days ago, and dey arrive las' night. Ah' show dem to yo whilst yo soak in de tub."

Willabelle immediately turned to the matter of helping her disrobe and showed a gentle concern for her condition. Even though the housekeeper had seen the bruises before, their appearance had grown even more unsightly with the yellowing tones mingling with the purple and blue. Others which had gone unnoticed had blackened and were clearly visible against the creamy skin. The slash across her back had taken on several small scabs and widened as the contusions became more evident.

"Lawsy, chil', yo look like yo was run over by both de team an' de coach."

Lierin sank into the soothing liquid and released a sigh as the heat banished the last of the chill. "I was sure that I had been."

The black woman chuckled. "If'n it di'n smell so bad, ah'd fetch some hoss liniment to rub on yo, but wid all dem fancy clothes de massa bought for yo, we cain't have yo smellin' like a hoss. Ah'll put some salve on dat place on your back though. It ain't a mite pretty."

As Lierin soaked away some of her soreness, Willabelle flipped open the couturier's boxes and displayed several delicately worked chemises, a stiff-boned corset, silk stockings, and lace-trimmed petticoats to her new mistress. A few fashionable gowns were taken from the larger boxes and draped over chairs, while matching slippers were also presented. In preparation for Lierin's leaving the tub, the housekeeper laid out a lace-embellished nightgown on the bed, then came with towel in hand to lend assistance to the young woman.

"Did Mr. Wingate select all those clothes by himself?" Lierin asked as the housekeeper gently patted her skin dry.

"Ah 'spect so, missus, an' Ah say he done a mighty fine job of it, too."

"Yes, he apparently has no difficulty selecting the right apparel for a woman."

Detecting a slight satirical inflection in her voice, Willabelle paused briefly, giving her a quizzical stare. "Don' yo like de clothes, missus?"

"Of course! It would be difficult not to. I mean, everything has been chosen so well." She pulled the nightgown over her head, speaking through it as she added, "Your master appears to be very talented at dressing a woman."

Willabelle smiled to herself as a small ray of understanding dawned. It was not uncommon for a wife to be suspicious of the way her husband gained such knowledge, especially when the man was as good-looking as the master. "Yo don' need to fret yose'f about Massa Ashton. Ah ain't never seen a man so taken wid a lady as he is wid yo. Reckonin' yo was dead nearly kilt him."

Lierin tied the satin cords of the dressing gown about her narrow waist as she asked, "Are you sure I'm really his wife?"

"De massa says yo is, and dat's good enough fo' me. An' if'n yo gots any doubts, take a gander at dat dere paintin' again. Dat oughta convince yo if it ain't done so already."

"Miss Rousse seems to think differently. I understand she was engaged to Ashton when he went down to New Orleans and got married."

"Humph!" The black woman rolled her eyes. "If Miz Marelda reckon herself engaged to Massa Ashton, it was mostly in her mind. Dat woman been ataggin' aftah him ever since she was a young kid comin' here wid her pa. Her folks died some five or so years ago an' left her wid dat big ol' house in town. It jes' seem like she got real anxious to be married aftah dat. 'Tain't hard to figger she's itchin' fo' Massa Ashton 'cause she's out here all de time. If Ah knows her at all, she be around fo' a spell more, even wid de massa sayin' yo is his wife. Seems like dere ain't no nice way to tell her to go."

"Mr. Wingate may not wish her to leave. She is a very beautiful woman."

"Dat'll be de day when de massa cain't make up his mind," Willabelle mumbled beneath her breath.

"Do you think I should be cautious about leaving my room?" Lierin queried. "Miss Rousse does seem to resent me."

Willabelle grunted. "Don' yo be scared 'bout dat, missus. In fact, Ah'm thinkin' yo better venture out jes' as soon as pos'ble 'cause if'n yo don', she gonna have de idea she gots Massa Ashton all to herse'f. She been like a cat runnin' up de walls dis whole week."

"Are you suggesting that I chase after him, too?" Lierin inquired in astonishment. "Why, I hardly know the man."

"Well, honey chil', if'n yo don' mind some advice from one who knows de man, yo ain't gonna find another like him fo' some time to come. He's a man, all right, an' yo is a mighty fine-lookin' woman, but like yo said, so is Marelda."

Lierin did not feel inclined to argue with the housekeeper. Neither would she be goaded into running after a man who was still very much a stranger to her. There were serious matters to take into consideration. Once she lifted the barriers between them and accepted him as her husband, she would have to face the matter of going to bed with him, and at this point in time she was not willing to run headlong into a situation she had some reservations about. She would just as soon take it slowly and avoid what mistakes she could. Hopefully the problem would soon be solved by the return of her memory.

Still, she was intrigued by the one who called himself her husband. He was an exceptionally good-looking man and comported himself well. This was made evident once more when he came to visit her in her bedchamber, which had become his morning custom.

In gentlemanly decorum he waited at the threshold as Willabelle announced his presence, and Lierin noticed how her own heart quickened its pace with the knowledge of his presence. The warmth in her cheeks could hardly be dismissed as lack of interest.

Willabelle had let the door swing back, allowing Ashton full view of the room, and his gaze found Lierin framed in the morning light spilling through the crystal panes. Her long hair seemed ablaze as it tumbled in loose array around her shoulders, and when their eyes met, a hesitant smile touched her lips.

"I must thank you for your gifts," she murmured. "They're very lovely. You've been very generous with me."

"May I come in?" he inquired.

"Oh, surely." She was amazed that he should require her permission.

Willabelle slipped from the room as he entered, announcing as she swung the door closed, "Ah'll fetch y'all some vittles."

Ashton moved across the room, drawn to his wife much as a freezing man is lured to warmth or a starving man to a feast. Her beauty filled his hungering gaze and lighted a fire in his blood, sending the cold chills of uncertainty fleeing from his vitals. Was it madness to awake in a world where nothing bore the touch of familiarity, where every face was that of a stranger, where even the bed she lay in and the clothes she wore bore no hint of her own world? Or worse yet, not being able to say what her own world was and having no recall beyond that moment of awakening? How could he even entertain the idea of madness when he gazed at her?

"May I say, madam, that you're looking exceptionally beautiful this morning?"

"Even with the bruises?" she queried dubiously.

"My eyes have been so long starved for you, I barely notice them." His fingers lifted to brush her cheek lightly. "Besides, they're fading now and will soon be gone." He lowered his head near the curling mass of gold-lit auburn and closed his eyes as her fragrance spiraled down through him with intoxicating effect, snaring his mind and his senses and blending them with memories of old.

Lierin felt his nearness with every stirring fiber in her being, with every tingling wave that washed through her body. Her eyes flicked hurriedly downward as the warmth of his breath touched her ear, and she stared in fixed attention where his shirt gaped open, partially revealing a firmly muscled, darkly matted chest. As he leaned closer, her nerves jumped, and she placed a cautious hand against that firm expanse, but the contact was explosive. It set her pulse leaping out of control. Feeling the heat of a blush in her cheeks, she stepped quickly away, rubbing her palm as though it had been scorched.

"I'm overwhelmed by the clothes you bought me," she stated breathlessly, casting a nervous glance over her shoulder as she lengthened the distance between them. It was safer that way. "I've been thinking that I must have some clothes of my own somewhere."

"It doesn't really matter if you have," he replied, contemplating her from beneath his brows. "Outfitting you with a wardrobe isn't going to put me into debtor's prison. We'll have to attend to its completion when you feel up to leaving the house."

Lierin experienced some bemusement of her own. "Aren't you afraid I'm only after your gifts and your wealth? Especially when there's still some doubt I'm your wife?"

Ashton laughed softly. "Who prattles about doubt?"

She answered with a tiny shrug. "Some think you're being fooled."

"Marelda has come to visit you?" he inquired and, at her reluctant nod, captured the wide, emerald eyes by the intensity of his stare. "Marelda never saw you before the other night, and she'd be the last person to admit that you're my wife."

"I wish it were as settled in my mind as it seems to be in yours." Turning away, Lierin pressed her fingers against her temples and shook her head in frustration. "I know the memory is there, waiting to be brought to the surface, but there seems to be a barrier that prevents it. There are so many things I need to know about my life." She heaved a sigh. "I'm a stranger even to myself."

"I can tell you a few facts," he murmured, moving near. "But our time together was so brief I fear they're not very significant."

She faced him and searched his face. "Please . . . tell me everything you can."

A warm glow came into the smoky depths as he stared down into her troubled face. He reached out a hand and gently smoothed an errant strand from her cheek. Then he stepped away, relating the facts as if he had memorized them. "You were born twenty-three years ago in New Orleans and named Lierin Edana Somerton. Your mother, Dierdre Cassidy, was of Irish descent, and your father came from England. You have a sister, Lenore Elizabeth Somerton, who was also born in New Orleans. . . ."

"Which of us is older?"

Ashton paused, glancing back at her with an apologetic smile. "I'm sorry, my love. I was so enamored with you, some details were left wanting."

The endearment and statement brought the color rushing back to her cheeks. Her voice was barely a whisper as she urged, "Go on."

Ashton stepped to the windows and, pulling the draperies aside, looked out over the grounds. "When your mother died, she left you and Lenore a coastal home in Biloxi. You also have a house in New Orleans bequeathed to you by your grandfather. The will was drawn up while you stayed with him, and although he died believing you had drowned, it was never changed." Dropping the silk panel over the window, he faced her, folding his hands behind his back. "So you see, madam, you have possessions of your own, and with your father a rich merchant in England, you're quite independent of my wealth." A slow smile touched his lips. "Indeed, were I a fortune seeker, you would be a very prime target for my attentions."

Her spirits responded to his humor, and in a half-shy manner, she gave him retort: "I'll have to consider that as a possible cause for your insistence in claiming me as your wife." She grew steadily braver as he returned a roguish smile to her. "I do perceive that you've been something of a rake."

"Madam?" His brow slanted up.

Her eyes briefly marked the gifts on the bed. "You certainly seem to know how to dress a lady." She gave him a look askance. "Or should I say undress?"

Ashton protested her charge with a lopsided smile. "I've been a blessed saint, madam."

"Hm." Lierin strolled about, tossing him a glance over her shoulder. "I wonder."

"Wonder no more, my love," he advised her with a lively sparkle in his eyes. "I swear to you that I savored no other wench while your memory burned in my mind."

"Burned in your mind?" She turned to him again with a quizzical smile. "Just how long did the fire of my memory last? A week? A month? A year?"

Ashton laughed with pleasure, cheered by the fact that he was seeing glimpses of a personality that was more like his Lierin. His gaze warmed as it raked her. "Were you not so badly bruised, my love, I would show you how desperate a man I have become."

Her smile slowly faded. "You have no doubt charmed many women out of their virtue, sir. I only hope I do not find myself a victim of some ploy you've contrived."

Ashton grew serious as he sensed that her worry was genuine. "What are you afraid of, Lierin?"

She heaved a wavering sigh and let a long moment pass before she replied: "I have this fear that I'm not really your wife, and if I let you become my husband, I will someday realize my mistake. By then, it might be too late. I could find myself with child. I might fall in love with you, and I'm afraid of being hurt."

Ashton went to her and stood before her, resisting the urge to take her into his arms. "I love you, Lierin, and I play no games with your heart. I married you because I wanted you for my wife. Whatever children our love may bear, they will have a proper name and a claim to all my holdings. I promise you that."

Though she wanted to hold him at arm's length for her own good, she was becoming increasingly aware of him as a man. Her spirit was nurtured by the comfort he so easily bestowed on her, and she wanted to draw succor from his caring attention. "It's difficult to accept the idea of being married, Ashton, when I know so little about myself."

"That's understandable, my love. We were together for such a brief period, you barely had time to get accustomed to the idea."

"And yet," she murmured thoughtfully, staring at the golden band on her finger, "I wear this ring. Do you recognize it?"

He lifted her hand and considered the circle of gold a long moment before replying: "I had no time to purchase anything but a plain band for you. If my memory serves me correctly, this is the ring I gave you."

She felt the warmth of his gaze on her face and dared to glance up. "Perhaps we are married, Ashton, and I'm just letting my fears blind me to that fact."

"Don't torment yourself, my love," he urged. "Hopefully, after further rest your memory will come back, and you'll know the truth."

"I await that moment anxiously."

"So do I, my love. So do I."

- Chapter Four -

The parlor was the gathering place for the Wingate family before the evening meal. It was a time for conversation and restful pleasantries, a goblet of sherry or a small draft of a stronger beverage, a few more tapestry stitches, or a tinkling melody played on the harpsichord. Sometimes the rich, mellow sounds of the cello flowed through the house, either as part of a duet of the two instruments, or singly, as it was played this evening. Marelda's hopes soared as she listened to the musical strains, for she knew Ashton was the only one in the household who could make the instrument come alive with such warmth. He was a man of many talents, a perfectionist who strove to succeed in all things.

Marelda paused in front of the hall mirror to give herself a last complimentary appraisal. Her black hair was artfully arranged to set off her sultry facade, having been swept in deep, lush waves to one side, where it was gathered in a cluster of ringlets that dangled prettily from behind her ear. She had worn the gown of dark red taffeta with the hope that Ashton would be at dinner, and now that she knew she would not be disappointed, she smiled smugly to herself. She considered the selection of the gown a stroke of genius on her part. The illusion of voluptuousness had been created by the use of padding sewn inside her chemise where it would press her small breasts upward. The shallow bodice seemed unable to contain the structured fullness and threatened to dip below the line of decency and reveal the darker hues of her bosom. A man would be hard pressed to ignore such a daring décolletage, and since Ashton was very much of that gender, she expected him to be susceptible. Of course, her display might shock the elder ladies, but if it succeeded in winning Ashton's regard and arousing his manly lusts, then it would be well worth her exposure. She would not sit idly by while the red-head made so much of her invalid state.

Moving steathily to the door of her adversary's room, she pressed an ear to the smooth panels and listened for any sign of stirring from within. Willabelle's voice was heard, but her tone was low and muted, making the words inaudible. It hardly mattered. Marelda had not expected the lazy twit to raise herself from her bed and join them for dinner. She had not made the effort all week, seeming rather to dote on the idea of her frailty.

The fool! Marelda smirked. While she languishes weak and pallid amid her lace pillows, I shall have my way with Ashton. He will surely have second thoughts about claiming her as his long-lost wife.

Marelda hummed gaily as she descended the stairs. She was feeling light of spirit with Ashton so close within her grasp. After all, she was quite a beautiful woman, and she was not unknowledgeable about seduction, having used it on other men at her whim. Though she had not been without certain pleasures, she had always been careful to maintain her virginity, gaining for herself the reputation of a tease. It was not that she was averse to yielding herself to such amorous adventures, but knowing the perils of total submission, she had been reluctant to endanger her chances of becoming Ashton's wife.

Wanting the surprise to be complete, Marelda softened her footsteps upon nearing the parlor and gained a vantage point at the door without being noticed. Amanda and Aunt Jennifer sat in a pair of chairs near the fireplace and were concentrating on their needlework as they listened to the music. Ashton sat closer to the entry and seemed equally absorbed in his effort. The slightly wistful expression that flitted across his profile hinted of some deep, hidden yearning, which she could not fully fathom. She was half-afraid it had something to do with the woman upstairs. That could not be allowed!

"Good evening," she bade warmly from the doorway and immediately gained the attention she sought. Ashton looked around, and the music stopped abruptly, causing the two siblings to glance up in wonder. Aunt Jennifer's eyes went to the door and widened, then narrowed with a sudden grimace as the needle pricked her finger. Sucking the abused digit, she stared at the younger woman with a disturbed frown.

"Good heavens," Amanda exclaimed beneath her breath and pressed a hand to her throat as she sagged back in her chair.

Only Ashton took their guest's entry in stride and rose to his feet with a smile of mild amusement. "Good evening, Marelda."

The brunette indicated the harpsichord. "Do you mind if I join you?"

"Please do," Ashton replied, lifting his own hand toward the piece in polite response. He waited until she had seated herself, then settled into his chair again. She ran her fingers over the keys in light practice, then paused, giving him a nod to begin, The entrancing melody began anew, filling the house with haunting refrains. Then the keys of the harpsichord intruded, and the flowing strains were quickly overwhelmed by the loud twanging notes that seemed either half a beat behind or ahead of the cello. Aunt Jennifer cringed as Marelda attacked the keys, and though she tried to concentrate on the tapestry she was creating, her effort won her several more jabs from the sharp needle. Amanda kept her pained frown averted, but her inclination to nod her head in a subconscious effort to urge Marelda into a more timely pace drew Ashton's notice. He subdued a smile and showed mercy on the two aging siblings by bringing the piece to a graceful end. For a moment he adjusted and tested the strings, feigning dissatisfaction with his own performance. As she waited for him to continue, Marelda left her bench and approached the sideboard where a set of crystal decanters resided on a silver tray. Keeping her back to Ashton, she took up a wineglass and poured herself a liberal brandy, then returned to stand before the man who consumed her interest.

Amanda glanced apprehensively toward their guest and found Marelda's bosom straining over the top of her gown. Her own cheeks grew warm at the immodest display of a magenta peak rising above the woman's gown. The huge grandfather dock chimed out the hour, and the elder woman gratefully consulted its face for a diversion. "Wherever is Willabelle? She's usually been in and out several times by now, fretting about the table or fussing about the slowness of the kitchen help."

Ashton answered without bothering to lift his gaze. "She's probably out there now, stirring Bertha into a nervous frenzy."

Here was a topic that had long roused Marelda's irritation. "You allow your people far too much latitude, Ashton. Willabelle runs the house as if it were her own."

Deliberately Ashton made the cello screech, driving the harping woman back a step, and then seeming intent upon his task, he bent closer to lend a careful ear to the tuning of the strings.

Marelda was not willing to dismiss the subject. "You pamper your servants far too much. Why, anyone would think they were family, the way you coddle them."

"I don't coddle them, Marelda," he stated quietly but firmly, "but I did lay out a goodly sum of money to purchase them, and I see no reason to devalue my investments by mistreatment."

"I've heard it rumored that you even allow them a credit for their services, and that after several years they have the chance to buy their freedom. Are you aware of the laws concerning the freeing of slaves?"

Slowly Ashton raised his gaze, briefly noting her display as his eyes traveled upward. He showed neither shock nor interest as he calmly considered her. "Any slave who wants his freedom above everything else ceases to be valuable to me, Marelda. At the first chance he gets, he's going to run away, and chains would make him useless. If any are set on going, I let them work off their worth, and then I ship them to safety. It's as simple as that, and I break no laws."

"It's a wonder you have anyone working for you."

"I believe we've already discussed the success of Belle Chêne. I see no reason to belabor the point." Halting further debate, he again stroked the strings with the bow, making them sing. He involved himself in a delicate air, soothing his irritation by slow degrees, while he filled his mind with thoughts of Lierin. He had paused at her door before coming down, only to be told by Willabelle that his wife was indisposed. He had felt a need to see her and, after his failure, had grown pensive, wondering how long she would hide from him and if she would ever accept the fact of their marriage.

He glanced around, and for a moment, he thought he was imagining the vision that had come to stand in the doorway. His hands paused and his breath slowed as the last trembling note of a plucked string slowly died in the sudden silent parlor. It was a sight the likes of which he had formed in his mind many times in the past three years, but now, it was very wonderfully real.

"Lierin!" Did he speak or only think the word?

Marelda swished around in surprise, sloshing the brandy over the rim of the goblet onto her wide skirts. She stared at the one in the doorway, and her mind moaned and roiled in abject frustration.

Just behind Lierin and alert to lend a hand or assistance, stood a grinning Willabelle, obviously proud of this creation and her own part in it. The housekeeper had settled the matter of Lierin's identity in her own mind, accepting her as mistress without reservation, and wanted to aid in her advancement to that position in whatever fashion she could.

Ashton came to his feet and could feel the quickening thud of his heart as he savored every detail of his wife's beauty. Her red hair had been gathered on top of her head in a loose swirl and formed soft waves where it had been brushed up and away from her face. The effect was as alluring as her gown, which seemed to float around her in a pale pink cloud. The long, voluminous sleeves were made of sheer silk and were bound at the wrists with satin cuffs that matched the band about her neck. A high, frothy ruff rose from the narrow collar and seemed prim to a fault, but he knew that the fullness beneath the bodice was all woman. Though pale from the exertion of reaching the parlor, she was a living portrait of feminine beauty. All thought of Marelda fled his mind. Indeed, it was as if only two people were in the room. Their eyes met and held, and all he could see was a lovely face with twin green vortices that threatened to engulf him.

A worried smile tugged at her lips, but her gaze never wavered from his, though she addressed them all. "Willabelle said it would be all right if I came down to join you for the evening meal," she murmured in half-apology. "I don't wish to impose, so if you've planned otherwise, I can dine in my room."

"I will not hear of it!" Ashton's words were almost an explosion as he set the cello aside and stepped forward to take her hand. Tucking her arm safely through his, he spoke past her: "Willabelle, see that another place is set."

"No need, Massa Ashton." The woman chuckled as she saw her charge delivered into another's care, and she shuffled off, continuing over her shoulder, "It already been took care of. Yassuh! Yassuh!"

"Please." Leirin lifted her gaze to the warmth of his. "I heard you playing. Will you continue?"

"If you will join me," he murmured.

"Join you?" Lierin suffered through a moment of confusion until he indicated the harpsichord; then she hurried to deny the possibility. "Oh, but I can't . . . or at least, I don't think I can. . . ."

"We'll see if it comes back to you." Ashton led her to the instrument and picked out a brief, brisk tune on the keyboard as she sank to the tapestry-covered bench. Tentatively she placed her fingers where his had been and ran through the same ditty. She laughed at her accomplishment and glanced up at him. With a growing smile, he played a longer portion, and she repeated it with rising enthusiasm. When he brushed her skirts aside, she quickly slid over on the bench, allowing him more room as he sat beside her. They played a short duet together, Lierin's pale fingers flicking over the higher keyboard, while Ashton dealt with the lower. Much to her own surprise, an amusing verse came to mind, and she sang it in a lilting voice, shrugging in amazement as the words seemed to flow unbidden from some unknown source. At its conclusion, they dissolved in laughter, and when his arm came around her and brought her close, it seemed a natural reaction to relax against him.

"That was most delightful, madam. Thank you."

"My pleasure, sir," she responded brightly.

Marelda ground her teeth as she saw her plans for the evening tumbling in a wasted effort around her heels. Listening to the sounds of their gaiety while she had to watch the two of them nuzzling each other almost made her nauseated. It was extremely humiliating to be sitting with her bosom overflowing her gown while she was ignored and all but forgotten by the same man whose eyes brazenly devoured the auburn-haired wench. If not for her pride, she would have risen to her feet and stalked out of the room.

Marelda's repugnance was not shared by all. Amanda was grateful for Lierin's presence, for the young woman had lifted her spirits as much as she had Ashton's. When Amanda considered the pair and how well they complemented the other, Marelda's attire faded from mind. Lierin was as beautiful and feminine as Ashton was handsome and masculine, and the good looks of each were enhanced by the contrast with the other. Truly, the match seemed without flaw.

Amanda exchanged a pleased smile with her sister, and no words were needed to communicate their mutual satisfaction. Their only regret was that it had taken so long for them to meet this delightful addition to the family, this Lierin.

Dinner was announced, and Ashton escorted his wife to the

place reserved for the mistress of the house, at the opposite end from where he sat. Marelda was left to make her way unattended into the dining hall, and following them, she suffered several jabs from the sharp horns of jealousy as she noted the way Ashton's hand lingered on the narrow waist and lightly stroked above it. Petulantly waving away Willis's help, Marelda waited beside her chair for Ashton to lend her aid. When he finally turned to give assistance, she let her handkerchief fall to the floor in the guise of carelessness and deliberately waited until he had stepped forward to pick up the cloth before reaching for it herself, thereby allowing him an unrestricted view of her bosom. The two older ladies were just entering the room and missed the exhibition, but Lierin saw the ploy for what it was. She realized Willabelle had spoken the truth concerning Marelda. The brunette was out to snare Ashton, and apparently she had no reservations about the tactics she employed.

Ashton's gaze did not waver as it passed the magenta-crested breasts and dropped to the handkerchief. Retrieving the delicate linen, he placed it beside Marelda's plate, then looked back to see Lierin's reaction. At her wondering stare, he gave a quick shrug of his brows, knowing of no other way to reassure her while they were in the other's presence.

"It's certainly good to have you with us, my dear," Amanda said as she paused at Lierin's chair and patted her arm affectionately.

"Oh, it is," Aunt Jennifer agreed.

Lierin was moved by their sincerity. She blinked back the sudden moisture that blurred her vision and smiled in gratitude. "Thank you."

During the meal Marelda found no relief from her anxieties. Even though she translated Lierin's shyness and demureness into caution and coyness and observed her with the eagerness of a snake ready to devour its prey, she failed to find any definite flaw that she could point an accusing finger to. She was distressed by the thought that this would be the way things went henceforth, that she would forever see this usurper at the focal point of attention, while she looked on from a distance. She could hardly ignore the eagerness of family and servants to accept the red-haired woman as Ashton's wife.

When the meal was concluded, Lierin's strength began to flag, and she begged to be excused, knowing how quickly total exhaustion could come upon her. Ashton asked the same for himself and, ignoring Marelda's glare, carefully assisted his wife from the room. Lierin had grown stiff from sitting, and her gait was cautiously slow. Ashton noted her difficulty and paused in the hall to lift her in his arms. He was just as observant of the grimace that briefly touched her features.

"I'm sorry." His face was touched with concern. "Did I hurt you?"

"It's nothing, really," she hastened to assure him. "Just a bruise on my back." Her cheeks grew warm as she settled cautiously against him and slipped her arms around his neck. Whenever she touched him, her mind was overwhelmed with a searing awareness of his hardened frame and the manly virility he exuded. She was beginning to understand Marelda's reluctance to give him up. In truth, the idea of being this man's wife was beginning to settle in with a multitude of pleasing aspects.

Ashton's brows came together as he recalled Willabelle's comments about the place on her back. "Do you know how you got the bruise?"

Lierin replied with a small shrug. "From the accident, I suppose."

"Willabelle thought someone might have hit you. Can you recall anything happening like that?"

"No, not at all. I can't imagine why anybody would do such a thing."

"Would you be averse to showing me the place?" he asked. He met her surprised and somewhat wary gaze, and his eyes sparkled into hers. "Only to appease my curiosity, my dear."

Lierin smiled as she teased: "Though I cannot be sure, sir, I suspect I've heard better excuses from several unworthy knaves."

His grin grew slightly roguish. "I haven't forgotten that you have a very nice back, madam, certainly one worthy of admiration. You can hardly blame me for finding an excuse to view it." Arriving at her door, he pushed it open and bore her across the threshold. "In fact, I remember quite distinctly that every part of you is noteworthy." His eyes dipped to caress her breast, halting her breath with his bold gaze. "You're very soft and womanly. . . ."

Lierin hastened to redirect his attention to something less disturbing. "I fear I've become a burden this evening . . . taking you away from your family and guest."

"On the contrary, my love, I am indebted to you for providing me an excuse to escape."

She gave him a slanted glance and could not resist a gentle gibe. "I thought you might have enjoyed her game."

Ashton's eyes took on a glowing sheen as they again touched her bosom. "I've seen better, especially when I've been privileged to entertain my present companion."

Her body tingled beneath his heated perusal, and she could not subdue a blush as a thrill rushed through her. Her voice was small as she reminded him, "I think you can put me down now. . . ."

Despite the gnawing ache in the pit of his stomach, Ashton resumed his jovial demeanor as he placed her on the downturned covers of the tester bed. "Delivered safe and sound to your bed, madam, and I judge, with no more bruises. Yet I would say you've a trifle overdressed for bed. Do you care for assistance?"

She declined his offer with a soft chuckle of amusement. "I think I'll wait for Willabelle to unfasten me."

"What? And ignore these willing hands? Madam, surely a husband can do such a service without tarnishing his wife's good reputation." His white teeth gleamed beneath a widening grin. "I promise to be a gentleman."

Lierin cocked a brow at him, conveying her distrust. "No doubt a married gentleman who takes his liberties seriously."

"Of course!" he teased. "How else should I take them?"

She laughed. "I really don't think I'm safe in here with you."

"Come now, madam. Will a man ravish his own wife?"

"If he's desperate enough," she replied pertly.

"I am that, madam," he freely admitted, "but where does trust begin? If I can restrain myself while unfastening your gown, will you not, then, be reassured that my first concern is for you and your rapid recovery?"

"I grow weary of the argument." She resigned herself with far less reluctance than caution demanded. Indeed, she almost felt as if she were throwing reason and security to the wind. What was there about the man that made her so pliable with him? He was handsome; none could deny the fact, but there was a quality of manliness that very much appealed to her. "Mind well your words, sir. Trust is very important in anyone's marriage."

Ashton chuckled as he began to struggle with the tiny fastenings, then a moment later he sobered as the back of the gown fell apart, revealing an ugly welt. He spread the opening wider to get a better view of it, causing Lierin to catch her breath.

"Easy, love," he reassured her in a serious tone. "I only want to examine this more carefully." He held the lamp closer as he inspected the strip of bruised and scabbed flesh that crossed her back from her left shoulder almost to the lower middle. He frowned sharply when the memory of the switch-wielding matron came to mind, but something heavier than a willow branch had produced this. "I don't think this was caused by any fall from a horse."

Lierin was totally confounded by the idea that she might have suffered intentional abuse before the accident. She could not imagine such an event, much less recall the circumstances of it. She turned to discuss the matter further and suffered some shock as she found herself beneath the unswerving regard of those smoldering hazel eyes. His mood had obviously changed; his questing concern had been swept away by the onslaught of his raging desire, and he made it quite evident what he wanted. The muscles beneath the darkly bronzed visage had tensed, while his nostrils flared with his heavy breathing. She felt her heart lurch forward in a sudden frantic beating, and her senses came abruptly awake. The heat of his gaze set a flame burning within her, and yet she felt all shivery inside. She was afraid he would touch her and she would yield herself in trembling eagerness. Seeking escape from his unspoken seduction, she sprang to her feet and fled across the room, taking refuge behind the dressing screen.

It was a long painful moment before Ashton regained enough control to ask, "Do you want me to send Willabelle up to you?"

"No. I don't think that will be necessary now."

"Perhaps I should lend further assistance to loosening your gown," he offered.

She laughed nervously, tugging the ties of her petticoats free and pushing the billowing folds down with the pink garment. "I think you have the heart of a rake, Mr. Wingate."

Ashton chuckled as he meandered about the room. "That's what you said three years ago."

"Then I haven't entirely lost my wits."

He met her gaze above the screen. "You're still as beautiful as ever."

"Will you hand me my gown and robe from the armoire?" she requested, avoiding the path where his statement might lead.

Ashton selected garments that would more readily reveal her curves and draped them over the top of the screen. As he waited for her to emerge, he doffed his own double-breasted dress coat and loosened his vest and shirt, tossing the cravat over a chair atop the coat. When she stepped around the screen, his hungry gaze devoured her softly clad back and swaying hips as she went to the dressing table. He followed her, feeling much like a rutting swamp cat prowling after a mate. Lierin sensed his approach, and her whole body tensed as he laid a hand upon her arm. A flooding excitement washed through her body, and she could not subdue the quickening pace of her heart as she was turned to meet the full force of his hunger. He studied her reaction as he lowered his face to hers. The green eyes flickered with uncertainty, then just before his open mouth captured hers, the eyelids came slowly downward and almost haltingly she yielded her lips to his. The kiss began as a gentle questing, with his mouth moving slowly upon hers, but the fires ignited like dry kindling in a roaring blaze. Passion sparked and flared ever brighter beneath his torching demands, turning her mind inside out and uncovering a need in her that she had not known existed. His hand slipped downward over her buttock, pressing her to him as his mouth slanted crushingly across hers, and with a soft moan she rose against him, molding herself more intimately to his body.

A knock on the door jolted them back to reality. Ashton raised his head with a muttered curse and tossed a glare over his shoulder at the offending portal. Though he was tempted to ignore the summons, it came again, this time louder and more insistent. With a growl he stood away from Lierin and moved across the room to the windows where he flipped a catch and pushed out the crystal panes to allow the night air to cool his mind and body.

Lierin found she had to settle her own jangled emotions before she could call out with any semblance of calm. "Yes? Who is it?"

An all too familiar voice answered through the closed portal: "Marelda Rousse. May I come in?"

Angrily Ashton ran his fingers through his hair, muttering sourly, "I'll wring that woman's neck yet!"

"Just a moment, Marelda," Lierin bade and, glancing back at him, waited for him to give a nod of approval before she went to open the door.

"I left a book of prose in here earlier this week," Marelda bubbled hurriedly as she pushed into the room. "I'd like to read it before I go to bed. It does so help to relax me." Her eyes quickly searched the room until she found the one she had come to fetch. "Oh! Ashton!" She managed to sound surprised in spite of her suspicions. She noted their relaxed attire, and though she kept her smile, her eyes grew cold. "I'm sorry if I . . . ah . . . interrupted anything, dahling."

Ashton's irritation had not eased as he returned her gaze with a frown.

"I'll get the book," she said, reading his annoyance. "I left it over there by the chair." She swept across the room and picked up the volume that she had seen on the table when she first visited Lierin. Though she had concocted the he out of desperation, knowing that Ashton would probably still be in the room, it had given her an excuse to get in and hopefully halt whatever amorous play might be taking place.

"Oh, Ashton . . ." Marelda paused at the door. "I thought I heard a ruckus in the stables before I came up. Do you suppose there's any trouble with the horses? Should I send someone out there to see? Or will you be going out?"

"I'll see to it," Ashton growled, by now thoroughly incensed with the woman.

"Do you want me to stay with Lierin while you go?" she offered in the guise of sweetness.

Lierin answered for herself, somewhat stiffly. "That won't be necessary, Marelda."

"Well, good night then. Pleasant dreams." Marelda fairly sang the words as she waltzed out of the room.

Ashton gnashed his teeth as he retrieved his coat from the chair and flung it over his shoulder. "She came in here on purpose."

Lierin was in full agreement, but having no wish to set spurs to his anger, she refrained from voicing her opinion. "I hope there's nothing wrong with the horses."

"Marelda probably made that up, too," Ashton replied. His mood softened as he brought Lierin close again. "It will be torture to leave you."

"It will be torture if you stay," she whispered back. "I'm not ready for this yet. Go," she urged, "see about your horses, and give me time to think."

Ashton glanced up from his ledgers as a soft rapping came upon his door. Almost in unison, the tinkling chimes of his desk clock began to herald the hour of eleven. He rose and stretched his arms over his head to release the knot that had formed between his shoulder blades. After he had been called out to the stables on a fool's errand, he wondered what other crisis awaited him outside his chamber door. Alas, it was far more than he had expected. Marelda had come brazenly adorned in a loosely flowing peignoir that hung open over a diaphanous gown. The gossamer cloth held nothing from his regard. Indeed, it was hardly more than a transparent web over her body. Her hair fell in a dark torrent around her shoulders, and when she moved forward into the room, his senses were assailed by a heavy, liberally used fragrance. Smiling seductively, she closed the door behind her and leaned against it, thrusting out her small breasts until they strained against the sheer cloth. The invitation in her eyes was for him to reach out and accept all that she offered. When he made no such attempt, she advanced toward him with a slow, undulating motion that was meant to captivate her audience, forcing him to retreat before the imminent threat of contact.

Ashton's brows twisted dubiously as he considered the woman. "I believe you've made a mistake, Marelda."

"No mistake, Ashton." Her red lips parted in a seductive smile as she slipped the peignoir from her shoulders and let it fall to the floor. "I have grown tired of chasing you betwixt your marriage and your infatuations. I have come to offer myself so you can no longer mistake what I have to give you. No other woman can fulfill your needs and your desires as well as I . . . because I know you far better than those strangers whom you seek out. They are no more than passing fancies. You'll grow tired of them eventually, but I shall always be here to love you."

He shook his head, bemused by her persistence. If he had pursued her in a heated passion at any previous time, he might have been able to understand her refusal to let go. "Marelda, I'm sorry . . . I'm . . . not the man for you, and even if I were, I'm not free to accept what you offer."

Not willing to yield the field, she cajoled in soft supplication: "You're as free as you wish to be, Ashton, and I have come willingly to give myself to you. You know you love me. Why do you deny it?"

Ashton stared down at her for a moment, somewhat astounded by her reasoning; then he let out a long, slow breath and tried to soften his words with a halfhearted smile. "The mistake is yours, Marelda. Truly yours. You must understand that I love my wife." He let his smile fade and then slowly, deliberately stressed his next words. "I love Lierin."

The truth of his words finally penetrated, and the metamorphosis was swift. The silken sultry smile became a snarl of rage. The dark eyes flared and then glared, and she fairly hissed as she came at him with fingers curled, ready to claw his face.

"Calm down, Marelda," he commanded sharply, catching her wrists and holding them away as she fought with wild-eyed fury. "This will do you no good."

A growl came from Marelda's throat as she jerked away. Snatching up her robe, she thrust her arms in the sleeves and wrapped the belt securely about her. The rouge and kohl stood out boldly on her rage-twisted face and made her resemble a rejected street hussy in amorous disarray. With quick, angry movements she knotted her long hair off her neck, and gave vent to several gutter-born epithets with a voice that was sharp and piercing. Ashton's brow arched in some amusement as he heard a brief dissertation on possible aspects of his parentage, birth, and rearing. She ignored no phase in his life until she reached the recent past.

"You river-running scum! You tempt me with your damned tight breeches and twitching buttocks until I'm led to disgracing myself by coming here! I placed my tender heart as a helpless offering in your hands, but you rend it apart and cast me aside like a shred of half-eaten fruit; then you turn away, smug in your conceit, leaving me to find solace at some stranger's whim." She laid a hand upon the doorknob, but hurled more insults before she left. "You vile bastard! Rogue! Bah! Men! Fools to the last!"

The door was snatched open and slammed behind her with a vengeance. A moment later her own closed with echoing finality.

– Chapter Five –

Marelda left Belle Chêne with all the outraged energy of a summer tempest. She gave minimal farewells to the elder ladies, who were somewhat dazed by her abrupt decision to be gone. Her large trunk was wrestled into the back of her landau, and when Ashton came to see her off, she gave him a curt nod, scorning his proffered hand before she turned to accept assistance from her driver. As the carriage departed, Amanda and Jennifer cast curious glances at Ashton, but neither gained any measure of understanding from his slowly widening grin.

Marelda seethed the entire distance to Natchez and mumbled curses against the master of Belle Chêne, hoping the earth would open up and devour him and his specious bride. As her rage and frustration mounted, she thought she would definitely revel in news of their mutual demise. Indeed, if such an announcement ever came to her ears concerning Lierin Wingate, she made a promise to herself that she would dance on the little tart's grave. She had suffered far too much at the hands of that twit. It seemed her best efforts had been frustrated by the family's willingness to be taken in by that feigned innocence, and she considered it highly unfair. She had been the one abused, not that chit!

The prior evening's scene was repeated over and over in Marelda's mind and did much to churn up animosities from the darkest pit of hell. Not only were the couple mentally cursed and castigated, but stripped and put on imaginary racks of torture, where she laid burning coals against their flesh for every offense they had caused her to suffer. She especially delighted in the idea of flogging the wench, while Ashton helplessly witnessed the torture. Thoughts of revenge only aggravated her hatred, and she began to conjure actual ways her venom could reach out and destroy them. Much to her sorrow, however, there seemed to be no successful way of escaping the backlash of her schemes. Justice would be blind to her reason, and whatever she set out to do she could only expect to feel the bite of her own fangs in the end. The threat of enduring reprisal dissuaded her from pursuing the matter further. Until she found a way to repay the pair without coming under condemnation herself, they would be safe from her plots.

The carriage rattled down a Natchez street and passed in front of a tavern where a group of men stood conversing on the boardwalk. Marelda gave no notice to the gathering until she recognized the short, stocky shape of M. Horace Titch on its outer fringe. The man bobbed up and down like a bird on his short legs as he maneuvered for a better position, but for the most part the other men seemed to ignore him. She had always considered him a rather comical character and had often made fun of him behind his back, but she had also noticed his adoring stares following her about. Perhaps she might be successful in persuading him to do her bidding with only a smile as a reward. She could hardly see how she could fail.

Marelda spoke a word to her driver, and the closed landau was brought to a halt beside the boardwalk. Leaning out the window, she waved her handkerchief to gain the squat little man's attention. "Mr. Titch! Yahoo! Mr. Titch!"

Horace glanced around and, seeing who hailed him, beamed in sudden delight. Immediately excusing himself from his companions, he hurried toward her carriage with his short-legged duck walk and was nearly breathless with elation when he arrived. "My dear Miss Rousse! Ah'm delighted to see you!"

The stage had truly been deprived of a great artist when Marelda chose to pursue the pampered life of a wealthy heiress. Her greatest act was that of the properly demure lady. Of course, even if she had been less skilled with her performance, Horace would never have noticed as those dark eyes swept downward above a coy smile. "You're very gallant, Mr. Titch. You make a lady seem so special."

"But you are special, Miss Rousse," he responded eagerly. "Very special."

"Why, Mr. Titch. You say the nicest things. I must be careful not to let you turn my head with such sweet flattery."

Horace was nearly bursting with enthusiasm. "Oh, it isn't flattery in the least! You're the finest lady in all of Natchez! And may I say the most beautiful?"

Marelda cast her eyes downward again and smiled, feigning nervous embarrassment. "I fear you'll make me blush if you continue, Mr. Titch."

Horace thrust out his rounded chest, threatening the buttons of his large checkered vest. Never before had he brought a heightened color to any woman's cheeks except of course by anger, and the idea that he could accomplish such a feat with the beauteous Marelda Rousse was an invigorating boost to his ego. As he bathed in this moment of bliss, the realization began to dawn on him slowly that a distressed frown had replaced her smile and that she had begun twisting her handkerchief between her hands in a distraught fashion. He finally remembered that she had summoned him and made a cautious inquiry. "Uh . . . may I assist you in some way, Miss Rousse?"

"Oh, Mr. Titch, I wouldn't want to trouble you. . . ."

"I assure you it would be my pleasure."

"Well, if you're sure it would not be too much of an imposition . . ."

"Certainly not, Miss Rousse!" he declared. "Ask anything at all, and if it's within my power, your wish will be granted."

Marelda affected a reluctant guise as she concocted the lie: "I just don't know where to turn. You see, my uncle is coming for a visit . . . and he has gotten into the habit of taking a toddy in the evening . . . for medicinal purposes, you understand."

"Oh, of course!"

In an exaggerated drawl fairly dripping with honey and cream she continued: "I clearly forgot to ask the servants to purchase a bottle or two for the larder, and here he'll be coming this very evening. I declare, with no man in the house to attend to such needs, I'm simply at a loss. The cupboard is bone dry, and if I don't serve him a little something, my uncle is bound to think the very worst of my hospitality. I hesitate to venture into a tavern by myself. You understand, don't you? It's such manly territory. But if I send my driver, he must leave the carriage unattended."

"Oh, please! Allow me, Miss Rousse." Horace swallowed the bait with vigor.

"Oh, would you, Mr. Titch?" Marelda loosed the drawstring of her purse, and a few coins rattled on the bottom as she began digging inside. "If you'll just wait a moment, sir, I have the money here."

Astounded by the opportunity to serve this beautiful woman, Mr. Titch hastened to object: "I'll not hear of it, Miss Rousse. I beg you to let me deliver this favor as a true gentleman of the first water. It's the least I can do."

Eagerly Horace set out on his errand, taking short, quick steps that were closely reminiscent of a duck crossing an icy pond. Intent upon this moment of glory, he reasoned as he went that if the lady would like one bottle, she might better appreciate two or even three.

Marelda's eyes took on a feral gleam as a whole series of thoughts enraptured her. Her love of money had not been satiated by the small fortune her sire had bequeathed to her, but here was a resource she had not considered before and one well worth tapping. The Titch family had money enough to balance out the faults of the little man, and Horace did seem incredibly pliant to her wishes. Hardly like that devil, Ashton, who had always been difficult to manage. She was so taken with the prospect of gaining greater wealth, it seemed only a few brief moments before the door of the tavern opened again and the short man teetered out, his arms filled with a large cloth sack. His rapid gait brought him to her carriage without delay, and after swinging the door open, he deposited the offering at her feet.

"Enough for a fortnight or more, Miss Rousse." He spread the top of the bag to display four bottles. "Your . . . uh . . . uncle should not go wanting during his visit."

"Why, Mr. Titch, I do declare. I believe you have put me in your debt and richly so. Would you like to ride with me? Perhaps I can drop you somewhere."

"The ride itself would be my pleasure, Miss Rousse, and any-where you choose to drop me would be fine." He gestured down the street to a black man who sat atop a waiting conveyance. "My carriage will follow." Hoisting himself aboard, Horace settled into the seat facing her, rather awed at being in her company.

Marelda waved her handkerchief to indicate the group of men he had left. "I hope I'm not taking you away from some important discussion with your friends."

"Important enough to rouse fear in the hearts of every man,

woman, and child in Natchez if they knew the truth. What we need now is some sort of action."

"My goodness, it sounds frightfully important." She fluttered her lashes to convey her bemusement. "What truth do you speak of, Mr. Titch?"

"Why, the truth about those half-wits escaping from the madhouse!"

Marelda was genuinely surprised. "Someone escaped from the asylum?"

"Haven't you heard?" Horace was impressed with his own ability to enlighten her. "The madhouse burned, and several inmates walked away. At this very moment they're roaming completely free around the countryside, and there's no telling what sort of danger we might be in."

"But when did all this happen?"

"The same night we were all at Belle Chêne awaiting Ashton Wingate's return."

Marelda leaned back in her seat and stared at him while her mind worked in a slowly turning cycle. Ashton had said Lierin might have escaped from a burning house, and here was news that the madhouse had gone up in flames. Was it a coincidence? Or a stroke of luck for her? She almost laughed as she mentally rubbed her hands in glee. Perhaps she had found a safe way to have her revenge after all.

Marelda assumed an expression of worry and concern as she focused her regard on the stubby little man. "Do you suppose that girl Ashton brought home might have come from the madhouse?"

Horace's bushy brows shot up in surprise. He hadn't even considered the wench. "Why, I suppose she could have. . . ."

"Ashton says that she's his long-dead wife come back alive, but how can anyone believe that?" Marelda could almost see the man's mind gulping down the tidbits she fed him. "How can she be his wife when everyone knows Lierin Wingate died three years ago?"

"Why . . . why would Ashton say that she's his wife when she's really not?"

Marelda managed a concerned frown before she shrugged. "I would hate to be the one who said it, but you know how Ashton is about a pretty face. With him knowing she might be from the asylum and the girl saying she can't remember, he's probably giving that excuse to make things convenient for him."

Horace stroked his chin thoughtfully. What the lady said might very well be true, but he would never dare confront Ashton and accuse him of lying. "I guess that's one of 'em who's found a safe nest."

Marelda was aghast that he did not jump at the opportunity she was presenting him. "What do you mean?"

"No one's going to interfere with Ashton," he said simply.

"But the girl might have escaped from the madhouse!" Dissatisfied by his lack of zeal, she threw his words back at him. "We could all be in danger!"

"I'm afraid we'll have to wait until she does something before we can take her from Belle Chêne."

"Does what?" Marelda had to curb her mounting irritation with the man. "You mean kill someone?"

"Or hurt somebody." It would take something drastic to prompt him to move against the man, and he could imagine there were others who felt the same way.

"I shall not be able to sleep a wink!" she declared, but those who knew her were cognizant of the fact that after a few toddies, the mighty Mississippi could change its course and sweep her house away without her being aware of it. "I could be murdered in my bed by that woman, and there'd be no one to rush to my defense!"

"I'd gladly lend you my protection, Miss Rousse," Horace offered magnanimously. "In fact, if it would make you feel better, I can come by 'most every day ... or ... ah ... evening and ... ah ... make sure that you are safe."

"Oh, would you, Horace?" Smiling warmly, she reached over and placed her gloved hand upon his. "You are a true friend indeed."

Now that it had received some nourishment, Mumford Horace Titch's infatuation with Marelda burgeoned well out of proportion. With the excuse he had provided for himself, he came to visit her as soon as he was assured that he would not intrude upon her uncle's visit, reluctantly letting a week go past before he approached her door. The maid let him in and looked him over with some skepticism before she showed him into the parlor, there bidding him wait until she had informed her mistress of his presence. Though the mantel clock showed less than two hours before midday, Horace, in his diligence to his newly acquired duties, had failed to consider that the lady was a late riser. A silver coffee service was brought to help him while away the time, and he drummed his fingers nervously on the porcelain cup as the clock ticked away the minutes. He was on his second cup of the dark bitter brew when Marelda finally came into the parlor, but the wait proved worthwhile, at least on his part. Her robe seemed hastily donned, and the thin gown worn beneath it displayed enough of her bosom to make the strong coffee go to his head.

"My most humble apologies, dear lady!" Horace stammered and came to his feet, nearly spilling the cup of steaming liquid into his lap. "I did not mean to disturb your sleep."

Marelda leisurely crossed the room and, pouring herself a draft, sweetened it with several spoonfuls of sugar and lightened the color with a liberal dribble of cream before noting that her guest's face was a reddish hue. His eyes seemed to bulge as they remained locked on her carefully arranged décolletage. Since his breaking point appeared imminent, she casually presented her back as she sipped from her cup.

"You mustn't give it another thought, Mr. Titch. It's just that I hadn't expected anyone at this . . . um . . . hour." She gazed lazily at the mantel clock, favoring him with a full view of her left profile, which she considered her best. "Had I any clue whatsoever that you'd really be coming to attend to my welfare, I would have prepared myself better." This was hardly the truth, but she ignored the inaccuracy and enjoyed the effect her state of dishabille was provoking in the short, pudgy man.

"Please," she murmured graciously, waving a hand to the settee from which he had risen, "make yourself comfortable." As he obeyed, she took a seat in a chair directly opposite him, letting him have a glimpse of an ankle before pulling her robe together.

Horace's head was still filled with swelling bosom, sleepy dark eyes, and ruby lips when this latest blast brought a light beading of perspiration upon his upper lip. He stretched his neck and twitched it to ease the sudden tightness of his cravat.

"I . . . that is . . . I mean, if we are going to be friends now, uh . . . "mister" sounds so . . . um . . . formal. Maybe . . ." He couldn't quite put such a bold proposal into words, and was relieved when the lady seemed to understand.

"Of course." She sipped from her cup and eyed him over its edge. "You may call me Marelda, and I"—she leaned forward and smiled seductively—"shall call you . . . Mumford."

It took a decidedly strong effort on his part to tear his eyes from her gaping gown and meet her gaze. It was terribly difficult to suggest that this beautiful creature could displease him in any way. "I . . . uh . . ." Openly sweating now, he ran a finger beneath his collar, feeling in dire need for a breath of cool, fresh air. "My . . . um . . . middle name is Horace, and I . . ."

"But, dahling," she pouted prettily, "I rather like Mumford, or even . . ."

Horace almost cringed as he sensed it coming.

". . . Mummy!"

"I . . . er . . . Horace is my favorite." His voice grew very small as he dared disagree with this delectable demoiselle. "My mother and Sissy always called me Mummy, and the other boys . . ." The memory of some of their taunts was simply too painful to express. He sat erect on the edge of the divan and stared at the buckles of his shoes while he fumbled with his cup and struggled to find a way to change the subject.

"Of course, my dear." Marelda set her cup aside and rose. "It shall be whatever you wish."

Horace scrambled to his feet as she stepped very close to him, and her sweet lavender fragrance set his brain swirling.

"You can see that all is well here and that I am in no danger," she stated matter-of-factly. She ran a hand down her side, smoothing the velvet robe to emphasize her words while noting how his eyes followed the gesture. "Since the hour is close to noon, I really must be getting dressed and seeing to lunch." The cook had better be well along with the latter, she thought. She was not a breakfast person unless she was visiting the Wingate estate, and she almost shuddered when she considered the hours those people kept. "Was there something else you wanted? Have you found out any information about that woman at the Wingates'?" Marelda took him by the arm and began leading him toward the door, casually pressing her breast against him. "I'll bet you anything she's one of those who escaped from the madhouse. Why else would she show up in a nightgown the very same night? It's really a shame someone doesn't at least bring that to Ashton's notice." He's taking a great chance with her living there. Suppose, if you might, that she set the fire at the madhouse, and she's just waiting the chance to torch Belle Chêne."

Somehow M. Horace Titch found himself outside on the stoop with no recollection of how he had arrived there. He had a vague recall of sweet lips curved in a tantalizing smile before the door shut them from sight, but the memory of the yielding softness against his arm overshadowed all else and filled his chest with a pounding heart. The cool air cleared his mind by slow degrees, and he found a hat in his hand. Since it had all the appearance of being his, he placed it on his head and began to walk toward the center of town. A rattle of wheels beside him reminded him that he had come in a carriage, and he climbed inside to review the idea of approaching Ashton Wingate on the matter of the mysterious girl and the possible reactions of the man if it were done wrongly.

The elements of Horace Titch's problem ricocheted around in his head, but whenever he settled on a tactic that seemed commensurate with diplomacy, his imagination ended the scene with chilling images of Ashton Wingate committing various forms of horrendous mayhem upon his person. His thoughts were still locked on this dilemma when the carriage passed a knot of men who had gathered on a street corner. A single word caught his attention.

". . . Madhouse!"

Promptly Horace rapped on the roof and bade his driver to halt. Keenly curious, he made his way to the edge of the crowd and turned an attentive ear to what was being said. A man holding the reins of a sweating horse was breathlessly relating the news.

"Yeah, they found him in one of the backrooms with the charred hilt of a knife stickin' from his back. It's the sheriff's guess that he was one of the keepers and that the fire was deliberately started to cover up the murder. My bet is that one of those inmates who escaped caught him unawares, grabbed his keys, and took off after setting the place on fire."

The men mumbled among themselves and grew angrier as conjectures about the escaped inmates became more lurid. As he listened, it became increasingly apparent to Horace that if these fellows were provided with the proper incentive, he would not have to face Ashton Wingate at all, for they would do it for him.

He glanced about him, sizing up many in the group as a bunch of ruffians who frequented the taverns and picked up odd jobs here and there to supply them with necessary coinage. By their rough garb, it was easy to assess that these were not part of the affluent class and might be impressed by the presence of a wealthy gentleman in their midst. Having worn his newest and best for Marelda's benefit, he was outfitted well enough to strike awe in the minds of these penniless yokels. His fine gray frock coat and trousers were imbued with light plum stripes, while the brocade vest was traced with a pattern of small plum flowers. Why, his garments, right down to the plum-and-gray-checkered silk cravat, might have even made the arrogant Ashton Wingate writhe in envy.

Horace cleared his throat to gain the others' notice, sensing that here was his chance to put forth his suspicions. "Men, listen to me. We've got to do something about those madfolk running around our community. None of us are safe, and it's a downright shame that the womenfolk of Natchez have to venture out at the risk of their very lives."

A low rumble of assent accompanied the nodding of heads, and after a moment the men quieted and again gave Horace their full consideration. Warming to his topic, the squat, would-be orator puffed out his chest and hooked his thumbs in his vest pockets. It was no mystery to him that several stared with jaws hanging slack, for he was sure his authoritative demeanor and costly garb affected some in that manner. If he heard, he gave no hint when one man commented to a companion:

"Gor! Ain't no man what dresses like that this time o' morn'n!" The fellow scratched a heavily stubbled chin. "He musta spent the whole night swillin' down gin. Prob'ly slept it off wid one o' Cottonmouth Maggie's girls down by the Trace."

"Look to yourselves, men!" Horace barked. "It's not only the women who are in danger. Reliable accounts have it that mad people sometimes have the strength of five or six men! They're likely to tear a common man apart for the pennies in his pocket!" He sought to find the magic words that would set them aflame with righteous fervor. "I say it's time we band together and search out these escaped madfolk before they do us some harm!"

Silence settled over the group as they realized he was actually asking them to do something. A few more curious souls had joined the gathering, and a jug was passed around and repeatedly tipped to moisten thirsty gullets.

"Now, it's been assumed that the escaped inmates were all men, but I've heard there was also a woman among them. In fact, the very same night the madhouse burned, Ashton Wingate brought home an injured girl who was wearing only a nightgown and was all muddied and bruised from trampin' through the swamp. What's a man to think when we all know it's only a few miles through the woods from Belle Chêne to the madhouse?"

He could see the responding nods and hear the growing buzz of comments.

"There's no tellin' what she might do to them poor folks out there or to those old ladies who stay alone when Ashton's away on business. Set another fire?"

The crowd could summon no great sympathy for the ladies, especially when they thought of that big black overseer who watched over the place. Ashton Wingate had made it clear some time ago that no one fooled with any of his, be it his kin, his slaves, or his property. They remembered a time when he had called out the sheriff to carry off a bunch of boys who had gone out to his place on a 'coon hunt, and after several hours behind bars, they had ended up having to pay for that cow, which at night and from a distance had really looked like a coon. There were other stories about how men were hired out there and expected to work right alongside the slaves. Why, it was common knowledge that a man couldn't earn a day's pay at Belle Chêne without churning up a sweat and nearly working his fingers to the bone. Any excuse to trample on the Wingates' lawn was to be taken advantage of, and this one seemed a far better excuse than most. It would feel sort of good to tweak Ashton's nose on his own front lawn. . . .

Horace cried aloud as if haunted by the horror of it all. "We just can't let this kind of thing go on! That madwoman"—the leap from suspicion to conclusion was easy—"could murder a dozen people or more if she isn't put away!"

This time there was a shout of assent, and when it died, Horace ranted on in his high-pitched voice.

"We'd just be doing all of them a favor and performing our duty to make it safe for everyone to sleep at night and for womenfolk and children on the streets."

"You're right!" The hue and cry was taken up. "Who knows their way around out there? We need someone to lead us out!"

Horace grew anxious as a sudden note of confusion seemed ready to sap the will of the crowd. "I do!" he yelled and became instantly aware of his folly. "I can draw you a map." His voice dwindled even lower as he added, "I . . . er . . . I'd go myself but I have no horse. . . ."

"Use mine! We need some one to show us the way!"

Horace stared at his hand where a pair of reins had suddenly appeared, and when he looked about, the owner of the horse had gone. The rawboned nag at the other end of the leather straps gave Horace gaze for gaze. The horse appeared to have been assembled by a neophyte who had randomly jammed long gnarled bones into a sagging, mottled brown, and mostly hairy hide. The steed's narrow eyes appeared to harbor an ill-disguised desire to wreak vengeance on any man fool enough to straddle his bony back. Horace shuddered as he recalled the pain that had accompanied his last attempt to ride a horse. That particular event had caused him to swear an oath to keep himself forevermore to the well-padded seat of a carriage.

"I . . . um . . . don't . . ." he murmured weakly, then turned away from that mean-eyed stare and managed somehow to gather some semblance of bravado: "There's no tellin' how violent that woman might be. Someone should . . ."

"Here!" A rusted antique of a long, double-barreled flintlock shotgun was thrust into his other hand. "She's primed and loaded, so's you treats her like a baby, see?"

Guns were another item Horace failed to understand. They had always left him hurting in one part or another. At first his father had scorned him because he could not shoot, then, relenting, had tried to instruct him in the proper use of firearms. An hour later the elder Titch had found himself seriously contemplating a savaged hat and shredded coattails while a doctor plucked buckshot from the lower portion of his backside. He had hastened to agree with the medical man that the son would likely fare just as well without a knowledge of hunting in his education, and the subject had never been broached again . . . until now.

"Come on!" someone shouted. "Let's be about it!"

All around him men were mounting horses that seemed to have been gathered from nowhere, and somehow Horace found himself in the saddle with the gun cradled in his arm. He hurt almost at once and, glancing around in dismay, searched for some trace of his driver or carriage. He noticed the sheriff's bewhiskered deputy surveying the happenings from a short distance away, but the man's tobacco-chewing reticence gave Horace no reason to hope that this ride would be terminated. Several men climbed into a wagon, and the whole entourage assembled behind the short-legged dandy, with a pair of buckboards bringing up the rear. Though he sought heartily to catch a glimpse of his carriage and promised himself that he would deal harshly with his driver whenever he found him, there was no escape for M. Horace Titch.

Someone slapped his horse, and they were off amid shouts and a noisy scramble. Horace was quite astounded by the fact that a steed could have such a bone-jarring trot. The corners of his mouth turned down in an agonized grimace as his backside bounced unmercifully against the saddle. To escape the abuse he tried to stand in the stirrups for a moment, but that position threatened to topple him head-first over the horse's neck. When he clamped his legs tighter around the horse's belly, it only seemed to excite and encourage the animal into a faster trot. Horace jerked on the reins to keep the pace slower, and the best the confused mount could do was a stiff-legged half-trot. Horace's dark head jerked with every downward motion of his body, and he became a mass of jiggling ripples from his jowls to his toes. It was a long way to Belle Chêne, and he was more than a little afraid that the ride went directly through hell.

The harpsichord took unto itself a new life under the slender, agile fingers that caressed the keyboard. Lierin was enthusiastic at her ability to play the instrument and, while the ladies napped upstairs, had slipped into the parlor to examine the extent of her talent. The sweet fluid notes had drawn Ashton to the room immediately upon his arrival home. He had seen to the last details of the steamboat's departure upriver and left his captain and Mr. Logan to the matter of boarding the passengers.

Breathing out the smoke of a long, black cheroot, Ashton leaned back in his chair and watched the vapors drift slowly toward the ceiling as the light, airy music filled his head and echoed through the house. He was bathed in a sea of bliss. He could name no other woman who could stir his emotions so completely and bring such pleasure to his senses. Her merest presence touched his life with happiness, and yet he realized she was still much of an enigma to him.

She had a great deal to tell him about herself and her life and where she had been for these past three years.

The mood was broken by a sudden and persistent knocking on the door. Lierin stopped playing and glanced around as if she had forgotten there was another world beyond the parlor. When Ashton called out, bidding admittance, he was amazed when one of the stablehands answered the summons and hurried in with hat in hand. It was unusual for Hickory to come into the house, and Ashton knew before the man spoke that a crisis was imminent.

"Massa," the groom wheezed and waggled a finger in the general direction of Natchez. "Massa, dey's a whole passel o' men acomin' dis way, ridin' lickety-split an' lookin' like dey's up to no good." The black paused to swallow and catch his breath before continuing: "Suh, Ah do believe dey's headin' here. Dere jes' ain't no other place fo' dem to go."

Ashton pondered the matter as he tapped the burning end of his cigar in a dish. "Perhaps we should see what kind of reception we can arrange for them. Do you have any more running left in those long legs of yours?"

"Yassuh, Massa Ashton." Hickory grinned and nodded an eager affirmative. "Ah was jes' up in de hayloft when Ah seen dem acomin'. Why, Ah gots at least a mile or more o' dust raisin' left."

"Judd is cleaning some of the brush away from the creek." Ashton rattled out orders in rapid-fire sequence. "You get down there and tell him to come back and bring every man he can lay a hand to. Tell him to come ready for trouble. I'll leave instructions with Willabelle in the kitchen. Best be on your way now, Hickory."

The man was already turning to leave, and the door quickly closed behind him. Ashton went to Lierin, who had risen from the bench. He smiled to ease her worried frown and took her hands into his.

"No need to fret, my love," he soothed. "Some of the boys from town get themselves liquored up once in a while and start cavorting around the countryside, seeing what kind of trouble they can get into. We've learned how to handle them without anyone getting hurt, so just continue to play. The sound of your music pleasures me greatly, and I would hear more of it. I must have a word with Willabelle now, and then I'll just step outside on the porch." He pressed a quick kiss on the back of her hand, then released her and left. Lierin returned to her music, but with Ashton's departure from the parlor, the delightful interlude had ceased to be. The luster of the moment had definitely fled with him.

The group of horsemen drew near the porch where the master of Belle Chêne awaited them. They dissolved into a roiling, struggling mass as each one jockeyed for a position. Of course, the loser of this melee had to be the rider least skilled in the art of horsemanship, in this case one Mumford Horace Titch. This stalwart who had led the hardy band came to a stumbling, scrambling halt with the hooves of his gallant mount almost banging into the bottom step. A shocked expression contorted his face at the last stiff-legged bounce, and he sucked in his breath through gritted teeth at the pure agony of the moment. He stood up in the stirrups, trying to ease his pain, and surreptitiously sought to untangle the butt of the overlong shotgun from the loose ends of the reins. The gaping twin bores of the eight-gauge swung in a wide arc, and there was a sudden scurrying as Mr. Titch's companions wisely concluded that their spokesman needed more room.

Horace finally succeeded in freeing the recalcitrant locks of the smoothbore from the tenacious leather straps and, glancing around for support, found that his allies had withdrawn several paces to the rear, leaving him solely in charge of delivering the elements of their complaint to Mr. Wingate. Since everyone seemed to be waiting for him to open the proceedings, he cleared his throat and, in spite of his bruised state, drew himself up to his full height, only to find that he still had to look up to meet Ashton's gaze. The sun-bronzed features hinted of that one's amusement, which severely unsettled Horace's composure. Nervously he cleared his throat again, but strive though he might, he could not lay tongue to a single sensible word with which to begin.

Ashton Wingate saved the day as he squinted at the sun briefly and then greeted his visitors. "Good afternoon, Mr. Titch." He nodded to the others. "Gentlemen." He leaned indolently against a pillar, his fingers jammed in the tops of his pockets. "You seem to have picked a fine day for a ride in the country."

M. Horace Titch tried to hitch himself a notch or two higher, then had to grab for the gun as it began to slip away from him. "I doubt, suh, that you will be able to deal with these good men through the use of inane pleasantries."

Ashton arched a condescending brow. "I have a feeling that you're about to correct my error, Mr. Titch. You can start by telling me what the lot of you are doing here on my lawn."

The fowling piece was growing heavy, and Horace shifted it to a new position before he answered: "That's just what I'm about to do, suh, and I warn you to be wary. I assure you that we represent the whole of Natchez and Davis County."

"Indeed?" Ashton let the single word convey his doubt.

"There's been a grievous wrong perpetrated upon the good people of our area." Horace was sweating heavily and would have wiped his brow had he found a free hand. "As you are well aware, suh, several of those madfolk escaped from the sanitarium when the place burned down. I have it on very good authority that you have involved yourself in this travesty. . . ." Horace noticed an almost imperceptible hardening of the hazel eyes, but he continued, encouraged by the presence of those behind him. Even Ashton Wingate would not think of standing against such odds. "It seems you have taken one of those crazy people into your home."

Horace almost held his breath as he awaited the man's reaction to this bold statement. Other than a slight tensing of the lean jaw, he saw no real sign of change and came to the conclusion that Ashton Wingate had either not heard him or had misunderstood his statement.

"I mean to say, suh, that the . . . uh . . . young woman you brought home a couple of weeks ago might just be one of them mad ones."

A murmur of agreement rose behind Horace, but Ashton only glanced at the sun again, and then consulted his pocket watch.

Seeing no threat forthcoming, Horace warmed to his topic and rushed on: "Really, Mr. Wingate, I can't understand why you would take such a risk by bringing one of *them* right into your own home. We must insist that she be delivered into the hands of the authorities." M. Horace Titch realized he had finally gained Ashton's full attention when he found himself under the unwavering regard of those penetrating green-brown eyes. He hastened to add, "Just until it can be determined who she is, of course . . . and only for the safety of the women and children around these parts."

Now that the demand was out, the rest of the men relaxed a bit. There was a full chorus of assents, with a lot of bobbing heads.

" 'At's right!"

"Way to tell 'im, Titch!"

"We gotta take 'er in!"

Ashton seemed strangely undisturbed by their proposition. "You men have had a long ride out here, and the day has been unseasonably warm." He called out to include the lot of them: "And you seem mighty uncomfortable on those horses. Why don't you climb down and rest for a spell?"

A pause followed as they considered this, and a general mumbling rose among them as they agreed that Ashton Wingate wasn't such an almighty ogre after all. As invited, they dismounted.

M. H. Titch was overjoyed at the prospect of standing on good, solid earth again. A considerable degree of havoc had been wreaked upon his posterior and anterior parts, and he was not at all sure that a walk back to Natchez was not preferable to another ride on this wretched beast. He tried several times to swing his leg over the saddle, as some of the others had so easily done, but the long weapon got in his way. Somehow he ended up sitting on top of the thing, and had the trigger assembly been any less stout, he might have lost his manhood or, at the very least, a part of his leg.

Horace considered his predicament for a moment, giving no heed to the gaping stares he had collected. If he could just hold the gun up high, he thought, then get his right leg free and over the saddle . . . Amazing! Of a sudden, he found himself standing in the left stirrup with nothing tangled or caught. He was not completely aware of the danger of having his foot deeply wedged in the iron when he began to lower himself from the saddle, but he began to have some inkling of this when he found his other leg too short to reach the ground. He hung there, debating his next maneuver, when the matter resolved itself. The weapon slipped from his grasp, falling between him and the steed, and on the way down, the outsized hammers raked him from breastbone to belly. Forgetting his tenacious grip on the horse's mane, he snatched for the evil weapon. At the same time his right foot shot underneath the belly of the nag, and with a thud and a loud "whoof," Horace hit the ground in an absolutely prone position. The weary steed craned its neck to view this latest inanity with a good measure of disdain. The gun teetered precariously on top of the dazed man's chest, and it was nearly a full minute before Horace came to his senses. Sudden visions of being dragged all the way back to town moved him to immediate action. Dust billowed up around the short, stout man as he struggled frantically to free his foot from the stirrup.

One of his companions had mercy on him and came to his aid. When the boot was untangled, Horace climbed slowly to his feet, using the gun for a crutch, and ruefully dusted off his new suit, causing an epidemic of sneezing fits to strike those nearest him. He slapped the beaver hat against his leg until it regained some semblance of its former hue, then settled it once more upon his head. With the completion of this simple toilet, he lifted his gaze to his host and immediately detected the fact that Ashton Wingate was regarding him with something akin to pity. He could have endured outright hatred far better; at least that emotion would have made him feel less like a bumbling clod.

"Suh, I must warn you," he began angrily, but had to pause to spit dirt out of his mouth. "We will not be put off lightly. We've come here to see that our community is made safe again."

The troop of unworthies began to exchange self-righteous comments as they regrouped behind their leader. They lifted clubs and guns en masse to affirm their agreement with what Horace had stated.

With calm deliberation, Ashton perused the crowd of men, then casually called over his shoulder for a bucket of cool water to be brought up fresh from the well and a jug of rum to accompany it. Unruffled, he waited until both had arrived and made a show of emptying the dark, potent brew into the bucket. He stirred the lot with a long-handled dipper, then raised the cup and took a long, slow sip, following his action with a smile of obvious pleasure.

The mob had grown strangely quiet as envious eyes marked his every movement. Dry tongues licked longingly over parched lips, while nostrils quivered to catch the scent. When he was sure he had gained their rapt attention, Ashton lifted the dripping ladle aloft and dribbled the liquid in a slow, tantalizing stream.

"The road from town is hot and dusty. I'm sure you men could use a bit of cool water."

Sighs of relief were quickly overwhelmed by shouts of assent, and a mass of burly bodies gathered near the stoop. Nudging elbows prodded slighter forms aside as each sought to receive his ration. Ashton stared down at them and almost smiled as he stepped back.

"Aye, that's the way, lads. Nothing like a good swig of grog to cut the grime in a man's throat."

They nodded eagerly in a rushing tide of agreement. Horace finally yielded to his own thirst and deigned to put the brimming dipper to his lips. He swirled the first draft around in his mouth and then spewed a muddy stream onto the lane before he quenched his thirst. As he passed the dipper on, he got back to the matter at hand. "Mr. Wingate!" He gained that one's rather skeptical regard almost immediately. "Do you intend to hand the woman over to us so we might deliver her to the sheriff?"

His cohorts suddenly recalled the reason for their visit and, since the bucket was nearly empty, clustered around their selected spokesman. Horace had never been leader of anything before, and he felt a surge of importance as he laid the gun over his arm and turned to survey his fellows. There was a wild dash for cover as the bore of the weapon swung with him.

Had Ashton been in a better mood, he might have found some humor in these antics, but he could manage no more than a coldly tolerant smile when the little man's round, dirt-streaked face confronted him again. He had not heard the harpsichord for some moments and could only hope that Willabelle had had the foresight to escort Lierin up to her room.

Horace cleared his throat. "You understand clearly why we've come, suh. If you would be so kind as to fetch the girl, we'll take her in to the sheriff and let him decide what to do with her. I'll see that no action is taken against you."

Ashton neither spoke nor changed his expression, but Horace's eyes widened perceptively as the front door swung open and Belle Chêne's huge black overseer, Judd Barnum, stepped casually out, with a pair of oversize horse pistols tucked in his belt. In the crook of his arm rested an ancient but well-kept, bell-muzzled blunderbuss, and across his chest he wore a wide leather strap from which dangled a dozen or so wooden charges for the awesome weapon. The black held his silence, but braced his feet apart and proceeded to dip into the large pocket of his waistcoat, removing a handful of small, jagged metal pieces, which he ceremoniously dumped into the muzzle of the blunderbuss. Laying the piece again over his massive arm, Judd glanced up to meet the startled and disturbed stare of the short man, then his gaze ranged leisurely over the rest of the gathering.

At least one of the onlookers shuddered as he conjured a mental image of the mayhem such a charge would cause. Bellies tightened and grumbled as they churned in sudden consternation. Somewhere the note of lighthearted fun had vanished from this afternoon's foray, and they began to have second thoughts about the wisdom of disturbing the occupants of Belle Chêne.

"You gentlemen are under a misconception," Ashton announced almost pleasantly.

Horace tried to form a question, but he found his mouth gone dry, this time with roweling dismay. He had heard that Ashton Wingate had a penchant for turning the tables on pranksters or any-one else who meant him harm, but he had not expected the man to stand firm against such odds and surely not to take the upper hand. Intensely aware of the threat that faced them, Horace could only stand and gape.

The hazel eyes flicked toward him briefly. "You most of all, Mr. Titch."

"Why . . . ?" The single word was strangled out.

"The lady whom you have so carelessly slandered is my wife, and you should know me well enough by now at least to guess that I'm not partial to having anything taken from me by force, especially when it is something I treasure."

"If'n she's your'n, why ain't we never seent her befo'?" The question came from a bearded, snaggle-toothed fellow who stood near the rear of the group.

"If Sheriff Dobbs has any questions he wishes to address to me, I will most respectfully respond, but I owe none of you an explanation."

"Ah . . . the sheriff's a friend o' his. Ol' Harvey ain't gonna do nothin' to upset his lordship here. We've gotta take care o' this mat-ter ourselves if'n we want justice done."

Once again nodding heads conveyed the general consensus of the group of men.

"Yeah! She might've been the one what murdered the attendant, an' she could kill again! Maybe one o' ours next!"

"Yeah! If'n he won't give her to us, we'll take her!"

There was a sudden surge toward the porch, but Judd stepped forward, snatching one of the pistols from his belt and driving them rapidly back as he swung the wide bore of the blunderbuss to face them.

"Ah di'n hear Massa Ashton say any o' y'all was invited on his nice clean porch," he said almost amiably. His big, square grin displayed a full set of gleaming white teeth. "Ah be careful about dirtyin' it if'n Ah was y'all. Massa Ashton's gots a mighty mean temper when he's riled. He jes' might tell me to blow a few heads off. It be a mess all right, but Ah gotta to do what he sez, 'cause he de massa. Y'all understand?"

"*You'd* better understand, nigger! You kill a white man, and you'll be hanged. You'd better think twice about that!"

Judd's broad grin never wavered as he met the man's glare. "Dat ain't gonna do yo no good, mistah, 'cause yo be six feet under befo' dey ketch me."

"Arrogant nigger!" an unkempt, slovenly fellow sneered. "Anybody'd think he's got a title or somepin'."

"There's enough of us to take 'em," another man urged from the center of the fray.

"Well, I seen the two of 'em clean ol' Sal's place out last year," one who favored caution argued. "We'd better think on this some more."

"Good advice, gentlemen," Ashton agreed. "Consider the odds carefully before making any hasty decisions."

"You don't scare us, *Mistuh* Ashton," a burly fellow jeered. "We're gonna make pulp outa you an' your black boy here."

Ashton raised his arm and beckoned to the right and left. "You men best show yourselves now before these fools get hurt."

Somewhere in the back one man nudged another, then jerked his head to one side. Other heads began to turn warily on suddenly stiff necks, while jaws began to sag. If the arrival of the massive black had not been enough to dampen the spirit of adventure, this latest development was well calculated to do the job. A steady stream of sweating black men came marching from around both ends of the house. Some of them bore scythes, while others carried pitchforks or axes, and a few had found pistols or other paraphernalia that could do injury to the common man. By the grins they wore, it was easy to determine that they were going to enjoy this rout. Willis's eyes were wide as he slipped out the front door, and the long weapon he carried matched the one Mr. Titch had so zealously guarded. Hiram came around the end of the house, and he too bore a firearm of some length and power.

Ashton leisurely strolled across the front of the porch and, turning, retraced his steps as he considered the suddenly troubled faces of his visitors. "You men know I'm not fond of trespassers, especially those who come to poach, steal, or destroy anything of mine. Some say I'm a hard man, demanding retribution for the slightest offense. Now, it's obvious that I can't hang all of you, because you haven't stolen anything or killed anyone yet. You're too many for the sheriff to lock up, and you'd only abuse his hospitality anyway. I could give each of you the thrashing you deserve for coming out here as an unlawful mob, but I have other affairs that demand my attention. However, I think a nice, long, reflective saunter back to Natchez will suit my purposes. . . ." He smiled tolerantly and, glancing over his shoulder at Judd, casually inclined his head. The black chuckled and, descending a step, raised the pistol and blunderbuss into the air. The bits of metal and shot went skyward with a roar, and in quick accompaniment those with similar weapons copied his manner. The blasts caused a horrendous cacophony that thoroughly startled the mounts, and to add to the chaos the falling debris rained down like a swarm of stinging bees on their hides. The bedlam was immediate and almost unbelievable. The frightened steeds snorted, whinnied, and bucked beneath the smarting shower. The reins snaked out of Horace's hand, and the nag, sensing his freedom, took flight. The rest of the men scurried to catch flying reins, manes, or tails before their own steeds followed the example. Iron-weighted hooves lashed out in every direction, and it was a wild dance to escape their abuse. Some stalwarts foolishly persisted and ended up yelping and jumping around while others grimaced in silent agony and staggered away, and all this to the chortling amusement of those who witnessed the melee.

Finally, the last of the steeds broke loose, and the herd stampeded off down the road, raising a plume of dust out behind them. They had no more than disappeared from sight than another group of horsemen swung into the long, tree-lined lane and approached the

house. Sheriff Dobbs rode in the van, and among those who followed was one who made Ashton frown. It was Peter Logan from the
asylum. The man's presence caused Ashton to regret the tardiness of
the steamer's departure.

Harvey Dobbs pulled his horse to a halt near the porch and
thoughtfully chewed on the stub of a cigar as he contemplated the
bedraggled rabble and the blacks who stood around with their various weapons. He peered down the dusty lane, then removed the
cigar butt and stared at it for a brief moment before flipping it away.

"I should've known you wouldn't need any help." Harvey gave
Ashton a lopsided grin, then inclined his head toward his deputy.
"Ol' Foss here heard the commotion in town, and we decided to
come out here and have a look-see."

The grizzled and bewhiskered deputy cocked a bushy brow at
the leader of the now horseless pack and spat a long spurt of chewing
tobacco juice in the dust near Titch's feet, making that one dance
away in outraged dignity.

"See here!" Horace protested and jerked his handkerchief from
his pocket to wipe away some of the dark liquid that had splattered
his boots. As he bent over, the barrel of the gun slipped downward.
He grabbed for the clumsy piece, unwittingly catching his fingers in
the trigger guard. The resulting force of both barrels firing into the
ground at close range rolled him over, right into the tiny puddle of
dark slimy spittle that he had so fastidiously avoided a moment
before. There was stunned silence for a moment, then the faces of the
gawking men began to break in sporadic waves as the sheriff's
chortling laughter infected them and they were able to see the
humor in the incident. When the guffaws grew louder, Horace's
cheeks took on a hue that was nearly as dark and red as beets. With
his lips pulled back in repugnance, he got to his hands and knees and
gingerly held his trouser leg away from him as he raised himself to
an upright position.

Sheriff Dobbs wiped his hand across his mouth, seeming to
smooth away his laughter. He swung down from his horse and, with
a nod, directed Peter Logan to do the same. Hitching up his trousers,
he stepped onto the porch beside Ashton and threw a thumb over his
shoulder to indicate the smaller man as that one came forward.

"Mr. Logan agreed to come out here and settle this matter before
he left, so no one"—he paused to frown at Horace sharply—"will

come out here again on this fool's errand. He needs only to see the girl to put this rumor to shame." Harvey gazed out over the heads of the men who were closely following the exchange and explained for their benefit. "Mr. Logan is from the asylum, so he should be able to identify those who escaped."

Ashton regarded the attendant briefly. "My wife has been indisposed this week. I don't wish to upset her."

Harvey Dobbs's brows shot up. "Your wife?"

Ashton nodded stiffly. "I don't care to explain now, Harvey, but it is Lierin."

"But I thought . . ." Harvey began, then frowning in bemusement, drew his large frame up slowly. "Are you sure, Ashton?"

"Yes."

The single word satisfied the lawman, but there were other factions to be considered. "For her future protection, Ashton, I think we ought to let Mr. Logan see her and end this thing right now. There's been a murder committed, and these men could take it in their heads to come here while you're gone."

"I don't wish to put her through this, Harvey. . . ."

The front door creaked open slightly, drawing Ashton's immediate notice. His heart gave a sudden lurch as he saw Lierin in the narrow opening. Willabelle stood behind her and was anxiously trying to coax her back.

"I have to know!" Lierin whispered urgently, resisting the woman's effort. Pushing the portal wider, she stepped out in the full light of the lowering sun. There were several audible intakes of breath, for she seemed almost angelic as she approached the three men who stood on the edge of the porch. Ashton thought she had never looked more beautiful. The gold and red rays stretching out across the heavens touched her hair and set the fiery strands aglow. The upswept coiffure and the pale blue of her high-necked, lace-trimmed gown created a soft and lovely setting for her delicate beauty. Her striking comeliness caused the onlookers to debate the wisdom of their leader, for it was clearly evident that this was no wild-eyed lunatic. No raving madwoman. She was only a pale, frightened girl.

A few of the brave hearties who had ridden out recalled some of the rudiments of gentlemanly courtesy and hastily snatched battered hats from mop-haired heads. Even Horace was struck with awe, but the compulsion to beg this one's forgiveness was promptly squelched by the sure knowledge that Marelda would not approve.

Lierin's smile wavered with uncertainty as she halted beside Ashton. Hesitantly she raised her eyes to the sheriff, who was taller by a full head and more.

"Did you wish to see me, sir?" she queried softly.

Harvey Dobbs cleared his throat and peered askance at Peter Logan, who had halted beside him. The smaller man stared agog at the one in question; then remembering himself, he tugged off his own soft cap and glanced up into Ashton Wingate's tense frown. The scowl seemed to bring him to his senses, and he directed himself to the sheriff, giving a quick, negative shake of his head. He repeated the same gesture for the benefit of their host, adding a smile and a wink.

Though the attendant's manner confused Ashton and made him wonder if the man could rightfully identify anyone, he felt a wave of relief wash over him. He had stubbornly rejected the idea of Lierin being the one from the madhouse, but there had always been the possibility that she had been unjustly imprisoned there. Henceforth no one would question the matter of where she belonged, for Peter Logan had given his answer, and she was safe. Relaxing now, Ashton slipped his arm about her and made the introductions.

"This is my wife, Lierin," he stated with a sense of pride swelling in his chest. "My sweet, this is Sheriff Harvey Dobbs, a friend of mine, and"—he gestured to Peter—"Mr. Logan, who will be traveling to Memphis aboard one of our steamers tonight."

"Did I understand them to say that you're from the asylum?" she asked, startling the three men with the inquiry.

"Aye, that I be, ma'am," Peter Logan replied.

"I couldn't help overhearing . . . I mean, the voices were so loud. . . ." She swept a hand to indicate the loose cluster of men. "I could hardly ignore them, and I heard enough to gather that I've been well defended from this mob of duty-minded citizens." Her eyes calmly rested on Horace, who hurriedly dropped his gaze and, in sudden discomfiture, shifted his feet. His embarrassment was hardly alleviated when she directed her comments to the sheriff. "Sir, if I'm not the one you seek, I urge you to consider the plight of those poor, unfortunate people who did escape and not allow this offense to be repeated."

"Yes, ma'am," Sheriff Dobbs respectfully agreed. "I shall surely do that."

"If there has been a murder committed, surely we must all consider that it might have been an outsider who did the deed. Would you judge the inmates guilty before giving them a hearing?"

"No, ma'am." The sheriff's adamant tone denied the possibility.

"I shall take comfort in your assurances and in the belief that no harm will come to the inmates while you're in charge."

"I'll do my best not to disappoint you, ma'am," he pledged with a smile.

"I'm sure you won't, sheriff," she replied graciously. "But what of the plight of these men?" Lierin scanned the faces of her audience and, with a slight frown, commented on the obvious. "They've lost their mounts, and I see no way for them to return to Natchez. Is it a long walk back?"

Ashton chuckled as those in the adverse party were reminded of their situation and began to mutter and grumble. Their shuffling movements raised a welter of dust from the drive, but having already been told their fate, no one dared voice a complaint. "Long enough to give them time to think, my sweet."

"Shouldn't we at least take them back to town?"

"She's a blessed saint," a man responded as a hopeful murmur rose up around him. Titch's followers were more than willing to accept some leniency from this woman and waited with bated breath as their host lifted an inquiring brow toward Judd. "Don't we have a wagon large enough to accommodate these men?"

The huge black pondered the matter in a sober manner until an idea struck; then a wide grin spread across his dark face as he caught the flow of Ashton's thoughts. "Well, dere is one, Massa Ashton, but de boys done got it hitched up behind de barn. Ah don't reckon it'd suit dese here gen'lemen at all."

"Anything's better than walking!" a rotund fellow declared. His feet were already aching from the strain of standing.

Ashton turned to speak to Hickory, who had come to stand near the end of the porch. "Go fetch the wagon from the stable. We can't have Mr. Titch strolling all the way back to Natchez and wearing out his new shoes."

Chuckling to himself, Hickory left at a shuffling trot, and the men responded with mumbled thanks at the prospect of being provided transportation back to town. They began to smile and laugh until a gasp from Horace drew their attention to what came around the end of the house. There was no question the wagon was large enough, for it was made with thick board sides attached to a stout bed and mounted on massive axles. The wide, heavy wheels dropped with a jolting impact into every rut as a pair of draft horses pulled it near. Lierin pressed a perfumed handkerchief over her nose and mouth as the staunch odor of fresh manure wafted to them on an errant breeze. Huge chunks of the stuff were thickly caked to the interior and covered the lowered tailgate. A cloud of distressed flies followed closely behind as if determined not to be left bereft of either home or sustenance.

It was Titch who seemed the most offended as he stared aghast at the contraption. "You can't be serious!"

"I have nothing else of comparable size, and there is quite a number of you," Ashton reminded him. "If you're unduly squeamish, you can always walk. Perhaps next time you will consider waiting for an invitation; then I can be better prepared, but for now, I would suggest you be on your way . . . whichever way you choose to travel."

Sheriff Dobbs faced the discontented pack with a widening grin. "You heard 'im, boys. It's time for you to be leaving. I might warn you also: The next time you presume to take over my responsibilities, I'll set a fine so stiff, you'll have to come out here and work for Judd Barnum to get enough to pay for it." He chuckled at his own humor. "You mosey on into town now, and mind you, if you're set on walking, don't dally on Mr. Wingate's lands. I'll be along in a moment to see that you abide by what I say. So get on your way."

Hickory sat on the high seat, clear of the stench and the flies, and whistled through his gapping front teeth and a wide, innocent grin as those who chose to accept the offering climbed in. After all, they reasoned, it was a long way back to Natchez.

Mr. Titch held back, stubbornly resolving to walk behind the conveyance. He cast dire glares toward his erstwhile host as the wagon trundled down the lane.

Sheriff Dobbs stood chortling as he observed their untidy departure. "A few miles down the road, and most of 'em won't know the wagon even smells, but heaven help Lower Town when they arrive."

"They should remember this for some time," Ashton remarked.

Harvey crinkled his brows. "Some of those boys are not too forgiving, Ashton. You'd better look to yourself and your own for a while. Sometimes, it's the ones who seem the most harmless who carry the biggest grudge."

Ashton dropped a hand on his friend's shoulder. "I'll try to take care, Harvey . . . and thanks."

"Anytime." The lawman grinned and turned to watch the departing band.

Several who had selected to walk went away limping, and the gallant Mumford Horace Titch, who had ridden in the fore on the way out, was now pushed to the rear in disgrace. It was much later when he relented and jumped up on the tailgate, where he clung tenaciously to the precarious perch until he was forced by discomfort to walk again. Needless to say, he had sufficient time to contemplate the error of trespassing on Ashton Wingate's property.

– Chapter Six –

The rattle of hooves faded in the distance as the sheriff and his men departed. The house settled back into a tranquil calm, but Lierin knew no such peace. She had returned to the parlor, allowing Ashton the opportunity to speak in privacy with his friend before the man went on his way, but as she perched tensely on the edge of her chair she was unable to stop shaking. An inner fear had attacked her when she heard the railing accusations, for she had been afraid that Horace Titch and his band of ruffians were right . . . that she was the woman who escaped from the madhouse. Since the day she had awakened from the void, she had never felt the anguish and frustration of her memory loss as much as she did now. It was like facing a blank door, knowing there was something on the other side and yet unable to find a latch or knob with which to open it. Beyond the barrier most of her life lay hidden well out of her reach. She wanted desperately to know where she had come from, who her family and friends were, and what events had led her to a collision with Ashton's coach.

Mr. Logan had spoken in her defense, and the matter hopefully was settled. But while she watched from the foyer, she had noticed something perhaps the others had not discerned. Though Ashton had given every indication that he would protect her to the death against the mob of men, he had seemed somehow reluctant to have the gray-haired attendant see her, as if he himself suffered nagging doubts concerning her identity.

She spread her trembling hands upon her lap and stared with fixed gaze at the thin fingers and the plain, golden band until a flash of pain made her close her eyes. Slowly she rubbed her brow with her fingertips, trying to massage away the ache, and behind her eyelids a vision began to form, that of a hand clasping a long, slim poker with a spike at its head. The iron was raised high, then it came slashing cruelly downward, again and again. Of a sudden her mind was filled with a twisted mask that progressively evolved into the face of a man. The visage was contorted by a gaping maw and terror-filled eyes that bore into her very soul. Cringing away from the horrible phantasm, she mewled in fear, wanting to be rid of these fantasies that kept tormenting her.

Lierin came to her feet with a strangled cry as a hand was laid on her shoulder. In a desperate attempt at freedom, she lunged away from the tall form, but an arm reached out, catching her about the waist and drawing her back against a solid chest.

"Lierin?" Ashton gave her a light shake as she tried to fight him, bringing her back to her senses. "Lierin, what's wrong?"

Staring up at him with wide, frightened eyes, she pressed a hand over her quivering mouth and shook her head. "I don't know, Ashton," she choked. "I keep seeing something . . . or remembering." She averted her face, hiding it from his worried gaze, and spoke through her tears. "I see a hand raised, and it keeps on hitting . . . hitting." Her shoulders trembled as she began to sob. "I wonder if I might have hurt someone. Perhaps you should have let them take me! Maybe I am the one they want, and Mr. Logan lied!"

"Foolishness!" Ashton took her by the shoulders and stared intently into the deep, tear-wet pools of emerald, as if compelling her to believe him. "There's nothing wrong with you but a simple loss of memory. You've had a shock, and you can't remember. You're letting the accusations of those churlish louts become your memory."

"Nooo!" she moaned. "You don't understand. I had a similar vision before those men ever came out here."

Ashton brought her close against him, enfolding her in his arms as he brushed his lips against her temple. "It's probably only a dream you've had and nothing to be taken seriously."

"I wish I could believe that." Lierin leaned her forehead against the side of his neck where she could feel the strong, slowly drumming beat of his pulse. Security seemed an almost tangible substance in his arms, and somewhere deep within her a yearning grew. As if her soul commanded her to speak, her thoughts came unbidden to her tongue. "I want so much to believe that the nightmare never happened. I . . . really want to believe I am your wife, Ashton. I . . . want to be a part of you and your family, to know with certainty that I belong here in your home. I have to know what the truth is."

Unfaltering in his effort to soothe her, Ashton gently cupped her face in his hands and probed the dark, translucent depths that were open to his gaze. "Then believe, Lierin," he urged in a whisper. "Accept what I say as fact and trust me. I mean you no hurt. If you knew how much I loved you, you'd not be afraid."

With deliberate care, his mouth lowered and covered hers in a slowly stirring kiss that continued unrelentingly until her fears were banished to the farthermost region of her consciousness. His lips moved upon hers, parting and playing and, with subtle persistence, demanding a response. Sleeping embers were fanned aflame, warming her and turning her mind slowly inside out. Her hands crept up his back, and she yielded her lips to his ardor. It was bliss. Heaven come down to earth. A sweet nectar that only lovers could taste. A potion to be savored leisurely and to its fullest, which indeed it might have been had the distant approach of clattering heels not warned them. Ashton raised his head, and the hazel eyes burned into hers, branding her with an unspoken promise. He stepped away and strode from the room, leaving her warmly flushed and totally unnerved. It was not a state she wished to be found in. Lifting her skirts, she followed Ashton's exit through the dining room and into the far hall, then blushed in confusion as he paused farther down the corridor to look back. His gaze seemed to touch her everywhere, stripping the pale body bare and snatching her breath with the boldness of his stare. His eyes flared as they plunged to the core of her being, and the evidence that he accurately assessed her condition became brazenly visible in those shining hazel orbs. With purposeful intent, he began to retrace his steps. Over the pounding of her heart, she could hear the chatter of the elder ladies as they entered the parlor, and she realized the way through the main hall was now clear. She fled, knowing that if she allowed him to touch her again, all reason would be swept away.

Breathless, she raced up the stairs and sought what safety her room afforded. She locked the door and, curling on the chaise longue, stared at the bleached wood portal, while her ears strained to catch the leisured stride of booted heels. They came unswervingly to her door and paused there as knuckles were lightly applied to the panel. She chewed her lip as she waited for the second summons to come. It was followed by a third. The knob was briefly tested, and finally the footsteps moved away. She might have breathed a sigh of relief, but a feeling of disappointment rose within her, displacing any small sense of victory she might have experienced.

Chilling winds swept in from the north, bringing with them a roiling mass of black clouds that snuffed the last rosy glow from the western horizon. Droplets began to fall, first in a light sprinkling that washed the dust from the air and brought the sweet scent of rain into the house. Then, as the lightning pranced closer in a flashing, sizzling display of the storm's power, a torrential downpour marched across the fields of Belle Chêne. Servants hastened to close windows and rekindle fires that had been allowed to die in the warmth of the day. Amusing speculations were made about the possible plight of Mr. Titch and his band of stalwarts. Everyone agreed that Hickory had sense enough to find shelter from the storm, but whether the rest could spend the night cooped up together in a barn without an outright war being waged seemed highly unlikely.

Willabelle came to help her young mistress dress for dinner, and though Lierin would have preferred to act the coward and keep herself hidden in her room, she gave herself over to the woman's care. The choice of gowns was simple since a journey to the dressmaker's had not yet been made, and the emerald green was the last of the evening creations to be worn. The garment was beautiful, temptingly so, but the neckline bared her shoulders above the full sleeves and swooped low over her bosom, while at the same time the stays of the corset pressed the higher curves of her breasts into view. For one who had been persuaded by the merits of caution, Lierin had to muse on the possible hazards of wearing such a gown in Ashton's presence. The décolletage was perhaps more modest than the gown Marelda had worn, but considering there was a riper fullness to be displayed, she could hardly claim to present a prudish illusion. The threat seemed well tempered, however, for it appeared unlikely that Ashton would make advances while they were chaperoned by his kin.

Her confidence rallied further when she descended the stairs and heard a soft, rich melody drifting from the parlor. She would be safe enough from those knee-weakening stares and casually bestowed caresses while Ashton played the cello, she thought. Indeed, while he was involved with the music, she would have the opportunity to observe him at her leisure.

The room was softly lighted by tiny flames that danced on the tips of a dozen tapers or more. On the hearth a cheery fire burned, adding its warmth and flickering light to the tasteful interior. Beyond the windows the lightning continued to frolic across the night sky as wild and chaotic winds swirled around the corners of the house, rattling the limbs of trees and shrubs that closely hugged the structure. Ashton sat with his back to the door as he played, and her gaze did not venture beyond the man as she approached. Even with only a view of his back, she could tell that he was impeccably garbed, which of course was not surprising. He seemed to have a flair for selecting clothes that were stylish and flawlessly tailored. Such was the case with the deep blue coat he was currently wearing. The garment was a superb fit, for the lines passed smoothly from wide shoulders to lean waist without a hint of an unsightly bulge to mar the styling. The merit was not confined solely to the garment, however, for his height and muscular slenderness complemented even the old riding breeches he was wont to wear while working his horses.

Not wishing to intrude, she had taken care to soften her footsteps, but as she drew near the music stopped, and Ashton came to his feet. Putting aside the instrument, he stepped around the chair and, with a widening smile, came toward her. His gaze savored the richness of her beauty and paused in obvious appreciation on the swelling bosom. Taking her hands into his, he lowered his head to capture her lips with his open mouth, immediately startling her with the light stroke of his tongue. She had hardly expected to be greeted with such a wanton kiss in the presence of the ladies. Unnerved, she pulled away.

"You'll shock your grandmother. . . ." she protested breathlessly.

A lazy grin curved Ashton's lips as his eyes caressed the delicate visage. "Tell me, madam, how I might do that when she's not here?"

"Not here?" Her gaze went past his arm to the pair of empty chairs where the ladies usually sat, then lifted to search his smiling face. "Where . . . ?"

"She and Aunt Jenny were invited to a neighbor's house for dinner." He shrugged casually. "The invitation was extended to us as well, but I made our excuses."

"Then . . ." She cast a worried glance about the room, and a blinding flash of lightning seemed to bring the truth home. "We're here alone?"

"Except for the servants." He raised a dubious brow. "Does that distress you, my love?"

Lierin answered with a slow and hesitant nod. "You've been very devious, Mr. Wingate."

Ashton laughed as he drew her to the sideboard where the crystal decanters sparkled beneath the gleaming tapers. He splashed a small draft of sherry in a glass, added a dash of water, and handed it to her. "What do you expect me to do?"

She sipped from the goblet and released a long, wavering sigh before she made her reply. "I think you intend to seduce me."

His white teeth flashed in a wicked grin. "The difference between seduction and rape, my love, is the simple word *no*. All you have to do is say it."

Lierin could find no adequate response. That particular word was much like caution, which was slowly losing its flavor and hardening into a dry, tasteless crust that gave her no pleasure. Though indeed simple, it was a word that was becoming increasingly difficult to use with him.

Ashton's gaze lowered to the swelling fullness above her gown, making her breath halt. His head came down, and her heart trembled as he dropped a kiss on her bare shoulder.

"You're very appetizing this evening, madam . . . quite a delectable morsel to savor. . . ." His tongue briefly touched her skin, drawing a shocked gasp from her and sending the pulse leaping through her veins again. He smiled into her astonished, sidelong regard and watched the flush of color spread downward into her pale breasts. "One taste is hardly enough," he murmured and bent lower to stroke his tongue lightly against the higher curve of that tempting roundness.

"Ashton!" She jumped as the wind scraped a branch against the window, and pressed a restraining hand upon his chest, whispering in shaky, urgent appeal, "The servants!"

Ashton chuckled as he straightened and bestowed a more proper kiss to her temple, greatly heartened by the fact that she had not denied him. "Ah, love, I'm so famished for the full feast, it's hard to restrain myself even with so many people in this house. I yearn to take you back to New Orleans, to that same room where we once made love, where we can be alone together."

A door slammed in the back of the house, and they moved apart as Willabelle came puffing into the dining room. "Lawsy, dat wind gonna blow dis house away if'n it gets any stronger." She cackled as she shook her head. "Why, it jes' mighta blown Mr. Titch clear into Natchez. Bet he ain't had such a bath in a month o' Sundays. Course, he be in need of it if he climbed into dat wagon. Ah jes' wish Ah could see him right now. Humph, he musta been a li'l tetched to think we gonna hand over de missus like she was some poor white trash or somepin. Yo sho' showed him, massa. Yassuh! Yassuh!"

The housekeeper chortled again before she turned to contemplate the table setting. She busied herself moving one place setting from the end to a position close to the head; then with a satisfied nod she bustled from the room. In a moment Willis appeared and decorously announced that dinner was about to be served. As the servant returned to the kitchen, Ashton presented his arm to his young wife and led her to the place Willabelle had rearranged, which, when they were seated, would bring her under his close scrutiny. His hand lightly stroked along her ribs as she stepped forward to take the chair, and when she glanced back inquiringly, their eyes held for a long, eternal moment.

Ashton was not a man to ignore an opportunity, and once more his lips found hers. When he raised his head again it was to probe the translucent green depths. Lierin felt as if she were being mesmerized by the hypnotic strength of his stare, and she was only distantly aware of his fingers gliding from her throat over her collarbone and then tracing downward. Her lips were parted with her rapid breathing as his mouth began a similar descent, and her senses swirled in a wild and giddy torrent. With casual ease his hand slipped down to cup her breast, but the scalding caress was enough to startle Lierin into full consciousness. Trembling, she moved away from his touch and settled into the chair, and when he had also taken his place, her eyes lifted to search his in worried appeal. She could not utter the words she wanted to say, the pleas that would caution him to take care with her emotions. She wanted love, but it was all going too swiftly. How could she clearly discern right from wrong when she had no sure knowledge of who she was?

During the meal Ashton's gaze never wandered far from the one who whetted his appetite, and it was not for that which was placed before them. As for Lierin, the sherry had been effective in subduing her qualms, and she began to enjoy the intimate dinner and the soft touch of his hand as it came to rest now and then upon her arm.

When they ventured back to the parlor, Ashton closed the french doors behind them, shutting off the dining room and securing their privacy. Lierin wandered back to the harpsichord and sought to plumb the depths of her memory as her fingers moved over the keyboard. Ashton stood close beside her, sometimes supplying the missing notes when she paused in confusion, but mostly admiring the delectable view of bare shoulders and soft bosom. She smiled up at him with glowing eyes as he brushed his knuckles along her nape and lost herself in the pleasure of his nearness. Her contentment diminished slightly as he moved away, but when he reached for the poker iron, a sudden horror seized her and her hands froze on the keys. A brief flash of an iron being brought down on a man's head rudely snatched her mind from the tranquillity of the moment.

Ashton glanced around in surprise as the melody halted on a discordant note, and when he saw the expression of frantic fright on her face and the slender, shaking fingers pressed tightly against her temples, he dropped the iron into the stand and ran back to her. Knowing full well what was tormenting her, he pulled her to her feet and held her close against him as he murmured against her hair. "It's all right, my love. It's all right. Try not to think of it."

"The poker iron . . ." Lierin shivered against him. "It's the same! Over and over! A man being hit by an iron. Oh, Ashton, when will it ever stop?"

Ashton held her from him as he questioned, "Do you know who the man is or what he looks like? Have you ever seen him before?"

"It's all a blur." Tears began to spill down her cheeks. "Oh, Ashton, I'm so afraid. I don't know why I keep seeing such a thing . . . unless . . . unless I'm being tormented by a memory of something I've done. Are you sure Mr. Logan . . . ?"

"You had nothing to do with that, Lierin," Ashton insisted. "The man was stabbed with a knife, and he was large, fully twice your weight and more. Even with the poker iron, your best effort would not have been good enough. He'd have turned on you before you could have done him serious harm."

"But the place on my back . . . you said it looked as if someone had hit me. Perhaps . . ."

Ashton stressed his words as he stared intently into the troubled green eyes. "Peter Logan said you were not the woman from the madhouse, Lierin. Accept that as fact. You're not the one! You're Lierin Wingate, my wife!"

His authoritative tone seemed to put matters in the proper perspective, and she took hold of her fears with a growing determination. If she was to survive this portion of her life with her sanity intact, she had to act with firm deliberation, refusing to be cindered beneath the weight of her trepidations. Calming herself by dint of will, she brushed the wetness from her cheek as Ashton stepped away to the sideboard and poured a glass of brandy.

"Here, drink this," he coaxed, returning to her. "It will help." He watched as she took a cautious sip of the strong spirits and smiled when she shuddered in distaste. With a finger beneath the glass, he urged it back to her lips again. "All of it, my love."

Lierin obeyed, reluctantly downing the fiery liquid in small gulps until only a few drops remained. With a last convulsive shiver, she returned the glass, already feeling the brandy's warmth spread through her. Ashton took her hand and led her to the settee where he leaned back in the corner and gathered her close. Lierin's emotions unfurled as she relaxed against him, and with a trembling sigh she snuggled closer, needing the tenderness he so freely bestowed upon her. It seemed natural to curl against him and rest her hand upon his chest.

A long and silently blissful time passed between them as the frolicking flames flared up and slowly died. The room began to take on a chill before Ashton reluctantly left her to throw several more pieces of wood on the fire. When he came back, he sat on his haunches before her and laid a hand upon her thigh, casually caressing it as he asked, "Are you going to be all right?"

"I think so." She was struck by the intimacy of his touch and, finding no cause to remove herself from it, accepted the tender feelings of contentment. Beneath his silent regard her cheeks grew steadily warm, and she turned her gaze toward the hearth to ease her confusion.

"There's another bedroom adjoining my quarters," he stated and

waited to continue until her gaze came back to rest on him in wondering silence. "I'd like you to move in there tonight." A lazy smile
accompanied his words. "I know the temptation will be greater for
me, but it's what I'd prefer . . . at least for the time being." His lips
widened into a teasing grin. "I think it's clear by now what I really
want. And it's not separate rooms."

Her eyes delved deeply into his as she whispered, "Have a care
for me, Ashton." Her smile turned wistful. "You have such a way
about you . . . I'm not sure I can resist you."

His brows came up in surprise. It amazed him that she would
make such an admission when she knew how anxious he was to test
the full measure of her resistance. "Madam, do you know what
you're putting into my hands?"

Lierin feigned sweet innocence. "Trust?"

His forehead twisted in an annoyed frown as the single word
seemed to squelch his hopes. "Mmm." He rose and offered a hand to
her. "Come, madam. I'll escort you to your new chamber before I
ravish you here and now."

"But I thought you said that trust is important in marriage," she
pointed out as he pulled her to her feet.

Ashton responded with a doubtful stare. "That word is coming
up much too often for my comfort, madam. I shall dispense with
your idea of trust by taking you back to New Orleans. It that fails,
there's no doubt I'll perish from wanting you."

She was unable to read his expression. "Are you serious? I mean,
about taking me to New Orleans."

"Yes, as a matter of fact, I am," he stated as the idea took deeper
root.

"But you just came back from New Orleans."

"This trip will be solely for our pleasure, madam," he assured her
warmly.

Lierin regarded him with an air of skepticism. "And of course
you intend to complete this seduction of yours."

"Aye, madam, and the sooner, the better."

He bent and lifted her in his arms, dropping a kiss against her
throat as she settled contentedly against him. He was fascinated with
the way the gown gapped from her bosom while her arms were
about his neck. It was a most tempting sight and one he repeatedly
reviewed as he carried her to his bedroom door. He turned the knob

and, with a shoulder, nudged it open to bear her across the threshold. They passed through the suite of rooms and paused in the bathing room where he stood her to her feet.

"You'll probably want to undress in here. The bedroom may be a bit cool yet." Ashton inclined his head toward a small chest where a neatly folded stack of clothing lay. "I had Willabelle bring in a few things while we dined."

Lierin recognized the garments as her own green robe and batiste nightgown and realized that the invitation to move her into a bedchamber near his own had not been a spontaneous offer at all. Not only had he given prior thought to the matter, but he had made arrangements, assuming she would agree. She regarded him with some amazement. "I think I underestimated you."

Ashton returned a lopsided grin to her dubious gaze. "I didn't think you'd object."

"Are you always so sure of yourself?" she queried, conscious of how deftly she had been maneuvered.

"It's a matter of logic, madam. The accommodations are more comfortable here. . . ."

"And handier to you."

"Yes, that, too," he admitted with rakish aplomb. Doffing his coat, vest, and cravat, he hung them on a wooden clothes tree near the door, then took her hands and brought them to his lips while his eyes played with hers. "I'll stir up the fire while you get undressed."

The door closed behind him, allowing Lierin a few private moments to settle back to earth. She was becoming increasingly aware of the fact that whenever she was with him, she gave little thought to resistance. He was like a strong magnet that drew her progressively nearer. He was totally a man, and having all the cravings of a woman, she found herself very susceptible. Despite her attempts at logic and restraint, she was beginning to relish the idea of being married to him. Whether it was reasonable or not, she desired the intimacy and the familiarity of a husband-and-wife relationship.

His robe hung with his other garments on the clothes tree, and beneath the stroke of her hand a clean, masculine scent drifted from the velvet garment, filling her whole being with soft yearnings. She drew in her breath, surprised at her wayward will, and deliberately set her mind to the matter of getting undressed. The nightgown slid with silken softness over her naked body, and distantly she wondered what it would be like to have Ashton make love to her, if she would find the moment pleasurable, or if the anticipation was far more entertaining than the actuality.

She stared dreamily across the small space of the room, doubting the possibility of such a thing happening. The man exuded an unceasing current of virility, which could not be denied. Though she could imagine the hazel eyes growing cold with rage, there was a fire that burned in the man which could be effective in thawing the resistance of almost any woman.

Lierin shook her head angrily. Once again her thoughts took her into reckless meanderings. Rather than rein in her wayward musings, she was letting her mind run far afield. It was illogical to think of coupling with the man when he was still very much a stranger to her. Why did she persist in these frivolous ponderings when she knew the wisest choice would be to keep her distance?

Belting the green velvet robe about her slender waist, she entered the adjoining bedroom and moved on bare feet across the luxurious carpet while she admired the fine furnishings and soft colors. The boudoir dwarfed the memory of the guest room in her mind, for it was everything a woman could wish for. Indeed, if she had viewed the accommodations first, she would have been reluctant to question Ashton's sincerity.

He had turned from the fireplace to watch her approach, and she stepped near, slipping her arm through his and giving him her answer with a soft smile. "It's beautiful, Ashton, and you were right. I could not have rejected it."

Lierin raised on her toes to press a kiss to his cheek, but he turned his face to meet her lips with his. She had no desire to withdraw and leisurely savored the rising warmth of his response. His mouth opened and snatched hungrily at hers, drawing and compelling her to answer. The hesitant intrusion of her tongue encouraged him, and he faced her, bringing her full against him. His embrace tightened, and the kiss intensified for a long, blissful moment. Torn between yielding and denial, she trembled in his arms, aware that he was becoming increasingly aroused. It came to her that if she did not immediately halt this whirligig world, she would not find the strength to deny him.

"I must have time, Ashton," she whispered pleadingly as she broke away from the kiss. "Please let me find myself."

Ashton's brows gathered in a pained frown as he set her from him, and she saw the agony of her denial in his face. Not knowing how to ease his plight, she followed him to the bed and waited as he folded down the covers. When he faced her again, he let out his breath haltingly and raised his hands as if to lay them on her shoulders. She waited expectantly, wanting him to, but he turned away with a heavy sigh.

"I'll go."

"Please, Ashton . . ." Her eyes pleaded with him to understand. "Won't you stay and talk for a while?"

Ashton responded with an abortive laugh. "Madam, you have either underestimated your charms or overestimated my ability to resist you. The temptation is beyond me. If I stay a moment longer, a simple *no* will no longer suffice." He jammed his hands into the pockets of his trousers, and his jaw tightened as he glanced away. "I am sorely beset with my passions, so please, madam . . . have a care. Just get in bed while I still have my wits about me."

Lierin dared not ignore his warning and hurried to comply, not even pausing to doff her robe before slipping under the covers. He went back to the fireplace, threw another log on the blazing kindling, then stood frowning down into the shifting orange and gold flames. She studied him against the brightening firelight, crushingly aware of how quickly she had come to desire him. Somewhere in the inner core of her being was the sure and unmistakable knowledge that she had experienced moments of intimacy with a man. If she closed her eyes, she could almost envision a man rising naked from a bed and moving away from her. Though vague and indistinct, the form left an impression of towering height, wide shoulders tapering to narrow hips, and short hair curling in feathery wisps against a bronze-hued neck. Willabelle had assured her that Ashton was a man among many, and she was swiftly coming to that same conclusion. Indeed, if she could accurately judge a man's merits in so short a time, he was just what she needed for a whole lifetime of loving and caring regard.

"Ashton?" Her voice was a soft murmur in the room.

He glanced around. "Yes?" Her answering silence drew him back until he stood beside the bed. "What is it, Lierin?"

She searched the handsome visage in the meager light of the room. She knew she risked much at this moment, for she was very vulnerable to his manly persuasion. She could be hurt in the outcome of it all, and yet she wanted him to make love to her. She yearned to feel that strong, firmly muscled body against her own and to give herself unreservedly to him. Her eyes were limpid pools of deep emerald green as her hand reached to the edge of the bed to pull down the covers invitingly. "I don't think you have to take me to New Orleans, Ashton. You can have everything you want right now."

The leap of Ashton's heart started the blood surging through his veins, and his long-starved passions seized control of his body. His eyes flared their answer in heated lust as his fingers moved to the buttons of his shirt. In a moment his brown shoulders gleamed naked in the candlelight, and he sat on the bed to remove his boots. Lierin rose to her knees, and her robe slipped from the end of the bed where she tossed it as she pressed close against him. She laid her arms over his shoulders, and Ashton's mind reeled with the ecstasy of her soft breasts rubbing against his back, tantalizing him and stirring his passions until they became a hot, sweet ache in the pit of his belly. This was Lierin, tempting, warm, responsive, capable of setting his very being on fire. The last boot thudded to the floor as her hands slipped down his hard chest, pausing momentarily as her right hand found a scar, then stroking firmly over the swell of muscles while her fingers threaded through its thick matting of hair.

"Hurry," she whispered in his ear and traced it teasingly with her tongue before she sat back on her heels. Reluctant to be parted, he sprawled back upon the bed, twisting slightly as he reached for her, pulling her down upon him. As his mouth reached to entrap hers, his hand wandered up, moving from her buttock to her breast, then further still, catching his thin fingers in the top of the gown before being joined by his other hand. She gasped in surprise as he ripped the garment apart, spilling free the ripe fullness of her bosom before his hungering eyes. His mouth touched her breast with a moist, burning heat that took her breath away and set her heart racing wildly within the cavity of her chest. She shivered, feeling consumed by the slow, licking flame of his tongue, and her whole being throbbed with each wet, languid caress.

With another tug he finished parting the nightgown and, pulling it from her, tossed it to the end of the bed. The hazel eyes struck sparks against her flesh, and with a hint of a mysterious smile she raised upright, taking his hand and drawing him to his knees until they faced each other on the bed with her limbs tucked within the spread of his. His hands slid about her waist and glided down over her buttocks, while her lips pressed light, eager kisses against his throat and the line of his jaw. The soft, pale peaks of her breasts brushed his furred chest, tormenting him with the sweet ecstasy of it.

"I think I've fallen in love with you," she breathed. Her fingers curled in the hair at his nape. "I want you. . . . Oh, Ashton, I really do. . . ."

His arms caught her close, and his mouth seized hers with a fervor that took her breath away. Their lips blended with a crushing urgency that readily conveyed the craving impatience of each. When they came apart, their eyes smoldered with a common heat. Her hands slid admiringly over his muscular ribs to the waistband of his trousers, and then stroked down lean thighs, while his own plucked the buttons free. His breath sucked in through clenched teeth as her fingers slipped inside the top of the loosened garment and teased him with a feathery light caress against his hard belly. The hot blood shot through his loins and thudded through him, cauterizing his mind with his ravaging needs.

He rose briefly to his feet, then came back in full, naked glory, taking her against him and pressing hard and hot between her thighs. His mouth came down on hers with a rapacious hunger, twisting, devouring, awakening passions she hardly knew existed. He laid her down, and his hands and lips glided over her silken flesh with the bold confidence of a man who had no doubt in himself. With purposeful intent he plucked at the strings of her senses, and she responded with soft, melodic sighs. Swept by building passion and brought ever nearer to that dam of restraint, she began to tremble and writhe. Their eyes melded in warm union as he braced himself above her, then came ecstasy, plunging in with the bold thrust of a knight's lance and forging them together in the knot of love. A flooding tide of emotions washed through Lierin, and her whole being came alive with pulsing joy. The strokes of his body were smooth and languid against her own until the lusting heat made them both greedy for more, and it became a wild, frenzied search for fulfillment. She arched against him, answering his hard, thrusting hips with a fervor that equaled his. She gasped as she was snatched to a lofty firmament, where the vapors were sweet and heady and where the stars blazed in a blinding, brilliant display. A myriad sensations fell like sparkling dust against her skin and burst in tiny shards of rapturous bliss. She clung to him and he to her as they were lifted ever higher on the crest of their passion. They soared together in this iridescent world until finally the heavenly spheres released them from their celestial orbit, and they descended on light, airy cushions of thistledown. Contentment gave fragrance to their sighs as their lips blended in the warm afterglow of their passion. The raindrops trickled down the panes of glass, but the pair gave them no heed as they sipped the sweet nectar of sated desires.

The master's suite was shaded from the morning sun, and only a minimum of light leaked in around the velvet drapes drawn over the french doors and crystal windows. Lierin stirred, reaching out a hand searchingly to the far side of the bed. Finding the place empty, she sat up and glanced quickly about the room, but to no avail. Though she listened carefully, she heard nothing to indicate Ashton was anywhere in the suite of rooms. Sometime during the night he had carried her to his bed, ending the matter of separate rooms with the firm declaration of where she belonged. It was a massive room, tasteful in its accoutrements and decor. Teal blues and soft taupes were in abundance, while velvets, tapestries, leathers, and deeply hued woods gave the room a masculine warmth. The fact that the accommodations belonged to a man with whom she had become enamored only made the prospect of being ensconced here more appealing.

Smoothing her tumbled hair away from her cheek, she leaned back into the pillows with a dreamy sigh. She had memories of the past hours to content her until he came back to her again. The master of Belle Chêne had seized her mind and body with his irresistible charm, and now her heart was hopelessly entangled with the man. Wrapped up in the rapture of her infatuation, she conjured an image in her mind of that sleek, bronze form with its rippling muscles, hardened belly, and iron-thewed thighs. Her face grew warm as her imagination completed the man with more intimate detail, and her lips curved into a secretive smile as she recalled the warmth he displayed beneath her exploring hand. Later, when he had moved away from her during the night to lay more wood on the fire, she had been fascinated with the play of lithe brawn across his back and, beneath the line that separated dark skin from light, the tautly muscled buttocks.

The opening and closing of the door in the far bedroom snatched Lierin from her musings, and she threw back the covers, recognizing Willabelle's heavy tread, then gasped as she was abruptly reminded of her nakedness. Grabbing up Ashton's robe from the end of the bed, she quickly donned the oversized garment, but paused to listen as the housekeeper entered the bathing room. The door was pushed shut, allowing Lierin to slump back on the bed in relief. She was reluctant to face the woman in such a state of dishabille only a short time after she had vowed not to be rushed in accepting Ashton as her husband. Still, she knew she would have to admit her status as mistress of the house sometime before the hour was out. She could hardly hide from Willabelle much longer than that, even in this huge house.

The activity increased in the adjoining room as other servants began bringing water for a bath. The housekeeper directed them in a muted tone, then the voices dwindled, and a brief moment later a light knock sounded on the door. Pausing to collect her composure before answering the summons, Lierin checked herself in the cheval glass, finding her hair wildly tossed and her cheeks as flushed and rosy as the body beneath the robe. Her appearance was so obvious, there would be little doubt that she had spent the night in sensual pursuits with Mr. Wingate, and any semblance of dignity would be difficult to maintain if Willabelle was less than discreet.

Resolving to give the occasion her best effort, Lierin opened the portal and found Willabelle laying out fresh linens and garments. The woman had been humming to herself, but turned to greet her young mistress with the usual cheery smile and chatter, putting Lierin completely at ease. The housekeeper seemed to accept her presence in the master's bedroom casually and as part of the routine.

In a short time Lierin was enjoying a deliciously warm bath, and had hardly settled in for a leisurely soak when the lower hall echoed with the rapid click of booted heels. Ashton strode toward the stairs, motivating Luella May to run down the upper hall and bestow a warning knock on the master's chamber door. Willabelle quickly slipped from the room and left her charge to whatever was about to befall her.

When Ashton entered his suite, he was drawn to the door of the bathing room by the soft, lilting melody that drifted from the cubicle. Leaning a shoulder against the jamb, he indulged himself in the pleasure of viewing this undraped beauty which was so charmingly presented to him. He considered his timing perfect. His lady was at her bath, and with the soft morning light filtering through the window and lending her ivory skin a radiance of its own, she seemed like some woodland nymph intent upon her toilet in a hidden forest glade.

Lierin finally glanced up, sensing a presence and yet expecting to find Willabelle. She suffered a start when she was greeted instead by a most wicked smile and warmly glowing hazel eyes. She was not yet at ease beneath the bold stare of a man and pinkened as his gaze dipped to her wetly gleaming breasts.

"You've made my day, madam . . . and my night."

Her color heightened at his reminder of their passionate involvement. He was garbed casually in riding breeches, tall boots, and full-sleeved shirt, and seemed to be the very epitome of the confident male, which made her all the more conscious of her own nakedness and timidity. Seeking to divert his stare and allow her pulse to slow its reckless beating, she indicated his attire. "Have you been out riding?"

"Only to look over a portion of land that is being cleared," he replied, watching the soapy runnels cascade over her bosom as she attempted to bathe and cover herself at the same time. "My plan for today is to take you into Natchez. You'll be needing clothes for our trip to New Orleans."

"But I thought we weren't going. . . ."

"On the contrary, my love." Ashton strode forward and sat on the wooden stool that had been drawn up near the tub. Taking the sponge from her, he dipped it into the soapy water and began to scrub her back, beginning low and slowly working his way upward. "A trip to New Orleans might help you remember, and of course we'll need some time to get acquainted again. What better place to do that than where it all began?"

Lierin half turned her head and sighed in obvious pleasure as his fingers began to knead her back and shoulders.

"Feels good?" he asked softly.

"Hmm, yes. Very," she murmured, forgetting her shyness as she leaned forward, the better to receive his administerings. He waxed bolder as he lathered her side, slipping his hand forward to soap and wash her breast. Her heart took on a trip-hammer beat, and with soft and limpid eyes, she turned her gaze to his. Bending forward, he nuzzled her ear and, brushing aside the loosely dangling curls that dropped coyly from the casually gathered mass, pressed light kisses upon her throat. His hand moved freely across her bosom, then slid beneath her as he lifted her from the bath onto his lap. Neither of them gave heed to the fact that his clothes were becoming soaked, for the heat of the moment had overtaken them. They were two beings enraptured with each other, and the rest of the world faded from notice.

Hearing the soft click of heels approaching the upper landing, Ashton glanced up to find a sight that completely nourished his spirits. For the outing Lierin had arrayed herself in one of the gowns he had purchased and with stunning results. Long ago he had realized she fulfilled every aspect of his long-held vision of a desirable woman. His memory had served him well during the past three years, but when he gazed at the living, breathing woman, he knew he had not grasped the full reality of her beauty. Was it a trick of his mind that she seemed even lovelier than he had remembered?

As she paused in indecision at the head of the stairs, he slowly smiled and lifted up a hand to her. His eyes touched her warmly as she descended, taking in every delicious detail. The gown seemed an added touch of perfection with its iridescent, blue-green taffeta bodice and off-white skirt of the same fabric. A crisply pleated ruff fanned out from her throat, and similar ruffles added trimmings at the wrists. The sleeves were puffed and full at the top, but closely fitting for the major portion of the arm. Scalloped cream lace formed a pleated lining for the tall-brimmed, blue-green bonnet, and a wide bow of the same hue was tied beneath one side of her chin, lending her a pert, saucy look.

"Madam, you would make the sirens of ancient lore thrash upon their rocks and moan in envy," he vowed.

Lierin laughed gaily and placed her arms around his neck as he settled his own about her waist and swung her from the stairs. He held her suspended from the floor while they exchanged an ardent kiss. Her tongue readily answered his, and it was a long, enjoyable moment before they parted. Ashton sighed and reluctantly set her to her feet. "I'm tempted to take you back to bed when you answer me like that."

Caressing his vested chest, she responded with an enticing smile. "We can always delay our trip."

Ashton groaned in mock agony. "Oh, madam, I've never been so wont to stay abed before, but I owe you a nightgown, remember." He smiled down into her sparkling eyes. "We'll need a goodly supply for the rest of the nights we can spend together."

She raised on her toes to whisper in his ear. "I can understand why Marelda hates me so. You're very nice to go to bed with."

Ashton peered at her skeptically as he led her across the hall. "Madam, Marelda would have no scale to judge that by. I've never been intimate with the woman."

Hugging his arm tightly against her breast, Lierin smiled into his eyes. "That makes me very, very happy."

Hiram stood waiting at the open door of the carriage. As they emerged from the house, he swept off his fine beaver hat and greeted them with a wide grin. "Lawsy, y'all sho' make a pair all duded up."

"Why, thank you, Hiram," Lierin replied blithely. "Mr. Wingate does look fine, doesn't he?"

"Yes'm, jes' like he always does," the coachman agreed, then chuckled as he expanded on his statement: "But he ain't nearly as pretty as yo, missus."

Their warm laughter rewarded him, and with a bright smile Lierin accepted her husband's assistance into the carriage. Settling into the leather seat, she lifted her skirts aside as Ashton sat close beside her. He laid his arm along the back of the seat behind her and, with a hand on her shoulder, urged her to nestle close against his side.

"I love you," he whispered.

The bonneted head turned to present a softly smiling visage to his loving gaze, and her eyes touched his face in a gentle caress. "The feeling is mutual, sir."

The landau swung around the curving drive, and the journey into Natchez took on a new measure of delight for Ashton, who had traversed the road on numerous and widely varied occasions. For the first time in many months he felt settled, both in mind and in spirit. The night of lustful pleasures had given him a release he had sorely needed, but the cause of his contentment lay in the person who snug-gled so willingly against him.

Lierin picked a piece of lint from his trouser leg, and her hand lingered to rub the firmly muscled thigh lightly. Lifting her gaze, she met Ashton's smiling regard and reached to receive his kiss when his face lowered to hers. The ride continued in a most delightful fashion until Hiram maneuvered the conveyance to a halt in front of the couturiere's.

Ashton assisted his young wife to the boardwalk and spoke a word with Hiram about the estimated time of their return before slipping his hand to the small of her back and escorting her inside the dressmaker's shop. Miss Gertrude hurried from the back of the shop, straining her long neck to see around the bolts of cloth that were stacked on the tables. When the gawky, parrot-faced woman saw who had entered, she threw up her hands and rushed forward to greet them.

"Oh, I've been so anxious to meet your young wife, Mr. Wingate," she warbled.

He made the introductions, and through the small spectacles perched on the bridge of her thin, hawkish nose, Miss Gertrude gave Lierin a careful inspection from bonnet to soft leather slippers, then smiled and nodded in approval. "Your grandmother was in here yes-terday morning, Mr. Wingate, and the way she was bragging about your wife, I thought she had been inflated with a lot of hot air, but I can see for myself that her claims are true."

Miss Gertrude took the slender hand into hers and patted it affectionately. "When the ladies see you wearing my creations, I shall be deluged with a brood of chirping biddies wanting to look exactly like you. I've done a few miracles in my time, Mrs. Wingate, but none of that sort. You're such a lovely thing, I can already see trouble coming."

Lierin laughed at the unorthodox compliment and gently teased, "Perhaps we should forget about the clothes if there's going to be such a problem for you."

Miss Gertrude's gangling form straightened abruptly, and she stared at the young woman in comic disbelief. "What?! And have you gowned by someone else? My dear, that is positively ridiculous. No one else will do you justice." Her mouth lifted in a lopsided grin as she shrugged. "They'll come all right, jealous as all get out, but have no fear. I can handle them."

Envious they would be. About that Miss Gertrude had no doubt. Long ago she had heard rumors about the handsome Ashton Wingate and all the beautiful young women who had set their caps for him. The most persistent of these had been Marelda Rousse, who had frequented her shop and often prattled about how much the man adored her. His hasty marriage had caused her a great deal of embarrassment, and she had given tongue to a multitude of rationales on the probability of Ashton having been forced into the marriage by some outraged father. When pressed as to how that might have been accomplished with the obstinate Mr. Wingate, the brunette had simply shrugged and said he must have spoiled some girl's maidenhead while he was drunk and then been prompted to do the honorable thing while in that same condition. The explanations had reeked of envy at the time, but once one chanced to view the lady in question, they lost all semblance of truth. If the tales had been factual, then in his drunken heat the man had blindly selected a jewel of unmatchable beauty.

The dressmaker gestured for them to follow and led the way toward the back of the shop. As the woman moved away, Lierin leaned near Ashton. "I do believe Miss Gertrude has a bit of blarney in her, especially if she tells the same thing to all her customers."

He chuckled and squeezed her waist. "Miss Gertrude has been known to be brutally honest at times, and I can't see any reason to believe she's filling your pretty ears with rubbish now. If you're not aware of it, madam, you're definitely a pleasure to look at. Indeed, it has become my favorite pastime."

Ashton had already taken note that it was other men's wont to stare at his young wife and admire her beauty, too. The reaction was the same among the male customers at a nearby inn where they later went to enjoy a light repast. The hour was well after midday, and the number of patrons had dwindled to a double handful of men who were scattered about the common room. A few were acquaintances of Ashton and pressed for introductions, then, clapping him on his back, offered their good wishes. Some were strangers who stared in mute appreciation, while others were bolder and openly ogled her. With a brow raised in deliberate challenge, Ashton stared these men down until they turned away. He escorted her to a table near the back and placed her where he could enjoy what he had not been willing to share with others. Even there he found he had to contend with the curious glances of the gaunt, rawboned innkeeper. Ashton knew the man as a somewhat dull individual who had never shown too great an interest in eyeing women, seeming rather to prefer to watch over his own meager wealth. His unswerving interest in Lierin seemed highly out of character, and Ashton was more than mildly surprised when the man approached them.

"Pardon me, missus, but did I overhear Mr. Wingate say that you're his wife?"

Lierin nodded hesitantly. "Yes."

The innkeeper scratched his head, seeming bemused. "I guess I was mistaken. I thought you might have been that lady Mr. Sinclair was looking for."

"Mr. Sinclair?" Lierin repeated in a questioning tone.

"Yes'm, Mr. Sinclair said his wife had been kidnapped from their home and brought here by the man who had taken her, but I guess you're not her, being Mr. Wingate's wife and all."

"I don't believe I even know a Mr. Sinclair," Lierin murmured quietly, feeling somewhat unsettled. "Why did you think I was the one?"

"Oh, she come in here, and I got to see her from a distance. She was a fine slip of a woman, just like yourself, ma'am. At first, I thought the man she come in with was her coachman, 'cause he was driving her carriage, but then, he got himself a room next to hers and they kept kind o' secluded while they were here. She seemed power-ful upset about something, but I never got to talk with her or see her up close. Whatever was goin' on, it had to be somethin' strange, 'cause they both seemed sorta nervous. He weren't much to look at, but that Mr. Sinclair is a right nice-lookin' dandy, he is. Anyway, when Mr. Sinclair showed up, the other man skedaddled out o' sight, taking her with him, I suppose. Mr. Sinclair searched for the pair of them for a while, then loaded his wife's trunks in her coach, hired a man to drive it, and left. I seen him in here a time or two since then, but he ain't from around these parts, an' he don't talk much."

"When did all this happen?" Ashton queried.

The innkeeper scraped a hand over his bristly chin as he mused on the matter. "Seems like it were shortly 'fore the madhouse burned." He thought a moment longer and then gave a decisive nod. "Yep, that's about it."

A nervous fluttering attacked Lierin's stomach. Though she kept telling herself the man had mistaken her for someone he had not clearly seen and she was really and truly Lierin Wingate, she was assailed by sudden doubts. If she did not bear some resemblance to this unknown woman, why had he made the inquiry? On the other hand, the portrait had given incontestable proof that she was precisely the one Ashton claimed her to be. Holding on tenaciously to that thought, Lierin regained her composure and thrust aside her qualms.

Ashton had watched her with gentle concern throughout the meal and was greatly heartened to see her cheerfulness return. He was presented evidence of this when they emerged from the inn, and she halted him on the vine-draped gallery. With a delicious grin, she slipped her arms about his neck and pulled his head down to press parted lips upon his. He was more than willing to cooperate and delayed the moment by lengthening the kiss into a more passionate play of mouth and tongue.

A sudden gasp startled them, and pulling apart, they turned to face a tall, sandy-haired man who stared at them in wide-eyed surprise. He seemed frozen with shock as he gaped at one and then the other. With an embarrassed giggle, Lierin ran past the intruder and Ashton followed with a grin and a murmured apology. Rushing to the thoroughfare, he beckoned to Hiram, and soon they were exchanging laughing comments about the astonished, dapperly attired young man in the privacy of their carriage.

That same gentleman was still on the veranda when a brief moment later Horace Titch strolled past with Marelda on his arm. The woman had seen the flight of the Wingate couple and was sharing her complaints with her escort as they neared the man.

"I simply don't know how that woman convinced Ashton she was Lierin Wingate, when all the time she's been claiming a complete loss of memory. Why, she said she can't even remember who she is or where she came from, and who knows if she'll ever remember again. I still say she's from the madhouse."

"But, sweetie, Mr. Logan swore that she wasn't," Horace dared to argue.

"Well, considering what Ashton did for the man, don't you think Mr. Logan said that only because he didn't want to upset Ashton? While you were out there with all those men, you should have insisted that she be taken in for the murder of that attendant, but, no, you let Ashton make a fool of you."

Horace clenched his pudgy hands into tight fists as he mumbled, "I'll never forgive him for that, and I swear someday I'll have my revenge."

"You'd better have a large army with you the next time you face Ashton Wingate," Marelda advised dryly. "He seems to thrive on gaining the advantage in such situations."

Marelda's eyes settled on the tall man and flared in bold admiration. Though younger and somewhat heavier than Ashton, there was something about the stranger that reminded her of the other. It was easy to surmise from the cut of his clothes that he enjoyed at least a reasonable wealth, but even without that added attraction, he was definitely more appealing to her senses than the company she was presently keeping.

The tall man tipped his hat to her, but his neatly clipped mustache barely twitched as he gave her a bland smile. Marelda was disappointed by his lack of response and wondered if some great problem of the world rested on his shoulders. She was accustomed to more zealous reactions to her flirtations and her sultry look of promise.

– Chapter Seven –

New Orleans! Crescent City. Gateway to the Mississippi. Lustrous pearl of the Delta. A city loved by saint and sinner alike, a place of lazy days and sultry nights, a rich and ever-expanding boomtown with a unique mixture of customs and cultures. A paradise where one could seek his own, a place of revelries, of sweet bliss captured in the darkest hours and nurtured beneath the warming sun, where time passed as effortlessly as the wide, muddy river that lapped at its banks. The sights and sounds gave flavor to the metropolis, while the aromas, both zesty and sweet, stirred the senses of all who strolled the streets. Sweet shrubs added a heady fragrance to the air, while azalea bushes provided a mass of riotous color across spacious lawns and behind closed gardens, wherever one was wont to look. It was surely an Eden for lovers.

From the time of the Wingates' disembarking, it became an adventure that produced memories rather than brought them to mind. The floating palaces were docked three deep along the city's levee, and as the *River Witch* nudged its way through to the quay, the drum of excitement began to beat with quickening rhythm in Lierin's heart. The whistle blew high above her head, adding to the exhilaration of the moment, while the tall smokestacks belched in satisfied relief. Eagerly Lierin searched the waterfront and could find no spot where the pace was leisured. Everywhere she looked there was some sort of frenzied activity. Straining teams of mules pulled away wagons heaped high with cotton bales or hogsheads of molasses and such, while stevedores hustled across planks and captains barked orders to their crews.

Whisked down the plank on the capable arm of her husband and handed into the open barouche of a hired livery, Lierin felt as if she were soaring as high as the sea birds that shrieked overhead. Glancing about with the enthusiasm of a child, she espied a small group of colorfully dressed quadroons waiting in a nearby carriage. They were quite elegant in their silken finery and lovely beyond the common meaning of the word. Their unusual attire and appearance fascinated her until she noticed their flirtatious smiles and glowing eyes directed toward Ashton; then she began to understand some of the jealousies provoked by these women. Ashton laughed as she snuggled closer, and accommodated her desire to show possession by laying an arm about her shoulders.

"I suppose it doesn't matter to them that you're married," she commented in a miffed tone.

"It matters to me," Ashton murmured with gentle fervor. He raised her chin and, while all the world watched, kissed her softly parted lips in a most loving manner, causing an eruption of giggles to come from the nearby conveyance.

Lierin's anxieties were completely appeased when he finally lifted his head. Her own eyes were warm and shining as they caressed his face. "Does the bliss ever stop, Ashton, or does it just keep getting better?"

He smiled. "Sometimes it takes hard work and tenacity to make love last. It can grow stale from misuse."

"It's been so easy loving you this last month," she breathed. "I can't imagine having to work at it."

"Would you like to see the place where I first saw you?"

Lierin nodded eagerly. "Oh, yes. I want to know everything that we did together. I want to relive those moments with you."

Ashton leaned forward and instructed the driver to take them to the Vieux Carré, then settled back to enjoy the ride as the horses clip-clopped their way across the cobbled wharf. He had been half afraid to take her on the steamer, not knowing how she would react or if he would be encouraging more nightmares. Though he had watched her closely, ready at any moment to give the command to dock, she had shown no qualms. Indeed, she had displayed as much exuberance as anyone going on their first excursion. Hoping that something would stimulate his wife's memory and encourage its return, he had made arrangements to have the same suite at the St. Louis Hotel wherein they had, as a slightly younger couple, explored the delights of their newly wedded status. The view of the streets would be the same, with similar sounds drifting in through the tall french doors. He would take her to the restaurants where they had dined and wander through the same shops, visit the parks where they had once strolled and attend theaters where troupes had entertained them. As much as could be controlled, all would be the same. It was the best he could do; he could only hope it would be enough.

Lierin leaned with comfortable ease against Ashton's side and took in the remarkable sights that whisked past in an ever-changing panorama on either side. She had no idea where they wended, but was content and happy in her place close beneath his arm. The barouche passed along a street where hotels and eating establishments abounded, and then turned down a narrow lane where myriad shops were adorned with ornamental iron lace and overhanging balconies. Ashton pointed, drawing her attention to a cluster of small boutiques that hugged the street.

"Over there! That's where I first saw you, but it took you a while to learn I existed."

Lierin responded with an amused chuckle. "I probably knew you were there all along and was just playing coy. I can't imagine any woman not being aware of you."

"Nevertheless, madam, you gave me a fright. I was sure my life had ended when you got into the carriage and rode away with your chaperone."

"Then where did we actually meet?"

"Ahhh, Providence was with me." Smiling, he nodded and gave another address to the driver. "A band of miscreants had cast a shadow of blame on my crew, no doubt to escape the penalties they justly deserved. They bribed a man to give a false account of pirates attacking other steamers and then taking refuge aboard my vessel. By the time the officials recognized the ploy for what it was, the blackguards had slithered free, leaving me outraged and determined to confront a particular judge who was reviewing the evidence against my men."

"My grandfather? Judge Cassidy?"

"Aye, madam. A wise man who allowed me to speak my piece until a certain young lady came to his defense. I shall be eternally grateful that he did."

The barouche entered a tightly turning passage where brick fences rose on either side. Wrought-iron gates hung beneath rounded brick arches, permitting a view of blossom-bedecked gardens and meandering stone paths. The conveyance swept out into a wider street where tall townhouses snuggled close against each other. As they progressed on their way, the houses became larger, with narrow spaces appearing between. The gardens became lawns, and the lawns widened, with moss-draped oaks and a variety of other trees shading them. The barouche passed every style of house, from columned colonials to dwellings found in the West Indies, and it was in front of one of these latter types where they finally halted.

Recognition might have been hindered by the fact that shutters had been nailed over the windows of the house, but the interior was hardly more comforting, for it was dark and rather morbid. Ashton opened several windows and pushed the shutters free, allowing the sunlight to spill into the rooms. Ghostly shapes of sheet-draped furniture stood like dreary sentinels about the room, but the presence of these lifeless creations apparently had not discouraged the entry of a recent visitor who had left signs of his passage in the layer of dust on the floor. The manly footprints wandered aimlessly through the lower part of the house, but in the judge's study it seemed the man had had a definite purpose in mind, for the tracks went directly from the door to a lowboy and returned to the portal in the same unswerving manner. On the wall above the table a pair of hangers were spaced wide apart, as if two paintings had once hung side by side above the piece. Ashton could only make a guess as to what might have hung there.

"When I received your portrait, it was accompanied by a letter which explained that the painting was one of a pair given to the judge by your father. The other was of your sister, Lenore, and they were both in your grandfather's possession at the time of his death. The one of Lenore might have been sent back to her, but these footprints are fairly recent, and as you can see"—he drew her gaze downward to the footprints—"once the man entered this room, he came directly to this table."

"What interest would anyone have in a portrait when"—she swept her hand about the study—"when there are other things of more value to interest a thief?"

Ashton chuckled. "I never saw the portraits while they were here, but if Lenore looks anything like you, I can understand why a man would want it."

"Now don't tease, Ashton. Someone must have had a more sensible reason than that for taking it."

Ashton shrugged. "I can't imagine any plausible purpose. No one had a right to come here except by our authority. Your grandfather made provisions to leave everything in this house to you and made no attempt to change the will even after he received word that you had drowned."

"But why didn't he do so?"

"Lenore and your father left here at odds with the old gentleman, and I guess he figured I was the only family he had left. At least, that's what he indicated when I came to see him. He was on his deathbed, and he muttered something about me inheriting everything that he had meant for you, so I guess he knew what he was doing." Ashton gazed thoughtfully about the room as if seeing it for the first time. "I couldn't bear to come back here while I believed you dead. This house held too many memories."

"I don't remember being here at all, and yet . . ." Lierin shivered as a sudden chill went down her spine, and she glanced around in growing dismay. "I sense something here. . . ." She lowered her gaze beneath his questioning stare and continued in a whisper: "It's almost as if the house were crying out in mourning . . . or warning. . . ."

"Come, my love," Ashton urged gently, drawing her with him to the door. "We'll go back to the hotel now. I can't see any reason for staying here if it upsets you."

Lierin let him lead her from the house, but at the front gate she turned and stared back at the house with its sloping roof and shaded galleries that stretched across the front of the house. Beneath the wide eaves of the higher porch, the dark, lusterless windows seemed to gaze back at her in sad reflection, as if they were compelling her to stay and bring them back to life again. The bolted shutters on the lower veranda were dusty and in need of repair, and nearby the flower garden was overgrown with dried weeds. A trumpet vine had obviously feasted well on the rich soil, for it stretched its tentacles skyward above the roof. Her eyes followed its thick mass to the lower porch, then flew upward again to one of the windows on the higher level. The glass was a dark void, frustrating her efforts to see beyond it, yet she could almost swear she had caught a movement there. Curiosity knitted her brow as she searched the other windows, but they were equally blank, providing no glimpse beyond their translucent panes. Was it only her imagination? Or simply a reflection of a bird flitting past the window?

"What are you thinking?"

Lierin turned with a laugh as the masculine voice intruded into her musings, and shook her head. "Spooks! They haunt me when I look at the place." She slipped her arm through his. "My grandfather must have loved this old place dearly. I can see where once a lot of care went into keeping the house and yard."

Ashton squeezed the slender hand that rested on his arm. "He'd have given it all away just to have you near him."

She sighed rather sadly. "It seems a shame to let it go to ruin."

"We can open it up and hire a few servants to maintain it if you wish, and on future visits, we can come here and stay."

"That would be nice."

"Who knows? Perhaps one of our children would like to make a home of it someday."

Lierin slipped her arms about his lean waist and smiled up into his sparkling eyes. "We'll have to make a baby first."

"I'm at your complete disposal, madam," he offered with gallant zeal.

"Perhaps we should talk about this for a while . . . say, in bed at the hotel?"

Green lights danced in his eyes as he stared down at her. "I was about to make that very suggestion."

"Shall we get started?" she inquired with a coy smile. "You've often mentioned how much fun we had together, you've made me inquisitive about our suite at the hotel."

Ashton grinned as he handed her into the waiting barouche, and as they leaned back into the cushioned seat, the driver roused the horses and clucked them into a brisk trot. The carriage flitted through the sun-dappled shade of the lane, and Lierin blinked as the flickering light evoked disjointed memories of another such ride, when she had sat beside a tall, darkly garbed man who had patted her hand . . . consolingly? She canted her head as she tried to grasp the mood of that moment. The haunting ride seemed somehow associated with another's death, but she could not be sure, for the feelings were as illusive as the identity of her companion. The shape of him was strangely familiar, but from some inner source she perceived that the man was not Ashton. The figure was slightly bulkier . . . and was there a mustache?

The images disturbed her, and she tried to push them from her mind, wanting nothing to mar her happiness, but they were like ghosts from the past playing a teasing game with her memory. They flitted through her mind, leaving impressions of a shadowy shape here and the low murmur of a voice there, but all the while resisting her efforts to draw them into the full light of her consciousness.

She heaved a sigh in frustration, and when Ashton glanced down at her with a questioning brow raised, she smiled and laid her arm along the length of his thigh. "I wish I could remember being here with you. I fear I've forgotten too many wonderful adventures."

"Aye, madam, you have, but we'll make new ones for you to take home."

The afternoon light filtered through the bed hangings and set the draperies aglow with a shimmering whiteness. Now and then an airy rush billowed the translucent silks and caressed the naked bodies that lay entwined. The breezes blended with murmured questions and softly spoken vows of love, while kisses and whispering sighs fell on willing lips. Manly fingertips brushed bare ribs and stroked pliant peaks and creamy breasts. Others, more dainty, traced down a lightly corded neck and the rugged swell of muscles in a brown arm, then ventured on to a flat, hard belly. Pale thighs yielded to dark as love welled up with a surging rush of emotions. It was a leisured feast of sensual pleasures, a blissful interlude that took place in the confines of a silken tent. It was a coming together of man and wife, and a renewing of all that had been and would be again.

The night was black and rather coolish with low clouds pressing a misty haze down upon the city. Ashton left his sleeping wife and, donning a robe over his naked body, stepped out onto the balcony. A lantern glowed with a halo of pale yellow light, like a lone beacon in the darkness, showing the streets devoid of life at this approaching midnight hour. From the distance drifted the elusive sounds of music and accompanying revelry which attested to the fact that there were those who clung to the moment and resisted the passing of time. So it would be with him if he could accomplish that magical feat. He luxuriated in this present, enchanting period so well, he became almost fearful of it being swept away from him again.

Drawn to the warmth of the one he cherished, Ashton returned to the room and paused at the foot of the bed to gaze down upon his beloved. Lierin lay curled on her side, lost in the deep slumber of the innocent. To his knowledge, nothing yet had prompted a recall, and the fact that she had forgotten every pleasure they had once shared rasped like a dull saw at the back of his mind. As for himself, he had the whole three years etched firmly in his recollection, even though there were quite a few events he would have chosen to forget. The night of horror on the river was one he would have banished to oblivion, and then, there were the long, agonizing days when he had lain in bed unable to move, and in every waking moment his yearning for her had savaged his mind. Even when the strain had overtaken him and he had fallen into exhausted slumber, he had awakened with the same word on his parched lips: "Lierin?" And the answer always came, "No sign of her. Not even a trace. Nothing. The river has swallowed her up." Then he went through weeks of healing, and when he could walk again, he had paced the floor in restless misery. The ravaging thoughts allowed him no more than a few hours of sleep at a time, and the long nights crept past with uncaring slowness until he had cried out and begged for the dawn to come. It came . . . and was worse than the dark, for he could see the empty chair at his table, the bed where only he slept, the place at his side that no other woman could fill . . . and in the cold light of day he finally had to face the tormenting reality that his love was gone forever.

The trip to her grandfather's had been a pain he had forced himself to bear after his convalescence. He had found the old man ill and bedridden. The news that Lierin would never return to brighten his day had been too much for the judge, and though they were bitter in his mouth, Ashton had affirmed the words, "Lierin is dead," then had shared the elder's grief, and a short time later the news had come to him that the old judge had slipped away.

Seeking a haven from his anguish, he had fled to the east and then further still, to Europe. He had avoided that part of the universe where Robert Somerton nurtured his hatred; not that he was afraid of the man, but because he had a need to put all the memories of Lierin behind him . . . if he could. Travel had failed to ease the hurt, and he had buried himself in work. The family businesses fared well under his forced attention. He had bent himself to the firm establishment of the steamer trade that plied the same river which had taken his most precious possession. Then, when the aches were just beginning to ebb, Lierin had by some miracle come back to him like a wraith out of the night, and here she lay in gentle repose where he could feast his eyes upon her. Yet he was plagued by the lost years, for he could find no plausible explanation for her extended absence. Why had she not come back to him?

"Sweet plaguing love, where will you lead me now?" His whisper was barely audible in the silent room. "I've been delivered from my torment, but if you should ever be taken from me again, what will I do?" It was impossible to think of existing without her. If such an event were to occur, it would be easy to surmise that he would plow the universe in search of her, never resting until death gave him ease. "Have mercy on me, Lierin, and stay forever by my side. Do not vanish from me again, for surely I would be no more a man."

How long he stood at the foot of the bed, he could not say. Finally he doffed his robe and, leaning down, braced his arms on either side of her, realizing that her eyes had opened and she lay watching him. She pushed the sheet away from her, then her arms reached up to encircle him. As his naked body lowered upon her own, her lips moved hot and eager beneath his kiss. Once again the ecstasy began, just as it had that night when he had found his love.

A tiny rosewood box was borne inconspicuously on the serving tray as Ashton brought his wife breakfast in bed. A small vase of yellow flowers obscured it until Lierin lifted the bouquet to test the fragrance of the blossoms. Discovering the ornately carved cubicle, she searched the hazel eyes for some clue to the mysterious box, but they gleamed back at her above mute, smiling lips. Quite carefully, as if she held a great treasure in her hands, she lifted the lid and stared in amazement at what the box contained. Nestled within a bed of velvet was an emerald and diamond ring of unique and extraordinary beauty.

"Oh, Ashton . . ." Tears gathered to blur her vision as she looked at him. "It's so very lovely."

"I was rather rushed when I bought the first wedding ring. I hope this will make amends."

"There was no need for amends. My joy is being your wife."

Ashton lifted her hand and slid the jeweled circlet upon her finger while his eyes caressed the soft visage. "With this ring I thee wed. . . ." His face descended, and Lierin's lips parted in anticipation of his kiss. "And what God has joined together," he breathed, "let not man put asunder . . . ever again."

Though the rich foods, luxurious accommodations, and festive sights provoked no memory of bygone events, Lierin bloomed beneath the care and loving attention of her husband. The azalea and camellia shrubs could not equal her radiance, and as was its wont when moments are pleasurable, time flew past on quicksilver wings. Soon the month was behind them, and the *River Witch* took them upriver once again. There they settled with effortless ease into the daily routine of master and mistress of Belle Chêne.

A grand fête was planned to introduce Lierin to family friends and to the community at large. It was to be a festive occasion with food and refreshments aplenty. A pavilion was erected on the lush grounds, and there the musicians would play their lively tunes and romantic waltzes for the dancers. Invitations were spread by word of mouth and by notices on every posting board in the county. Soon the countryside was aflutter with preparations. Seamstresses worked day and night as the ladies prepared their finest or ordered new, depending on their status.

The frenzy increased as the appointed date drew nigh, and the hive of activity was centered around Belle Chêne. A wide variety of confections were made, and crocks of fermented wines and kegs of cider were brought out of storage. Sides of beef and pork were turned on spits above trenches where aromatic woods burned with a low, steady heat. As the time waned to a matter of hours, whole spits of fowl, goose, and turkey were added to the fires, and fruits were carried to the tables.

The first carriages began to arrive, and soon the sprawling lawns were filled with running children and strolling couples. Lierin braved the throng on her husband's arm and approached the first few introductions hesitantly. She took heart from the jovial well-wishers and their open acceptance, and, with a growing sense of belonging, greeted them with gentle warmth. The couple pushed through a rapidly growing crowd to greet others until at last they could only stand and let newcomers advance as best they might. In a moment of respite Ashton wondered if he could think of any particular acquaintance who was not in the crowd that surrounded them. He felt a minor sense of irritation when he recognized a few he had hoped would not attend. Still, he was hardly surprised to see Marelda. She came on the arm of M. Horace Titch, who approached the reception line with considerably less zeal than she portrayed. Indeed, he seemed downright fearful. He twitched nervously as Ashton made the presentations and then stumbled away in clumsy haste. Marelda jerked the squat man's arm, disappointed that she had not been permitted enough time to taunt the couple with subtle gibes, and began to berate him soundly on his lack of manners.

"I really don't understand you, Horace. You act as if we don't have any right to be here, and everyone knows that Ashton invited the whole countryside to this affair. Why are you such a coward?"

M. Horace Titch flinched beneath her ridicule and glanced about sheepishly to see if there were any witnesses to this verbal abuse. Sometimes the pain of being with Marelda was almost too much to bear, yet adoring her as he did, he could never deny her smallest request even when she carelessly stripped him of his pride.

Throughout the introductions and the feast Lierin became aware of the unswerving regard of a man who had made no effort to come forward and present himself. She felt a vague sense of recognition and finally realized he was the same man she had shocked by kissing Ashton outside the inn. She made an effort to dismiss his bold interest as something his fantasies had fermented, yet it was hard to ignore his unrelenting stares.

The rich hues of the sunset had spread over the sky when servants began setting out lamps and lighting lanterns. As if by some unspoken command the guests grew quiet, and all eyes were drawn to the portico of the mansion. There, they found the couple they had come to honor. The two had changed to evening attire, and for once, the elder ladies of Belle Chêne were struck to dumbness and could only admire their charges in silent awe. Willabelle loudly sniffed and wiped at her eyes with a knuckle, while Luella May stood off to one side, her palms pressed together with the fingertips touching her lips, as if she prayed that nothing would destroy the poignancy of the moment. Ashton's proudly smiling eyes caressed Lierin's face for a brief moment, then he moved forward, leading his lady slowly down the steps and giving all an ample opportunity to admire her grace and beauty. The guests gave way before them as he escorted her across the lawn and up the steps of the large pavilion. At his nod the musicians began a waltz, and with an arm about her seemingly fragile waist, he swept her in the opening steps of the dance. Bathed in the rosy colors of the sunset and the security of their love, they swirled about while the guests gathered around the perimeter to watch and murmur in admiration. When the last notes of the music finally ebbed, the onlookers erupted in an enthusiastic applause. Ashton held his wife's hand at arm's length while she dipped into a deep and gracious curtsey. His voice rang out with pride as he began the announcement.

"Ladies, gentlemen, and friends. I would like to present my wife, Lierin. . . ."

"Sir . . ." a man's voice intruded. "I think there's been a dreadful mistake."

The tall, sandy-haired stranger elbowed his way through the midst of the guests and came to stand near the steps of the pavilion where he drew the confused stares of the Wingate couple. Ashton frowned down at the man, troubled by his statement. The stranger cast a glance over his shoulder at the puzzled faces that surrounded him, and then once again addressed his host.

"I fear, sir, you are under the wrong assumption. This woman whom you have introduced as your wife is not Lierin. . . ."

Startled gasps came from all who listened, and Lierin clutched at Ashton's arm, feeling suddenly weak.

"She is Lenore Sinclair, the twin sister of your late wife. . . ."

"*No!* That is impossible!" The denial exploded from Ashton. "She is Lierin!"

"I'm sorry, sir," the stranger apologized crisply. "The mistake is yours."

"How can you possibly know?" Ashton demanded. "Who are you?"

"I am Malcolm Sinclair," the man stated boldly. "The lady's husband."

Lierin's breath left her in a rush, as if someone had struck her a fierce blow, and she sagged in a dizzy faint. Trails of light swirled about her as the pavilion reeled in a drunken orbit. She hardly knew the moment Ashton lifted her in his arms, but distantly she was aware of a flurry of confused conjectures sweeping through the guests. Somewhere in the crowd feminine laughter peeled with the sound of triumphant victory, and she assumed it was Marelda, gloating. Ashton carried her to a chair and she sagged weakly against its tall back. Dr. Franklin Page had separated himself from the crowd and came to lend his assistance, producing a vial of smelling salts. As Lierin turned her face away from the caustic fumes, she found herself staring into the brown eyes of Malcolm Sinclair as he stood a step or two beyond Ashton.

"Are you all right?" Ashton whispered in anxious concern as he pressed a dampened cloth to her brow.

"Is it true?" Her question was barely audible. "Am I really his wife? Or am I yours?"

Ashton squeezed her hand reassuringly, then straightened to face the man. His jaw was set, and so was his mind. "I know this is Lierin," he stubbornly declared. "I married her three years ago in New Orleans. . . ."

"It cannot be." Malcolm Sinclair was equally adamant. "Your wife drowned in a riverboat accident those same number of years ago, sir. I tell you now this is Lenore, the woman I married. She was taken from our home by force, and after a careful search I found the trail led here to Natchez. I couldn't find her, and I thought she was lost to me forever until I happened upon you two outside the inn. The shock of seeing my wife kissing another man overwhelmed me, and I was too stunned to tell you then." Turning to Lierin, he spread his hat and hand in pleading supplication. "Lenore, my love. Set this thing to rest. Tell them you're my wife."

"I . . . I cannot. . . ." Lierin stammered, her mind a maelstrom of confusion. "I know . . . I mean . . . I think . . . I really think . . . I am Lierin."

"Your sister is dead," he insisted. "Don't you remember?"

"No," she whispered miserably. "I can't remember anything."

"What has he done to you?" Malcolm cried. He whirled on Ashton in an angry heat. "I don't know how you managed this. . . ."

"Ashton had nothing to do with her loss of memory," Dr. Page interjected almost calmly and squinted up at the young man. "But what she says is true. She can't remember you or anything else . . . and she may never recall her life before the accident."

"Accident?" Malcolm seemed bemused. "What accident?"

Ashton offered the information reluctantly: "She was struck by my carriage."

"I didn't know," Malcolm murmured and faced Lierin again, his eyes dark and troubled. "As I stand here, I swear to you that you are Lenore Sinclair. My wife."

Lierin twisted her hands in her lap and turned away from his pleading gaze as tears began to stream down her face. She fought against her mounting fears and the building pressure that threatened to send her sobbing across the lawns.

"Have you something to substantiate your claim?" Ashton challenged. "You obviously know something about the Somerton family, but what proof do you bear? I say she is Lierin, and you vow she is Lenore. Am I simply to take your word that she is Lenore?" He laughed caustically. "You will pardon me, sir, if I will demand more evidence than just your word."

"I have nothing with me. . . ."

Ashton smiled sardonically. "There could be a very good reason for that."

"I do have proof!" Malcolm Sinclair insisted. "If you will allow me to return, I shall present enough evidence to convince you."

"I would be interested in seeing what you have," Ashton stated. "Return at your convenience, but remember that it will take a great deal to sway me from my belief that she is my wife."

Malcolm clapped his hat upon his head and, turning on a heel, strode through the guests as they opened a path for him. In the painful silence that followed his passing, Ashton stood with a hand upon his wife's trembling shoulder, hardly aware of the guests moving away from the pavilion. Aunt Jennifer and Amanda came to give comfort, but words of reassurance seemed empty and without substance. The laughter was gone from the evening's revelries, and only the smirking smile of Marelda Rousse greeted the couple as they made their way toward the house.

"I told you, didn't I?" she taunted. She flung up her head and chuckled as she saw the turmoil twisting behind Ashton's face. "What's the matter, dahling? Have you lost your tongue? Don't you have something to say?"

Seeing the tensing muscles in Ashton's lean jaw, Horace Titch squirmed uneasily and tugged at Marelda's sleeve. "We'd better leave now."

The brunette tossed him an impatient glare. "Really, Horace, don't you have any backbone at all?"

The short man shriveled in shame, unable to ignore this latest cut while Ashton Wingate was within hearing range. He stepped awkwardly away and patted his plaid coat, as if unable to decide what to do with his hands. Marelda sighed heavily and relented, taking his arm as she left with him. She had to consider that there was still much to be gained by keeping the man on a string.

Lierin returned to the master bedroom, and Ashton closed the door quietly behind them. She moved about the room as if in a daze and undressed as a matter of rote. His heart heavy with dread, Ashton sat in a chair and watched her, knowing she was confused, but unable to say more than what had already been said.

She came from the bathing room, her face freshly washed and her hair tumbling loose about her shoulders. The satin peignoir she had donned hugged the softly curving figure and dipped low between her breasts to reveal the enticing cleavage. Though she seemed oblivious to her dishabille, he was not. Its effect was perhaps even more devastating now that Malcolm Sinclair had cast a shadow of doubt between them.

"Do you think I played you false?" he murmured as she paused at the window to stare out in thoughtful reflection.

Lierin turned slowly, shaking her head. "Malcolm Sinclair hasn't proved anything yet."

She came to him, her eyes touching to the depth of his soul. His thighs parted to receive her as his arms slipped about her hips, bringing her close against him. He pressed a kiss upon the inner curve of her breast and then leaned his head back to savor the sweetness of her lips. The silken sash that bound her waist came free beneath his plucking fingers, and the robe fell open, allowing his mouth to roam the hills and vales of her scented flesh. She trembled as he awakened her senses, and for them life began again, thudding through their veins with renewed vigor and leading them on to greater heights than they had ever known before.

It was two days hence that Willis came to the parlor. The butler's disquiet was obvious to the family members who waited tensely for him to make his announcement.

"Massa Ashton . . ." His dark, sorrowful eyes moved about the room, meeting the apprehensive stares that rested upon him. "Dere's two men at de door wantin' to have a word wid yo an' de missus. One is dat Mistah Sinclair who comed here befo', and de other says he's Miz Lierin's pa . . . 'ceptin' he says she's Miz Lenore."

A feeling of despair knotted within Lierin's stomach and left her cold and shaking.

"Show them in, Willis," Ashton bade, all humor gone from his face. "What they have to report can be said in front of the whole family."

"Yassuh, Massa Ashton," the black man replied solemnly and, with drooping shoulders, left the room.

Aunt Jennifer plied the needle to her tapestry, paying no heed to where she stitched, while Amanda carefully observed her grandson as he went to stand beside Lierin's chair. The girl seemed frozen as she stared with fixed attention at the door. When Ashton's hand came to rest upon her shoulder, the stiffness went out of her spine. She rubbed her cheek against his knuckles and gazed up at him with soft, liquid eyes. In the waiting stillness, the approaching footsteps sounded more like the roll of drums that heralded an execution. Immediately the starch returned to Lierin's spine, and she raised her chin to meet the visitors with a serene air.

Malcolm Sinclair entered the parlor first, carrying a small bundle of papers in his left hand and in his right a rather large, cloth-covered painting. A step or two behind him came a white-haired, dapperly dressed gentleman. The elder man gazed curiously about the room until he saw Lierin, then he hurried forward to take her hand in both of his. Searching her eyes, he struggled for composure as his mouth trembled and his features threatened to crumple; then with a single sniff he regained control and gave her a brave smile.

"I've been beside myself with worry, wondering what had become of you and not knowing whether you were alive or dead. All Malcolm knew was that you had been kidnapped, but we had no hope of ever finding you again."

Lierin removed her fingers from the well-manicured hands and stared into the troubled gray eyes. She wondered if he had been weeping, for they were red and watery, and his nose bore the same hue. The thick mass of waving hair and the mustache that curled upward at the corners of his mouth were starkly white against the aging bronzed skin. He was nearly half a head shorter than the man who now stood behind him, and his slender frame was well turned out in a brown cutaway tailcoat, buff vest and trousers.

"I'm sorry, sir," she murmured. "I'm afraid I don't recognize you."

The white-haired man turned to stare in amazement at Malcolm, who stepped to his side and laid an arm comfortingly about his shoulders. "Lenore," the younger man said softly, as if afraid of upsetting her, "this is your father, Robert Somerton."

Lierin glanced around, seeking some denial from Ashton. "Is he?"

Ashton felt the stares of the other men and could only shake his head. "I'm sorry, my love. I cannot answer that. I never met your father."

"Perhaps this will help convince you of my claims," Malcolm said, thrusting the bundle of papers toward Ashton. "These are the marriage documents confirming the fact that Lenore Somerton and I spoke the vows together more than two years ago."

Ashton took the papers and, briefly scanning them, found that they did indeed attest to such an event. He handed them back with a brusque comment: "I have a similar certificate verifying my marriage to Lierin Somerton. However, neither of these records proves who she is."

Malcolm's eyes blazed with ill-suppressed ire as he indicated the white-haired man. "But this is her father!"

"Perhaps," Ashton replied with a noncommittal shrug, "but I can't guarantee your statement as fact because I never met the man."

"Good heavens! What will it take to convince you?" Malcolm's ire rose in the face of the other man's unyielding resistance. "Why in the bloody devil would I come here claiming she is my wife when she's not? It doesn't make any sense."

"I can't think of a reason," Ashton answered, "but I can't ignore what I feel, and I sincerely believe this is Lierin."

"Show him the portrait, Malcolm," the elder man bade. "Perhaps he will see his error."

The younger man placed the framed painting on a nearby table and held it upright with one hand, leaving it covered for a moment as he spoke to Ashton. "Were you not sent a portrait of your wife?"

Ashton responded with a slow nod. "Yes."

"And did you have any question that it was a painting of Lierin?"

"No." Ashton's spine prickled as the other smiled smugly.

"Then I ask you to view this painting very carefully and give me your comments." He lifted the cloth covering, bringing gasps of surprise from the members of the Wingate family. The portrait was similar to the one that had been shown to Lierin, but there were subtle differences in the facial features of the woman, for they were more delicate and refined. Though the other painting had closely resembled the one who sat in the parlor now, there was no question that she had been the subject of this portrait.

"The other painting, which you have, is of Lierin . . . your wife, but this one is of Lenore, *my* wife." Malcolm almost smirked as he watched the play of confusion on the other's face. "Now tell me that you have not made a mistake, sir."

Amanda and Aunt Jennifer were equally distressed and wondered at Ashton's frowning silence.

"Perhaps now you will allow me to take my wife home where she belongs. . . ."

"Please!" Lierin gasped, turning to Ashton for solace. "Please, I don't remember them. . . ."

Ashton gave her shoulder a comforting squeeze. "Don't fret, my love. I'm not about to let them take you."

"What are you saying?" Malcolm barked angrily. "You have no right to keep my wife here!"

"This matter will have to be settled in a court of law," Ashton stated. "I will not give up my claim to her without a thorough investigation into this matter. When Lierin fell from my steamer three years ago, no further trace was found of her. . . ."

Malcolm snorted derisively. "It's not the first time the Mississippi has failed to yield its dead."

"I know that, but I must be thoroughly satisfied that every effort is made to clear up the question of Lierin's identity."

"Lenore!" Robert Somerton corrected.

"I will send agents to the family home in England and then to Biloxi and New Orleans to see what can be found."

"But that kind of investigation can take months!" Malcolm protested.

"I don't care how long it takes!" Ashton returned sharply. "My only concern is for Lierin and the outcome of the investigation. If I am proved wrong, I can do naught but comply with what is truth. I will bend to nothing less."

"And do you think you're going to hold my wife here all that time?" Malcolm raged.

Ashton smiled blandly. "She obviously wants to stay."

"I will not allow it!" The brown eyes snapped with fire as Malcolm glared at Ashton.

"Then it will have to be settled by a judge's ruling."

"I've heard about you in Natchez," Malcolm sneered. "They say you're a bullheaded and obstinate man, but let me tell you that before this is finished, you will have heard of me, and you will know that I am more than a match for you. Indeed, a duel may settle this. . . ."

Startled gasps came from the women, and they sought a denial from Ashton. He gave none.

"I await your pleasure, sir," he responded calmly. "Shall it be today?"

Malcolm's eyes narrowed. "I'll let you know when the time is convenient for me."

"Please do," Ashton urged. "Perhaps such a contest will abolish the necessity of an investigation and save me a great deal of trouble."

Malcolm sneered derisively. "For one who has already been shown that he's wrong, you seem much too sure of yourself."

"Maybe I have reason to be."

Malcolm's eyes were as cold as the frigid north. "Conceit never won a duel."

Ashton shrugged casually. "I'm willing to be tested."

"Think of Lenore," Robert Somerton cautioned, laying a hand on Malcolm's arm. "I'm sure this discussion about duels is upsetting to her."

"You're right, of course," the sandy-haired man agreed, seeming to dismiss the matter with ease. He stepped to the table and began rewrapping the portrait, but halted when Ashton came to his side.

"That painting was in Judge Cassidy's house not too long ago. How did you know it was there?"

"Does it make any difference?" Malcolm questioned caustically.

"Everything in that house belongs to Lierin or to me. You broke into it to take that painting."

"If you're trying to accuse me of thievery, this is the only thing I took. I knew it was there because Lenore had told me her father had given the two portraits to the judge. When I saw the other was missing, I assumed you had taken it." With that, he lifted the object of their discussion and crossed the room, pausing in front of Lierin's chair. "I don't fully understand your memory loss, Lenore, but remember this, my dearest, I shall always love you."

Turning, he strode from the room with Robert Somerton following in his wake. The sound of their booted heels striking the marble floor as they progressed across the hall echoed in the silence of the manse, and the unhesitating stride of Malcolm's footfalls seemed to declare that he would meet whatever challenge was presented him.

- *Chapter Eight* -

The sun lowered toward the western horizon where it was obscured by a gathering mass of dark clouds. As night draped the land with its blanketing cloak of blackness, lightning began to flicker in the distance and was followed by a low rumble of thunder. The storm advanced in slow degrees, grumbling and stamping its way across the leaden landscape and finally reaching its peak in the early hours of the morning. It seemed bent on thwarting Ashton's attempt at sleep, but he could hardly blame his lack of slumber on the thundering crashes. He hated the small bed in the guest room where he had grudgingly agreed to stay until a judge could decide the matter of Lierin's identity. Neither he nor Lierin had wanted the separation, but for the sake of appearances and to ease the minds of the elder ladies, they had thought it best to sleep apart. It had been a week of unparalleled torture for Ashton, for he had been haunted by the fear that he was about to lose Lierin all over again. He found no rest in his lonely bed. He missed her warmth and her softly curving form snuggled close against him; he missed reaching out and touching her in the middle of the night; he missed holding her in love.

The fury of the storm was mirrored in his mood as he tossed and turned in a tempest of his own. A blinding flash of lightning bleached the darkness from the night, setting the rain-drenched windows aglow. A sharp crack of thunder trod on its heels, bringing Ashton upright with a curse. His temper had reached its zenith, and he threw himself from the bed. With long, irate strides he crossed the floor to the bathing room and, quickly traversing the cubicle's narrow width, entered the master bedroom. The play of streaking lights beyond the crystal panes lighted the chamber and showed him the slender, white-garbed figure sitting in the middle of the huge four-poster. Her arms were wrapped about her folded limbs, and her knees were tucked beneath her chin. Her gaze was unswerving as she watched him come forward, and when another bolt of blinding brightness seared a path across the ebony sky, her eyes flicked downward to his naked loins. She showed no alarm at the passion he displayed, but calmly waited until his knee came upon the bed and the mattress dipped beneath his weight. His hands slipped to the hem of her gown, and she lifted her arms as he drew the garment over her head. With a soft sigh she sank back beneath his encroaching weight, and their lips began a leisured search as they savored the bliss of their love. He cupped her face between his hands, staring down into her eyes through the darkness, and realized her hair was slightly damp.

"Where have you been?" he asked in wonder.

"I couldn't sleep," she whispered, "and I stepped out on the balcony."

"In the rain?"

She nodded. "I was so lonely I hardly noticed."

He pressed a kiss to her cheek. "You should have come to me."

"I wasn't sure you wanted me."

"Good heavens, madam!" he responded, feeling rather astounded by her statement. "Have I been so lax in telling you how much I love you . . . and want you? How can I convince you of what my heart feels . . . ?"

"Just show me," she breathed.

His head lowered to her breast, and her mouth came open in a soundless cry as his tongue caressed a soft peak. His hands moved with unhesitating boldness over her body, while her own explored the familiar sinews that rippled beneath his warm flesh. He lifted her hips to his, and they merged as lovers who were bound to each other for all eternity. His hard-thrusting passion drove her beyond the flickering lights of the present world, took her to a haven where a myriad of images danced through her mind. Other flights of sensual pleasure flashed in twinkling rapidity through her consciousness, teasing her with brief glimpses of a naked man whose face and form eluded the grasping efforts of her concentration. Strive though she might, she could not bring the darkened visage into focus, but the man was as bold and lustful as the one who was with her now.

She came slowly to herself again, and the illusions disappeared in a vapor as she felt the thudding beat of Ashton's heart against her breast.

"I was hoping you would come," she sighed. "I've been so miserable this week, having this huge bed all to myself."

Ashton braced on an elbow and gazed down into the glistening sheen of her eyes. "I couldn't stay away another moment."

"What are we going to do now?" she asked quietly. "How can I ever stop thinking I'm your wife and accept the idea that I belong to Malcolm?"

"I'll have difficulty with that myself," he sighed and brushed his lips against her ear. "I'm not willing to let you go."

"But you must . . . if I am Malcolm's wife."

"I can't believe that you are," he groaned and rolled onto his back. He rubbed a hand over his brow. "It's too painful even to think of letting you go. I nearly ceased to function as a man when I thought you were dead, and now that I have you again, how can I possibly allow another man to take you?"

Lierin rose above him and lightly traced a finger over the scar on the side of his chest. "I feel safe here with you, as if it's where I belong."

His long fingers slipped beneath the weight of her hair and gently kneaded her nape. "We can go to Europe. . . ."

She shook her head, and a long tress tumbled over his arm to fall in a thick curl upon his furred chest. "You're not a man who runs from the truth, Ashton."

His hand moved downward until it lay soft upon her breast. He could feel the warmth and smoothness of her flesh beneath his palm and was aware of the reawakening fires in his own body. He thought no more of losing her when loving her took hold of his mind. Her mouth came down to meet his, but the kiss was but a heartbeat away as a distant pounding intruded into the silence of the room.

Ashton glanced toward the mantel clock, but its blackened face gave no hint of the hour. "Who the devil . . . ? It must be two or three in the morning."

The summons came again, this time louder and more insistent. A voice called, and the words were faint but clear: "Massa, wake up! Yo warehouses are burnin' in Natchez!"

"Damn!" The expletive exploded from Ashton as he leaped from the bed. He ran naked across the room, tore through the bathing room, and, hastily thrusting himself into a robe, flung open the far door. Willis stood before the portal with a nightcap sitting askew on his head and the neck of a nightshirt showing above a long, hastily donned robe. His eyes stared in wide-eyed alarm above the flickering flame of the candle he bore.

"Massa Ashton," the butler addressed him in anxious tones. "Dere's a man at de front door, sayin' one o' yo warehouses down by de waterfront done caught fire in de storm, an' he say dat most likely by de time yo gets dere, de others be goin' up in smoke, too."

"Send someone to fetch Judd and tell him to gather some men to fight the fire! I'll be down as soon as I can throw some clothes on."

The black hesitated. "Massa, if'n it's all right, Ah'd like to go wid yo. Ah is pretty good at totin' buckets."

"Be quick about it then. We don't have much time to spare."

"Yassuh!" Willis jumped to action before the door slammed shut.

Lierin entered the bedroom, tying the belt of her dressing gown about her narrow waist. "What's happened?"

"I've got to go into Natchez," Ashton replied, jerking out of his robe. "My warehouses are on fire!"

She hastened to lay out his clothes as he tugged on a pair of trousers. "It's raining pretty hard. Can we dare hope that it might stop the fire from spreading to the other warehouses?"

"How I hope!"

As he shoved the tail of his shirt into the waistband of his pants, she stood beside him holding his coat. "Whatever happens, be careful," she pleaded.

He brought her close against him for a moment and crushed her lips beneath a quick, hard kiss, then spoke in a husky voice: "You can forget about separate bedrooms from now on. I'm not giving you up. Malcolm Sinclair will have to kill me before I'll allow him to take you from me."

A blade of fear stabbed through her heart. "Oh, Ashton, don't say that!"

"It's what I mean!"

Tearing himself away, he ran from the room and down the hall. Near the stable Judd was already gathering the men into a wagon, and a tarpaulin was being spread to protect them from the elements.

Pulling down the brim of his hat and tugging up the collar of his oil-skin coat, Ashton squinted toward the eastern horizon where the sky was still black. There was no hint of dawn behind the mass of dark clouds that roiled across its face. He climbed up beside Judd on the driver's seat, and beneath the crack of a whip, the team plunged forward, setting themselves to a muddy, reckless race into Natchez.

All the while Ashton dared to hope, and at the end of the trail, he found cause to be grateful for the rain that had thoroughly soaked them on the road, for the downpour had also confined the fire to the middle shed, leaving the adjacent buildings unscathed. He stood with Judd and the warehouse boss under the tin roof of an open-sided shelter and surveyed the thickly smoldering ruins.

"Did we lose much?" Ashton asked.

"Enough, suh," the manager answered above the steady drum of raindrops pelting the metal roof. "But it could've been a lot worse. So happens, a boat picked up a whole load of cotton just yesterday, so there were only thirty or so bales on hand, maybe a dozen bales of flax, a few barrels o' molasses, and some odds and ends. That's about it. If it weren't for the fact that lightning probably started it, you can consider yourself a lucky man, 'cause without the rain everythin' would've gone up in flames."

"Pardon me . . ." a gravelly voice intruded from behind them. "Any o' you fellers Mistah Wingate?"

They turned to find a short, straggly-haired beggar standing close. His clothes were wet and ragged, and he wore badly worn boots that turned up at the toes.

"I'm Mr. Wingate," Ashton replied.

Sniffing, the vagrant rubbed a dirty sleeve across his nose and gestured toward the gutted warehouse. "If ye've got an extra coin in yer pocket, I can tell ye somethin' 'bout how that there shed caught on fire."

Ashton patted his pockets and found them empty. His manager had a similar lack of luck in his search and shrugged as he apologized. "Guess I got dressed in a hurry."

"I'll have to owe you," Ashton pledged.

"Seein' as how it's yerself doin' the promisin', Mistah Wingate, I'll take yer word for it. I guess I owe ye that much."

"What do you mean?"

The beggar shrugged and chortled. "For some time now, I've

been beddin' down in that there shed o' yers. I always slipped in through a broken window in the back, an' I'd find a cotton bale that weren't too hard. It's always been nice an' dry in there, kinda cozy on a night like this. . . ."

"You said you could tell us how the fire started," Ashton urged.

"Yes, suh. I'm gettin' to that. Ye see, I was tryin' to catch a few winks when I thought I heard some voices right outside that there broken window. Well, it sorta startled me, an' I sidled on up to the window to listen for a spell. Then it come to me. They were plannin' on firin' up the place. Well, the idea o' bein' caught inside scared me plum peaked. I nearly swallowed my tongue thinkin' 'bout it, but how could I leave while they were there to catch me?"

"How many men were there?" Ashton probed.

"Three or four maybe. I think I've seen at least one of 'em down at the Razorback Saloon a time or two, but I can't be sure it was him. It was real dark outside until the lightnin' began to move in, an' that's when I saw the biggest feller had two fingers missin' from his left hand. Well, it reminded me o' that mean ol' bruiser I seen once down at the saloon."

"You said there were others?" Ashton pressed.

"Yeah." The man scratched his bristly chin. "One was a short, squat feller . . . dressed kinda fancy . . . and seemed to have a nervous twitch or somethin'. . . ."

Ashton glanced at Judd. "Sounds strangely like Horace Titch."

The black frowned thoughtfully. "Do yo reckon he got 'nuff gumption to be a party to dis?"

"With Marelda urging him," Ashton replied derisively, "anything is possible."

"Yo reckon dis was done fo' revenge?"

"I don't know why it was done, but I'm going to find out." Ashton raised a questioning brow to the black man. "Are you with me?"

Judd grinned broadly. "Ain't Ah always been?"

Willabelle crossed the room almost hesitantly and stood nervously smoothing her apron until her mistress glanced up. Lierin had never seen the woman so unsure of herself, and a prickling of apprehension warned her that she had not come on some simple errand.

"What is it, Willabelle?"

"Missus . . ." The housekeeper's dark eyes conveyed her concern as she struggled to make the announcement: "Dat man what say he yo pa is downstairs askin' to see yo."

A coldness congealed around Lierin's heart. The dull gray light of the storm-plagued morning had failed to cast its shadow over her memories of the bygone hours with Ashton, but now a sudden depression descended to strip away those feelings of contentment.

Almost hopefully Willabelle asked, "Can Ah tell him to come back later after de massa returns?"

Lierin rose from the small writing desk. Her limbs were trembling, and a lump had formed in her throat, but she managed a calm facade. "No, Willabelle, I'll hear what he has to say. It's the least I can do."

The housekeeper rolled her eyes skyward. "Ah knowed dis was gonna be a bad day when Ah opened mah eyes dis mornin'," she mumbled. "First de warehouses burnin', an' now dat man acomin' when de massa ain't home."

"There's no need to upset yourself, Willabelle," Lierin comforted her. "Just tell him I'll be down in a moment."

"Yas'm," the black woman replied glumly and waddled from the room. When she entered the parlor, she found the man had already helped himself to a glass of brandy and had lighted one of the master's cigars. His audacity grated on the servant's good humor, and she glared at him before he faced her. She conveyed the message stiltedly: "De massa, he ain't home, but de missus say say be right down."

"When do you expect Mr. Wingate to be returning?"

"Ah don' know," the woman muttered, "but de sooner de better."

Robert Somerton arched a querying brow at the black. "Have you something against my seeing my daughter?"

"Miz Lierin, she done been mighty upset by all dis commotion 'bout her bein' another man's wife. . . ."

"Her name is Lenore." He flicked the ash from his cigar, casually aiming for the porcelain dish on the table and missing it by a wide margin. "Remember it if you can."

A dark fire had started smoldering in Willabelle's eyes even before she witnessed the carelessly tossed ash, but now flares of anger were beginning to ignite in their black depths. She went to the table where the tiny cinders had fallen and swept them off into her hand as she stated, "De massa, he say she Miz Lierin, an' dat suits me jes' fine."

Robert laughed with rancor. "Then I'd say you are as blind and foolish as your master. He demanded proof, and we gave it to him, but he has ignored good common sense. Mark my word, he will not continue to use my daughter's illness for his own ends. I'll see to that! He took her sister and abused her, but now he will be stopped!"

"Ah gotta tend some chores," Willabelle announced bluntly.

Robert swept his hand in a gesture of dismissal. He didn't know why he had stooped to argue with a servant anyway, especially one so obstinate. "Then you'd better be about them before your master comes home and beats you."

Willabelle puffed up like an enraged toad. "My massa, he ain't never laid a hand on any of us!" she squawked in outrage. Lifting her nose imperiously, she stalked from the room, rattling the crystal insets in the china cabinet with her heavy strides as she crossed the dining hall. Her ire was sorely strained, and in that moment she could understand quite vividly why the master had remained reticent about his father-in-law. There was nothing good to be said about the man.

A few moments later Lierin entered the parlor, her manner subdued and almost fearful. She tolerated the man's kiss of greeting upon her cheek and allowed him to lead her to the settee, then listened in the manner of a dutiful daughter as he related stories of their past life in England. He showed her a painted miniature of twin girls, and she had to concede she bore a striking resemblance to both of them, but it was not until he brought out a sketch of a Tudor-style manor home drawn on a hill beyond a body of water that she began to sense a familiarity with the things he showed her.

"You drew this yourself," he said, gesturing with his replenished drink to the etching. " 'Tis our home in England."

Lierin carefully studied the drawing and, in that moment, could almost imagine herself skipping through the mansion's long galleries. She could envision walls lined with portraits, lances, and shields, and long tables placed between tall, majestic chairs.

"I think I've been there before," she acknowledged. "The place seems familiar to me."

"Aha!" Robert cried in jubilant victory. "Now we're getting somewhere! Perhaps you'll even concede that I might be your father. . . ."

Her shoulders lifted in a small noncommittal shrug. She was

reluctant to go that far, for doing so would give him and Malcolm Sinclair the advantage over Ashton, and she knew with whom her loyalty abided. "Whether I am Lenore or Lierin, you could still be my father, but how can I really claim you are when I don't even remember you?"

Robert was thoughtful for a space of time, and when he began to speak, he chose his words carefully. "I honestly think you need time and a quiet place to consider this without any interference from either Malcolm or Ashton. Why don't you let me take you to Biloxi? We have a place there on the beach. You have your own clothes there and everything else you need."

She frowned, distressed at the thought of leaving Belle Chêne . . . and Ashton. "I'm happy here. . . ."

"But you won't be if you start remembering what Ashton Wingate did to your sister. She's dead because of him, and you vowed one day to have your revenge on him. In fact, I don't understand how you can hate this man so much and still think of him as your husband."

"I don't hate him," she protested. "I . . ."

He peered at her closely, waiting for her to continue, but his curiosity was left wanting. "You know of course that Malcolm is planning on calling him out in a duel."

Her heart stopped in sudden fear, and she stared at him with eyes wide and searching.

"Malcolm is very good at firearms," Robert stated. "It's doubtful that Ashton will escape."

"You've got to stop them," she urged.

"How am I going to stop them?" he inquired in amazement. "You're the only one who can do that."

She moaned and wrung her hands, feeling the trap closing in on her. "If I stay with Ashton, Malcolm will insist upon a duel. If I go with Malcolm, Ashton will come after us and demand the same thing. I know him. He's already said he won't give me up. And I don't want anyone killed."

"That's why I say your only safe option is to do what I suggested . . . go with me back to Biloxi. It's not likely they'll call *me* out in a duel."

Wearily Lierin slumped on the settee, hardly relishing his proposal, yet accepting the merits of it as reasonable. It offered her what was perhaps the only possible escape from her predicament. "I'll have to think about it."

"You don't have much time, my dear," he advised. "Malcolm is making arrangements to come out here and challenge Ashton very soon. If you delay, it could mean death for him." He shrugged. "Of course, I wouldn't mourn his passing, considering he took Lierin from us."

"Can a father mistake his own daughter?" she asked in a tiny voice, and lifted her gaze to his bemused countenance. "Are you sure that I am Lenore?"

He flung up his hand in an impatient gesture. "What's a father to do when his own daughter won't believe him? How can I make you understand? The mistake is not mine but Ashton's! Or rather some ploy of his. It's got to be a trick he's playing on us all. He knows Lierin drowned."

Slowly Lierin pushed herself to her feet and passed a shaking hand across her brow. "Aunt Jennifer and Amanda are resting upstairs. It's probably better if I leave now without them being aware of it. If you'll wait in your carriage, I'll just go upstairs for a moment and write a note to Ashton."

"You won't tell him where we're going. . . ."

"No," she sighed. "That would only be an open invitation for him to come after us. I'll just ask him not to interfere." She left the room and climbed the stairs, feeling as if her whole world had come to an end. With tears blurring her vision, she composed a brief letter, signed it "Lenore," and brushed a kiss upon the wedding band and placed it on top of the missive. Taking only the clothes on her back, she retraced her steps to the lower level and slipped out the front door, glad that she had not had to confront Willis or Willabelle before her departure. Tears trailed down her cheeks as she gazed back at the house, and she wondered if she would ever return.

Ashton pushed open the tall, swinging doors of the Razorback Saloon and took two steps into the smoke-filled, crowded room before letting the panels rattle shut behind him. He had taken a leisured meal at the inn, and then had gone to the *River Witch* to wash and garb himself in fresh attire. Judd had joined him there to review the possible whereabouts of those who had torched the warehouse, and they had both decided that a visit to the Under-the-Hill tavern was worth the effort.

Rather than give the impression that he was seeking a fight, Ashton had come dressed much like a riverboat gambler in black coat, cravat, and trousers, with a crisp, white shirt setting off his silver-and-gray-brocaded vest. His tall, rakish figure drew the admiring stares of the harlots who serviced the place, and they greeted him with sultry smiles as he paused inside the door to consider his surroundings. The ceiling was low but the room was wide, with the space broken by large posts that supported the upper floor. A stout bar, pockmarked from a multitude of brawls, angled across one corner of the hall, while the open area was crammed with small tables and crude chairs. A good many of these were filled with patrons, and a pair of scruffy characters leaned against the bar. A more sensitive nose might have turned away from the stench of sweaty bodies, soured ale, tobacco, and mold, but Ashton was no pampered prig. He had seen both sides of the world around him, but it was times like these when he felt very fortunate for his own way of life.

Ashton strolled across the room and selected a dimly lighted table where he pulled out a chair facing the door. Almost before he settled into it, a gaudily dressed strumpet was at his side. Her cheeks were heavily rouged, and when she braced her arms on the table and leaned toward him with a smile, letting the bodice droop away from her breasts, she presented him with a full view of other areas where the red color had been applied.

"What's yer favor, handsome man?"

"Tonight," he responded, drawing a deck from his vest pocket, "only a game of cards and a drink."

The trollop shrugged. "If ye're only aftah a drink, mistah, I'll send Sarah over here to serve ye. I can't waste no time with a man who won't buy, even if he is pretty. But if ye should change yer mind, me name's Fern. . . ."

Casually Ashton began to shuffle the cards while he slowly scanned the faces of the men who watched him. They were a disreputable lot, and one by one they turned away as his gaze touched them. The reputation of this man had preceded him, and they were not fooled by his unthreatening mien or his fancy coat and spit-polished boots. A fire had destroyed a warehouse that morning, and the word was already out that it had been set. They also knew whom it belonged to and could smell trouble brewing. No one bothered with Ashton Wingate's property or possessions without meeting the man; it was like sending out an invitation.

Ashton felt a presence near his elbow and, leaning back in his chair, peered up into the bone-thin face of the woman who stood awaiting his attention. In the smoky haze it was hard to discern the color of the pale, lusterless eyes or the hue of the snarled hair that was drawn into a crude bun at her bony nape. Rags were tied around a badly worn pair of oversized shoes, securing them to her feet, and the coarse blue dress had obviously been made for one a good twenty pounds heavier. He made a rough guess as to her age, placing it somewhere near his own, but he had a feeling she looked much older than she actually was. When she spoke, her tone was flat and void of emotion.

"Fern said you were wanting a drink."

"What's the best one in this place?"

"Ale," the serving maid returned promptly. "It's the only thing that can't be watered much."

"Give me an ale, then . . . Sarah?" He looked at her inquiringly and received an answering nod. "And in a clean mug if you can find one."

"You'd have better luck finding one at Belle Chêne," she advised. "And you'd be a whole lot safer, too."

Ashton's brows lifted in surprise. "Do you know me?"

Sarah cut her eyes toward a group of men who had gathered near the bar. "I heard them talking about you and how you took a mad-woman into your house and claimed she was your wife. Those are some of the same ones who came out to your place looking for her. They're saying they lost some good horses because of you."

Ashton responded with a soft chuckle. "Then why don't they come and make their complaints known to me?"

Her heavily lined brow puckered into deeper furrows as she pondered his question. "I guess they're afraid of you, but I don't understand why. There's more of them."

"Just find a place to hide if they manage to gather up their courage," he suggested.

"You'd be wise to take your own advice. I haven't been here very long, but I've seen what some of these ruffians can do. In fact, you'd be wise to leave now."

"I came looking for a man, and I haven't found him yet. He has two fingers missing from his left hand. . . ."

"No one in this room fits that description," she stated and moved away. Beneath the ragged hem of her gown, her loose slippers made a slight flip-flop sound on the sawdust floor. Her appearance seemed very much a part of this desolate life, and yet as he studied her, Ashton wondered if she might not have known a different way once. She carried herself with a subtle grace the harlots could not match. While they slumped and sauntered their way among the men, trying to provoke some business for the night, she moved with the delicate air of a queen, albeit a ragged one. Even the way she talked hinted of some tutoring.

Coming back to his table, Sarah set down a sparkling mug and a tin pitcher of lukewarm, foamy ale beside it, then stood back and folded her hands as she waited patiently for him to lay out the necessary payment. When he did, her eyes widened in astonishment at the shiny gold color of the coin.

"Oh, that's far too much, sir, and I doubt if I can get the proper change from the barkeep. He's sure to raise the price and keep as much of it as he can."

Ashton reached into his pocket and placed the larger, duller coin on the table beside the gold piece. "This is for the barkeep; the gold is for you . . . for finding me a clean glass."

She hesitated briefly, seeming bewildered by his generosity; then with tears in her eyes, she gathered the coins into her hand. "Thank you, Mr. Wingate. I won't forget this."

Ashton sampled the ale from the mug and then wrinkled his nose at the acrid taste of the brew. If this was the best drink in the house, he mused with repugnance, he would certainly be hard-pressed to sample any other.

With unhurried aplomb he settled his black, low-crowned hat upon his head, disregarding the manners of a proper gentleman, and laid out the cards again, playing with the casual air of one ultimately bored. He continued in this vein for some time, and was just about to give up his watchful vigil when a group of four men pushed open the swinging doors. The leader was a thickset hulk of a man whose forehead sloped toward bushy brows and narrow, recessed eyes. A remarkably large, purple-veined nose jutted out and downward over thick, sneering lips. Just inside the door he halted and braced his left hand on a post while he surveyed the crowd. Ashton was quick to note the absence of two fingers from the meaty paw, and he felt a prickling on his neck when the piggish eyes settled on him.

The hulking brute straightened and squared his shoulders, straining the seams of his short jacket as he thrust out his barrel chest. He hitched up his trousers over his protruding belly and then raised both hands to settle his knit cap at a jaunty angle on his head. He strolled ponderously forward, swinging his heavily muscled legs wide with each step before planting his large feet firmly beneath him. Ashton stiffened as the ungraceful fellow approached, for the man seemed to be leading his cronies directly toward his table. His tension eased considerably when the miscreant settled at a table next to his, and he let out a slow breath of relief.

" 'Pears we've got the hoity-toity folks from Upper Town acomin' down to our digs these days." The huge lout chortled as he jerked his thumb in Ashton's direction.

Ashton surmised that it would not be long before the foursome found some excuse to set upon him, yet it was as if some perverse patience urged him to wait them out. Lazily bracing a booted foot on the rung of a chair, he continued his game of solitaire, but was no less primed for action.

The bear-sized giant banged a beefy fist on the rough planks of the table as his voice rose to an ear-numbing bellow. *"Here now! Where's a servin' wench? Bring us some ale!"* He lowered his voice and sneered aside to his companions: "H'it's gettin' so's a man has to beg to get a drink 'round here."

The strumpets kept their distance, having a care for their continued good health, and it was Sarah who hastened to fill large pitchers and bring them brimming to their table. They ignored the mugs she provided and reached for the tins, but halted as Sarah cleared her throat and announced, "The barkeep said you have to pay before you drink."

The leader glared at her, but she returned his stare unflinchingly. Finally he dug into the pocket of his jacket, bringing out a handful of coins from which he laboriously counted out a sum and laid it on the table.

"That's enough for only three pints," Sarah informed him smartly. "You received four."

The pinheaded lummox grudgingly added more coin to the rest, then with a leering grin added a single penny to the heap: "And a little somethin' fer yerself, me dearie."

The woman gave him a wan, unenthused smile and reached out to sweep the coins into her hand, but before she could draw back, the two fingers of the maimed hand closed with vicious intent upon her upper arm. With a cry of pain she jerked away from the hefty bully and glowered at him as she rubbed the already darkening bruise.

"You mindless red-neck!" she snapped. "Keep your dirty hands to yourself!"

"Eh, now!" he hooted. "I likes a woman with spirit. Why don't ye go find one o' them fancy gowns what yer sisters are wearin' an' dress yerself up fer me? Ye wouldn't be half bad to look at in the proper clothes."

"The same certainly can't be said of you," Sarah retorted and sidestepped his sweeping slap, saving herself another bruise, but her agility seemed to challenge the man's own questionable spryness. Half rising from his chair, he snatched her skirts and spun her around into his embrace. She screeched in outrage as he pulled her down onto his lap, and almost immediately his hand settled between her thighs. The abused woman's eyes widened, and she gasped at the affront while she struggled desperately to escape his grasp.

Now Ashton had been taught at an early age to respect womankind whatever the circumstance, and he had generally subscribed to that ethic. This display of beastliness was simply too much for him to endure. Rising to his feet, he tugged down his vest and stepped to the other's table to confront the uncouth lecher.

"I beg your pardon, sir, but I believe the lady desires to be free of you. Why don't you save us both a lot of bother and release her peaceably?"

The swinish one spilled the ragged woman to the floor in some astonishment. No one had ever had the gall to interfere with him before. Reaching down, Ashton assisted the serving maid to her feet and pushed her toward the bar as the calloused rapscallion came out of his chair with an apoplectic purple mottling his face. The man had not yet attained a state of balance when Ashton's fist swung around, with his full weight behind the blow. He caught the burly one on the jaw and sent him sprawling backward across the table into his companions. Chairs splintered asunder as the three progressed rapidly to the sawdust floor, with loud "whomphs" and "whoofs" attesting to the force of their landing. The quartet struggled up, grasping for knives, clubs, or whatever weapon came quickly to hand. Ashton forestalled their efforts by kicking the table, along with its contents, on top of them. Ale spewed out of tin pitchers, stinging eyes and filling flaring nostrils. Snarled curses filled the air as the foursome went down again in a thrashing tangle. Unrelenting, Ashton added confusion to the melee by sailing his own table toward them with a lusty heave. The brawny leader had rolled and risen to his hands and knees when the wooden piece caromed off his backside, launching him headlong into his cohorts.

More unfriendly shapes approached through the gloom of the place, forming a veritable wall of darkness that crept ever closer. Ashton recognized the vengeful gleam in their eyes, and cautiously backed away, snatching up the broken leg of a table as he went.

"Ssst! Mr. Wingate! Over here!"

Quickly Ashton glanced behind him to see Sarah crouched in an open doorway. Leaping over a fallen chair, he accepted her invitation with proper haste and charged through the portal, slamming it closed behind him and ramming home the bolt. The pair of them fled through the stacks of provender that filled the dimly lighted room until their flight was halted by the stout rear door that was stuck fast in its frame. Ashton lent a shoulder to open the reluctant barrier as the uproar rose in the tavern behind them. Finally after another forceful shove, the outside portal swung free, allowing them to escape. The alley was narrow and slippery with mud, but his guide knew every bend and puddle. She was little more than a dark shape flitting through the shadows as Ashton paused to barricade the rear exit. He followed apace and was within a step of a corner when the stout door crashed open again. The sudden shouts of the unruly gang attested to the fact that they had been seen, and the chase was on.

Ashton caught the slender arm of the woman and pulled her along with him as he raced around the corner of the shanty. They ran up the sloping incline of Silver Street, pushing every ounce of energy into their limbs. The way was muddy, and the wet mire sucked at Sarah's ragged slippers, impeding their progress. With the pursuing ruffians rapidly closing the distance between them, there was no time to bend down and free the shoes from their cloth bindings. A wagon had been drawn across the street on the upper part of the hill, and they dashed around it, no more than a few short strides ahead of the following band. Shouts of victory were already being raised as the rowdies sensed the imminent capture of the pair. They followed around the end of the van, but slid and skidded to an uncertain halt as a slightly larger collection of darker shapes rushed out of the shadows into the lantern light. Sarah gasped as she found herself in the swarm and threw herself behind her champion, only to hear him chuckle.

"It's all right. They're friends."

"You mean they were waiting here all along?" she questioned loudly as the two forces came together.

Ashton chuckled. "I always like to plan ahead when I can."

He sobered abruptly as a bearded man seized his lapel, and he spun about, driving a hard fist into the other's belly and following with a cross to the chin. The man's head snapped back with the force of the blow, but Ashton was given no respite as another pressed for attention. Judd entered the fray with a zeal that nearly shriveled the valor of their adversaries. Not only was he quick and powerful, but with his long arms he could reach out a goodly distance and land hard blows, which his opponent had to survive in order to strike back. Not to be outdone, Sarah jumped on the back of another would-be attacker and clawed at his face from behind. A bite on his ear made him yowl in pain, and he redoubled his efforts to shake off the she-cat who rode him.

From every aspect it was a wild and mucky melee. Mud was plentiful, and with the momentum of hard-driving fists, many were sent sprawling or sliding through it on their backs or bellies. The dark ooze soon coated friend and foe alike until it became a chore to discern who was who in the meager light of the street lanterns. There were more than a few who took on the appearances of river monsters as large globs clung to them and created awesome shapes. Brief queries began to precede blows, and many, realizing their mistakes, turned away from companions to fight back to back against the enemy.

Still, the ranks of the Lower Town antagonists began to dwindle as one by one they slithered senseless into the muck or crept away, unable to summon the proper incentive to endure further punishment. Ashton was beginning to feel some hope for the outcome when a bellow of glee made him spin about. He found four ominous shapes advancing upon him from the edge of the fray. They were relatively untouched by the filth as if they had held themselves apart from it, but in any circumstance the four would have been recognizable by the broad, square shape of the one who led them. They hefted heavy cudgels in meaty fists and spread out as they moved in.

"Mr. Wingate, suh," the brawny one addressed him with a chortle, "you're 'bout to meet your maker."

"Fo' 'gainst one?" a deep voice questioned from nearby, and Ashton felt a measure of relief as he recognized it instantly as Judd's. "Somehow dat seem a mite unfair, but jes' a mite, mind yo. How 'bout makin' it fo' to two?"

The heavy man gave no pause, but lunged at Ashton. He had been shamed in the tavern and relished the idea of delivering a death stroke to this one. Ashton sidestepped his rush and swung a smarting clout to the man's head as he passed. The eager one bellowed in pain and lurched around like a wounded bull. Ashton struck again, this time a chopping blow at the arm that bore the bat. The weapon fell to the ground, but the bearlike assailant closed and grasped Ashton in a crushing embrace. He felt his ribs creak with the strain and heaved upward with his arms. The other's grip slipped slightly, and Ashton heaved again until he found enough space to move his arms. He drove the knuckles of both hands up under the man's lower ribs and was rewarded by a howl when the fellow staggered back with his arms spread in agony. Ashton followed his retreat and repeatedly slammed his fist into the other's face, flattening the bulbous nose, then driving a blow into the flabby belly and another to the chin. Still, the man reached out to grasp with those massive arms. Ashton stepped back and, with all his weight behind it, sent a fist straight into the sagging mouth. The man's head jerked back with the blow, and he staggered away in a daze. He had no time to clear his thoughts before three stumbling forms rushed past. Catching their cohort's arm, they dragged him along with them as they fled, slipping and sliding down the hill. Ashton turned in wonderment to find Judd grinning broadly. The black man stood in a victorious stance with legs spread and arms akimbo.

"What happened?" Ashton asked in bemusement.

The black shrugged casually. "Ah reckon dey figger de odds was too much fo' dem."

"As usual, you took care of more than your share of the battling," Ashton said with a grin.

Judd chuckled. "Ah ain't sure what my share shoulda been, so Ah jes' took what was left over."

Ashton clapped him on the back and laughed. "Feel perfectly free to help yourself to any leftovers like that you might find."

Judd gestured down the street at the fleeing rogues. "Yo reckon we oughta go aftah dem? Dere ain't no short dandy among 'em, but Ah noticed de big one missin' two fingers."

"I'll inform Harvey of their whereabouts and let him drag them in. I don't have any more fight left in me." He walked over to the wagon where Sarah was sitting with chin in hand. A cudgel dangled from the other hand, and it was obvious from the small heap of bodies that lay in the mud near the forward wheel that she had used the bat with wicked intent.

"There's been times in the past year or so," she muttered, "when I've wanted to do something like this, especially when I thought of the brute I had for a husband."

Ashton cocked a brow at her in amusement. "Madam, I pity the man if you ever lay your hands on him."

"Humph," she responded. "I won't pity him. I'll probably have him drawn and quartered, not only for what he did to me, but for what he did to my family." She blinked at the moisture that suddenly filled her eyes and, in some embarrassment, thrust her hand into the pocket of her muddy skirt. Dragging forth a ragged kerchief and applying it to her wet cheeks, she sniffed and composed herself. "I'm sorry, Mr. Wingate. I didn't mean to bother you with my problems."

"No bother at all, Sarah," he said and, with gentle concern, inquired, "What will you do now? It will be too dangerous for you to go back to the Razorback Saloon."

"I don't know," she answered quietly. "I have a brother who sailed to the Far East several years ago. I'm not sure when he'll return, and he was always something of a black sheep anyway. He rebelled against the idea of taking over the business affairs when my father passed on." She laughed without humor. "Believe it or not, Mr. Wingate, I was born into wealth. My father made a fortune maintaining several general stores and supplying them with goods he shipped in on his own vessels. I used to keep his books for him, so I know he was successful. Now my family has been utterly destroyed. My father is dead, the fortune is gone, and I don't know if I'll ever find my brother again." She stared into space, as if her thoughts had taken her far beyond the moment; then she heaved a long sigh. "I think I only exist to see the day my husband receives his due."

Thoughtfully Ashton wiped a glob of mud from his sleeve. "If you've had some experience keeping journals, I can give you work at the office of my shipping business."

Sarah stared at him in wonder. "You don't have to feel responsible for me, Mr. Wingate. What I did back there at Razorback Saloon I did out of gratitude. The fight started because of me, and you owe me nothing."

He peered at her with a slowly spreading grin. "My business has a need for someone with a talent for ciphering and keeping books. If you don't think yourself capable, I'll try to find someone else."

Her thin face took on a glow that nearly equaled the moon shining high overhead. "I'm capable, Mr. Wingate. I know I am."

"Good." The matter was settled. "You'd better come back with us to Belle Chêne tonight. It will be safer there. In the morning my wife can take you to get some clothes." He smiled. "She's not really from the madhouse, you know."

Sarah smiled rather sadly. "I know that, Mr. Wingate."

The hour was late when Ashton paused outside the back door to shed his muddy boots and as much attire as he dared. He had accomplished the first and had shrugged out of coat and vest when he became aware of muffled sobs coming from the kitchen. With worry crowding his mind, he leaped up the steps and entered the room in stockinged feet. Willabelle turned about with a start, clasping the hem of her apron over her mouth. From her eyes streamed a torrent of tears, and the red-eyed stares of Luella May and Bertha convinced him that they also shared in the sorrow. When Willabelle recognized the mud-smeared visage of her master, she drew a deep breath and began to sob with renewed vigor.

"Why are all of you crying?" he demanded. "What's happened?"

"It's Miz Lierin, massa," Willabelle moaned, and the other two dissolved in a fresh spate of sobs and sniffles.

Sharp talons of dread raked Ashton's heart, and his mind began to race. "Where is she?" he cried. "Has she been hurt?"

Again Willabelle supplied the information as she wept in her apron. "Gone, massa."

"Gone? Gone where?" He was completely bewildered.

The housekeeper sniffed loudly and, wiping her face with the apron, drew a quavering breath as she struggled for control. "Ah don' know, massa. Dat Mistah Somerton, he come out here an' talk wid her for some time. Den Mis Lierin an' him jes' up an' left widout nobody knowin'. Yo grandma an' Miz Jenny . . . dey took to deir beds wid a powerful case o' de mulligrubs."

"But why?" Ashton asked, confused and hurting. "Why would she go?"

Willabelle lifted her massive shoulders in a helpless shrug. "Ah don' know, massa. Maybe Mistah Somerton, he worked her into believin' she was Miz Lenore."

A great weight descended on Ashton's shoulders. Of a sudden he was tired, and his body ached from the abuse it had taken. His mind labored to sort out the realities, but he felt the pressing burden of a mountain he could not climb. Blinking at the gathering moisture in his eyes, he turned away and blindly made his way to the door. "I'll find her," he mumbled. "I'll start the search in the morning." He paused in the portal and lamely gestured toward the back door, remembering that he had left Sarah somewhere outside. "I brought a woman home with me. Take care of her and give her something to wear."

The wails began anew, and he turned his head to bend a gloomy regard on the housekeeper.

"What is it now?"

"Nothin', 'ceptin' Miz Lierin done gone off widout her clothes," Willabelle choked out. "All dem purty gowns you bought, she left dem all behind. She left jes' like some ghost, needin' nothin' an' takin' nothin' wid her."

– Chapter Nine –

Lenore or Lierin. Which was it to be? The woman who was presented the choice debated the matter from the moment she left Belle Chêne. It was a cruel quandary she found herself in. She could hardly accept Lierin as her name without closing her mind to the presence of her father and the proof he had presented. If she selected the appellation of Lenore, she was denying all hopes of a future with Ashton. It was a war between emotions and reality, and no matter how she wanted it to be otherwise, the facts seemed to be tilting the scales heavily toward Malcolm Sinclair. The naked truths of life had a way of ignoring the longings of one's heart. Ashton had thought his wife had drowned, and so had many other people. He had never found her, and in the three years following the accident, she had not been seen or heard from again. Surely, if Lierin had loved him and she were alive, she would have braved the fires of hell or the frigid climes of the North to come back to him. It was what she, the woman with one name too many, would have done.

Enter Malcolm Sinclair. Even before they had met the man, they had heard about his search for his wife. The innkeeper, having seen her, had thought she was the one. The portraits suggested that she looked more like Lenore than Lierin. Her father had also insisted that Malcolm was telling the truth. What more proof did she need?

The journey from Natchez to Biloxi gave her plenty of time to mull over the problem in her mind. It also gave her cause to lament that she had not brought a change of clothes. Had they traveled from Natchez to New Orleans by steamboat and then by ship to Biloxi, they would have greatly reduced their time en route, but Robert Somerton had brought a fine carriage to the city on the bluff, and by this mode he would return. They stopped two nights along the way, the first one finding whatever rest they could alongside the road, and the second acquiring questionable accommodations at an inn, the question being whether or not it was an improvement over the previous night.

The way was hot and dusty, but her father seemed immune to the discomforts. His nose and cheeks grew red with the aging day, but it had little to do with the heat, rather with whatever was in the silver flask he frequently tipped. At the Pearl River he sought to gain a free crossing by challenging the ferryman to a drinking contest, which would likely have seen them both under the table in a drunken stupor. His daughter strenuously objected and frowned her displeasure until he relented and doled out the necessary coin.

It seemed part of the routine that by midafternoon he was feeling high of spirit. She was amazed at the endless repertoire from which he was able to draw, for he recited long and varied verses with a silver-tongued flair that softened his crisp English accent. Well into his cups, he was very garrulous and would start to relate stories that seemed foreign to his life as a merchant; then with a chortle he would slash his hand back and forth before him as if to erase the tale and explain, "That was before I met your mother, my dear."

Occasionally he napped, and his loud snores filled the confines of the well-appointed conveyance until his daughter was tempted to nudge him to awareness again. She wished she could have found that same depth of slumber for herself, but whenever she closed her eyes, Ashton was there waiting. He haunted her through every waking hour, and when she fled in exhausted relief to the arms of slumber, her dreams took up the chase. Perhaps it was because she had no prior memories of her life that she cherished these recent ones with Ashton so much. Whatever the case, she was frustrated by failure when she sought to direct her mind to other things that might have been less disturbing.

By the third day she was nearly spent, and her frayed nerves could no longer deal with the constant conflict within her. She deliberately set herself the task of accepting this man who rode with her as her father, striving diligently to cast aside any doubt that he could be mistaken, while at the same time making a concerted effort to regard herself as Lenore. After all, if anyone knew who she was, surely it would be her father. Still, when she considered his constant tippling, she wondered if he really had enough presence of mind to tell who she was.

It was by dint of will that she took on the name Lenore, though the conflict of her identity still raged within her. The application of her resolve further sapped her energies, and by the time they reached the large house on the shore and the carriage swept up the curving drive, she was totally drained, both mentally and physically.

Robert Somerton stepped nimbly down to aid in her descent as a maid hurried across the porch. Lenore accepted his helping hand but avoided meeting his gaze, and without pausing she moved up the path toward the wide steps, letting her eyes sweep over the graceful facade of the two-story house. Dark green shutters trimmed the french doors and windows that were positioned in symmetrical order along the porches on both levels. Wood railing closed the area between square-columned supports and swept up the curving stairway that led to the upper veranda. Though it did not come close to the beauty of Belle Chêne, the house was not without appeal, and she felt a strange kinship with it, as if it had once offered comfort and security.

The cheery-faced maid dipped into a quick curtsey as Lenore mounted the steps to the porch. She guessed the woman's age to be at least ten years older than her own, but her manner was sprightly and energetic, as if she held the secret of eternal youth within her grasp. Her blue eyes twinkled kindly above a bright smile.

"Me name's Meghan, mum," the maid announced. "I be hired by Mr. Sinclair to see to the needs of the household, if ye be havin' no objection, mum."

"Mr. Sinclair?" A delicate brow arched in question. "I was not aware that Mr. Sinclair was lending his authority to the management of this house."

Meghan appeared momentarily confused by her comment. "Well, seein's as it be yer house, mum, isn't it right fer yer husband to attend to such matters in yer absence?"

Lenore half turned to regard her father with open suspicion. She had been assured that only the two of them would be living in the house with the servants.

Clearing his throat, Robert hastened to speak in a hushed tone to his daughter: "Malcolm said he would move out, Lenore, so there's no reason to get upset."

"I hope not." Her tone was perhaps somewhat less than gracious, but she was leery of being pushed into a situation she was not ready to accept. "As I've tried to explain before, I will need time to adjust." She reiterated her stance while wondering how many times she had done so thus far. On the trip her father had been effusively complimentary about the younger man, as if trying to sway her toward an early acceptance of their marital state. At the moment, she had no desire to become intimate with Malcolm, for her heart was still much entangled with Ashton, and that is where she feared it would remain for some time to come.

"Come into the house, mum," Meghan gently urged. "Ye've had a long journey, an' I know ye must be tuckered clear to the bone."

Lenore entered the hall as the maid held the door and halted just inside to let her eyes adapt to the darker interior. Despair congealed in the pit of her stomach when her vision adjusted, for what she saw made her sure that she had been in the house before. She could name neither the day nor the year, but she had the distinct recollection of having been in this same hall many times before. The narrow corridor ran the full length of the structure, with a staircase laid against one wall and then curving to the other for its ascent to the upper level. The decor was tasteful and uncluttered, with cool, serene colors providing a sense of space and airiness. Rugs of varying sizes adorned the wooden floors in the hall and the adjoining rooms. The largest of these nearly filled the spacious parlor on her right and lay beneath a grouping of several chairs, small tables, and a settee. Across the hall and in the opposite direction, a pale-hued Persian carpet was spread beneath the dining room table and chairs.

"We've had some lemonade cooling in the well, mum," Meghan stated. "Would ye be wantin' me to bring ye some, with maybe a few teacakes to nibble?"

Lenore smiled. "That sounds very tempting."

"Ye rest yerself in the parlor, mum," Meghan encouraged. "I'll be back shortly."

In the ensuing silence Robert Somerton peered at his daughter and finally came to stand beside her. "Well, girl, do you find anything that seems familiar to you?"

Without committing herself to an answer, Lenore entered the parlor and approached the french doors that offered a panoramic view of the shore. Aware that her father watched her closely from the hallway, she opened one, allowing the tangy salt smell of the sea to waft in on a fresh breeze.

"The servants haven't been here long, have they?" she stated matter-of-factly.

His wispy brows shot up as his gray eyes fixed her with a questioning stare. "How come you to arrive at that conclusion, my dear?"

"Meghan introduced herself to me." She shrugged casually. "If she had been here all along, she would have known me."

"The old servants were let go when you were kidnapped. Malcolm had to hire new ones in their stead."

She turned to him in bemusement. "Were there none who returned? No favored one who came back to work?"

"Ah, no . . . I think they had all found employment elsewhere." Robert wiped the back of a shaky hand across his mouth, while his eyes searched about the room. He spied a set of crystal decanters on the sideboard, and for a moment it seemed as if he battled a strong urge as his tongue flicked out to wet his lips. Nervously smoothing his coat, he yielded to the impulse and hurried across the room to pour himself a liberal glass of whiskey. "I don't really know the detail of it. I came here only a short time ago myself." He tossed down a goodly draft before he faced her again. "After you . . . and Lierin . . . left the nest for your respective homes, I did some traveling. Then I decided to visit here and see how you and Malcolm were getting along. I guess it's lucky I did."

"Lucky?" Lenore whispered the word distantly and gave him a wan smile. "That remains to be seen, doesn't it?"

Robert looked at her closely. "Whatever can you mean?"

Thoughtfully Lenore drew off her gloves and doffed her bonnet, laying them both aside before strolling leisurely about the room. She inspected the appointments, hoping some minor object would encourage a deeper recall. She eyed her father in much the same manner, wanting to know with unmistakable conviction that he was blood kin. "It's only that Malcolm will take some getting used to. I had begun to believe that I was Ashton's wife, and it was a considerable shock to learn that it might have been a mistake."

Her father stared at her in consternation. "Are you saying, young lady, that you actually . . . shared a bed with the man?"

Lenore felt an insidious warmth creeping into her cheeks. How could she tell him of all the nights she had spent in Ashton's arms?

How could she allow those moments, which were still precious to her, to be aired and sullied by him and Malcolm Sinclair? She had given herself to Ashton, believing she was his wife, and she would not reveal that knowledge just to appease their curiosity.

"I've been here before," she acknowledged, ignoring his question. "I know that. Everything seems familiar." She inclined her head toward the sea and, for a brief moment, watched the surf lap lazily at the pale shore. "I've felt the waves rush across my bare feet as I walked along this lonely stretch of land." She swept her hand about the room in an encompassing gesture. "I accept the idea that this is my home . . . but . . ." She came around and stared at him with eerie effect as the setting sun, shining in through the crystal panes, stripped away the deep green hue of her eyes and imbued them with a shining light until they seemed like two crystals glowing between jet lashes. "But . . . I still don't remember you."

Staring into those bright orbs, Robert Somerton felt the hackles prickle on the back of his neck. A chill seemed to penetrate to his inner soul, and he had to shake himself from the spell of it. He gulped down another hearty portion of whiskey and straightened his back indignantly as he turned from her. "It's a terrible thing when a daughter forgets her own flesh and blood." He rubbed the back of his hand beneath his nose and sniffed as if he fought a sudden battle with tears. "I must say, Lenore, it grieves me deeply that you've thrust me from your mind."

"I don't remember Malcolm Sinclair, either," she murmured in a small dejected voice. She discounted the carriage ride in New Orleans that had stirred a recall of a man with a mustache, for the memory had been too vague and general. There were a goodly number of men who could fit that description.

"And that's another thing. Forgetting your own husband." Somerton swung around and stared at his daughter, as if astounded that such words had come from her lips. He sipped from the glass and, rocking back on his heels, shook his head in sorrowful lament. "I don't know what's taken hold of your senses, girl. The men who've held you most dear you've pushed from your memory as if we meant nothing to you . . . as if we were no more than a speck of froth on yonder sea." He drained his glass in a single gulp, then sucked in a deep breath as the liquor traced a fiery path down his throat. "In the same course, you've taken to your heart a man who led your sister astray, then discarded her as worthless trash when he had had his will with her. Ashton Wingate might not have murdered Lierin himself, but if he didn't, he's at least responsible for her death. If he hadn't taken her off, she'd still be with us today." He plumbed the depth of her clouded gaze as if trying to find some hint of agreement. "Don't you remember how we mourned her loss? Don't you recall your vows of revenge?"

In roweling distress Lenore shook her head, rejecting his arguments. "Ashton loved Lierin. I know he did! And I will not accept your claims that he deliberately murdered her or is responsible for her death."

Robert Somerton went to his daughter and, in a conciliatory manner, reached out to lay a comforting hand on her shoulder, but with a small cry, Lenore shrank away from his touch. A weary sigh slipped from him as he returned to the sideboard. He refilled his glass and, savoring the spirits, began to pace the room in pensive concentration.

"My dearest Lenore." He assumed the lecturing tone of a disturbed father, speaking slowly and carefully so that each word would carry its full impact. "I do not wish to distress you unduly. Heaven knows your mental state is delicate enough. I only wish to point out several facts that you must already know. The man is an accomplished roué, and I can understand why a helpless and confused young girl could be easily swayed by his intense persuasion, but, my dear child," he chuckled lightly, "I cannot accept the idea that such a man believes in ghosts. 'Tis more reasonable for me to believe that he knew who you were all the time." He took a deep draft and smiled in what could only be satisfaction with his own logic. "Can you not see room for some error in your conclusions?"

A wearying perplexity nagged at the edge of Lenore's mind. Her father made it seem so simple, but she could not and would not doubt Ashton's passion for his Lierin, and she was far too tired to explain her reasons to her father. Her hands became white-knuckled fists as she clenched them in her lap. Slowly she shook her head from side to side. "I will hear no more of this." A trace of anger crept into her voice. "You will refrain from degrading Ashton Wingate in my presence ever again. He is a man of honor, and despite what you say, he is a gentleman!"

"What's this I hear? Is it possible that you're in love with the man?"

Lenore stared at her father while she fought the urge to cry out, "*Yes . . . oh, yes!* I love him!" She wanted to scream the declaration to the world at large, and her eyes filled with tears as she thought how her statement would be crushed beneath the stern heel of criticism.

Her father considered her with a lazy smile. "Malcolm had better not hear how you've fastened your fancies on another man. You know what will come of that?" He nodded as if he knew she understood. "That's right. A duel."

Of a sudden Lenore found herself running from the room. She had heard enough!

"Lenore!"

Her father's cry only spurred her on. Her cheeks were hot with the flow of tears, and her chest ached as she struggled to contain the sobs. She fled across the hall, nearly colliding with Meghan, who was approaching with a tray of refreshments. She brushed past the maid, hardly caring that she had not partaken of a meal since daybreak, and flew up the stairs.

The journey had taken its toll, but this latest abuse nearly rent her soul. As she reached the upper landing, the sobs burst from her in a torrent of emotion, and she ran, giving no heed to her direction as she turned down the hall to her right and burst through an open doorway at the far end. Her gaze chased wildly about the room as she entered, and through a teary blur she saw a tall four-poster and other furnishings appropriate for a large bedchamber. The french doors and windows were open to catch the cooling breezes from off the ocean, and like the parlor below, the room was suffused with a light that now had begun to take on a pinkish cast. The delicately hued floral wallcovering seemed to glow with a soft sheen that was both inviting . . . and familiar. Smothering her sobs beneath a trembling hand, she stumbled across the room to the french doors and there leaned her head against a frame as she stared out with misty gaze upon the crashing surf. The burden in her breast seemed unbearable, and a ragged sigh did not ease the pain. Though the view could have been appeasing, she yearned to have the lush green lawns of Belle Chêne in sight and to know within her mind that she was Ashton's beloved, no matter what name she bore.

Her chin lifted, and her heart quickened as she detected a man on horseback riding at a full canter toward the house. For a moment she held her breath, wanting it to be Ashton, but all the while know-ing it could not be.

She fell further into despondency as the rider came nearer. The man's body was too thick, and he rode without the skill of the other man. Recognizing Malcolm Sinclair, she waited with quaking heart as he dismounted and came into the house. Eons seemed to pass before she heard the scrape of his boot against the stairs. His foot-steps came down the hall, pausing before each door as if he searched for her in the other rooms. A rising panic took hold of her as he drew near, and she cast her gaze about for someplace to hide, but she forced herself to remain where she was, knowing that reality had to be dealt with and that she would have to face the man sooner or later.

Malcolm paused at the door of her bedroom and cast a glance inward, then seeing her, entered with a rather sheepish smile. "I thought you might have forgotten which room was ours." He spread his hands. "I've been waiting here, hoping your father would be suc-cessful in bringing you home and yet fearing that Ashton would not let you go."

Lenore appraised him with a reserved air. He was as tall as Ash-ton, a stone or two heavier, and perhaps five or so years younger. He had to be considered handsome with his brown eyes and tawny hair. His mustache was neatly trimmed, lending him a rakish look. He was dressed in the height of fashion, and his riding apparel obviously had cost him a considerable amount, but he failed to do for them what Ashton did for his old riding garments. He did not carry himself with the same proud, straightforward stride of the other man. There was almost a careless swagger to the way he moved, a slight rolling of one shoulder or the other as he sauntered forward.

"I know this is my room." She gathered her courage and forced herself to meet his gaze. "But I can't recall sharing it with anyone." She managed a meager smile. "I'm sorry, Malcolm, but I just can't lay hold of any memory of you in my life."

"That's easily solved, my love." He laughed softly and, laying his hands on her waist, tried to draw her near, but Lenore broke free as a sense of desperation filled her. She quickly stepped away, widening the distance between them as she moved across the room, conve-niently taking a place behind a chair.

"I'll need time to adjust, Malcolm," she said firmly. She was even more serious now than she had been when she had pleaded with Ashton for the same consideration. "Even though I've been assured that you are my husband, I am unable to turn my thoughts around and accept the idea of our marriage right now."

As if his mind could not fully grasp her meaning, he stared at her, and slowly lowered his arms to his sides. "Are you saying that I must find another bedroom for myself?"

"Not only a bedroom, Malcolm, but another house," she stated boldly. "I only came here because my father assured me that you would not be living with us. He said you were willing to move out until I've had some time to adapt."

A troubled frown came to his brow. "That will be difficult to do, Lenore."

Some intuitive suspicion that she was being duped made her wary of his answers. There was no question in her mind that she would have stayed with Ashton if she had known she would be pressed to abide with this man. Her gaze was cool and unswerving as she inquired, "Why would it be difficult?"

Malcolm shrugged his broad shoulders and casually sauntered about the room, halting beside the chair she stood behind. "There's just not another place in Biloxi where I can stay."

"Surely you can find a room at the inn," she argued.

His pleasant demeanor was momentarily transformed into an irate frown as he looked at her sharply. "Did you also insist upon living apart from Ashton Wingate? The two of you seemed cozy enough, what with your kissing him in broad daylight."

His jealousy and hatred of the other man were apparent, and knowing full well that he could still challenge Ashton to a duel, she carefully avoided giving him any insight as to what really had happened at Belle Chêne. "I was put in a guest room after the accident, and while I was there, Ashton comported himself as a perfect gentleman. He never at any time forced me to accept the idea that I was his wife."

Malcolm digested this a moment, but whether he accepted her answer or not could not be determined as he turned his back to her. Dropping into the chair, he stretched his legs out before him. "You say, Lenore, that you don't remember anything about me. I am trying to understand, but it's difficult when I remember how close we once were." Leaning across the space where she stood, he patted the cushioned seat of a nearby chaise. "Sit, my love, and let's talk about this for a while. I'm sure we'll both gain some insight into this problem of yours if we can discuss it together."

Lenore lowered a cool stare to the back of his tousled head, feeling no desire to comply with his request, but finding no polite way to avoid doing so. Reluctantly she moved between the two chairs and felt his scrutiny as she settled with stiff-backed caution on the edge of the chaise.

"Relax, my dear," he cajoled. "I'm not a monster who will tear you to shreds." He raised himself from his chair to fluff the silk pillows against the back of her chaise. "Come, lean back," he urged, dropping a hand upon her shoulder.

In abrupt reaction Lenore pushed away his arm and, feeling suddenly closed in, moved quickly in the opposite direction until she sat at the far end of the cushion. She stole a wary glance at him, unable to explain her sudden panic even to herself, and found him staring back at her in surprise. She forced a weak smile. "I'd rather sit here if you don't mind, Malcolm. I get dizzy when I lie down." She could probably lay the blame for this recent malady on her fatigue, but it seemed an appropriate excuse to use to avoid being confined to an area in close proximity to him.

Malcolm dropped into his chair again and regarded her for a long moment, seeming completely bewildered. "Are you afraid of me, Lenore?"

"Do I have reason to be?" she asked quietly.

He ran his fingers through his tousled hair. "I can't think of one, but you seem so . . . so distant."

Remaining aloof, she returned his gaze without giving him the benefit of a reply. Beneath her steadfast stare, Malcolm sighed and glanced around, feeling at a loss.

"You've always intrigued me, Lenore," he murmured, searching for the appropriate words that would draw her from her shell. "I am indeed fortunate to have such a beautiful wife. I remember the first time I saw you, you were wearing green . . . the same color as your eyes. I stopped and stared, but you were with another man, and I couldn't intrude. . . ."

"Who was the man?"

"An older man." His broad shoulders lifted casually. "A cousin, perhaps. I really can't say. I was too involved with watching you to pay much attention to your escort." He closed his eyes and smiled in dreamy reflection as he leaned his head back against the chair. "I can still remember how your skin gleamed beneath the lamplight and how tantalizing the curves of your breasts were beneath your gown...."

Lenore lifted a palmetto fan from a table near the chaise and leisurely applied its function toward the cooling of her cheeks, prompting Malcolm to open one eye and peer at her with a confident smile. She averted her face from his amused regard, irked that he should find any pleasure in her blush.

"If it was a cousin of mine, then we must have been in England. I don't have any kin here in America anymore." She issued the statements as if she were reading a humdrum report, and then glanced up at him with an inquiry, fervently hoping to find some gap in his story. "Can you describe the interior of the manor house in England?"

He placed the fingertips of both hands together as he delved into reflections. "I was there only briefly as a guest, so I didn't see all the rooms, but there was a large central room ... or, as your father called it, a great hall. Next to that was a long room with a huge hearth and stone stairs."

"Do you remember if there was anything on the wall?"

He paused a long moment in deep thought. "Portraits of your ancestors, I think, and some shields and crests." He canted his head as another memory came to mind. "There were also two other portraits hanging there, one of you and the other of your sister ... larger replicas of the ones your father gave Judge Cassidy."

Lenore shivered inside as his words struck a familiar chord within her. She could almost see the pair of paintings mounted side by side above the hearth. "Where did you say they were?"

"Above the fireplace, I think." He nodded after a thoughtful search of his memory. "Yes, that's where they were."

Her hopes sank to a dismal level with his affirmation, and she felt drained and listless as she continued the interrogation: "You undoubtedly knew my portrait was at my grandfather's house, but I've been wondering how you came by that information. Were you there before?"

"We went there together, my love. Don't you remember?"

Lenore frowned as she failed to recall the event. "No, I don't."

He seemed amazed that she should forget. "Don't you recall how upset you were when you learned of your grandfather's death? The house was closed up by then, and you kept blaming yourself for having left him as you did."

Lenore raised her head in alert attention. "How did we get there? I mean, did we walk . . . ?"

"We took a barouche, and you were sobbing so much I wondered if I'd have to find a doctor to give you some laudanum."

The piece fit neatly into the puzzle, but it gave her no pleasure to know that it was Malcolm who had comforted her in that faraway memory. She was earnestly trying to assimilate this latest bit of information when another question came to haunt her: "Where did you say we were married?"

"Here in Biloxi," he replied easily. "I came to live here, and it was not very long after that that you decided to move from England and also take up residence here." He gave her a slow grin. "I like to think you made that choice because of me." He detected a small, puzzled quirk in her frown and let a long sigh slip from his lips as he lifted his gaze toward the ceiling. "We've known each other for some time now . . . three or so years, I guess. I keep thinking, all the years . . . forgotten. It seems like such a waste."

"I'm sorry if my condition distresses you, Malcolm." Her tone held no emotion. "It distresses me even more."

"I'm sure it does, my love," he murmured softly, lowering his head to stare at her. "But there's no reason why we can't renew some of those memories."

Lenore took a warning from his warming smile. His eyes had grown dark and now smoldered with a light that made her fearful of what the next moments would bring. Flicking downward in one bold caress, his gaze seemed to strip her bare, and there was almost a leer lifting the corner of his lips when he raised his eyes to meet hers again. "There are times when a man needs to be reassured, and it's been some time since we've made love. . . ."

By some inner strength Lenore subdued her quaking and attempted to appear casual as she deliberately misread his meaning. "What assurances do you need, Malcolm? If you still have any qualms about Ashton, I told you that he was very polite while I was there." She lifted her shoulders in a shrug and for his consideration put forth several conjectures that would hopefully ease the impact of her rejection: "I don't know, but it's possible that Dr. Page said something to Ashton about the delicacy of my condition and persuaded him to treat me gently. It's difficult to say how I might have reacted had I been forced. Surely the shock would have caused me to suffer serious trauma. Even now, whenever I'm upset, I start to have strange visions. I even imagine a man being beaten and murdered. . . ."

Malcolm's eyebrows came up in surprise. "Murdered?"

"Oh, I know how strange it sounds, Malcolm, but during moments of stress, I begin to hallucinate. I really can't say whether I begin to recall, in visions, events I've actually experienced or if it's just my imagination creating horrible illusions. Whatever the case, it's very disturbing." She hoped fervently that a small part of her father's talent for acting had rubbed off on her and that she was being successful in convincing Malcolm of her frailty. It would ease her mind considerably if she could live in the house without fear of rape. "Can you understand how I might have been affected if I had been coerced?"

"Yes. Yes, of course." He seemed almost eager to placate her fears. "I wouldn't want you to be upset about anything, my dear. I want you to get well as quickly as possible."

The brisk clatter of heels came along the corridor and halted at the open door. They looked around to see a young maid pausing at the threshold. Her uncertainty was obvious. Beneath their combined stares she seemed to debate whether to make a tactful retreat or chance an advance.

"Come in," Lenore invited, extremely grateful for the interruption.

The girl entered hesitantly, casting an anxious glance toward each of them. Her black hair, blue eyes, and soft fair skin delicately touched with a blush were a striking combination, but she seemed naively unaware of her comeliness as she nervously straightened her cap. Trailing strands of dark hair had escaped the starched headpiece and were hanging about her face. Though her apron was crisp and clean, it was slightly misaligned with her dark blue gown, lending her a rather untidy demeanor.

"Excuse me, mum," she apologized, dipping her knees in a quick curtsey. "I be Mary, the housemaid. Meghan sent me up to ask if ye'd be wantin' a bath."

Lenore flashed a look toward Malcolm, who was thoughtfully

rubbing a finger along his chin. He stared at the girl, but he seemed lost in his musings, as if he were still mulling over her comments. Perhaps she had given him reason to fear her sanity, but if it would keep him at bay, it was what she wanted. She also desired a bath, but she was leery of giving an affirmative answer while he was still in the room.

Malcolm finally became aware that he was being observed, and with a debonair smile he faced the green eyes that rested on him. "If you will excuse me, my love. There are some matters in town that need my attention." Rising to his feet, he took her hand and dropped a kiss on the tips of her fingers. "Until this evening, then."

Graciously Lenore nodded, immensely relieved that he was leaving. She only hoped that, while he was gone, he would reconsider and find another place to live.

Not since her first bath at Belle Chêne had Lenore felt such a need to soak away her stiffness and the ache in her muscles. The journey from Natchez had been a grueling ordeal, for she was sure the carriage wheels had found nearly every rut and crevice in the road. Slammed and jostled about the interior, she had been left both bruised and battered. As she sank with a long, grateful sigh into the steamy water, she closed her eyes, and let her mind wander at will. A definite path seemed laid out for her thoughts, however, for she was soon remembering when Ashton had attended her bath and the resulting play of passion that had led him to strip off his wet clothes and press his hard, naked body full against her own. Though she knew she was letting her mind travel a dangerous course, she savored the recollections. Otherwise, she would have sunk into the pit of despair and been overwhelmed by sorrows.

Memories of another toilette wandered with ghostlike grace through her mind as she continued her bath. It seemed that the hour was late, and she had just traveled a long distance and was preparing for bed. . . .

Her mind took up the path in visual recall, and she found herself clothed in a nightgown with a cloak thrown over it. She was walking through darkness; then a burst of light intruded, and she recoiled in sudden fear as the too-familiar nightmare came upon her. The poker lifted, but now it was as if she were standing afar off watching the event from a distance. The silhouette of a darkly cloaked man flitted across a narrow space, and gloved hands brought the iron down on the shaggy head of another.

She almost screamed as she came upright in the bathtub. Slowly the fear waned, and as it did, her thoughts became crystal clear. Of a sudden she was struck by the realization of what she had just envisioned, and the full force of that revelation nearly snatched her breath.

"It wasn't me!" she whispered in amazed relief. "I didn't do it!" She glanced about the room as the peace of that knowledge drifted down upon her, while at the same time the condemnation of her fears was lifted from her shoulders. For the first time in many weeks she felt free, as if she had been saved forever from the gallows of death and hellish retribution. She wanted to cry in relief and at the same time shout with joy, and yet the tragedy of that moment still plagued her. She sensed more than ever that what her mind had given her was not a dream but the actual murder of a man. But whose?

She shook her head as she failed to find an answer for that question. If Malcolm's tale was true, she had been kidnapped from this very same house and spirited away to Natchez. Her father's wealth might have been a cause. . . .

Below the surface of her memory she felt a twinge of another vague recall. Leaning back in the tub again, she closed her eyes and gave deliberate attention to that feeling. At first she was able to grasp only a faint flicker of a shadowy illusion, but then, images of a group of men began to form in the roiling, confused haze of her reflections. Their appearance was rough and their speech liberally spiced with profanities. She cringed in distaste as one of them sauntered near to leer into her face.

"Awh, ya'll bring us a handsome purse, ya will, missy," he boasted between chortles. "But what's stickin' in me craw is why in the bloody hell can't we have some fun with ya first? Ya're a right fine-lookin' lady, ya are, an' seein's as Ah've never bedded a real lady before, I'm 'bout as curious as a stud sniffin' after a filly. Ah ain't alone, Ah tell ya. Me friends are of the same mind."

A soft rap on the door put fantasy to flight, and Lenore sat up in alert attention. Rising from the tub, she wrapped a towel about herself and moved carefully to the door. Her questioning call was promptly answered by Meghan, and with a great deal of relief,

Lenore twisted the key in the lock and stepped back, pulling the door open to admit the woman. The securing of the portal was a measure she had taken to ensure that her bath would remain private, just in case Malcolm turned curious or, worse, amorous. With her father continually praising him, she was not sure if she would have an ally in the house, and she felt a need to be cautious.

"I found this in yer trunk, mum. I hope it will do," the maid said, carrying in a pale blue organdy gown over her arms. She spread the garment on the bed for Lenore's inspection and stood back to give it her own critical appraisal. "What with yer clothes bein' wadded up and left in the trunk these many months, it took a bit o' ironin' to get all the wrinkles out. Someone must've been in an awful hurry when they packed for ye."

Lenore paused as the words of the innkeeper in Natchez came clearly to mind. She distinctly remembered him describing Malcolm's departure: ". . . loaded up his wife's trunks in her coach, hired a man to drive it, and left."

Meghan heaved a sigh. "An' such a nice new trunk, too. All fancy an' fresh inside an' large enough to hold yer gowns without nary a wrinkle. I can well understand why the mister let go the help, doin' yer lovely gowns that way. They ought to been ashamed o' themselves."

"It doesn't really matter now, Meghan. You've made the gown look new again." Indeed, Lenore could find no flaw in the maid's work or the creation itself. The rounded neckline was trimmed with appliqués of satin leaves, delicately worked with embroidered veins, and a spattering of seed pearls resting like dewdrops over the foliage. Though voluminous, the pale blue sleeves ended midarm with similarly adorned bands. A satin sash would cinch the elevated waist and, like the layered skirt, bore a sparse trailing of leaves down its length.

The woman beamed. " 'Tis a lovely gown, it is, mum, an' ye're sure to look like a bride wearin' it."

Lenore tilted her head as something very fleeting flashed through her consciousness. Did she glimpse a wall of smiling faces surrounding her? And was Malcolm Sinclair standing beside her, looking very much like a groom while he accepted the congratulations of these others?

Suddenly atremble, Lenore sank to the seat of a nearby chair and tried desperately to discern what she had viewed in her mind. Was she the bride in that gathering? And was Malcolm truly the groom?

A multitude of questions formed in her mind, but she found for them no firm answers. And yet, it seemed, since she had arrived at this house, she had started hallucinating more or, hopefully, recalling actual events from her past, some of which came only in bits and snatches, while other parts seemed clearer. It truly saddened her that they were not in accord with the desires of her heart. She had found a memory of Malcolm in her life, but thus far she had not been successful in finding a place for Ashton.

Disconcerted, she lowered her head in her hand and closed her eyes, wanting to banish the recollections back to oblivion. Her failure to find any recall of Ashton swept away any hopes of a joyful conclusion to her malady and left her weak and listless. Although she knew she had to face the truth, her heart still cried out for him. Sweeter by far were the moments she had spent with him.

"Mum?" Meghan reached out a hand to lay it gently on her shoulder. "Are ye all right, mum?"

A long, weary sigh slipped from Lenore as she leaned back against the chair. "I don't know. I haven't been feeling at all well this afternoon."

"Come lay down on the bed, mum," the maid coaxed. "I'll fetch a cool, wet rag so ye can bathe yer face whilst ye rest."

"Shouldn't I be getting dressed for dinner?" Lenore tightened the towel across her bosom, but could not find the energy to begin the actual dressing.

"There's plenty o' time, mum. Just ye slip on yer wrapper an' lay down till ye're feelin' better. What with ye an' yer father travelin' all the way from Natchez, a little sleep might do ye good."

Obeying the woman's suggestion, Lenore donned a light cotton wrapper and stretched out on the bed. The sheets were cool and freshly scented, and the comfort of the down-filled tick soon swept her into the dark sea of slumber. For a time she drifted in a nirvanic limbo where reality was but a mere haze behind long, undulating veils. Dreams began to filter through, and in carefree abandon she floated from one to another, then slowly, almost imperceptibly, the fluttering draperies closed in around her and began to glow, as if suffused with sunlight. A broad-shouldered form came to her, at first indistinct and dark; then her heart tripped a beat as Ashton's sun-bronzed features came into focus. He leaned his head down to press a lover's kiss upon her naked breast, and before her eyes his visage slowly broadened and changed. A thin mustache appeared above leering lips, and she found herself staring into the warm regard of Malcolm Sinclair. The veils became flaming walls that surrounded her, and she writhed in agony as their fiery tongues flicked out to torment her. Then from the core of the flames human forms emerged and pressed in close around her, squeezing the breath from her lungs. Everywhere she turned she was met by a myriad of smirking faces. Goblets were lifted in tribute, as if to celebrate her descent into this roiling pit of hell . . . except for one man who stood apart from the proceedings. He was more like a frightened ferret scurrying about from one hiding place to another, moving stealthily but ever closer to her. Then suddenly his countenance filled her vision, and his soundless scream echoed through her brain.

Lenore came awake with a gasp and stared wildly about the room, unable to tear herself from the nightmare. Any second she expected to find that tormented visage hiding in one of the nooks and crannies of her room, and her heart quaked in fear as she braced herself for the discovery. A dark shadow seemed to hover close beside the bed, and when reality slowly returned, she realized it was Meghan who stood there. Gazing down at her with sympathic gaze, the maid smoothed the tumbled hair away from her brow and cheek.

"Ye've been tossin' an' mumblin' like ye were havin' a bad dream, mum, an' I think ye've got a wee bit o' fever."

Still apprehensive, Lenore cast a wary glance about the room. "Is someone with you?"

Meghan frowned in bemusement. " 'Tis only yerself an' me here, mum. There's no one else."

A trembling sigh slipped from Lenore's parched lips as she leaned back into the pillows. "Yes, I must have been dreaming."

"Aye, mum. That ye were," Meghan agreed, placing another moistened cloth across her forehead. "Ye rest yerself some more, an' I'll wake ye when it's time to dress for dinner. If ye're not better by then, I'll tell yer father ye won't be comin' down."

"I am tired," Lenore admitted.

"O' course ye are, an' ye've a good reason to be."

Lenore sighed and let sleep overtake her again. It was vague and restful, with only a fleeting moment of distress when her dreams wandered through a confused maze and she heard a cacophony of muted voices, the snarled curses of an angry man, the muffled weeping of a woman, and the slurred oration of a drunken poet.

Startled, Lenore sat upright, wondering for a moment where she was. Then as memory returned, she rose and allowed herself to be dressed in the gown that Meghan had laid out. Opening the chamber door, she slipped out into the corridor and crept down the stairs.

The illusive night sounds of the marsh drifted in through the open windows, blending with the soft, distant crashing of the waves on the beach. The french doors of the parlor stood wide to catch the cooling breezes, but as Lenore approached the room, she felt a chill sweep over her. The fever had not left, and reality seemed rather indistinct, but Meghan had done her best with dressing her hair, and her lackluster mood was not revealed. The fever filled her cheeks with color and brightened her eyes while the blue gown did much to compliment her fair skin.

The slightly slurred voice of her father came to her ears as she paused in the hall near the parlor: "What is this chiding? Have I not done well by you? The Bard said it well, he did. 'It is a wise father that knows his own child.' "

Malcolm's reply seemed rather brusque. "Happy is the child whose father goes to the devil."

"Tsk! Tsk!" Robert shamed. "Have you no respect for your elders, man?" A moment of silence followed by an appreciative sigh gave evidence that Somerton had just taken a long sip of his favorite tipple. He chortled as he gave a warning: "Be careful now. I'll leave me fortune at some other's door, and you'll be hard-pressed to find another."

"You're drunk," Malcolm chided.

"Am I now?" Robert sucked his breath in through his teeth and might have delivered a retort if Mary had not come into the hall with a tray of clean glasses for the parlor and greeted her mistress.

"Good evenin', mum. 'Tis good to see that ye be feelin' better."

Lenore smiled lamely, not wishing to correct the young woman. Then since Mary hung back, Lenore preceded her into the parlor. Malcolm quickly rose from his chair and came forward, wearing a strange smile as his eyes caressed her. Stiffening slightly as his hand slipped behind her waist, she pressed trembling hands against her skirt to quell the urge to draw away.

"Come join us, Lenore. We have been severely starved for your beauty, and now you have given us a feast. It is difficult to take in such radiance with just a mere glance. Let us savor it at our leisure."

Robert pushed himself rather clumsily from his chair and held up his glass in salute to her. "I must agree. Surely the loveliest daughter a man could want." He liberally indulged himself in the toast, then with a knuckle lightly whisked both ends of his mustache upward. Clearing his throat, he stared down into his empty glass and then beckoned for Mary to fill it. "Be a good girl now and fetch me another whiskey."

Malcolm's forehead crinkled into a reproving frown as he escorted Lenore to the settee. "Shouldn't you wait until after dinner?"

With a casual wave of a hand Somerton dismissed the younger man's suggestion and spoke directly to the maid. "A splash or two more won't hurt, me dearie."

Uncertain as to what to do, the maid looked to Malcolm for approval and then, at his reluctant nod, replenished the libation. Rubbing his hands in anticipation, Robert chortled as the servant brought him the glass, and being in good spirits, began to recit a little verse. "Yestre'en the queen had four Marys, This night she'll hae but three; There was Mary Beaton, and Mary Seaton and Mary Carmichael, and"—he winked at the girl as he changed the ending to his liking—"and thee, me sweet Mary Murphy."

The young woman clapped a hand over her mouth to squelch a burst of giggles and hurried from the room. Malcolm observed her flight and, shaking his head at the antics of the pair, took a place beside Lenore on the settee. His gaze warmed as it rested upon her.

"Strange that you should choose to wear that gown this evening, my dear," he murmured, flicking the soft flounce with a finger.

"Strange? How so?" A small, worried frown flitted across her brow. She could not shake the notion that she had worn it for an important occasion. "Is there some special significance to this gown?"

A tender smile touched his lips. "You could say that, madam. It happens to be the gown you wore when we were married."

His words fell with a thud against her heart, heralding doom for all her romantic aspirations. She could only whisper a weak reply: "I didn't realize the gown was that old, or perhaps I've misjudged the time we were married. When did you say . . . ?"

"We married shortly after we met, madam. The gown has been kept well-preserved."

"Meghan found it wadded up in the trunk," she commented distantly, trying to remember when he had said they had become acquainted.

He dropped a hand upon hers and squeezed it in an affectionate manner. "I gave no heed to the details of packing while I worried for your safety. I had no idea where that madman had taken you."

Her gaze moved dully about the room, hardly caring what object it settled upon. A fireplace had been built into the east wall between two windows, and above the mantel hung a landscape that was not particularly exceptional. In fact, it was of mediocre quality, and it seemed somehow out of place with the rest of the fine furnishings. At the moment the presence of that painting exemplified her sentiments toward the two men. Despite repeated confirmations to the contrary, she felt as if the pair did not belong in her life. She wanted Ashton!

– *Chapter Ten* –

The soft, fuchsia hues of the breaking dawn swept outward in undulating rays from the eastern horizon and skimmed over the tossing surf, touching the white, foamy crests with a pinkish cast and awakening Lenore's heart to the beauty of the morning. Idly brushing her hair, she strolled out onto the veranda to view the sight at a better vantage point than her bedchamber allowed. The servants were in the kitchen, preparing the morning meal, and beyond her room the house was quiet except for the muffled snores drifting from Robert's room. She had come to think of him as "Robert" or "Mr. Somerton" rather than "Father" or some other endearment, for without a memory of him in her past, he meant nothing more to her. He was simply Robert Somerton. From the comments Ashton had made, she had known her father would be a hard man to deal with, yet she had not been prepared for his fondness for whiskey. He began each day with brandy-laced coffee, and from there it seemed any brand or variety would suffice as long as he had it in hand.

Her pale dressing gown swirled about her as an ocean-scented breeze swept across the porch, and she inhaled deeply, savoring its fragrance. Although it had scarce been more than a fortnight since her arrival, it seemed as if an eternity had passed since she had left Belle Chêne behind her and traveled to this house by the sea. She had spent several days in bed, wavering between reality and delirium; then at last the fever had left her, and she had been able to move about and acquaint herself with the house, with those who lived there, and with the surrounding area. It had not taken her long to realize that she had once loved this house and that she had been comfortable here. She knew every corner of it, every pleat of canopy and drape, the windowpanes framing trees that were now cast in summer's green array, but which she knew she had seen in autumn's hennaed splendor and in dreary winter's nakedness. She drew pleasure from the sound of the rushing waves and the sight of the seabirds swooping down to pluck tiny morsels from the shallows. She had glimpsed mere specks on the horizon and seen them advance toward land and become large ships with their white sails gleaming beneath the sun. When they swept in closer, she could almost feel the rolling deck beneath her feet and the full run of wind through her hair. More disturbing, she could also imagine a manly form pressed against her back and strong, sun-bronzed arms encompassing her.

Lenore turned with a trembling sigh and entered her room. It seemed of late she could not have a thought without the intrusion of that dream. It did not ease her plight to know who lurked behind every spoken word or conscious thought or to realize the yearnings of her heart could not be set aside.

Once again she went to the small writing desk and, with quill in hand, tried to compose a letter that would explain her position and circumstance to Ashton. She wanted the missive to be of such irrefutable logic that it would solve her dilemma before it reached the catastrophic proportions she feared it would. Though she struggled, the brilliant, clarifying phrases failed to come to mind, much less flow from pen to paper.

Shaking her head in mute frustration, Lenore leaned back in the chair and tried to focus her mind on the task at hand. Like playful children her thoughts drifted elsewhere, unwilling to go where she was wont to lead them. Absently she lifted the quill and spun it between her fingers, watching the play of light and shadow on the pearl white plume. A face formed in her memory, a strong, appealing visage that grinned rakishly as it drew near and turned slightly as a parting mouth reached to meet hers. . . .

"Ashton!" Her lips formed the name with a sigh, but her imagination plunged on in wild and reckless haste. She could almost feel the warming excitement of his hand moving beneath her robe and cupping her breast while his thumb lightly danced a rousing game upon its burning crest.

Breathing a small, helpless moan, she threw aside the quill and rose to pace the room. Her cheeks were hot with a blush, and she could not slow the thudding beat of her heart. Whenever she loosened the restraint on her will, her mind was wont to fly away with her, and she had begun to wonder if a willful Lierin wasn't hiding just behind the door of her memory, awaiting the opportunity to come forth and claim her mind and body.

The long mirror in the corner reflected her image, and Lenore paused to consider the soft, liquid glow in the eyes and the taut peaks, erect and thrusting beneath her gown. She rubbed her brow and resumed her restless meandering. As long as she yearned for Ashton so desperately, she knew she would never be satisfied as Malcolm's wife. His failure to find other accommodations had caused her a good measure of concern. The knowledge that his room was just down the hall had convinced her of the necessity of locking both the hall door and the french doors that led from her room. The resulting warmth and stuffiness was almost unbearable, but she did not dare ease her plight for fear of inviting a worse disaster.

Even now, she was wary of his whereabouts, for he seemed to come and go with the stealth of a disembodied spirit. He could, at will, walk across a room without her even sensing his presence. It unnerved her to turn and find him watching her with unswerving attention, and in that moment she knew exactly how a tiny mouse felt under the steady regard of a sleek and hungry cat. His eyes could undress her in a brief flicker, while his slow, self-assured smile gave promise of other abilities that could not be spoken of in good manner. He seemed to delight in flaunting his masculinity, as if this would entice her to his bed. The cut of his trousers might have been more generous than Ashton's, no doubt to accommodate the heavier-muscled buttocks and thighs, but the way they clung to him, she could only assume he wore nothing underneath, and the effect was intentional. The exhibition only made her more cautious and prompted her to barricade her bedroom doors with chairs, lest he try to prove his manhood with a more physical advance. She knew there would come a time when she would have to acquiesce and become the mate for this strutting peacock, but right now she would just as soon keep their relationship simple, at least until she learned the secret of getting Ashton out of her blood.

She was beginning to sense there was some underlying quality about each man that reminded her of the other, but as yet she could not quite decide what it was, whether it was something in their physical appearance, their mannerisms, or their personalities. Ashton was sensual and hot-blooded, but his appeal was more refined than the other man's. Perhaps his age accounted for his suavity, but with only a trace of a smile and a look from beneath those magnificent brows, he could emit waves of masculine attraction, yet at the same time catch her heart with a subtle essence of boyish charm. With his aristocratic features and princely bearing he was certainly the more handsome and appealing of the two.

Malcolm, however, was not without charm. He was good-looking, and at times she suspected it was something in his visage that stirred a memory of Ashton, yet when she studied his broader cheeks and full, sensual lips she gained no insight into the illusive mystery. She had no doubt that he had instigated many a carnal thought in the minds of women. It seemed exactly what he solicited by his cocky manner. There was a sternness in him too, which she glimpsed when her father imbibed too much or was wont to be effusive or to spill Shakespearean phrases in his cups. There was no big outward show of this, only a hardening in his eyes and around his mouth whenever he looked at the elder man. His irritation could be understood; Robert could test the patience of a saint at times, and she was not without her moments of sensitivity. Whenever the elder man maligned Ashton's character, she felt tempted to shred apart the concept of parental honor and give him a lambasting he would not soon forget. If he thought he was of such perfect reputation that he could defame the Wingate man, then he needed a clearer insight into his own flaws.

The thunderous approach of horses' hooves jarred Lenore from her musing and brought her flying to the french doors just in time to see the carriage careen up the drive and come to a skidding halt in front of the house. She knew the signature of Malcolm's reckless arrivals, for he was the only one who urged the driver to such a head-long pace. Although the height of his excitement or agitation was usually indicated by his haste, he needed no excuse to whip the horses into a frenzy. He seemed to thrive on speed, and the faster the race, the better he liked it.

The fact that he was returning at this early hour could only mean that he had spent the night elsewhere, and although this did not grieve her, Lenore could only wonder where he had finally found a room or with whom he had stayed. He had ridden off shortly after her father left with the carriage the night before. Much later she had heard the elder man's stumbling progress as he made his way to his room. In whatever fashion Robert had returned, it was without the benefit of the landau, and here was Malcolm coming home in it, with his horse tied behind.

She heard the thud of Malcolm's boots across the porch, the slam of the front door, which rattled every window in the house, and then his racing climb up the stairs. She braced herself as he came down the hall, wondering what she had done to set him off. Much to her surprise, his footsteps halted at the door across from her own, and without so much as a knock for admittance or regard for the one who slept inside, slammed the portal wide and barged into Somerton's room. If his entry did not wake the slumbering man, then his loud shout was meant to do just that. The men's voices engaged and then lowered to a muffled drone, broken now and again by Malcolm's angry bark. From somewhere deep within her Lenore sensed that her father of yesteryear would never have meekly submitted to such an attack, no matter the cause. It nettled her that he did not rouse himself from this subservient attitude and take firm hold of the argument. She was even more piqued at the cavalier manner with which Malcolm treated him. If her father was one to tolerate it, she was not.

Fastening the top frog of her dressing gown, she left her room and crossed the hall. At her knock the door was snatched open, and she found herself staring into Malcolm's blazing eyes. It was clear the spurs of rage still goaded him, but as his gaze fell on her, his manner changed abruptly to a more pleasant mien. For a leisured moment his gaze swept the curves the dressing gown could not hide; then he stood back, sweeping an arm inward.

"Come in, my dear," he bade with a smile. "I was just having a discussion with your father."

"So I heard," she rejoined dryly as she accepted his invitation.

Malcolm lifted a questioning brow at her disapproving tone. "Perhaps I should explain, madam. Your father made the rounds of all the taverns last night, forgetting where he had told the driver to wait. I not only wasted a whole night searching for him and the carriage, but at this early hour I have also heard some of the rumors this drunken braggart has invited upon us."

Lenore glanced toward the bed where her father sat in much humbled dejection. His shoulders were slumped, and his head hung low in shame. She could not justify the sight in her mind. Indeed, it would have seemed more natural to her if he had thrown Malcolm out on his ear for having dared insult him. She could not grasp any reasoning for that particular impression, but one thing she could clearly discern from the situation, and that was something in her own character. Despite the recent times he had irritated her, she was still his daughter, and she felt a strong inclination to defend him, just as she would any of her kin.

"I would be pleased, Malcolm, if you would take into consideration that he is my father. This is my house, and until I have some recollection of you as my husband, I can only think of you as a guest here. I don't care at the moment what rumors he has started, but I would greatly appreciate it if you would give him more respect, or at least stop abusing him in such a manner. If you cannot, you may leave . . . posthaste."

The dark eyes hardened perceptively as Malcolm returned her stare, and he opened his mouth as if to retort, but immediately squelched the desire and responded with a stiff smile: "Forgive me, my dear. I shall try to be more respectful in the future. I was only concerned about our reputation here in Biloxi and how your father might have damaged it."

Lenore smiled stiffly in response and, feeling a pang of pity for her father, considered his sorry state. He seemed bewildered by her defense and stared back at her with doleful eyes rimmed with red and bordered underneath with dark bags. His cheeks were limp and flaccid, much like the jowls of a hunting hound, and beneath a sagging chin his dewlap hung slack. A bristly stubble grayed the jaw, and the shirt he wore was soiled and rumpled, as if he had slept in his clothes. Growing restive beneath her regard, he tried to smooth the wrinkles from his vest and cast an anxious glance about for another container of that strong, amber liquid. To him, it was the restorer of joy in that it provided a blessed numbing for his conscience.

"I . . . ah . . ." He licked a mottled tongue over dry and cracked lips and cleared his throat. "I didn't mean to create a disturbance, and I can surely understand Malcolm's annoyance with me. No need for you to harp at him, girl. 'Twas all my fault. I should never have forgotten myself like that."

She glanced at Malcolm to receive his gratified smile and felt a strange inclination to wipe the smirk from his face with some caustic retort. She disliked his arrogance and the confident leer that came into his eyes when his gaze dipped to her bosom. The question of whether or not he was seeing something there which might have warranted the lustful gleam prompted her to issue a vague excuse and depart their company. Much to her consternation, Malcolm followed a few, brief moments later, bringing a thin valise and her father to her room. The older man stumbled in and brought himself up before the writing desk where she sat. Beneath the mildly questioning frown that marred her smooth brow, he twisted his hands self-consciously and gave an explanation for their visit.

"I . . . uh . . . Malcolm has . . . ah . . . some affairs he wishes to discuss with you, my dear." He swallowed heavily against the thickness in his throat, while his gaze roamed the room for the whiskey he had yet to find.

With the quill Lenore gestured toward the washstand. "There's some cool water in the ewer if you'd like a drink."

Somerton had difficulty subduing the tremor in his hands as he poured the liquid, and the lip of the pitcher rattled shakily against the rim of the glass. He could not suppress a shudder of distaste as he downed the unfermented draft, and when he glanced up, he was met with Malcolm's disdaining sneer. His ruddy cheeks darkened, and sheepishly he lowered the glass to stare down at it in shame.

Malcolm's displeasure took on a facade of gracious charm as he came to the desk. He bent to bestow a kiss upon his bride, but Lenore turned her face aside, and his lips fell upon her cheek. He cocked a wondering brow as she rose and moved to the other side of the desk.

"You had a matter you wished to discuss?" she probed.

Malcolm rested the thin valise on the table and removed from it a sheaf of formal papers. "I had a meeting with our attorneys in town this morning, and they informed me that these documents should be signed by you."

Casually Lenore swept her hand to indicate the desk top. "Leave them there, and I'll read through them sometime today." She glanced up as Malcolm shuffled the papers awkwardly and cleared his throat. Wondering what disturbed him, she asked, "Is there something wrong with that?"

"Nothing except the lawyers wanted them back by this afternoon. Your father has examined them all and given his approval. It's nothing too important, only some loose ends that need tying up."

"If you're in a hurry to return them, I can look them over now and let you take them back. It shouldn't take too long." She reached out a hand to receive them, but he frowned.

"Actually"—he returned the documents to the case—"I came back to get your father to sign them. We were both reluctant to leave you alone with just the servants here, and thought your signature might save us the trip." He snapped the case closed with finality.

Robert had turned his back upon the couple and, stepping out onto the veranda, flinched when the sunlight struck him full in the face. Retreating quickly into the shadow of the overhang, he leaned against the outer wall, needing its sturdy support. He let his gaze sweep the broad expanse of gray-blue sea beyond the beach, and then suddenly he straightened in alert attention. "What the blazes is that?"

Malcolm seriously doubted the possibility of Robert seeing anything worthwhile in his condition. Tucking the valise under his arm, he crossed to the french doors and paused there to speak to the elder. "Come on, Robert, you'll have to hurry and dress if we're going into . . ." He glanced out toward the sea as the elder continued to stare, then threw the cigar aside and ran to the outside balustrade. "What the bloody hell!"

Wondering what strange malady had affected the men, Lenore joined them on the porch and looked out to where a plume of black smoke was being belched into the air through tall, twin stacks that perched atop a black, gold, and white edifice. The riverboat labored against the tossing waves, but even as Lenore watched, an anchor splashed off the bow and another was tossed from the stern, tethering the craft several hundred yards offshore and squarely in front of the beach house.

"The *River Witch!*" Her lips formed the words, but no sound issued forth. She had no need to read the letters on the side of the steamer to recognize that huge white bulk with its black-and-gold trim. A sheathing of boards and canvas had been added to the outside of the lower railing, no doubt to keep the waves from washing over the deck.

The paddle wheel stopped its churning, and the ship lay back gently against her anchor chains. A tall figure emerged from the pilot house and paced aft a few steps to stand and stare toward the house with hands braced low on narrow hips. The strength dissolved from her limbs, leaving her knees quivery and weak as she recognized the stance. It was one she had often admired with the lusting eyes of a woman in love. Her heart began to beat with an overwhelming intensity in her breast, and she had to breathe in small gasps, for the fragrant air of jubilation was far too rich to savor all at once.

"It's him!" Malcolm showed his teeth in a savage snarl. "It's that bastard Wingate!" He bent an accusing stare first on Robert, who shrugged lamely, then upon Lenore, and his eyes flared with jealous rage as he questioned her: "Did you know about this? Did you send for him?" His eyes swept inward to the small desk where she had been sitting, taking in the trimmed quills in the ink stand and the paper. "You wrote him!" he accused. "You told him where we were!"

"No!" Lenore shook her head and did not dare show the emotions she was experiencing. Joy. Excitement. Pleasure. They ran together and mingled with a wildly racing exhilaration. Ashton was near! Ashton was near! Her mind kept repeating the words over and over. He had come to show his colors boldly and make it known to all that he wanted her, that he would not give up the battle so easily.

"But how could he . . . ?" Malcolm's voice trailed off as he frowned in bemusement; then he glanced up at her sharply. "Did he know you had a house in Biloxi?"

Lenore shrugged and spread her hands to convey her innocence. "I didn't have to tell him. He already knew."

"I should have known he'd find out," Malcolm muttered. "And that bastard found us, just like a hound smelling out a bitch in heat." He swung his head back and forth like an raging bull. "I know why he's come. He thinks to steal you back." He flung out a threatening finger toward the vessel as he loudly declared, "But he won't stay! I'll see to that! I'll get the sheriff and have him moved!"

Robert carefully lowered himself into a porch chair as he made comment: "I don't think there's anything you can do about it, Malcolm. The man's well in his rights. This may be our property, and if he dares trespass, we can have him seized, but the open sea belongs to anyone bold enough to venture upon it."

With irate strides Malcolm passed from the veranda and left the room, but in a moment he was back on the gallery with a twin-barreled hunting gun. "Just let him try coming ashore. I'll have him shot before he can set foot to dry ground."

Lenore's elation was promptly smothered beneath Malcolm's threats. There was no telling how far his hatred would push him, nor could she expect his anger to ebb before the two men met. Somehow she would have to warn Ashton not to come ashore, but how could she manage that?

"The only thing about firearms," Somerton mumbled, "is that one can never be quite sure of the other man's abilities. We heard that Wingate is a dangerous man to tangle with. If he's as good a shot as they say, I'd advise you to take care."

Lenore stared at her father in surprise, remembering the afternoon when he had come to Belle Chêne and boasted of Malcolm's skill with firearms. Now here he was warning that same man of his rival's reputation. What sort of game was he playing?

"He may be good," Malcolm sneered, "but I think not good enough." He looked smug as he caressed the barrel of the weapon. "The only way Wingate will be able to leave here without confronting me is to turn that damned boat around and go back to New Orleans."

"Do you plan to watch the steamer all the time?" Somerton inquired in amazement.

Malcolm turned to glower over his shoulder, bestowing it on the elder man. "No, *Papa*, you're going to help me."

The winged brows shot up in surprise and then gathered in a disturbed frown. "I'll watch for you, but I won't touch that fowling piece. I don't know the first thing about guns."

Malcolm smiled blandly. "You won't need to. I intend to keep that pleasure for myself."

A strange, brooding uneasiness crept over Lenore and settled as a cold lump in the pit of her stomach. Something was wrong, but she was not quite sure what. She could only lay it to her concern for Ashton and expressed her worry in a timid question: "You wouldn't really murder him, would you?"

Malcolm's answer was cold and deliberate: "It won't be murder, my dear. I have a right to protect what is mine, and it should be obvious to all of us what the man intends. He's come to steal you away from me."

"Perhaps if you let me talk with him," she cajoled. "I'm sure he'll leave if I explain that I'm here of my own free will."

Malcolm tossed his head up with a short, jeering laugh. "I've heard about your precious Mr. Wingate. Nothing can deter him if he wants something badly enough." He strode along the balustrade without taking his eyes off the distant vessel and slowly retraced his steps in the same manner. "The man has his gall, anchoring offshore like that, right there where he can spy on us." Becoming more incensed, Malcolm threw a hand toward the steamer. "Look at him! He's even gotten himself a glass!"

Somerton squinted bloodshot eyes toward the vessel, trying to focus on the one who provoked them. The long brass cylinder glinted beneath the sun as the other stared through it, making it easier for Somerton to spot it. "By jove, so he has."

Lenore could hardly keep her own gaze from wandering to that tall figure. She could almost feel the touch of Ashton's unswerving stare through the glass. Her cheeks were flushed, but it had naught to do with the morning heat.

"I wish I had a dozen cannons right now," Malcolm ground through his teeth. "I'd blow that bloody fool out of the water just to see him come sailing down in tiny pieces."

Lenore felt a desperate need to try again. "Would you let me send him a letter?"

"*No!*" Malcolm barked. "He can sit out there until I figure a way to get to him; then I'll make sure he won't bother us ever again. He'll soon know which of us is the better man."

Joy was as irresistible as the tide. It came sweeping back upon Lenore when the men left her to her thoughts. The knowledge that Ashton had cared enough to come after her made her almost giddy, and for a time she thrust aside the qualms that Malcolm's threats had provoked and relented to the pleasure of knowing that Ashton was near. She pressed both hands to her mouth to squelch an insane giggle of sheer happiness, while her shoulders trembled with the effort to suppress the urge. Meghan was puttering about the room, readying her bath, and it seemed foolish to rouse the woman's suspicions when she had found no cause to trust her. Still, it was difficult to contain her elation, especially when the maid would glance toward her as if she sensed some change. Finally curiosity had its way.

"Be ye feelin' all right, mum?" Meghan inquired.

Lenore nodded eagerly and tried to hide the threatening smile as she lowered her hands to her lap. "Yes." She cleared her throat to disguise the laughter in her tone. "Why do you ask?"

Meghan pursed her mouth as she regarded her mistress. During these last weeks she had watched the young woman and been saddened by the way she had resigned herself to her fate and dutifully gone through the motions required of her while in the men's presence, but in her chambers the girl had moped and stared wistfully out to sea as if longing for something more. Now the green eyes danced with a lively élan, and for the first time since coming to the house the mistress seemed really alive. Earlier the angry voices of the men had carried into the house from the veranda, and Meghan had found it hard to ignore them. They had declared there was a man on board the steamer who intended to take the lady, and as Meghan considered the transformation, she determined it would not be entirely by force.

"Ye needn't be afraid o' me, mum," she assured her mistress. "I've formed no loyalties to Mr. Sinclair, if that's what ye be thinkin'."

Lenore stared at the maid, somewhat taken aback by her perception, and sought to hide behind a cloak of innocence, afraid to reveal the secrets of her heart. "Whatever are you talking about, Meghan?"

The woman folded her hands over her apron and inclined her head toward the stern-wheeler. "I know there's a man out there who's come here for ye, an' by the shine on yer face, I'd say ye're not too disappointed."

Lenore's eyes widened in alarm. She bounced from the bed and, rushing to Meghan, grasped her arm with an intense admonition: "You mustn't tell anyone that I'm glad he's here. Not anyone. Especially Mr. Sinclair or my father. Please. They both hate Mr. Wingate, and I don't know what either of them will do."

"Rest yer worries, mum," Meghan soothed, taking the slender hands within her own. "I was in love once meself, so I understand what ye be feelin'."

Lenore was still careful. "How much do you know about me?"

With a shrug the maid replied, "Oh, I've heard the men talkin' an' know about ye losin' yer memory an' maybe thinkin' ye were married to someone else." She paused as a realization dawned and looked at her mistress closely, meeting that one's hesitant gaze. "It's him, isn't it? I mean, it's that Mr. Wingate ye thought was yer husband?"

Lenore lowered her eyes from the other's probing stare and could see no reason to lie when the woman read her so well. "Yes, and I love him, but I'm trying hard not to. . . ."

"A real task ye've laid for yerself, mum. I can see that."

A slow nod of agreement came from Lenore. To cease caring for him would be difficult indeed, if not totally impossible.

*   *   *

The small desk clock had struck the second hour in delicate tones, while the larger timepiece in the downstairs hall seemed to echo its refrain in the silent house. Lenore did not pause as she carefully molded the shape of the pillows beneath the sheet. A moment later she stood back to survey her handiwork. A silvery shaft of moonlight streamed in through the windows, casting enough light over the bed so that anyone who came to look would have a view of her form. Under casual inspection, the pillows would add to the deception that she was still asleep, granting her enough time to slip out of the house and carry word out to Ashton that he must not come ashore. Malcolm's threats had taken on a more serious note at dinner, and uncertain as to what he might do, she had made the determination that Ashton had to be warned. The chore boy had left the small dinghy near the water's edge when he had gone fishing the day before, and it would provide her a way out to the *River Witch*. At her request, Meghan had borrowed some of the lad's clothing but had carefully refrained from asking why she might have need of them, preferring to remain ignorant of her intentions.

Lenore stuffed the long, softly curling mass of auburn hair beneath a cap and wrinkled her nose in distaste as she checked her appearance in the standing mirror. The clothes were hardly the sort a genteel lady would wear. The shirt had no buttons to speak of, and she had tied it in a knot at her waist to hold it secure, leaving a deeply plunging décolletage. The breeches fit well enough, but were worn thin by age and use. The placket had no other fastenings except the cord that drew the garment tight about her waist. In all, she presented quite a wanton sight, and if she were caught, she might be accused of blatantly inviting rape. Just to be safe, she added a worn canvas coat.

As she prepared to leave, she paused beside the hall door and held an ear against the panel to listen. From the loud snores emerging from her father's room, she could suppose that Malcolm's chastening had convinced him that he should stay home for the night. That of course left only Malcolm to be wary of, but he was the one she feared most. He would not accept lame excuses. If she was caught, he would know immediately where she was bound.

Taking up a pair of string sandals, she slipped out onto the veranda and paused in the shadows to watch for any warning signs of movement. None were seen, and she continued her careful flight, easing down the stairs one slow step at a time. The bottom tread creaked slightly as her weight came upon it, and with bated breath she waited for a commanding shout to halt her flight. When none came and the flow of life returned to her fear-numbed body, she sprinted across the lower porch and hurried down the steps. She paused on the last to slip her feet into the sandals, then took off again across the lawn. The dinghy had been pulled up on the sand, and she placed the oars in the oarlocks and, with a fierce determination, dragged the heavy boat into the softly lapping waves.

Several lanterns had been lighted on the decks of the steamer, and the windows of Ashton's quarters showed a faint glow. Turning her back on those directing beacons, she began to row out, now and then casting a glance over her shoulder to check her direction. It soon became apparent that she had misjudged the distance between the shore and the stern-wheeler. It was not long before her arms began to tremble and ache from the unaccustomed labor, and when she reached the craft, she rested over the oars, letting the dinghy bob against the side of the steamer while she waited for her strength to return. The tremor would not leave her arms, and it seemed only an effort of will would overcome her lagging energy. Gathering what she could from that source, she chose a dark spot near the stern to make her ascent, just in case Malcolm or Robert glanced toward the steamer, and with painter in hand pulled herself up, climbing over the planks that protected the lower deck. The difficult feat of boarding accomplished, she knotted the rope around a post and sagged against the deck to let some of the tension ease from her arms.

There were no lanterns nearby to reveal an approaching form, and she was not quite sure when she began to sense someone standing over her, but when the full realization struck, she rolled with a startled gasp, trying to avoid the hands that reached down to seize her. One grabbed her knee, while another the collar of the loose coat. Her panic was spurred on by the painful grasp, and she gave no thought to explaining her presence as she struggled frantically to free herself. Like a slippery eel she slithered out of the garment, leaving it in the man's hand. She fell forward with a grimace as he tightened his hold on her leg, then his free hand dipped down to catch the back of her shirt, and her eyes widened in sudden dismay as she felt the knot come free. The armholes bit into her skin as the shirt caught, and then there was a long, rending tear as the garment split and made its departure. With a muffled cry she ducked and gathered her arms close over her naked bosom, trying to twist away before her modesty was completely savaged. The man growled a low curse and caught her again, this time by the arm while he hooked his other hand inside her belt. He snatched her up, nearly jerking the breath from her as the rope bit into her waist, and gave her a harsh shake.

"Who sent you out here, boy?" the man barked in her ear.

"*Ashton!*" Her gasp was one of relief as she recognized the deep voice. Never in her limited recall had she heard such a beautiful sound.

"What the . . ." The hard fingers relaxed their grip immediately. "Lierin?"

Even with the covering of darkness she could feel his closely peering perusal. A blush warmed her cheeks as his gaze dipped to her bosom, and timidly she hugged her arms across her chest.

Ashton knew not what miracle had brought reality to his dream, and though he was most appreciative of her apparel, or the lack of it, there was a need for haste. "For whatever reason you've come, my love, I'm deeply grateful," he murmured huskily, "but I think we should adjourn to my quarters, considering the man on watch will be making his rounds along this deck any moment now."

Lenore was spurred to action at the idea of being caught in such disarray and made an abbreviated plea as she hurried toward his cabin. "My shirt . . ."

Ashton swept up the garments and followed, stepping close behind her when she halted at the door and fumbled with the knob. His arm came around in front of her to perform the service, and Lenore closed her eyes and shivered with suppressed longings as his hard, furred chest pressed against her bare back. The contact was no less explosive for Ashton. It sent the hot blood rushing into his loins, and somewhere between the opening and closing of the door, her coat and shirt left his other hand. Her pale shoulders gleamed in the golden glow of the cabin lamp, inflaming his mind with the sight. His arm curled about her, gathering her close, and a low moan slipped from Lenore as his hands began a questing search of her soft breasts. The cap tumbled to the floor as she leaned her head back against his shoulder and the loosely curling tresses spilled free, filling his head with a heady fragrance. The thin breeches gave her little protection from the burning heat of his arousal or the hand that stroked beneath them. This was not what she had come for, but every nerve and fiber of her being cried out for him to take her, to make her his own again. It was agony to think of denying him.

"We mustn't . . ." she pleaded in a frail, weak whisper. "Ashton, please . . . we cannot do this thing now."

"We must," he breathed against her ear and pressed fevered kisses upon her throat. To have her close again fulfilled every notion of what was right for him. "We must . . ."

He bent and lifted her in his arms. In two long strides he was to the bed, that same haven wherein they had in times past enjoyed the full tide of rapturous bliss. He laid her down, and his burning gaze swept her in a longing caress; then he was there beside her, taking her in his arms again. Lenore placed a hand upon his naked chest and turned her face aside, trying to avoid his heady kisses before they besotted her mind. "I only came here to warn you, Ashton." Her tone was one of desperation. "Malcolm will try to kill you if you come ashore. You must go away."

Ashton lifted his head and stared down at her with hungering hazel eyes. Sometimes love could come and go like the errant winds that were wont to sweep the shore; then again, it could be a timeless thing that distance, years, and hardships could not defeat. For Ashton it had been around for more than a trio of years, and she was rooted at the very core of his life. The note she had left was meant to convince him that she was Lenore and that she was doing the right thing, but how could he agree when she had taken his heart with her? "Forget Malcolm and all he's tried to tell you. Stay with me, Lierin, and I will leave here. If need be, I'll take you to the ends of the earth."

Tears began to course down her cheeks. "Oh, Ashton, can't you see? You want her and not me."

"I want *you!*"

"I'm not the woman you think I am, Ashton. I'm Lenore, not Lierin."

"Your memory . . ." he began hesitantly, almost fearfully. "Has it returned?"

"No." She did not dare meet his gaze. "But I must be Lenore. My own father has said I am."

"Your father hated me, remember. He has cause to hold us apart if he can."

"He wouldn't go that far," she argued.

Ashton let his breath out in a long sigh. "If you insist, I'll call you Lenore, but it changes nothing. In my heart you're still my wife . . . you're still part of me."

"You must leave here," she urged anxiously. "You must go and save yourself."

"Will you come with me?" he pressed.

"I can't, Ashton." Her voice was tiny. "I must go back. I must know the truth."

"Then I will stay . . . and I will fight for you until this thing is settled."

"Oh, please . . . please, Ashton," she begged wearily. "I won't be able to bear it if anything happens to you."

"I can't go back. I am bound to stay."

She shook her head in exasperation. "You're as stubborn as they say you are. Why don't you accept the inevitable?"

"The inevitable?" He rolled on his back with a harsh laugh and stared up at the low ceiling above his bed. "For three years I searched, but I could find no woman to take your place. I was a man, and yet I could not settle back into the relaxed standards of a rutting bachelor. I had this burning hunger in my loins that haunted me, but I could find no release. Call me bedeviled. Call me mad. Call me hopelessly and completely in love with a dream that only you can fulfill." Rolling his head on the pillow, he gazed at her. "I know what it was like without you, and I want no more of it. I have come to fight, my love, and fight I will."

Lenore raised herself until she rested on his chest. She made no effort to pull the sheet between them, but allowed her naked breasts to press upon that bare and broad expanse. Her eyes were tender with devotion as they caressed his face, and her lips curved in a wistful smile. "We make a pair, the two of us, wanting what we cannot have. I must go back, and you are determined to stay. Yet if I could, I would persuade you differently." She hesitated a moment; then somewhat ashamed of the proposal she was about to make, she continued without meeting his gaze: "If I give myself to you now, for the moment allowing that you may be right in thinking I am your wife, will you leave before some harm comes to you?"

Ashton lifted her until she lay full length upon him. There was no mistaking his ability to accept her offer, but he slowly shook his head. "I cannot make such a pact, my love, even though it would serve to ease my present desire. I love you too much to be satisfied with a parting gesture. I want all of you, and I will settle for nothing less."

She heaved a weary sigh. "Then I must go."

"There's no need to leave now. Stay with me for a while. Let me love you."

"It's not right anymore, Ashton. I belong to Malcolm now."

A deep scowl drew his brows down sharply, and he glanced away, tormented with jealousy. The muscles in his cheeks twitched as he resisted the urge to tell her how he had found the precise location of the house. A tour of the taverns in Biloxi had turned up not only a handful of Robert's drinking cronies but an interesting array of strumpets as well. It seemed more than a few had serviced the libertine Sinclair. "I don't like the thought of your going back to him."

"I must," she whispered. A light brush of her lips against his, and she slipped away from him. Smiling down into the eyes that watched her, she donned the torn shirt and jacket and gathered her hair beneath the cap.

"I'll take you back," he sighed, swinging his long legs over the side of the bed and rising to his feet.

The memory of the exhausting trip was fresh in Lenore's mind, and she was not anxious to argue with him. "But how will you get back?"

"I'll tie another dinghy behind and return in that." He reached for a shirt and felt her hand glide admiringly over his flexing ribs as he slipped it on. The gentle caress made him tremble with longing, and he stared down at her, wanting to take her in his arms but knowing there would be no turning back if he yielded to the desire. His mouth moved to whisper the words that were aching to be said: "I love you."

"I know," she murmured quietly, "and I love you."

"If I didn't think you'd grow to hate me, I'd keep you here, but it's a choice you'll have to make. Until you do, I'll be near enough to come to your aid if you should need me." He placed a small derringer in her hand. "I've shown you how to use this. I can hear a shot from the house. Just keep out of harm's way until I get there."

He took her back to shore, and after a last parting kiss, Lenore made her way to the upper veranda. She leaned against the balustrade as she watched him row out, then entered her room, heaving a forlorn sigh. She was already lonely.

- Chapter Eleven -

The muffled weeping became a reality that intruded into Lenore's slumber with the same rude gall as the morning light that pierced the panes of the east windows. Both were annoying and equally difficult to dismiss as she sought to retreat to the sweet solace of sleep. After returning from the *River Witch*, she had drifted immediately into a peaceful bliss of dreams. She dearly longed to spend the morning in that same languid slumber, letting the rest of the world pass by. It was not to be. One hazard of having a room with numerous windows and wide french doors that faced the sea and sat at an angle to the southern hemisphere was its vulnerability to the rising sun. The dawning rays spread across her bed in a radiating brightness, while the sorrowful sobs relentlessly pursued her beneath her pillow. There, the realization finally penetrated that someone on the porch was grieving.

Coming fully awake, Lenore flung herself from the bed and snatched on her dressing gown as she flew to the french doors. She ran out onto the veranda and, casting her gaze along the porch, saw Meghan standing near the balustrade. Heavy sobs shook the woman's shoulders as she stared teary-eyed toward the beach. In much bemusement Lenore followed the woman's gaze and saw Malcolm and Robert near the dinghy. Two other men were peering under a piece of canvas that was spread across the boat, something which had not been present when she and Ashton left the craft. She was puzzled by their apparent interest in the boat and even more confused by the servant's weeping.

"Meghan, what's wrong?" Lenore went to the maid and laid a comforting arm about her trembling shoulders. "Whatever is the matter?"

The woman struggled to form the words to answer her mistress, but her efforts seemed in vain as tears continued to spill down her plump cheeks. "It's Mary, mum," the servant finally managed. "The chore boy was going out early this morning to see if he could catch some fish for tonight's supper, and he found Mary dead and naked in the boat. The sheriff says she was murdered."

"Murdered?" Lenore stared at the woman, too stunned to grasp the realization. Mary had seemed so sweet and eager to please; she could hardly believe that anyone would want to hurt her. She blinked at the moisture that welled in her own eyes and spoke in a tone of dismay: "But I took the dinghy myself and rowed out to the *River Witch*. Mr. Wingate brought me back about four this morning."

"Oh, mum, ye'd better not tell the sheriff that. Mr. Sinclair is claimin' that she was killed by someone on the *River Witch*, an' if he finds out yer man was here on shore, he's sure to accuse him."

"But that's nonsense! I saw Ashton row back to the steamer in his own boat. I had a better chance at murdering her than he did."

Meghan shook her head dolefully. "She was raped, mum."

"Raped?" Lenore repeated the word with a gasp. "But who would do such a thing?"

"I don't know, mum. I was fast asleep meself, an' it weren't until the lad come screamin' through the house that I had any inklin' o' what had been done to that poor, dear chil'. What of ye, mum? Did ye see anyone on the beach after Mr. Wingate left?"

"No, no one at all," Lenore answered. Nor had she heard any sound out of the ordinary, only the muffled snores coming from her father's room. Once within the comfort of her bed, she had been lulled into a sweet, dreamy oblivion, thinking of Ashton, and nothing had disturbed that peace. "What is the sheriff going to do?"

"Well, mum, I s'pose he's goin' to be questionin' the lot o' us an' then yer Mr. Wingate an' his crew. Mary an' the coachman were sweet on each other, so Henry might be the one to really catch it. He seems like such a nice man, though."

Lenore's knees turned to jelly as invading impressions sought to push their horror upon her. The vision of the man being beaten by a poker was now familiar to her, but in a momentary glimpse she saw the darkly cloaked form of the murderer begin to whirl upon her with the iron still clasped in his hand. A cold sweat made her skin clammy as the illusion faded, but it was a full moment before she could clear her mind of the haunting fear and return her thoughts to the present moment. She took several deep breaths to slow her racing heart and made a belated observation: "The murderer doesn't have to be any of the men around here, Meghan. If Mary was working in Biloxi before she came here, she could have attracted someone from town."

Meghan wiped at the wetness on her cheeks. "Mary didn't know too much about this area, mum, so if she was here before the master hired her, it wasn't for very long. Seems like she was born around Natchez or one of the neighboring towns there."

"Natchez?" Lenore's attention perked up. "That's where Mr. Wingate is from. Perhaps he might have known her."

"Ye can bet the sheriff will be askin' him that, mum, an' I s'pose we'll just have to wait to see what he finds out." The maid gave a nod toward the men who were now approaching the house. "They're comin' to begin their inquiries."

Suddenly reminded of her dishabille, Lenore drew the collar of her dressing gown close about her neck. "I'd better make myself presentable."

"I'll fetch some water for ye," Meghan said with a wavering sigh. "It'll do me good to be about me duties an' get me mind off Mary."

A half hour's progress in the toilette saw Lenore gowned in a pale blue gown and the maid smoothing the auburn tresses into a sedate chignon. Lenore had been expecting Malcolm to bring her news of the girl's demise, and she was not surprised when a light rapping sounded on her door. Admitted by the maid, he strolled across the room to the dressing table and casually leaned a shoulder against the wall where he reflected on the beauty of the one who sat before the silvered glass. She seemed cool and serene, like the snow queen he had come to think of her as. There were times when he was tempted to break through that thin barrier of ice and have his will with her, but the uncertainty of how she would react made him subdue those lustful urgings. One day in the near future he fully expected to reap the rewards of his caution and patience.

"I guess Meghan has told you about Mary." He posed the statement with a brow raised in question and waited for the affirmative nod before he continued. "The incident has us all in shock. First, it was your kidnapping and now this has happened. I don't really think the two are related, but for the sake of caution, it would be best if you didn't venture out alone. Especially while that steamer is out there."

"Malcolm . . ." Lenore braced her hands on the edge of the dressing table as she prepared herself for delivering the truth. "I know you're going to be angry, but I went out to the *River Witch* during the night. . . ."

"You *what!*" Malcolm barked, startling Meghan, who dropped the brush. "You went out there behind my back! To that debaucher! To your sister's murderer! You gave yourself to him, when there's no telling what he might have done to Mary?"

Lenore came to her feet with green sparks of rage flashing in her eyes. Before she released the full tide of her anger, she glanced toward Meghan, who was wringing her hands in consternation and gestured her from the room. "Leave us, Meghan. I have something to discuss with"—she formed the words with reluctance—"my husband."

Meghan hesitated out of concern for her mistress, but the slender hand waved again, giving her no choice in the matter. Stepping from the room, the maid closed the door behind her, and though she was not one to eavesdrop, she stayed near, just in case there should be a need. Though she had never married, she knew how men could be about their wives, especially with one so beautiful, and Meghan was fearful that the clash between the two would prove harmful to the lady.

"How dare you say those things to me in front of a servant!" Lenore stormed. "For your information I did not give myself to Ashton. I only went out there to ask him to leave." Hot and seething, she turned and flounced across the room as she poured out her fury. "Since I have been in this house, I have heard his name defamed at every turn, and neither you nor my father knows anything about him."

"Ah, but you do," Malcolm flung back at her, equally incensed. He had no idea what there was about the other man that so intrigued her, but she had loved *him* once. He was sure of it, or she would never have married him. "You rebuke us, but all the while you're wanting him. Tell me it isn't so!"

Lenore bit back the retort that would have confirmed his accusation. She wanted to admit her love, but she also knew the folly of doing so. "I came to respect Ashton while I was at Belle Chêne. . . ."

Malcolm slammed his fist down on the dressing table as he shouted, "I say it's more than respect you feel!"

Her chin lifted in a lofty manner. "I resent the fact that you're trying to put words in my mouth, words that I have no intention of saying," she declared. "Since the accident with Ashton's carriage, my memory has been closed up in a dark box within my head, and I have no way to open it. I remembered nothing about you, but Ashton was kind to me, and while I was at Belle Chêne, I truly believed I was his wife. It seemed natural. . . ."

"But it's not natural for you to think of me as your husband," he interjected accusingly. "Isn't that what you're trying to say?"

"You keep jumping ahead of me and reconstructing my statements without hearing me out," she protested. "I wasn't going to say that at all."

"You've said it before," he retorted. "Maybe not in the same exact way, but the words all mean the same."

Lenore closed her eyes and rubbed her temples where a dull ache had begun to throb. Her tension was mounting, and confusing visions began to assail her. Through a long, dark tunnel she saw Ashton leaning against the railing of his steamer, and then gnarled hands stretching forth to seize her and snatching her by her long hair. Laughing faces pressed down upon her, while thick fingers tore at her clothing. She could almost taste the threat of rape, and in her mind she screamed. Then, quite clearly, she saw Malcolm above her, tossing the men aside. Almost gently he reached down to lift her in his arms.

A light frown touched her brow as she peered at him in bewilderment. Was it a memory of him she had glimpsed, or something she had conjured in her imagination? He had never spoken of a time when he had rescued her.

"Listen to me, Lenore. Hear me out," he demanded. "Whether you remember me or not, I'm still your husband, and I will not tolerate you sneaking out to see that man again!"

"With all your threats of killing, what was I to do?" she cried. "Stay in my room and watch you murder him? Never!"

"Lower your voice," Malcolm cautioned curtly. "The sheriff is still in the house, and you might give him ideas."

"Good!" She was becoming reckless, but she was too fired up to care. Her eyes glittered with ill-suppressed ire as they met his challenging glower. "Perhaps he'll decide to lend Ashton some protection after hearing how you've threatened him."

"Shush, woman. We'll talk about this later." He cut the conversation short with an angry slash of his hand.

Outside the door Meghan scampered quickly away as she heard footsteps approach the portal, and for the first time that morning a smile touched her face. She had been fearful that her mistress could not hold her own against Mr. Sinclair's sometimes overbearing nature and, now being of a different mind, admired the spunk of the young woman.

After the argument with Malcolm, Lenore found the sheriff's interrogation much like a pleasant stroll through a park. He was polite, if somewhat direct. After introducing himself as James Coty, he asked what was her association with the owner of the *River Witch* and if she thought any of the crew were capable of the murder.

"Mr. Sinclair has no doubt explained my loss of memory to you." With his verifying nod she continued: "Ashton Wingate believed that I was Lierin, my twin sister, whom he married three years ago. For a time I was also convinced of that. As for the men on the steamer, I have traveled with them, and while I did, they treated me with the utmost respect. I can't believe they'd abuse a woman in such a manner, but even if they had, they'd have had little time to do so, because I took the dinghy out to the *River Witch* myself and didn't return until after four in the morning." She met his surprised gaze squarely and without shame. "I went out to the steamer with the hope of persuading Mr. Wingate to leave before trouble started between him and my husband. If my word is not enough to convince you, ask the man who had the watch on board the steamer. He might have noticed someone else leaving the craft after we did."

"You say you didn't return until after four?" he asked and thoughtfully stroked his chin. "That only makes me wonder when the crime was actually committed. Obviously Mary was killed somewhere else and then dumped into the boat."

Lenore overcame her reluctance and plucked up her courage to ask, "Can you tell me in what manner Mary was murdered?"

"Strangled," the sheriff replied bluntly. "The man choked her so hard he broke her neck."

Recoiling in shuddering revulsion, Lenore sank into a nearby chair and clasped a shaking hand over her brow. Feeling faint and queasy, she could give no more than a nominal reply to the lawman, who assured her that he would not rest until the man was caught. Sheriff Coty took his leave, and listlessly she dragged herself to her bed where she remained for most of the day, too sick to lift her head from the pillow.

The cemetery was small, and even with the green touch of summer, it seemed drab and somehow forlorn. Gowned in black, Lenore felt as if she blended in with her surroundings. Her cheeks were pale, and dark circles made her eyes look that much larger. She waited in the landau with her father until the minister arrived, not willing to subject herself to any unnecessary movement when it was so stifling hot. A few light whiffs of the smelling salts seemed to clear her head and settle her queasiness, enough at least to allow her to leave the safety of the carriage. Solicitously her father escorted her to the graveside where Malcolm was waiting. Carefully avoiding the dark hole where the coffin had been placed, she lifted her gaze to the large knot of mourners who had gathered on the far side and, except for the sheriff and his deputy, found no familiar face among them. Since word had spread swiftly throughout the area, she judged many of these were curiosity seekers and nothing more. Behind the family and somewhat to their right Meghan stood with the coachman, and both added a sorrowful note with their muffled weeping. Lenore glanced back in sympathy to see how the grieving woman was faring and was startled when her gaze swept beyond them and found a short, dark-haired man with liquid eyes.

"Mr. Titch!" She barely breathed his name, but she drew Malcolm's inquiring regard.

"Did you say something, my dear?" he asked and leaned his head down to receive her reply.

Her nod surreptitiously marked the short man. "I was just a little surprised to see that man over there, that's all."

Malcolm turned his head to look over his shoulder and raised a brow in amused condescension. "Ahh, Mr. Titch."

"Do you know him?" she queried in surprise, unable to remember a time when she had mentioned Mr. Titch or the trouble he had caused.

"Gossips are as abundant in Natchez as in Biloxi or anywhere else, madam. I've heard of him, and if Horace has wandered through any of the taverns where your father has been, I'm sure he knows as much about us as anyone here. If you aren't aware of it, my dear, we've become quite the topic around here. Especially with that high-and-mighty Mr. Wingate sitting on our front door. . . ." He paused as his gaze lifted above her head, and the dark eyes hardened and became cold and piercing. "Speak of the devil."

Lenore glanced around, wondering who had darkened his day so abruptly; then her heart began to race as she saw the one who brightened hers. Ashton! The name filled her mind with sudden pleasure and somehow strengthened her for the task ahead.

A slight twist of those firm lips produced a vague smile, and with gentlemanly manner Ashton tipped his beaver hat to them before his eyes met hers with warm communication. The unspoken words of devotion were there, waiting for her to seize and take close to her heart. She did not let them go to waste, but thoroughly savored them.

Now that he had been discovered by the couple, and he could not peruse them unaware, Ashton strolled to a spot near the end of the grave where he hoped his presence would rub like a burr against the other's composure. There, he could also watch Lierin . . . or, as she would have it, Lenore. If he should choose to use that name, it was by no means indicative of any concession he was making, merely a temporary compromise until the truth of her identity could be cleared up. In his heart she was still Lierin, and if the investigation proved him wrong, he would be hard-pressed to bow out gracefully. Whether Lierin or Lenore, he knew he loved the woman herself, for the memories of the past were being overshadowed by the more recent ones they had made together.

Although unobtrusively, Lenore regarded him in return, admiring the fine figure he presented in his coal-gray coat, coal-and-pale-gray-striped cravat, and muted striped trousers of a slightly lighter shade of gray. As always, his shirt was crisp and white, and the boots, showing beneath the long, narrow-fitting trousers, were polished to a glossy black sheen. The summer had darkened his skin until the hazel eyes seemed to sparkle with a light of their own behind their sooty lashes. They put a shine in her own when once again their gaze merged and held.

The small, somber group waited in solemn silence as the minister sprinkled a handful of dirt over the casket and droned the words "Ashes to ashes and dust to dust . . ."

Lenore reached up a hand to brush away the tears that streamed down her cheeks and swallowed against the sorrow welling up in her chest. A smothered sob came from Meghan before the maid turned to console the coachman, who dissolved into harsh weeping. Robert Somerton reached inside his coat and, pulling out a flask, tipped it to his mouth with quick, short jerks. Malcolm was inattentive to the proceedings, for his stoical regard was centered on Ashton and was only broken when the latter brushed past and moved behind them again. A quick glance over the shoulder assured Malcolm that the other was moving toward Mr. Titch, and if he showed any sign of relaxing, it was in the slight drooping of his heavy shoulders as his tension eased.

"'Morning, Mr. Titch." Ashton greeted the man with a meager nod; then leaning his head back, he cast an eye toward the gloomy gray heavens as he casually remarked, "An appropriate day for a funeral, isn't it?"

"I suppose," Horace mumbled, directing a clandestine glance toward the taller man. "A bit hot for my taste, though. Maybe a rain would cool things off."

"Either that or make it more humid," Ashton replied pleasantly, noticing the sweat trickling down the other's round face. He wondered if that was due entirely to the heat, or if something else was stirring up Mr. Titch's lather. "I was quite surprised to see you here, Horace. Are you visiting relatives?"

"Yes . . ." Horace bit his lip as the lie slipped out. He would have told it gladly, but he was afraid that Ashton would carry the tale back to the sheriff, and it would start a whole avalanche of investigations. He dusted off his sleeve, striving to appear as nonchalant as his adversary, but for some reason he always missed reaching that goal when the other was around. "Actually, Marelda wanted to come to Biloxi . . . to see the ocean . . . or something."

Ashton reflected on the man's answer, remembering when he had told Marelda about Leirin owning property here. Knowing the woman as well as he did, he could not believe that it was only chance and coincidence that had brought the couple here. Marelda could be a woman of positive action sometimes, and he was most curious as to what had compelled her to come. Ashton watched the other closely as he asked, "Did you perhaps know the young woman who was murdered?"

Horace sniffed pompously. "Have you now taken on duties as sheriff, Ashton, that you think you can question me?"

"Not at all." Ashton observed the stilted anger of the squat man. "Sheriff Coty showed me the girl's body, and at the time I remarked that she looked familiar, but I couldn't place just where I had seen her before. Then when I saw you here today, it began to come back to me." He caught the nervous tick at the corner of the man's eyelids and watched the stubby hands mop at the heavily sweating brow. "Am I wrong in thinking that Mary worked for your sister for a while?"

The eyelids lowered over those dark, liquid pools as Horace silently cursed himself for coming. That had been so long ago, he had thought no one would remember. Reining in his panic, he put on a show of bravado and glared up at the other. "What if she did? You're not going to lay this murder on me."

"Horace, I believe you protest too much. The thought never entered my mind. The girl was raped, if you haven't heard, and I just couldn't imagine you doing such a thing."

Horace found cause to take offense at his statement. "Are you suggesting that I'm not a man?" His voice increased in volume: "I'll have you know . . ."

Realizing he had gained the attention of the other mourners, Horace slowly closed his mouth. As the recipient of their stares, he stretched his short neck out of his collar, raised up on his toes, and then settled back to a flat-footed stance, just like a little rooster ready to crow . . . or burst, which might have better described his present disposition. If he bragged about his prowess, which might have been viewed as questionable by other men, he would have invited the sheriff's suspicion. The other alternative of letting Ashton Wingate believe him incapable was just as bad. He could not tell them that Corissa had let Mary go for the girl's own good after he had dragged her down to the woodshed. He vividly remembered the resulting squabble he had gotten into with his sister about treating the servants and slaves in a more worthy manner. After all, there were other planters who used their slaves for their own convenience, he had argued, and he felt he had a right to be like other men. To be considered a man was the thing he most desired. There was no need to prove his manhood with the very young, and until Marelda had deigned to bestow some attention upon him, it had always been the innocent child-girls he had gone after. And Mary had been very young once . . . and very inexperienced.

Ashton smiled blandly. "I'm sorry if I disturbed you, Horace."

"You just don't know how much you have disturbed me." The short man flapped his arms as he worked himself up into an outraged fervor. "Of late, 'twould seem that I am being continually harassed either by you or by some of your friends. For instance, Harvey Dobbs came out to my place and asked me if I knew anything about the burning of your warehouse."

Ashton's expression did not change. "I've been wanting to question you about that myself, but lately I just haven't had time to give the matter as much attention as it deserves."

"Yes, I can see what's kept you busy," Horace sneered as he tossed his indefinable chin toward Lenore. "Not that I care, but you're going to get yourself killed sniffing after another man's wife. Or are you still trying to convince everyone that she's your long-lost Lierin?" Horace felt the surging thrill of success as he saw the sarcastic gibe hit its mark. He could hardly believe he had found a weakness in the other's steel-plated hide.

The muscles tensed in Ashton's jaw as he stared down at the little man. He was tempted to take him up and shake him just to hear him squeal like a frightened piglet. It was all he could do to control the urge and to give the man nothing more than a curt reply: "We'll see what the end brings, Horace, both for you . . . and me."

Ashton set his back to the man and joined the rest of the mourners as they began making their departures. Malcolm remained near the graveside with the sheriff, no doubt attempting to persuade the lawman to take some positive action against him. A wry smile touched Ashton's lips. The man would do more good explaining his own whereabouts during that time, since Lierin had chosen to tell the sheriff of her visit to the steamer. The watchman had helped him aboard when he returned to the steamer, and no other boat was sighted leaving the vessel after that.

Hickory glanced down from his lofty driver's seat as Ashton paused beside the carriage. As instructed, the black had brought the smaller landau with a two-horse team to Biloxi and had led his master's favorite stallion on a tether behind the procession. He had found lodging at the town's livery stable, where he could attend them while he waited for the next move in this game. Mr. Wingate had casually compared his maneuvers to a game of chess, the object being to capture the queen, and should the occasion arise and the lady be willing, Hickory would serve as knight and whisk her to safety while Ashton stayed behind to challenge the adversary. On this day Hickory had been summoned to the shoreline by a signal from the steamer and, meeting his master, had conveyed him to the cemetery.

"De missus looks kinda peaked, massa," the black observed.

"I was thinking the same thing myself," Ashton mused aloud as he observed her careful progress to the Somerton carriage. Her father assisted her, and as they paused, she reached out a hand to steady herself against her father's arm.

"Yo reckon dat Mr. Sinclair treatin' her all right, massa?"

"He'd better be if he values his life," Ashton muttered.

Lenore slowly raised her gaze to her father. "I'd better rest a moment," she whispered as she tried to subdue the waves of nausea that threatened to overwhelm her. The hot, sultry day had become almost unbearable for her, and she felt stifled by the muggy heat. "I'm not feeling well at all."

Robert patted her hand in a rare display of affection while the red, watery eyes hinted of a compassion she had not thought him capable of. "I'll fetch Meghan, dear. Perhaps she can help you."

As he hurried away, Lenore leaned her swimming head against the outside wall of the carriage and closed her eyes, wishing desperately that she were already home. She dabbed at her cheek with a lace handkerchief, but, small and dry, it did little to ease her plight.

"May I be of assistance?"

The thickly lashed eyelids opened wide as the familiar voice filled her brain. Ashton was there beside her, hardly more than a heartbeat away and, as always, ready to be gentle. The dark, chiseled face showed caring concern, and the eyes were soft and tender as they touched her.

"Are you ill?"

The deep pools of emerald moved beyond him to the man who was striding toward them. "Please go," she pleaded in an anxious whisper. "Malcolm is coming."

Ashton ignored the approaching man and the gawking

bystanders as he opened the carriage door. Bracing it with a shoulder, he lifted her in his arms and swept her inside.

"What is the meaning of this?" Malcolm demanded, coming to a halt beside the carriage. He jerked at Ashton's elbow to bring him around and was met with a sardonic smile.

"Excuse me, Malcolm. The lady appears to be ailing, and I didn't see you rushing to her side."

Malcolm's hawkish face reddened to the line of his tawny hair, and the dark eyes became piercing, like those of an eagle which had just spotted prey, except that this quarry would not be frightened off by a mere display of outrage and was much too dangerous to attack outright. Were he to challenge the man, Malcolm knew he might find himself the victim.

Seeing nothing more threatening than an angry frown, Ashton stepped back and tipped his hat to the lady. "Good day, madam. I trust you will soon be feeling better."

"Thank you," she murmured in a small voice and cast a worried glance at Malcolm as he watched Ashton return to his own carriage. The hatred he bore Ashton was clearly visible in the cold, dark eyes.

Lenore flew down the stairs, giving no heed to the showing of her slender calves beneath the uplifted hem of her nightgown. The tails of the dressing gown spread out behind her like oddly fluttering wings as she raced with a pace that matched her heartbeat. She had just been about to start her morning toilette when she had heard Malcolm's enraged bellow reverberate throughout the house. She had no need to be told that Ashton was at the core of her husband's fury and could only wonder what he had done this time to set the younger man off.

The front door stood open, and as she drew near the entry, she saw Malcolm standing on the porch with the hunting gun in his hands. A towel had been flung across a naked shoulder, and it was evident that he had been in the process of shaving, for one cheek was still covered with thickly lathered soap. His hair was wildly tousled, and his feet were bare against the wooden flooring. Nearing the portal, she slowed and eyed her husband cautiously. Intent upon watching some activity that was taking place beyond her range of vision, he seemed oblivious to her approach. She frowned, unable to see what had roused his ire; then her heart jumped as he snarled a savage curse and took a flying leap from the porch.

With quaking heart Lenore ran out onto the porch, fearing that he was about to carry out his threat to shoot Ashton. A pair of small, supply-laden boats were skimming in to shore on the other side of a narrow inlet, and as they slid home, Ashton and a half dozen of his men jumped from the boats. A few grabbed bundles as their cohorts pulled the craft ashore. One man glanced around and sighted Malcolm racing toward them with the weapon. He shouted a warning to his mates, prompting the men to scatter in several different directions. Ashton stood his ground and stared at the oncoming man as if he dared him to fire. Lenore screamed, fearing Malcolm would do just that, and when the seething man lifted the weapon to look down the sights, Ashton dove to one side, just as the gun went off with a deafening roar. A small geyser of sand sprayed up as the blast of buckshot buried itself in the beach, just beyond the spot where Ashton had been.

Malcolm took aim again, following Ashton's zigzagging flight among the wind-fashioned dunes. With a devious laugh, he slowly tightened his finger against the trigger plate, unaware of Lenore closing the space between them in frantic desperation. As she reached him, she swung both arms upward beneath the gun, knocking the barrel skyward. Another ear-shattering explosion rent the silence as the gun discharged, this time harmlessly into the air. A brief second later Malcolm's arm swung around, knocking her backward into the sand. A blaze of lights flashed in her brain, and again she saw the darkly cloaked villain of her visions whirl with the poker iron raised in his hand.

"You bitch!" Malcolm growled, throwing aside the gun and stepping near to seize her. "I'll teach you to interfere with me!"

He yanked her up by the shoulders and drew back his arm to bring the flat of his hand across her face, but from the corner of his eye, he caught a movement and glanced around to find Ashton charging toward him with a snarl of determination fixed on his face. Malcolm shoved Lenore aside and braced himself to meet the attack, but had little time to prepare before the other launched himself in a flying leap. Ashton's shoulder struck him in the chest, bowling him over into the sand. Immediately Ashton rolled and, coming to his feet again, hooked the towel around the back of Malcolm's neck and jerked him upright. Malcolm was off balance and stumbling when a hard fist slammed into his belly and another blow caught him against the cheek. Though heavier than his adversary, he was no match for the speed and agility of the other, and it soon became apparent which of them was more experienced in a fight. While Malcolm's fists flailed out in a vain effort at defense, Ashton continued to deliver punishing blows to his face and body; then he crossed the ends of the towel and wrenched the linen tight around the thick, corded throat.

"Touch her again, and I'll kill you!" he growled savagely and gave the dazed man a teeth-rattling shake. "Do you understand me?"

Malcolm's eyes bulged as he fought for breath, and in panicking fear he clawed at the cloth around his throat. Ashton gave him another shake, demanding to be answered, and Malcolm managed a hoarse croak of assent. With a derisive sneer, Ashton shoved him back, letting go and sending him sprawling into the sand.

"Take care that you heed my words," he snarled, the muscles in his cheeks flexing angrily.

Gasping air into his lungs, Malcolm struggled up on an elbow and rubbed his bruised throat.

Stepping to Lenore, Ashton reached down to help her to her feet. Their eyes met briefly, and in hers he read the gratitude she mutely conveyed before she busied herself brushing the sand from her clothes.

"Are you ready to leave with me now?" he murmured.

Lenore glanced toward Malcolm, fearing he might have heard the invitation, then gave a small shake of her head. "I must find out what is right, Ashton."

Robert had joined the gathering unobserved and, bending down to assist Malcolm, glared around at Ashton. "Why are you trespassing on our property?"

A slow grin spread across Ashton's lips, as if he were suddenly amused. " 'Twould seem I am not trespassing at all." He met the confused stares of the two men and casually shrugged. "If you both insist that Lierin is dead, then this property is partly mine. Lierin and I were married in Louisiana, and by the laws there, I am rightful heir to all her holdings. Since this house and land were willed to Lenore and Lierin by their mother, that's the way it stands. If you would like, you can keep the house, while I take the land around it in a fair exchange."

"I'll see you in hell first!" Malcolm croaked.

Ashton gave him a tolerant smile. "If you're so anxious to go there, I can accommodate you. A duel might satisfy this whole argument."

"*No!*" Lenore wailed, grabbing Ashton's arm.

Malcolm smirked. " 'Twould seem the lady is concerned for my welfare."

"I don't think she realizes you're as clumsy with weapons as you are in a fight."

The insult brought Malcolm scrambling to his feet. "I'll show you!"

Ashton's eyes gleamed in anticipation. "You'll show me what? How to use a pistol at twenty paces, I hope?"

Malcolm was again reminded of the gossip about the Natchez man being a skilled marksman and hunter and could not quite find the nerve to answer the challenge.

"Come now, man," Ashton urged. "What is it that you're going to show me?"

"I'll discuss it with you later," Malcolm growled. He liked it better when the odds were totally in his favor. He gave a curt excuse. "There's no reason to upset Lenore."

The hazel eyes hardened behind lowering lashes as Ashton stared at the man in sneering contempt. A little bloodletting might have eased some of the rage he felt toward the other. "Then you agree that I should take the land?"

"No! . . . I mean . . ." Malcolm knew the law as well as the other and could find no way out. "We'll talk about it later, I said!"

"I'm sorry, we'll have to discuss it now," Ashton insisted. "Either you move out of the house, or I take the land. Do you have any doubt as to my rights?"

Malcolm opened his mouth to object, but slowly closed it again. He could not put forth an adequate argument. "We must keep some land for passage back and forth, unless you wish to make us prisoners here."

"I'll give you an easement to use a small strip. I'll have my men stake out what I consider mine, but I warn you not to trespass beyond that area." He smiled as he added, "Of course, the lady may come and go as she pleases . . . but only the lady, no other."

"Her father?" Malcolm peered at him inquiringly. "You mean, he will not be allowed to venture where he chooses?"

"Her father and I do not share a common bond. He gave over any rights he might have had to this land when he permitted it to be given to his daughters. I claim Lierin's share, and he will have to seek my approval before treading on my soil."

"You have a reputation for being a difficult man to deal with," Malcolm retorted.

Ashton returned a bland smile to the other's menacing glower. "I do what I must do."

"You're a snake," Malcolm sneered contemptuously.

Ashton was unperturbed. "I've been called worse."

"I'd like to, but there's a lady present."

A casual shrug of dismissal was the only answer Malcolm received before Ashton lent his attention to Lenore. Almost in a caress he brushed a snarled tress from off her cheek. "I'll be near if you should need me."

Stepping back, he strode away and gestured for his men to return to their labors. "Let's get those supplies unloaded now. We've got a day's work ahead of us."

Malcolm stared after the man, his face twisted with loathing, and then tossed a glare toward Lenore as she cast an uncertain glance his way. Seeing his displeasure, she quickly turned and ran back to the house, all the while hiding the joy that bubbled up within her. She felt like kicking her bare heels together, but Malcolm would not approve. Only when the door of her room was closed behind her did she dare grin and hug herself in brimming jubilation.

– Chapter Twelve –

The crew from the *River Witch* set about clearing the brush from the land across the shallow inlet. Setting short posts, they spiked planks to the sides and, over the whole, laid boards to form a sizable platform some eighteen inches above the ground. Upon this the men began to erect a large canvas shelter, and like a mushroom, it kept expanding until Malcolm had visions of a tent large enough for a sheikh and his harem. His snide speculations were not far from the truth, for Ashton had acquired his would-be quarters from a man who had once traded with Bedouin Arabs and had given the tent to Ashton after that one had befriended him in a time of trouble. For several years Ashton had despaired of ever finding a use for it. Now he considered owning it a stroke of good fortune, for the sumptuous shelter was precisely the touch he required to rub salt in an open wound.

Malcolm went out to view the proceedings from the lower porch, and this time it was he rather than Robert who quaffed a strong whiskey. He tossed a warning glower at Lenore and her father when the pair came out to join him, daring them to make any comments that would ignite the powder keg of emotions that roiled within him. They carefully refrained from doing so.

As the hours passed, the area across the inlet took on more of a look of permanency. Other men came to bend their backs to the labor, and supplies continued to arrive from off the boat or from town. Fine pieces of furniture were brought along with Oriental rugs, a standing mirror, and Ashton's personal baggage. There was even a bathtub! As the wagon delivered it from town, Lenore chewed a knuckle to hide her amusement as Malcolm's scowl darkened perceptibly. She could almost imagine the steam coming from his ears as he silently seethed.

A somewhat smaller tent was erected nearby for the cabin boy, Hickory, and the horses. The black arrived close to noon, driving the carriage and bringing behind him a pair of wagons, one loaded with a large supply of hay and the other with boards for the construction of makeshift stalls. As he passed the house, Hickory wore a smile that was so broad it seemed to stretch from ear to ear. Malcolm noticed the gleam of white teeth from the porch, and the sight started an angry growl deep in the corded throat until the guttural utterance promptly reminded him of its rawness.

"We can't have that damn nigger living here on our property," he rasped in protest. "He'll steal us blind."

The emerald eyes settled on him with cool disdain, while the softly curving mouth managed a smile of comparable warmth. "Hickory is as honest as a man ought to be, Malcolm. You'll have nothing to fear from him."

Malcolm dismissed her statement with a caustic comment: "He's probably just like that pack of thieving murderers Wingate has for a crew. There's no telling what crimes they're apt to commit. Sheriff Coty ought to do something about them before it's too late. To be sure, we'll have to set out guards to watch over you while those men are out there"—his square chin jutted toward the *River Witch* and then in the direction of the tent—"and that fool, Wingate, is here so close."

Lenore could well imagine how closely she would be watched while Ashton was near. If the idea did not distress her so much, she might have found cause to laugh. "I hope you won't trouble yourself too much, Malcolm."

"Whatever the cost, madam, it will be worth it," he replied, choosing to ignore her sarcasm. "You're too rare a gem for me to put at risk." He considered how fresh and lovely she looked in her cream-colored gown trimmed with embroidered lace and took special note of the rosy glow in her cheeks. He might have blamed her carefully groomed state on the proximity of the other man, except that she had always dressed well and had remarkably good taste in clothes, seeming to know exactly what to wear to complement her beauty. The soft blush in her cheeks, however, had been all but absent until Ashton Wingate had ventured into the area.

"You seem to be feeling better, madam," he stated bluntly.

Lenore was tempted to retort that she might have been feeling a lot worse if Ashton had not come to her defense that morning. Instead, she gave him a serene smile, blandly agreeing with his observation. "Better than I have for some time, thank you, Malcolm."

Hot anger shot through the dark eyes before his eyelids narrowed to mask it. Somerton gestured with his glass, directing the younger man's attention to the working crew. "It looks like Wingate's settling in for keeps."

Lenore went to lean against the porch railing and, from there, watched as Ashton instructed his men in the placement of potted shrubs and the planting of others near the tent. Oaken barrels had been sawed in half to accommodate the larger greenery, which included a wide variety that had been selected when the clearing had begun. Around the wooden planking that now served as an informal courtyard were smaller bushes which from a distance looked suspiciously like jasmine shrubs in bloom. In all, the landscaping provided a certain lushness around the porch, and it was not long before a wrought-iron table and chairs appeared to finish the setting.

Toiling in the sweltering heat, the crew of men shed their shirts, threw off their shoes, and rolled up their trousers. Ashton seemed like a prince among paupers as he remained garbed in fawn-hued riding breeches, low-crowned hat, tall boots, and loose-sleeved shirt opened to the waist. He was continually on the move as he directed the project. Giving orders to some or turning to answer the inquiries of others, he was ever in demand, and by the time the sun lowered in the west, he had with the aid of his men created quite a fine sight for anyone to behold. With such elaborate lodging, it was clear he intended to stay as long as he deemed necessary.

The stoical gloom of the evening was keyed to the somberness of Malcolm's dour temper. Lenore took note of it as soon as she joined the two men in the parlor. Her husband sulked like a punished lad and went as often to the decanter as his father-in-law. He was forever strolling out onto the veranda and peering westward where a faint glow marked the location of Ashton's tent. His mood lightened as the intoxicant began to take effect, until finally he broke the cautious, stilted silence with a derisive chortle.

"At least that beggar will be supping alone tonight in that great gaudy tent of his."

Robert was sober enough to pick up on Malcolm's comment and offered some observations of his own: "Aye, and if a little blow comes off the gulf, he just might find that damned boat of his sitting in his lap."

The two waxed almost gleeful in their contemplation of possible disasters that might befall their new neighbor. Lenore found the macabre bent of their humor annoying and did her best to ignore them. Even when they went out to lounge on the veranda, it proved a difficult task.

"Behold!" Robert's hushed tone of amazement came drifting through the open french doors. "What ventures out from yonder craft? Some sweet surcease to ease the varlet's plight?"

His mixed prose was less than pure Shakespearean and more than slightly slurred, but it was enough to stir Lenore's curiosity. Lifting her sherry glass, she strolled out onto the porch where she could view the object of their attention. Pointedly keeping her distance from her companions, she chose a spot near the railing and leaned her back against a post as she turned her gaze out to sea.

Beyond the tumbling surf a lighter nudged out of the dark shadow of the *River Witch* and skimmed through the moonlit waters, heading for the lantern that marked Ashton's encampment. As the lighter neared the beach the rhythmic creak of oars came softly to her ears as the two men bent their backs to the rowing. Soon the boat scraped the sandy bottom of the shallows, and the two dragged it ashore. The pair of servants, complete with white-coated uniforms, lifted a huge, silver-domed tray from the prow and quickly bore it to the courtyard table. Setting to work, they lighted torches and staked them on poles around the deck, making every corner of the platform visible, much to Malcolm's chagrin. A white cloth was spread and upon it the necessary accoutrements were placed for an elegant setting, complete with a silver candelabrum and two place settings for a full-course dinner. All were curious to see who the expected guest might be and waited in anticipation, Lenore no less than the others.

The first mellow strains of the cello drifted on the wings of the night breezes, and everyone on the porch paused to listen. Lenore kept her face carefully blank as Malcolm's eyes settled on her and hardened. The chords wandered through a brief medley, then settled into one they had shared as a favorite. Restlessly Malcolm paced along the veranda and paused at the far end to stare at the brightly lighted area. Lenore leaned forward to catch the soft, musical refrains and closed her eyes as she luxuriated in the memories she had of Belle Chêne and its master. The music filled her heart with a soft bliss until her pleasure was soured by Malcolm's return.

Chafing, he glanced around at her father as his lips curled in contempt. "Would you listen to that wailing? It sounds like a wounded swamp cat caught in a trap. And you can guess what part they caught."

Robert sniggered into his glass. "Nay, lad. 'Tis only the guts they string out on a fiddle."

"It's not a fiddle," Lenore corrected crisply, irked at their crudities.

Her father peered at her dubiously. "A modicum of wit ye have tonight, lass. Have ye no laughter in ye?"

"It's that rutting tomcat yowling and prowling about out there, working her up into an itch," Malcolm jeered. "She'd like to join him."

And why not? Though silent, the retort flared through her mind. She would gladly have traded the inanities of the men for the affectionate attention that she longed for and which she knew Ashton would freely bestow on her.

A servant stepped to the door of the tent to speak to someone inside. The music halted, and Lenore held her breath as Ashton emerged, quite alone and quite handsomely groomed. He paused beside a jasmine shrub and, picking a blossom, laid it on one of the plates. He settled in a chair across from it, and a wine was poured into his silver goblet. Ashton sipped it, nodded his approval, and the full-course dinner progressed while the place across from him remained untouched. Finally Lenore understood the significance of the jasmine on the plate. It served as an invitation to her. Whether she was Lenore or Lierin, and when or if she ever chose to join him, she would be welcomed.

Malcolm also caught the impact of Ashton's boldness and turned upon her with a glare of seething outrage. She met it without flinching and smiled softly into his burning eyes. Still, when Meghan stepped to the french doors and announced their own dinner was to be served, she breathed a pray of thanksgiving that the diatribe would be forestalled. Throughout the meal she held the warm, tender feelings of love close to her heart, giving no heed to either the heated stares of Malcolm or the disapproving frowns of Robert.

* * *

The next morning Lenore sent her excuses to the dining room via Meghan and indulged in a light, peaceful repast in her own chamber. This seemed to vex Malcolm sorely, for a short time later she heard him storm out of the house in a high raging temper, leaving Robert to ensure that the two lovers were kept apart, Lenore to her house and Ashton to his tent. The distance was there, separating one from the other, but their minds seemed well in tune, for when Lenore strolled out onto the upper veranda to view the splendor of the morning, Ashton lifted the flap of his tent and stepped out, almost in unison with her. As he turned to glance toward the house, she appeared at the railing, and for a moment in time they stared across the space, totally aware of the other. Even with the stretch of land between them, she felt his eyes caress her, while her own gaze completed an admiring appraisal of him. A narrow breechcloth covered his loins and provided a minimum of modesty as it bulged over his manhood. The heat crept into her cheeks at the sight of him standing there like some bronze-skinned Apollo. From her memory she reconstructed details left obscure by the distance. The light furring of his muscular chest dwindled into a shadowed line as it trailed down his belly, which was flat and, as she knew, hard as oak. The legs were long and straight, lightly corded with muscles, and as finely toned as the rest of his body.

The long-endured ache of suppressed passions began to spread through her, stirring a quickness in her blood, and she wondered if he also was consumed by a lusting hunger, for he lifted a large towel from a wrought-iron chair and flung the long cloth over his shoulder, letting it hang past his loins. Her eyes followed and lowered to the flexing buttocks as he strolled out to where the waves lapped lazily at the shore. Dropping the towel beside the water's edge, he waded out toward the deep; then, arching his back, he plunged out further with a clean dive. His arms stroked the waters relentlessly, heedless of direction. She could almost sense his reasoning, his need to work out his frustrations. An ache was there in the pit of her own stomach, and she wished she might have been able to wear herself out in such a way, at least to an exhausted complacency. Instead, she had to endure the craving lusts and hope in time that she could come to accept Malcolm as easily as she had accepted Ashton.

She rubbed her brow, hoping to find a breach in that restricting wall that encased her memory and open it for a thorough examination. If only she could find a place for Ashton, some cherished moment remembered, but even before her attempt she knew it was useless. He was of her present, not her past.

The sun blazed down in shimmering heat waves, and slowly a mirage formed in her mind. She was on a sunny beach somewhere faraway. An auburn-haired girl played with a sand castle and a small doll. It was she. Or was it Lierin? Her vision was limited, as if she stared through a short tunnel, but she knew she ran and played with one who looked like her. The children, perhaps six or so of age, laughed and squealed as they chased each other to the water's edge. Then from afar a woman's voice called:

"Lenore?"

The young girl turned and shaded her eyes.

"Lierin?"

Her own vision widened, and she saw a woman she knew as Nanny standing on a grassy knoll. A mansion of generous proportions loomed behind her.

"Come now, the two of ye," the ruddy-faced woman bade. " 'Tis nigh unto noonday. Time for a wee bite to eat an' then a nap before yer father returns."

The illusion swirled and faded, and Lenore blinked as reality once again presented itself. She was almost afraid to bring the fantasy back, yet the question blazed. Was that moment really a part of her past? Or had she conjured it from the fabric of her fondest hopes? If the other girl had answered true . . .

She paced the porch and tried to summon something more. Some hint. Some clue. Something to point out the truth to her.

"Lenore!"

A prickling shivered along her spine as the name tore through her concentration; then she glanced around, realizing reality was there and coming in the presence of a dapperly garbed man who was hurrying up the stairs. Robert Somerton's cheeks were scarlet, and his agitated state was most apparent.

"You shouldn't be out here in your nightgown where everyone can see you, girl," he admonished, drawing her attention to her light apparel. "Go in and get dressed before some harm comes to you."

Lenore started to comply, then noticed how his eyes kept nervously flitting toward the beach. Her curiosity aroused, she turned her gaze outward and saw the reason for his unrest. Ashton was wading from the water, and if he went in looking good, he came out looking marvelous. His hair was wet, and the beads of moisture that clung to him glistened beneath the sun, giving his dark skin a lustrous sheen. She could imagine what embarrassed and worried her father the most. It was the skimpy cloth covering which now was molded wetly to Ashton and came very close to indecent display as it sagged slightly with the weight of the water.

"The man has lost his wits." Robert's sensibilities had been unduly shocked. "The very idea! Prancing about out there like that and flaunting himself before you! What does he think you are, anyway? Some hussy off the streets? It's surely no sight for a lady!"

Lenore hid a smile of amusement as she moved away, but from beneath her lashes she stole one last, admiring glance at that tall, muscular form before she entered her room and closed the french doors.

Robert Somerton's sense of propriety had been severely challenged, and he hurried down the stairs again, intending to confront this near-naked strutter. It was one thing to see the bare thighs and bulging flesh of a woman in places of ill repute, but quite another to have a man showing himself in such a manner before a lady. . . . And before such a fine one, too! It was too much!

Somerton flicked the ends of his mustache up in an outraged gesture as he hastened to intercept the lewd rascal who casually sauntered toward his tent. "Here now! I want a word with you," he called, commanding the younger man's notice. That one raised a brow in wonder as he turned and waited for the other to reach him. Halting before him, Somerton shook a shaming finger beneath his nose. "You have your nerve coming out dressed like that, offending my daughter with your display. I'll have you know, sir, that she is a lady."

"I know that," Ashton agreed pleasantly, taking some of the wind out of the other's sails.

The white-haired man searched for another form of attack. "Well, sir, you are no gentleman, I can tell you that!" The elder man swept his hand to indicate the long length of Ashton's form. "Look at you! All but naked, you are! Flaunting yourself in front of my daughter!"

"She's a married woman," Ashton responded with a tolerant smile.

"Not to you!" Robert shouted, catching the subtle drift of his meaning. "What more proof do you need to convince you?"

"Nothing from you or Malcolm," Ashton replied promptly and, toweling his hair dry, continued on his way. The stride of his long legs made it necessary for the shorter man to hurry to keep up with him. Although it was but a mere step or two to the courtyard, by the time Robert reached it, his face had taken on a deeper shade of red, and he was ready to accept the cool libation Ashton offered him. He slipped out of his coat, loosened his collar, and, after being offered a chair, sank into it with a sigh of gratitude as he sampled his drink. Ashton excused himself a moment, and in his absence, the elder gazed about him, realizing that the architect of the porch and dwelling had had enough foresight to place them both under the sprawling limbs of a huge tree, which offered a soothing, cooling shade. In his contemplation of the intelligence of the younger man, he managed to down more than half of the drink before Ashton returned in more modest attire.

"You've done well by yourself here," Somerton remarked, encompassing the encampment with a sweep of his hand. " 'Twould appear you've thought of everything."

Surprised at the unexpected compliment, Ashton glanced at the man. The anger had certainly fled from his countenance, and he seemed almost amiable as he surveyed his surroundings. The credit for the change had to be given to the lulling affect of the mint julep, and Ashton was not of a mind to deny the man when he asked for a refill.

"I used to be young once," Robert reflected after some length. After a thoughtful pause, he chortled and, draining the glass, held it out for a second replenishment. "I've even turned a few lady's heads in my time. Maybe not like you've managed to do with the girl over there." He gestured casually toward the house. "She's taken with you, all right, and Malcolm's bent on making her love him again."

"Did she ever?" Ashton posed the question with a hint of sarcasm, but the white-haired man missed the thrust of the subtle gibe.

"Malcolm believes she did . . . before she lost her memory." Robert scratched his chin thoughtfully. "Sometimes I wonder how it's all going to end. She's a good girl, she is. A little hot-tempered at times. Came charging to my defense when Malcolm was lambasting me for getting drunk."

Ashton smiled as a memory came winging back. "That sounds like her."

"Well, there I was, deserving everything Malcolm said about me, and she fairly set him back on his heels." Robert shifted the lower part of his jaw out to the side as he sat a long moment in pensive silence. "She deserves better than me for a father," he said and nodded his head as if agreeing with his own logic. "And maybe, just maybe, she deserves better than Malcolm for a husband."

Ashton's eyebrow rose sharply. "I'll agree with that outright, but I'm not convinced she is his wife."

"You're a stubborn man, Wingate," Robert observed wryly. "The fact that you're here proves it."

"I'm not denying it," Ashton replied readily. "Malcolm stole something from me I cherished above all else. I still say he has yet to prove his claim."

"But he has!" Robert insisted. "Don't you think I can tell the difference between my own daughters?"

Ashton shrugged as he watched the other drain another glass dry. "A father should be able to."

"Of course, and I tell you I have done just that!" Robert hiccuped and leaned back in the chair as he contemplated the now empty crystal. The warmth of the day and the rapidly imbibed whiskey were beginning to show their effect. "I know what you're thinking." The slowly reddening eyes lifted and tried to focus on the crisp, handsome features. "You think I drink too much, don't you, and that I've made a mistake. Well, I'll tell you a secret, my friend. It takes a lot to make me lose my wits. That's one thing Malcolm knows that you haven't learned yet. I am a man who knows the part he plays in this life!" To emphasize his statement, he slammed the goblet down on the surface of the wrought-iron table, and then gasped in pain as it shattered, and the pieces jabbed cruelly into his palm. Turning his hand over, he stared down in horror as the blood gushed forth from the wounds. His face twisted and contorted as if he saw some evil there in his palm. " 'Out, damned spot!' " he whimpered. " 'Out, I say! . . . Hell is murky! . . . What need we fear who knows it, when none can call our power to account?' "

Ashton arched a dubious brow at the man and, reaching across the table, plucked the broken slivers of glass from the rent palm. Quickly assessing the damage, he fetched a linen napkin from inside the tent, then pressed it into the other's palm. Attempting to reach through the other's stupor, he directed in commanding tone, "Now make a tight fist and hold it, do you hear? Hold it!" The order penetrated, and with a hand beneath the other's arm, Ashton lifted Robert to his feet. "Come on, I'll take you home. Lierin can clean up those cuts for you."

"She's a good girl," Somerton mumbled distantly and weaved unsteadily when Ashton let him go. "She deserves better . . ."

Ashton saw the hopelessness of the man's condition and, supporting a good part of the man's weight against him, escorted him back to the house. The short journey seemed too much for the besotted older man, and he sagged limply against the younger as Ashton took him across the porch. Stepping through the front door, Ashton glanced around and, seeing no one, called out. "Lierin? Lierin, where are you?"

"Ashton?" The gasp and the sound of running feet drew his gaze to the upper balustrade as Lenore came into view. He smiled a greeting while his eyes admired the vision she presented in a pale lilac gown. Her own eyes were wide with surprise, and her lips slightly parted, but the sight the red splotches on her father's white coat sent tiny shards of fear shooting through her.

"What's happened?" she demanded, but did not wait for an answer as she lifted her skirts and flew down the stairs. Her voice came in a tone of worry even as she descended. "Oh, Ashton, you haven't hurt him, have you?"

"Upon my honor, madam, I have not," he assured her with a lopsided smile as she left the last step and ran to them. She began searching for a wound under Somerton's coat until Ashton took her wrist. "Your father only cut his hand, Lierin. Believe me, he's all right."

"His hand?" She straightened and, with some bemusement, took the mentioned extremity. She lifted the cloth and wrinkling her nose in a grimace she began to examine the cuts.

"I thought you should clean it," Ashton suggested, leaning close. He would seize upon any excuse to be near her. He noticed the sweet smell of her as his eyes touched the soft nape, and he was reminded of his wont to kiss that delicate spot.

"Take him into the parlor," she directed. "I'll have Meghan fetch a pan of water and make some bandages and be right back."

Ashton complied and helped the elder man to a chair. Somerton clasped the napkin tightly again and cradled his wounded hand against him. "She would tend me," he whimpered like a child lost and confused. "Gentle angel though she be, and me the foulest wretch . . ." He brushed at the rush of tears that invaded his eyes and, sniffing loudly, drew himself up with a proud air, dropping his good hand on a knee. "A good child, she. Don't you agree?"

"Definitely more than a child," Ashton murmured as she came into the room. His eyes touched the soft womanly beauty of her and lingered when she knelt before the old man and gently began to tend him.

A thundering of hooves approached the house, and the three paused to listen, Lenore and Robert in some alarm. In his usual fashion Malcolm charged his mount head-on to the house; then coming to ground, he rushed up the steps.

"'By the pricking of my thumbs, Something wicked this way comes,'" Robert moaned. "'Open, locks, Whoever knocks!'"

Malcolm slammed the door wide and strode into the hall, stopping short when he saw the threesome. His narrowing eyes searched the worried countenances, then flew to the brazen, confident smile of Ashton Wingate.

"What the bloody hell are you doing here in my house!" he raged, sailing his hat down the hall in a fine display of temper. He would have charged the man and done battle with him, but the memory of his most recent defeat made him wary of such a foolish attack.

"Lierin's father cut his hand and needed assistance," Ashton explained. "I gave it."

"You gave it, now get out!" Malcolm flung his arm to indicate the front portal. "Now, I say!"

Ashton strolled leisurely to the door and paused there to make a parting comment. "I wasn't invited, so you needn't take your anger out on Lierin or her father. . . ."

"*Lenore!*" Malcolm shouted, rattling the panes of glass. "She's my wife! Not yours!"

Giving the man a passive smile, Ashton turned and left. As he made his way across the porch he noticed a pair of men riding toward the house. The larger of the two looked distantly familiar, but Ashton could not quite place where he had seen him before. It seemed as if it had been aboard one of his steamers and that the fellow had been part of the crew. Ashton mentally shrugged. It was useless to try to keep account of all the faces that had come and gone. There had been too many.

"The minute I'm gone"—Malcolm began his ranting, and his voice did not dwindle in strength as he gave full vent to his fury— "the pair of you bring that scoundrel in here. Well, I won't have it, do you hear? I've hired guards to protect this house and all that's in it from him and his kind!"

Lenore decided that she had had enough of waiting in the carriage. It was hot and stuffy, and she could not be sure just when Malcolm would return. A light dappling of perspiration moistened her upper lip, and she felt the cloying wetness of her fine muslin gown against her back. The landau was parked alongside the boardwalk, precisely where Malcolm had told them to wait, but there was no shade, and the horses were as hot and restless as she was. They swished their tails at the annoying flies that buzzed about them and nervously stamped their feet, now and then nudging forward when one of the tiny demons alighted and bit.

Stepping down to the boardwalk in something approaching a heated huff and not caring that she had left her bonnet behind, Lenore asked Henry to convey her whereabouts to Mr. Sinclair when and if he should happen to return. Malcolm had seemed most adamant when he had asked her to wait, and she had done so, until she had not been able to bear the torture another moment. The driver was quick to make an affirmative reply to her directive, and Lenore stalked into the nearby general store, plying her lace kerchief in a jerky, fanning motion as her heels struck the wooden planks of the boardwalk. Once she passed through the door, she replaced her frown of annoyance with a smile.

"Why, good mornin', Mrs. Sinclair," the storekeeper greeted her as he turned from stocking the shelves. "How are you? My goodness, it's been some time since I last saw you."

Lenore tried to bring some recollection of the man to mind, but as always she could not place the face. Almost hesitantly she asked, "Do you know me?"

"Why, yes . . . I mean . . ." The shopkeeper displayed his uncertainty before he made further reply. "I thought you were Mrs. Sinclair. Am I mistaken?"

"No," Lenore returned quietly. "I guess not."

Confused by her reply, he studied her closely. "Aren't you feeling well, ma'am?"

She fanned herself with her handkerchief, this time with leisured strokes. "It must be the heat."

The kindly man indicated several chairs that sat against the wall at the back of his shop. "Would you care to rest yourself for a moment?"

"No, I've sat too long as it is." Her lips curved gently upward as she rejected his offer. "I was waiting in the carriage for my husband to return. I guess his business took a little longer than he expected."

The man chuckled and nodded. "I know how that can go."

She glanced around, wondering how she might dare ask him his name without having to explain her malady. He had seemed so befuddled by some of the questions she had already asked him. "I've thought of writing a journal to keep an account of everyone I know here in Biloxi." She had seriously contemplated doing so, just to see if there were any names that pricked her memory. "And, of course, you would be a part of that list. . . . I was wondering how you spelled your name."

"B-l-a-c-k-w-e-l-l." He said the letters proudly. "J-o-s-e-p-h Blackwell."

Blushing lightly, she waved her handkerchief before her warm face and laughed. She might have felt better had he a more difficult name, and she was half afraid she had given him the impression she was something of a dunce. "Just as I thought."

"You must be planning on staying around these parts for a while if you're thinking of writing a journal," he observed.

"Oh, yes," she replied. "At least, my husband hasn't talked about going any other place. Besides, my father is staying with us."

"Oh?" Joseph's bushy brows raised in surprise before he chuckled. "How did you persuade your father to leave England? I thought you said he hated it here and refused to refer to the States as anything but the colonies."

Her slender shoulders lifted in a small shrug. "I guess he just changed his mind."

The shopkeeper nodded understandingly. "He probably couldn't stand being away from his family. Sometimes it's difficult for a father to admit that his daughter has desires contrary to his. It must have been a real blow for him when you decided to move here from England, coming all this way to live by yourself. By the way, how is your sister?"

A sad, wistful look replaced Lenore's smile as that girl-child of her dreams flickered back through her memory. "She's dead."

"Oh, I really am sorry, Mrs. Sinclair." The man spoke softly in sympathy. "I didn't know." He shook his head sadly. "First your husband, and then your sister. I've got to admire your spirit for being so brave after such losses."

She glanced up at him in wide curiosity. "My husband?"

Joseph looked at her strangely. "Why, yes. You were a widow when you first came here." He scratched his head in bemusement. "At least, that's what I thought you said, but I could be wrong. We really never talked much, only to pass the time of day now and then. Why, it was hardly a month or so ago that I actually learned about your marriage to Mr. Sinclair."

Her head swam with a flurry of confused images. From the vague, featureless forms, she knew instinctively that one was her father. Though he remained hardly more than a shadow, he stood with outstretched arms, bidding her to come and be comforted. A phantomlike form moved beside her, seeming to urge her toward the elder man, and this one she knew was Malcolm.

"There you are!" The familiar voice came from behind her.

Blinking, she turned as Malcolm hurried toward her, and for a brief moment, she had trouble sorting reality from illusion. In her mind she saw him being clapped on the back by a sturdy male hand.

"I didn't know you were going to leave the carriage," Malcolm chided a bit crisply. "You worried me, leaving like that."

"I'm sorry, Malcolm," she murmured. "I didn't mean to upset you, but it was very hot out there."

Malcolm realized Mr. Blackwell was watching them in a curious manner and reluctantly explained, "My wife has been sick. I hope she hasn't bothered you too much." He ignored the startled glance his wife shot him. "She's been a bit confused lately and can't seem to remember too well."

"I'm sorry to hear that," Blackwell responded kindly.

Malcolm smiled stiffly. "If you don't mind, we must be on our way now." He made the appropriate apologies. "I'm sorry. I had arranged to meet her father at a certain time, and we're late now. Good day to you, sir."

Holding Lenore's arm in an almost painful vise, he escorted her out and across the boardwalk, then handed her into the carriage. He frowned at her when he took the place beside her. "I told you not to leave."

"It was hot out here," she complained with rising ire. "And you were taking your own good time. I think the only reason you wanted me to come is because you were afraid of what Ashton would do while you were gone."

"I'm not afraid of that bastard," Malcolm muttered.

"I can't see why you were so persistent about me staying here. I had a nice chat with Mr. Blackwell."

"Oh?" His eyes were cold as they came upon her. "What did the old man have to say?"

"Something interesting." A light frown touched the creamy visage. "Why didn't you tell me I was a widow when you married me?"

Malcolm's brows lowered in pique. "I thought it would only confuse you more if you knew. That's one of the reasons I've been trying to shield you from the gossip in town. I just didn't know what kind of trauma it would cause." He seemed most inquisitive as he asked, "What else did your friendly storekeeper have to relate?"

"Nothing, really. From what he said, I gathered he didn't know me too well. We didn't have too much time to talk before you came in."

Relaxing back in the seat, Malcolm lifted his hat and wiped a handkerchief across his brow. "It is hot," he stated in a more pleasant tone. "I'm sorry I wasn't more considerate. I just got tied up and couldn't get away."

Lenore's curiosity had not yet been appeased, and she ventured, "Do you know anything about my first husband?"

The heavy shoulders lifted casually. "I think some kind of fever took him shortly after the two of you were married. Beyond that, I don't remember too much of what you told me about him, except that he lived on an island in the Caribbean."

"His name . . . do you know his name?" Lenore pressed.

Malcolm ran the handkerchief along the inside of the hatband and glanced at her askance as he replied, "Cameron Livingston."

"Livingston . . . Livingston . . ." She rolled the name over and over on her tongue, finding that it had a familiar ring. "Yes, I think I've heard the name before." The delicate brows came together as she tested her given name with it. "Lenore Livingston? Lenore . . . Livingston. Lenore Livingston! Yes! I know I've heard it before." She laughed, pleased at her accomplishment. "Perhaps I'm beginning to remember again. Oh, that would be so nice if I could."

The dark eyes turned to her above a wan smile. "It's been some time now since your accident. I'm beginning to wonder if your memory will ever come back and if you'll remember what we once meant to each other."

"I remember more than I did when I came here," she admitted. "It's coming back slowly, but at least I'm making progress."

Malcolm reached for the thin valise that he had tossed on the far seat. "There are some papers here your father wants you to sign. We're going now to meet him. Are you up to it?"

"Do you suppose we can make it another day?" she asked. The intolerable heat had drained her. "I don't feel up to reading right now."

"You really don't have to read anything, my dear. Your father has taken care of that for you."

"My father brought me up better than that. He'll expect me to heed his advice." She canted her head, wondering where that notion had come from.

Malcolm sighed impatiently. "Really, Lenore. The documents are not important enough that they must be read over in detail."

"I'd rather not attend to the matter just now, Malcolm," she stated, rather firmly. She resented being pressured by him. "If my father wishes to bring the papers home, I'll read them there. That is the most I will promise."

He responded with a derisive snort. "You've gotten very high-minded lately, especially since that nigger lover has roosted on our front lawn. Don't forget, madam, that I am your husband . . . not Ashton Wingate. You'll give me the respect that is due me."

Lenore's amazement was complete. She saw no reason for him to fly into a temper over her delay in signing papers that he had said himself were not important. "Malcolm, I only ask to be allowed to read the papers."

"Well, it's almost an insult the way you insist. It sounds as if you don't trust me . . . or your father. We're only seeking what is best for you."

"My father taught me long ago to look after my own interests."

"To hell with your father!"

"Malcolm!" She stared at him in astonishment. "I see no reason for this display of temper."

"I can!" he snapped. "I ask you to do one simple thing, but you refuse. I bet if your precious Mr. Wingate were here, you'd fall all over yourself doing what he asked."

"Your jealousy is showing," she said soberly.

"Isn't it the truth?" His dark eyes fairly snapped as he threw the accusation at her. "If you had the chance, you'd take that bastard into your bed."

"Malcolm, you're going too far," she warned.

"By doing what? Calling him a bastard or you a bitch?"

Lenore gasped in outrage and, now in a high-flown temper herself, rapped the handle of her parasol crisply on the small door behind the driver. "Henry, you may let me off here, please," she requested when the tiny portal came open. "I have some further shopping to do."

"You're not getting out!" Malcolm protested as the servant brought the conveyance to a halt. "I'm going to take you home."

"Then you'll have to kill me here and now, Malcolm, because if you don't let me out of this carriage this instant, I'm going to create such a scene that you won't be able to stay in this town another day." The words were slowly and carefully enunciated and the determination in the emerald eyes convinced him that she meant everything she had said. If he did not use caution and let her go, he could expect to take the consequences.

"If you get out, then you'll have to walk home," he threatened.

"Gladly!" Lenore glared at him. "Just move out of my way."

Her face was flushed and angry as she pushed open the door. Without a backward glance, she descended to the rutted thoroughfare and, snapping open her parasol, marched toward the boardwalk, heedless of the activity on the road. To an oncoming team and wagon, she gave little regard except a brief, cold-eyed glare that might have done much to shrivel the pride of the stout team. They had made large men scurry out of the way, but this trim lass did not display a flicker of fear. The team's driver sawed hard on the reins, turning the pair aside and shouting as he passed her. "Are you crazy, lady? You almost got yourself killed!"

Lenore mumbled beneath her breath. "Rude despicable lout! God only knows why I ever married him! I wish I had never seen him."

She stepped onto the boardwalk and walked briskly past several shops. A tall, nice-looking man who was leaning on a storefront ahead of her saw her coming and, with a sudden gleam of admiration in his eye, gallantly swept off his tall, beaver hat.

"Good morning, miss. Can I be of assistance?"

Ignoring him, she stalked past, and with a hurried twist of his body, the roué fell in behind. He ogled the shapely back as if the stylish clothes did not hinder his view of the slender body they covered and smiled broadly when she tossed a glower over her shoulder. She passed another doorway and drew a long, slow whistle from the barber, who was plying his razor to the well-lathered face of a customer.

"She's a redhead, all right," he commented in appreciation. "Hotter'n some of them peppers the Cajuns grow in Louisiana."

The one he attended raised his head to view this sight, and even with a hurried glimpse of her profile through the window, Ashton could not mistake that fair face.

"Lierin!" He threw himself from the chair, and, snatching the towel from his neck, used it to wipe the soap from his face. He dodged several chairs and men on the way out, causing one to start when he dropped the soapy linen in his lap.

"Your coat, sir!" the barber called after him. "You're leaving your coat!"

"I'll come back for it!" Ashton flung over his shoulder. He ran after the sprightly stepping woman, gaining the attention of the man who was following closely in her wake. That one frowned and set his arms akimbo in obvious vexation when Ashton ran past him.

When a hand came upon her arm, Lenore came around, ready to jab the pointed end of the parasol into the one who boldly accosted her until she looked up and recognized the handsome face that grinned down at her.

"Ashton! What are you doing here?"

"I followed you and Malcolm into town," he admitted, "and then when I saw you get in the carriage, I decided I'd get myself a shave."

She laughed as she rubbed a streak of soap from his cheek. "I don't think you waited for the barber to finish."

Ashton scraped a hand over his bristly chin. "Forgive my appearance, madam. I left in a hurry this morning." He tossed a glance up and down the street. "What are you doing here? Where's your carriage?"

Lenore lifted her slim nose into the air, still miffed at the one who had caused her anger. "I sent Malcolm and our carriage on their way."

A sparkle of interest began to gleam in Ashton's eyes. "Malcolm left you here alone?"

"I suppose my father is still here somewhere." She gave a flippant shrug. "Though I really don't care one way or the other."

Stepping aside, Ashton laid a hand behind her shoulder and swept an arm before them. "If you'd allow me time to get my coat, madam, I'll be more than happy to escort you wherever you desire to go."

The handsome roué stood stock-still in the middle of the board-walk, his feet braced apart and his hands set low on his hips. He might have been slow with his approach, but this wench was clearly one to squabble over. He made no move to step out of their way. Ashton met his challenging gaze with hardening eyes, then lightly handed the lady past the man. When she was securely beyond all danger, Ashton came back with his arm, sharply jabbing an elbow into the man's chest, right below the rib cage. The fellow staggered back, surprised at the tenacity of this one who had whisked the lady right from under his nose.

"Begone with you if you have a care for your hide," Ashton growled low. He was not about to endure another man's interfer-ence. "This one is mine."

The man regained his breath and caught Ashton's shoulder, ready to make a protest. "I saw her first . . ."

The frilly parasol was snapped shut in a second, and the pointed end quickly found a tender spot in the roué's ribs. He yelped in sud-den pain and, deciding the pair were too much for him, stepped into a stance of surrender.

"If you insist!" he cried, holding his arms outspread. He backed away, immediately relinquishing any claim on the fine-figured filly. It was obvious she had chosen her escort.

- Chapter Thirteen -

Eyes turned to regard the handsome couple as they strode along the boardwalk, and Ashton smiled with both pride and pleasure, having been successful in capturing the queen, at least for the afternoon. He beckoned to Hickory to bring the carriage around and, handing his lady in, settled close beside her and took her hand, gently encompassing the fine-boned fingers with his own. Lenore looked at him, unable to deny the warm feeling of contented bliss that quickly enveloped her whenever she was with him. His eyes glowed and brought a light blush to her cheeks as he took in every detail of her with a slow and exacting perusal. When he spoke, his murmur was soft and husky and bespoke of the yearnings that were readily visible in those hazel eyes. "You're a most pleasurable sight, madam, one that I've not had enough of seeing lately."

Her light laughter threaded through his mind. "My father and Malcolm think you've been seeing too much of me . . . and I of you." The corners of her lips twitched in amusement. "My father was quite shocked by your penchant for exhibiting yourself."

Ashton chuckled. "Aye, your father said as much when he came to rebuke me. He thought you too fragile to view what I had displayed. Obviously he isn't aware that we were living as man and wife before you left Belle Chêne."

The rosy color deepened in her cheeks beneath his querying regard. "I couldn't tell them, Ashton," she murmured, lowering her gaze to her lap. "They would have made it seem like something dirty." She released a long sigh. "Everything you have done is despicable in their eyes, and my father still blames you for taking Lierin from him."

Ashton squeezed her fingers in gentle understanding. "He's a troubled man, and despite myself I'm beginning to feel some sympathy toward him."

Her love for him welled up, spilling over the walls of restraint that she had tried so hard to construct as she lifted her head and searched the tanned visage. "You're a good man, Ashton Wingate."

With a chuckle Ashton tossed his hat upon the far seat and gave her a doubting look. "Why? Because I harbor no malice for an old man who thinks he has reason to hate me? It's useless to waste my resentment on him. I never knew of his fondness for whiskey, but it's clearly taking its toll. He almost lost touch with the world when he cut his hand, and I realized, then, that he's only a weak, empty shell of a man, worthy only of pity. My anger is better spent elsewhere."

"On Malcolm?" she inquired in a small voice.

Ashton's face hardened, and above the line of his jaw the tensing muscles vibrated, making ridges and hollows flex in his cheeks. "Now there's one who is deserving of my hatred."

Seeing the writhing turbulence of his animosity, she rubbed a hand over his arm soothingly. "Let's not talk about him," she cajoled. "Tell me of your plans. How long will you be keeping the *River Witch* here?"

"As long as I have to . . . or until you send me away."

"I've already asked you to go," she reminded him.

He lifted her hand to his lips and kissed the pale fingers while his eyes warmly probed the deep green crystals, finding there a myriad of emotions all wrapped up in love. "When your eyes tell me to go, my love, I'll go. Not before."

Lenore lowered silky lashes over the dark, translucent orbs, wondering if her yearnings were so visible. It seemed pointless to deny her love for him; it was not an emotion that could be easily set aside. He rested their entwined hands upon his thigh, and she sensed they shared similar cravings when she felt his thudding pulse. His free hand came to lift her chin, and his fingers slowly stroked her throat as he stared into her eyes.

"I want you," he breathed in a husky murmur. He moved her hand, making her aware of his needs, and he saw the wide-spreading confusion come back in her face. She shook her head in an almost pleading gesture of denial, mutely appealing for mercy, and tried to pull free, but the name Lierin, sighing from his lips, stilled her weak struggles. He pressed her head back upon the seat near his shoulder, and she stared with helpless entreaty into those smoldering green-brown eyes as his face loomed above her own. His mouth lowered, opening and slanting before covering hers, and she lost herself in the wild, sweet pleasure of his kiss, all the while knowing this should not be. The side of her hand burned where it rested against his loins, and the awareness of his inflamed desires made her tremble. Murmuring words of love and passion, he pressed fevered kisses upon her throat and cheek and lightly touched the fragile eyelids that quivered downward to receive his featherlike kiss.

"I wander helpless through the night," he whispered in agonized torment, "wanting you and knowing you are beyond my reach. My vitals roil in helpless frustration as I think of you up there in the house . . . and Malcolm between us, claiming you. Aye, I seethe when I think of him, and I realize how fiercely jealousy has taken root in me. It tears me apart when I see you with him. I beg you to have mercy on this wretched soul, my love. Leave with me now. Let me take you back home where I can love you . . . and cherish you. . . ."

"Oh, Ashton, Ashton," she moaned as tears welled in her eyes. "What would I be if I went back to Belle Chêne with you? Never knowing for sure whether I am Lierin or Lenore, I would be caught in an eternal conflict, wondering if I were committing adultery or just fulfilling my rightful place as your wife. This house here in Biloxi holds the key, and I believe it can unlock the secrets of my mind and free it from this turmoil. There are ugly things I see in visions, hateful things, and if I don't find the answers for them, they will hound me to my grave. I yearn to give myself to you now; I do want what you want, but I cannot go with you without knowing myself . . . who I am, where I've been, and what I've done." She removed her hand from his grasp and, placing it in her lap, slowly stroked it with her other, as if soothing her burning skin. "I must go back, and I think it would be well for us both if you take me home now. . . ." She turned her face away to hide a fresh rush of tears as she added, "Before I yield myself to you."

All too aware of the loneliness that would settle down upon him when they were parted, Ashton sought to persuade her: "Stay with me for a while more. Have dinner with me, and then I'll take you back later." She looked at him again almost pleadingly, and he smiled sadly, taking note of her reddened eyes, and relented. "Perhaps I ask too much of you right now. I know you are troubled." He let his breath out slowly, attempting to cool his mind and body. "I'll take you back. There'll be another day when we'll meet."

Relieved by his acquiescence, Lenore sniffed and, with her handkerchief, wiped the brimming wetness from her lashes. He knew how to appeal to her senses, and he was so hard to resist, she had found herself in a quandary, wondering if she could. Even now she had difficulty forgetting what had just passed between them and the scalding heat that had seared her hand.

Ashton gave Hickory instructions and, leaning back in the seat again, indulged himself in the pleasure of watching her rather than the scenery they passed. "I'm letting some business associates here in Biloxi borrow the *River Witch*." He saw her surprise and explained, "They're planning a social affair, with all the wealthy people in the area being invited to the gaming tables." Actually, he had initiated their interest, having seen how well the occasion would fit into his schemes and aid in his advancement toward a lasting seizure of the queen.

Lenore saw the sparkling gleam in his eye and could not resist an inquiry. "What has that to do with me?"

A roguish grin readily showed the contrast between his dark skin and white teeth. "You and Malcolm will be invited, of course."

"Malcolm will never go on your steamer." The very idea seemed preposterous. "He hates you too much."

"Ah, but I've been informed that Malcolm is quite fond of the gaming tables and likes the idea of easy money and associating with wealthy people. He doesn't appear to be as well off as I had first supposed. In fact, it's rather difficult to decide where he does get his money."

"I don't know anything about his work," she murmured distantly, realizing Malcolm had never made any attempt to inform her of his past, his family, or his activities. "In fact, I don't know very much about him at all."

"I've had some of my men watch him, and his business dealings seem to radiate from a room above the tavern."

"You mean"—a blush crept into her cheeks as she sought a delicate way of asking—"he's keeping company with . . . purchased ladies?"

Ashton chuckled. "If he were, my love, I wouldn't be telling you of his indiscretions." He shook his head as he continued. "No. He meets with other men there, and they're an unworthy-looking bunch from what my men report. The lot of them usually scatter after the meeting, going off in different directions, and then in a few days they're back again to meet with Malcolm."

"When Malcolm leaves the house, he only tells me he's going to meet with the lawyers, and then he comes back with papers for me to sign."

"What sort of papers?"

Her slender shoulders lifted briefly. "I don't know. He's never let me read them."

"Have you signed them?" Ashton asked in sudden worry.

"No," she replied, somewhat confused by his concern. "And I won't until he lets me read them."

"That's a good girl."

"What do you think they might be?" she queried.

"I don't know, but if he could, he would have you sign a complaint against me. He'd like nothing better than to see me arrested for Mary's murder."

"Who do you think killed her, Ashton?"

"Horace Titch, perhaps." Ashton shrugged. "Mary used to work for his sister. I really can't say otherwise. That stretch of land near us is not entirely isolated from the rest of the world, you know. A stranger could have wandered in, seized the girl, and left her in the dinghy after he killed her."

A shudder went through Lenore. "I never heard anything."

"The attack on her probably happened while you were out with me, and it frightens me when I think you were on the beach alone about that time." His eyes fondly traced the delicate profile as he murmured, "Have I thanked you yet for the alibi, madam? I didn't expect you to tell the sheriff you were with me."

Lenore stole a timid glance at him. "I couldn't see saving my reputation and letting you be arrested."

His finger teased a softly curling wisp that lay against her nape. "Where did you leave your bonnet?"

Surprise touched the lovely visage as she looked up at him. "It was so hot I left it in the carriage, but how . . . ?"

Ashton finished the question for her: ". . . did I know that you were wearing a bonnet? I saw you leave the house this morning, remember? Besides, I notice everything about you. If I hadn't seen you with the bonnet on, I would probably have wondered why your hair is a little mussed. . . ."

Suddenly self-conscious, Lenore quickly reached up to repair her coiffure and then realized he was teasing her when he chuckled. Lowering her hands to her lap again, she smiled through a blush as he gently squeezed her arm.

"I've seen your hair in wilder disarray, my love, and you have taken my breath away with your beauty."

Unable to resist his nearness as he laid his arm on the seat behind her, she leaned against his side. "Did you perchance know that I was a widow when Malcolm married me?"

Ashton's face displayed his astonishment. "You mean Lenore . . . ?"

"Yes, me." She nodded. "I was married to Cameron Livingston before I married Malcolm."

"If you *ever* married Malcolm," Ashton gently protested.

"Will you ever stop insisting that I'm Lierin?"

"Only when I have irrefutable proof, madam."

"Lierin Livingston just doesn't sound right."

"Lierin was not a widow when I married her." Shaking his head, he smiled down at her rather roguishly. "She was a virgin when I took her to bed."

"The same was not true of me when we made love at Belle Chêne," Lenore murmured, then wished she could recall the words when she realized how inane the statement was. Whether she was Lierin or Lenore, she had come to him as a married woman. The only question was, whose wife?

Ashton chuckled softly as he pressed his lips against her hair. "By then, my love, the damage had already been done. It happened in one single moment, at least three years past, and I can truthfully say that when the sun rose the next morning, we were most definitely man and wife."

"Comin' home!" Hickory shouted from up front, and Ashton peered out the window at the gray-blue sea that stretched out across the horizon. Hickory had made good time in bringing them back, and it was a disappointment to both of them. Lenore's fingers readily snuggled into his as Ashton reached to take her hand.

"Malcolm will be receiving an invitation for the party aboard the *River Witch*. I'd like you to come. Will you?"

"If it means that much to you, yes."

"It does . . . because I'll want to be with you. And when you see the *River Witch* leave, don't be upset. I haven't left you."

"I'll miss seeing her from my balcony."

A soft chuckle accompanied his reply. "There'll be another vessel coming in its stead, madam. Just be patient."

Lenore was truly amazed. "Shouldn't your boats be trading elsewhere? Aren't you losing money letting them sit out there idle in the gulf?"

"When a man's heart is not content, madam, riches mean nothing to him." Ashton glanced out the window again, fretting because they had so little time left. They were only a short distance from the lane that led up to the house now, and he turned back to her with eyes that burned in anxious appeal. Lenore never really knew if she leaned forward or if he pulled her close, but in the next moment she was pressed hard against him and his lips were moving passionately upon hers. Though brief, the kiss stirred up a whole caldron of cravings, and by the time the landau turned up the lane, they were both beset with a burning need to continue. Lenore was sorry she had bade him return so early. She shivered in longing as his hand came around her side and covered her breast; then he pulled away, and for both it was a difficult struggle to maintain a serene mien. It was a lengthy moment before Ashton managed to subdue the rutting lust and step down. Taking her hand, his fingers squeezed hers and quite properly he helped her down.

They had barely reached the front steps when the portal was flung wide, and Malcolm came striding out, his face dark with rage. Lenore ignored his glare and though she was still very much annoyed with the heavier man, she spoke in a guise of sweetness. "Mr. Wingate was kind enough to bring me home, Malcolm. Wasn't it nice that I didn't have to walk?"

Though Malcolm's hands remained lowered, they clenched into tight, meaty fists, while his eyes fairly flashed with indignation. He loathed the tolerant smile the other man returned to him, and wished he had been able to throttle Ashton right there on the front lawn. "Get in the house." He tossed the command at Lenore as he jerked his head in that direction. "I'll talk to you later. Right now, I have something to discuss with *Mister* Wingate."

Lenore complied, but upon entering the house, she went into the parlor and stood near the french doors, where she could overhear the exchange. Malcolm was making a valiant effort to control himself, but he was clearly upset with her and Ashton. If the circumstances warranted it, she was ready to throw herself between the two men to halt a violent end to their confrontation.

"Just when in the bloody hell do you intend to leave here?" Malcolm demanded of the other man. "You accost my wife at every turn—"

"Accost *whose* wife?" A mildly questioning quirk lifted Ashton's brow.

Malcolm became more incensed at the sardonic gibe. "Damn you! You know whose wife she is!"

"Aye, I know," Ashton replied easily, "and I've come to fetch her home where she belongs."

"There's no talking to you!" Malcolm complained angrily. "You've shut your mind to the facts!"

"Only to your whining, Malcolm."

"You can't even recognize the truth when you see it!"

"I've been called stubborn, but I'm always willing to review the truth. Thus far, I haven't been convinced that you're right in claiming Lierin. . . ."

"*Lenore!*"

A light chuckle shook Ashton's shoulders. "We shall see, Malcolm. We shall see." He placed a foot on the carriage step, but paused a moment to look back at the enraged man. "Even if she were Lenore, you wouldn't deserve her."

He climbed into the landau and, closing the door, settled back into the seat to await the next moment or two when Hickory would again halt the team, this time in front of the tent.

Wherever Lenore wandered, Ashton was sure to follow. It was a caustic taunt that Malcolm frequently used when he once again realized Ashton was hounding their heels. If Lenore stayed at home, then Ashton remained near his tent and was ever watchful of any opportunity that might bring them together while Malcolm was away. If she left with Malcolm, he moved behind them like a shadow, keeping a close surveillance.

While Ashton's nearness grated on Malcolm's nerves, it seemed to amuse everybody else. Behind her employer's back, Meghan mutely cheered the Natchez man on, and her eyes sparkled with glee whenever she saw him ride out after the mistress's carriage or when his own landau swung onto the road behind them. The only time she was a bit unnerved by his presence in the area was when he took a swim in the ocean. At such times she kept her gaze carefully averted, not wanting anyone to accuse her of secretly admiring such a magnificent manly form.

Even Robert Somerton began to take Ashton's proximity in stride. He ceased to rage when he saw the younger man stroll out for a swim wearing naught but a skimpy loincloth, and on a few occasions he wandered over to share a libation or two with Ashton, though generally it was only coffee the latter imbibed.

Lenore enjoyed it all. His closeness. His unswerving tenacity. The sight of his brown body gleaming beneath the sun. It seemed quite an unladylike desire, but she yearned to feel again those flexing buttocks beneath her hands, to stroke those hard thighs, and to rouse him with her touch. With each passing day, her battle for control slipped another degree, and she realized she was completely abandoning her attempt to think of Malcolm as her husband.

It was during this time that the *River Witch* slid out of view. Malcolm was confused but elated. It appeared that Ashton's men had deserted him; then bright and early on the morrow Malcolm's spiraling hopes were dashed upon the rocks of despair again. There, anchored where the steamer had been, was an oceangoing vessel. This new ship which had come to haunt him was the *Gray Eagle*, and from it, a dinghy was launched, bringing ashore the captain, the men to row it, and a woman. Malcolm's interest perked up as he watched the latter come ashore. Hoping she might be pretty enough to stir Lenore's suspicions and perhaps endanger her fondness for the other man, he observed the visitor carefully as the captain escorted her toward Ashton's tent, but from a distance he had to conclude that she was just another employee. Her dull red hair was pulled back into a severe knot at the nape of her neck, and the dark gray gown hung from thin shoulders. She had no bosom to speak of, and though she was neat in appearance, she was not of a quality that would give another woman cause to worry. Still, he was curious. She seemed slightly familiar, and yet he could not place her. He rarely wasted a second glance on a woman who looked as old and worn as she did, and he quickly decided it was not important if he knew her or not.

Ashton came out to greet his guests and accepted the account books Sarah handed to him.

"All of your journals are in order, Mr. Wingate," she reported, pleased by her accomplishment.

"Excellent, Sarah. You've proved your value beyond anything I had ever imagined."

She blushed with pleasure at the compliment. "I enjoy the work, sir. It helps me forget."

Ashton smiled wryly. "Some strive hard to remember, others to forget. I await the day when Lierin remembers."

"And I await the day when I totally forget . . . and perhaps forgive, though I don't think I'll ever do that."

Captain Meyers offered the wisdom he had gained in his advancing years: "Forgiveness is the secret of a contented life, Sarah. You'll only hurt yourself by carrying hatred in your heart."

Ashton frowned slightly, realizing he had a problem of his own in that respect. His head lifted, and his eyes grew cold as he fixed his gaze on the one who roused that ire. "It doesn't help me when I see the foe so often."

Sarah followed his stare to the man who stood on the distant porch; then she frowned, wondering what mirage the morning heat had conjured up. She shook her head, dispelling the possibility, and turned back to the men.

Ashton indicated his not-so-humble dwelling as he presented an invitation to the pair. "Would you care to come in and look around? I borrowed the cabin boy from the *River Witch*, and he's made some tea and coffee. There are some sweet cakes, too, if you care for them."

They passed through the open tent flap, and for both, it was like entering a world of make-believe where sheikhs were plentiful and flamboyance was proof of success. The somewhat bedazzled captain chortled merrily as he was shown about, and Sarah followed, much agog. The sumptuous bed had been created from several feather ticks and was extravagantly covered and draped with black silk patterned with gold leaves, the same sort an Arab prince might envy. The sheerest gold silk hung from a round frame high above the bed, forming a mosquito netting that was possibly without equal, at least anywhere in Mississippi. Rich pillows were plentiful and formed a luxurious headrest for the mattress. The opulence they saw was hardly in keeping with the excellent and subtle tastes of their employer, but it was amusing to see such a setting in the local territory.

"When they told me you were living in a tent, Ashton, I never dreamed it would be anything like this," Captain Meyers exclaimed. "I had visions of you huddling under a tiny piece of canvas and trying to find comfort on a narrow pallet. Did you design these lavish appointments yourself?"

Ashton chuckled over the rim of his coffee cup. "It's for effect, Charles. Malcolm Sinclair seems to like everything gaudy when he's away from home, if you can understand my meaning." He had seen clear evidence of this in the company of harlots the man was wont to entertain. For all of their attempts at grandeur, none of them could come close to matching the elegance Lierin had in her little finger. "I thought I'd make Malcolm feel right at home, should he ever decide to saunter down this way and have a look-see."

Captain Meyers's eyes gleamed as he wiped a hand across his mouth. "The man likes his women, eh?"

"You might say that," Ashton replied dryly.

"Malcolm Sinclair?" Sarah repeated the name in a tentative query. "Who is he?"

Ashton jerked his head toward the house. "He lives up there . . . with Lierin. Except he claims she's Lenore."

"My husband's mother was a Sinclair," Sarah stated distantly as she wandered to the open flap of the tent. She peered out, but the man on the porch was gone. With a sigh, she came back to sit upon the soft cushions and, taking her cup and saucer in hand, sipped the tea before directing a statement to Ashton: "You might be interested in hearing that Horace Titch was down at the river looking over that new stern-wheeler you recently purchased. While he was there, he also looked around your warehouses and seemed most curious about the one that burned. I didn't know what to do, so I thought it would be wise if the sheriff knew about it. Sheriff Dobbs said he'd keep an eye on the man."

"Horace was here," Ashton stated as he went to refill his cup from the silver coffeepot. "He might still be, for all I know. Harvey asked him some questions, but there's no real proof that he had anything to do with setting the fire. I thought of putting out some men to watch over the house, just to make sure nothing happens to Lierin while he's here." Ashton laughed in wry amusement. "But Malcolm has put out some rather unsightly pawns to perform a similar service . . . mainly to keep me away from her."

"Pawns?" Charles frowned thoughtfully at the characterization. "Are you playing some kind of game here, Ashton?"

"Aye, Charles. A game of chess, except my heart is caught up in this one."

Now that Ashton had visitors, Malcolm saw a chance to whisk his young wife into Biloxi without the other man being aware of it. When he strolled down the hall to her room, he gave no heed to the fact that Meghan had not yet awakened her. The door was locked, but his insistent knock brought Lenore stumbling sleepily to the door. She groaned in mute agony when she saw him dressed and ready to be about his affairs, which she hoped had nothing to do with her. As he pushed his way into the chamber, she returned to her bed and pulled the sheet high over her head, wishing she could dismiss him from the room as easily as she had banished him from sight.

"I have some business to attend to in Biloxi this morning, madam, and I would delight in your company. If you can extract yourself posthaste from the comfort of your bed and get dressed, I would greatly appreciate it."

"Oh, Malcolm," she moaned. "Please go without me today. I am truly sick, and I don't relish the idea of waiting in the carriage for you when I'm feeling this way."

"Come now, Lenore. You'll feel better once we're under way. The ride will do you good." Malcolm held up a hand, halting any argument she might have made as she lowered her arm and, with it, the sheet. "I'll hear no more of it, my sweet. I'll send Meghan up with some tea, and she'll help you get dressed. Please be quick about it. My appointment is important, and I'd like to be there on time."

He stepped into the hall and closed the door behind him, giving her no opportunity to deny him. As his footsteps moved away, Lenore stared listlessly around the room. The breeze wafting through the open windows was warm and humid, giving no relief from the sweltering heat that consumed the days. Her gown clung to her clammy skin, while tiny beads of moisture trickled down between her breasts. Gingerly she pushed away the sheet and rose from the bed. She waited, hardly daring to breathe as her stomach rebelled against the motion; then she carefully crossed the room to the washstand. One glance in the small mirror, which hung above it, confirmed the fact that she was not feeling her best. She looked tired and pale, and the usual sparkle was gone from her eyes. She heaved a long sigh, resigning herself to a day of activity, and splashed tepid water on her face and arms, hoping it would revive her flagging energy. The effort proved of meager benefit, and it was not until Meghan brought tea and biscuits that she was able to make a somewhat firmer resolution to endure the outing. The toilette, however, was almost her undoing, and she had to fight against an overwhelming revulsion when Meghan offered an open vial of perfume for her to sample.

"Please," Lenore murmured, turning her head aside and thrusting up a hand. Its sweet, flowery essence sent a shudder through her. "Something lighter today, Meghan, please."

The maid studied her young mistress closely and watched her press a wet cloth to a wan cheek. "Mum, if ye don't mind me askin', do ye know what be ailin' ye?"

Lenore shrugged the question away with a lame excuse. "This heat. I don't know how you can bear it so well, Meghan."

"I guess I do all right, mum, but then, I've nothin' else botherin' me."

Lenore could not meet the woman's gaze as she asked cautiously, "Do you think there's something else bothering me?"

"Well, mum, I've had none o' me own, but I have a sister what acted the same way as yerself whene'er she got with babe."

The silky lashes fluttered downward as Lenore released a quavering sigh. Had she still been at Belle Chêne with Ashton, she would have gladly welcomed her childbearing state, but now the problems associated with her condition loomed monstrously large and foreboding before her. She could only foresee serious difficulties in store for her, and she was not quite sure how she was going to handle them all. It might have been better had she admitted her intimacy with Ashton from the beginning; then her condition at least would have been considered a possibility, and the two men would be braced for the news. She could only wonder how long it would take them to notice without an announcement. If she held silent for a while and gave herself a little time to prepare, perhaps she could figure out a way to avoid a violent scene. It seemed logical at least to make an attempt. "Meghan, I must ask a favor of you."

"Yes, mum?"

"I beg of you to keep this matter a secret between us until a more appropriate time. I doubt if Mr. Sinclair will appreciate the idea of my being with child."

"I understand, mum," the maid responded kindly. "An' ye can count on me keepin' me tongue."

Lifting her head, Lenore stared at the gently smiling woman. "Do you really understand, Meghan?"

The servant nodded slowly. "It's that Mr. Wingate, isn't it? You're carrying his child."

Lenore hid her worry, hoping the two men would not be as perceptive as the maid. The fear of what Malcolm might do or at least attempt to do to Ashton literally sickened her, and she flung out a shaking hand in mute appeal to Meghan as the nausea came in a sudden wave. The servant quickly interpreted the gesture and scurried to present a basin. A long moment passed before Lenore dared to raise her eyes, even to Meghan's sympathetic gaze.

"I'll never make it through the day if I have to go with Malcolm," she declared weakly.

"Never ye mind 'bout that, mum," Meghan soothed, removing the basin. "I'll deliver the message to Mr. Sinclair that you won't be able to go, and if he insists, then perhaps he needs to be shown proof."

Lenore shook her head, aghast at the workings of the maid's mind. "You wouldn't . . ."

"Ye need yer rest, mum," Meghan insisted. "An' there may be no other way to convince him." Having formed a dislike for her employer for the callous way he treated the mistress, she mumbled beneath her breath as she left the room, " 'Twould serve him right if it raises his gorge a mite."

The days were noticeably longer now with summer fully upon them. Dusk was short, and there were only shreds of the spectacular sunset left when Ashton stepped from his tent. He stretched his arms over his head and surveyed the darkening sky and the multitude of stars that were gathering in the heavens. The slim, sleek silhouette of the *Gray Eagle* lay against the deepening magenta hues on the western horizon, and the dim glow of the watchman's lantern gave proof that his orders were being followed and they were keeping wary of any intruders. Beyond the ship the waters of the gulf stretched endlessly on into the horizon.

Somewhere in the swamp that lay behind him, the brassy call of a heron broke the quiet as Ashton turned his gaze toward the house. He searched the lighted windows, hoping to glimpse a shadow of the one he longed to see, but he saw nothing which gave him relief from the gnawing, aching loneliness in his breast. Lighting a cheroot, he strolled down to where the ebbing tide left a strip of wet sand along the water's edge. The tidal creek lay like a dark barrier across the sand, setting a boundary between him and his love. The cheroot died in his fingers as his gaze again lifted to the house.

Lenore! Lierin! Lenore? Lierin? Though the face remained the same, the names blurred in his mind. . . .

He ground his teeth and angrily tossed the cigar into the softly lapping waves. He felt an overwhelming urge to lash out at something . . . or someone. Malcolm preferably. But he had not yet returned. There was no one to receive his anger, only the calm, uncaring sea and the yielding sand that now bore the print of his boots and which on the morrow would be featureless again.

A slight movement caught his eye, and he peered into the darkness until he could make out the vague glow of a white-clad figure. Like an illusive wraith it moved with soundless tread toward the narrow strip of sand along the shore and there paused to gaze out toward his ship, seemingly unmindful of the encroaching waves. He scarcely breathed while the longings of his heart yielded to the quickening surge of hope. Was it . . . ?

"Lierin!" The word was barely a whisper, taken from him by the rising wind, but in his mind it was a shout of acclamation as he recognized the pale, slender form. It was she!

He leaped across the stream, and his loneliness was banished to the far ends of the earth as he ran toward her. He saw her turn with a start as he drew near and realized she wore a nightgown and nothing else. The bottom part of it was wet where the waves had splashed up against her legs, and that which was dry was being whipped about by the wind. Her hair was loose and flying out all around her, and with the moon adding a soft luminous nimbus around her, she seemed like a fairy queen caught in alarm.

"Lierin." The name came from his lips in a softly whispered caress and with all the pent-up longing of a man in love with a dream. It was the almost imperceptible crack in his voice that screamed with the agony of his frustration.

"Lenore," she whispered in a desperate plea.

Though Ashton could not see her face clearly or discern the movement of her lips, he heard the choked sadness, and it wrenched his heart. "Whatever name you bear, you're still my love."

She raised a hand to brush the errant tresses back from her face and gazed up at him with desires of her own. The moon shone down upon him, and where the shirt gapped open, she could see the firmly muscled expanse of his broad chest. The sight evoked memories of a time when she had nestled there in love's sated bliss and felt the tickling of his breath against her brow. Oh, what torture is love, she thought. Was she ever to find peace with it?

"I really didn't think you were out here," she murmured. "My father said he had seen you rowing out to your ship, and he invited the guards in for a drink."

"One of my boatmen brought me some supplies," Ashton replied gently. "Your father probably saw him returning."

"Oh." Her voice was tiny, dejected.

"Is everything all right in the house?" he asked in concern.

She took a deep breath and released it in slow degrees, trying to cool her brain and subdue the tormenting concupiscence that had made a torture rack of her bed. "I was just restless and couldn't sleep, and I decided to take a walk." She paused, knowing there was something else that had made her abandon her room, and she told him in a trembling voice: "I dreamed Malcolm took me and showed me your grave. I even saw a tombstone with your name chiseled into it. The wind was blowing, and it was raining. It all seemed so real, it frightened me."

"It was nothing more than a dream, my love," he soothed. "I don't intend to die and leave you to him."

The silence dragged on, and Ashton peered down at her, trying to see her face clearly. He sensed her unrest and, with a great deal of meaning in his words, rephrased his earlier question: "Is everything well with you?"

Lenore opened her mouth to deny the possibility that there might be anything wrong, then slowly closed it again. Shaking her head as she felt a rush of tears, she turned from him and began to make her way along the narrow strip of sand. She sensed rather than heard him walking beside her. Indeed, it would have been difficult to ignore him when every nerve awoke to his presence.

"You are pensive tonight, madam," he stated with surety. "Can you tell me what's wrong?"

Lenore resisted the urge to brush at the tears streaming down her cheeks and, facing the sea, finally relented to his probing inquiry and spoke quietly into the wind: "I'm . . . I'm going to have a baby."

Ashton stepped toward her, joy snatching his heart and flinging it high, but he halted, suddenly unsure of how he stood with her. She seemed cold and distant, as if she hated telling him. He was close behind her, almost touching, and the turmoil that roiled within him made his hands shake. It was a long time before he could speak the single word: "Whose?"

The question stung. Lenore could see no need for him to ask. Wiping at the now flooding tears, she spoke over her shoulder. "Malcolm and I have not been together since I've been back."

With infinite care Ashton slipped his arms about her, one to slip beneath her bosom and hug her close, while the other hand settled over her stomach. He could feel the firm flatness of it through the cotton fabric and marveled at the gift of life that in less than a year's time would bring forth a babe. His head bent, and his lips brushed her ear as he asked, "Now will you go home with me?"

Her breath slipped from her, and it was somewhere between a moan and a wistful sigh. "The baby solves nothing, Ashton. I can't go back not knowing who I am. There are too many things I must remember. How can I accept you as my real husband when I am haunted by visions of my being toasted as Malcolm's wife?"

"Visions, my love, not necessarily reality. How can you be sure what you're seeing is the truth?"

She sighed shakily. "Because Malcolm confirmed what I saw without being aware of it. He could not have seen into my mind."

Ashton's voice was hoarse and ragged. "You can't expect me to stand aside and let another man claim you and my child."

"Give me a bit more time, Ashton," she pleaded, stroking her fingers over the hand that held her close. "This house holds so many secrets. If I leave it, I may never know who I am!"

"Then let me send Malcolm away," Ashton suggested. "I fear for your safety being in the house with him. He shows no care for you when he loses his temper. And your father is no protection."

"I know that, and I intend to be careful, but Malcolm has been a part of my life, too."

"What of me?"

Staring out into the dark horizon, Lenore rolled her head upon his chest. "I don't know, Ashton. I hope . . ." Her mouth quivered, and the welling tears filled her eyes. "I hope for the child's sake that you are something more than my present. I go to bed at night, and when the lamps are out, I remember how it was with you. I feel you beside me and the touch of your hand upon me and I ache. . . ."

"Aye, madam. I know the pain of unsated desires only too well."

"But I must be sure of myself." She cast a worried glance toward the lane as she heard the distant rattle of a carriage and the thudding hoofbeats of an oncoming team. "Malcolm is returning. I must go."

Ashton caught an arm closer about her waist, delaying her. "Don't leave me without a kiss."

Her breath wavered in a ragged sigh as she felt his manly form pressing close against her back. "You must think I'm far stronger of will than I am."

Reluctantly Ashton let her go, and watched until the darkness of the night consumed her. The night was lonely again, empty as if something meaningful had left it. The moon was only a pale, drab glow in the sky. The clouds hinted of rain to come, and the tide was beginning to flow, washing up on the beach and erasing all signs of their meeting.

- *Chapter Fourteen* -

It was a quiet afternoon, and Lenore was restless. Although she knew Ashton was somewhere within calling distance, she felt very much alone. She wanted him near, and she was sure he would have come to her had she yielded to her desire and beckoned him. Thoughts of the baby nestling within her womb were coming more and more to mind, and she wanted to talk at length and to share the secrets of her musings with someone who cared and who would love them both, but to summon him would be disastrous with the two guards ever-watchful of his approach, although she was beginning to think Ashton could handle anything that came his way.

Robert had journeyed to New Orleans on business and had planned to remain there for a couple of days. Malcolm had stayed in the Biloxi area, but was on another one of his trips to town and, as usual, had left no word as to when he would be back. Though of late he was inclined to leave and return without word of warning, his manner with her seemed almost careful, as if he had taken a deep interest in her well-being or, more likely, feared losing her to the other man.

The invitation to the gaming night on the *River Witch* had been sent out, and to her amazement Malcolm had accepted it with enthusiasm. He even suggested that she have a new gown made for the affair, so he might show her off in style and impress the other guests, who purportedly were some of the most affluent in Mississippi and neighboring states. There was of course no need for her to venture into Biloxi; he would send out a dressmaker to perform the service. It was destined to be an unusual affair, and Malcolm did not want to be found wanting by the other guests, even if they were friends with that dreadful Ashton Wingate.

Lenore roamed aimlessly through the lower rooms of the house, dearly longing for some activity that she could engage in, or at least occupy her mind. Malcolm had suggested that she find a needle and thread and then busy herself with woman's work. The idea of stitching a sampler in the parlor did not fit her mood, yet it was in that room where she settled to read. She had found a book of plays her father had left in the dining room only that morning and, seeing the binding worn and well used, opened it with care. Puzzling at the illegible writing scrawled across the title page, she studied the scrolls and embellishes closely until she realized it was nothing more than a signature, but the name seemed of no importance to her. She had never heard of Edward Gaitling before. Still, there were many names that had been erased from her memory and perhaps this was one of them, or simply the name of an actor who had autographed the tome for the Shakespearean enthusiast.

Reading made her drowsy, and she let the volume rest in her lap as she sipped the tea Meghan had brought her. As she did so, her eyes lifted above the rim of the cup and settled on the landscape painting above the fireplace. A tiny frown troubled her brow as she again puzzled at its presence. It still seemed out of place.

Growing inquisitive, she rose and went to examine the oil more closely. Although large in size, it definitely would not have drawn a high price in an art salon.

Lenore pressed her fingers against her temple for a moment, puzzling at her thoughts. How would she know that? And just how many art salons had she visited that she could be aware of the value of a painting?

Her mind drifted back to the sketch her father had shown her at Belle Chêne. He had said she had created that bit of art. Therefore, she must know something about different works by other artists and had some knowledge of their worth.

The possibility that she was an artist sent her flying to the parlor's writing desk in search of pen and ink. The long, narrow drawer in the middle held a supply of parchment, and when she explored further, she found that a side compartment contained something that looked like a collection of unfinished sketches, which were neatly bound with a ribbon, as if someone had cherished them enough to keep them. Taking care, she untied the bow and began to peruse each one slowly, desperately hoping the drawings would reveal something about her and who she was. She found more sketches like the one her father had shown her of the manor house, and there were landscapes that meant nothing to her, but which were all quite good, she concluded, wondering if she complimented herself with that judgment.

Her interest swiftly advanced when she came to an intricate drawing of a woman dressed in a riding habit. The pose was slightly rakish, with booted feet braced apart under a cocked hem. A plumed cap sat at a jaunty slant over a smooth coiffure, and a crop was clasped at a horizontal angle in front of the skirt, with the ends clasped in gloved hands. It was not the form that intrigued her so much as the face, for it appeared to be a likeness of herself . . . or Lierin. In hopes of determining which of them it might be, she examined the drawing with meticulous care and discovered, half hidden in the flowing lines of the skirt, the name that claimed the art: "Lenore"! It seemed unlikely that she would have created such a careful image of herself; therefore she had to conclude the sketch was of Lierin and several years old.

She propped the piece against the oil lamp where she could view it as she worked and, dipping the quill in ink, began to follow the example set before her. Working diligently, she sought to re-create the fluid lines of the old drawing on the new parchment, then frowned in dissatisfaction when the quill refused to flow with her desires. It left splotches of ink to mar the strokes and, with its unwieldiness, seemed to thwart her attempts. In frustration she grabbed up the sheet and, wadding it into a ball, tossed it aside. Again she tried, and again the quill failed her. The difference between the old sketch and the new made her decide that she would have to find a better implement with which to apply the ink, for her talent was being badly hampered by what she had.

Neatening up the desk, she rose and put all thoughts of art behind her as she made her way upstairs. In the hallway outside her door she paused, not really wanting to while away the afternoon with a volume of plays, nor was she interested in a nap. Ashton had appeased her woman's curiosity and, in doing so, had made it hard for her to forget. In bed her mind was wont to bring back detailed memories of a broad chest, muscular ribs, and flat, hard belly. And that was only the beginning of her torment!

She glanced up and down the hall in desperation, seeking some diversion; then a point of interest caught her questing eye. All the other doors in the corridor were set in pairs, but at the opposite end of the hall from her bedroom and across from an unused chamber, there were three in a row. Relieved to have a puzzle to occupy her for a time, she made her way to the center portal, curious to know where it led. She was disappointed to find it locked and without a key in evidence, but it was hardly a secret of houses that some of their keys could be used interchangeably. Fetching the one to her own bedroom door, she applied it to the lock and was rewarded when the latch clicked free. She laid a cautious hand upon the knob, and when she pushed it, the door moved inward with a ponderous grating of hinges. A long, narrow cubicle lay beyond the portal, and on one wall a steep stairway led to a trapdoor in the ceiling. A rope dangled beside the door by which she had entered, and when she tugged on it, the trap door lifted, opening a crack as a heavy counterweight slid down the wall beside the stairs. She had sudden visions of a dark, bat-infested attic, which would fill a foolhardy woman with many trepidations, but a thin sliver of light shone from above, and the sight buttressed her courage. She began to tug at the rope again, this time twining it around the cleat that was secured into the wall, and the trapdoor slowly rose to welcome her advance.

The stairs were steep and clumsy, but sturdy enough to bear her weight. As she gingerly climbed she listened for the telltale flutter of wings that would send her scurrying back down the flight again. None came, and when her head rose above the level of the upper flooring, she realized her fears were for naught. She found none of the leathery hided creatures flitting about. The square vents beneath the gabled peaks were closely louvered, and thin slats were spaced inside to prevent the possibility of the detested denizens' intrustion. Absent, too, were the thick layers of dust and cobwebs she had expected, and she could only surmise that the servants cleaned the attic at least on a yearly basis. Planks had been nailed above the ceiling joists to form a floor for the attic, and on this were the usual heaps of discarded treasures. Several trunks and old traveling bags were pushed to one side, and near them the parts of an old bed were braced against a post. A collection of cloth-covered paintings stood upright between supporting beams, and a couple of wooden boxes were filled with an odd assortment of knickknacks.

The heat had been entrapped in this upper space and brought a glistening of perspiration to her skin as she climbed up to the flooring. She gently prodded the old trunks with her toe and received a hollow sound until she tested one that looked newer than the rest and which was strangely familiar. Wondering what might be inside, she loosened the straps and sought to lift the top, but again found a lock barring her way. A growing certainty that this chest belonged to her sent her searching through the wooden boxes for a makeshift tool with which to pry open the metal flap. The best she found was a broken letter opener, and the sweat of her labors plastered her gown to her back before she gave up the attempt. Whatever was in the trunk would remain a secret until she found a sturdier wedge.

She moved on, this time examining the paintings. Several in front were average scenes, but toward the back a large one was covered with a cleaner cloth. She slid it out and, removing the covering, propped the portrait where the light would fall upon it. The painting was of an older man, perhaps around Robert's age, and the face was rather squarish with clean, straight features and a mop of gray-streaked dark hair waving softly away from it. Though the expression was rather stern and forbidding, there was something in the green eyes that bespoke honesty and a fair sense of justice. She considered the portrait from every angle, but found nothing in the visage that stirred a recall. Returning the painting to the stack, she stepped away, then paused as she was suddenly struck with an image of the landscape downstairs. Mingled with it were brief flashes of the man's portrait hanging in its stead above the fireplace.

She turned back and, retrieving the portrait, made her way carefully down the narrow stairs and to the parlor. There she set the painting aside while she dragged a straight chair to the fireplace. Taking the landscape down, she replaced it with the oil of the man, then stood back to evaluate its importance to the room. The landscape had been like a large gall on a tree, out of place and totally unappealing, but now the parlor seemed complete, well in tune with its surroundings and the rest of the house. Not really knowing the history of the landscape, she did not want to upset Malcolm if perchance it had been a gift from him, and she resisted the urge to leave the portrait hanging there.

Returning the painting to the attic room, she made a mental note of just where she placed it, then descended the narrow stairs again. At the lower portal, she released the rope from the cleat, slowly closing the trapdoor. Stepping into the hall, she locked the door leading to the corridor and removed the key.

Boredom set in once again as she went to her bedchamber. A light, freshly scented breeze sweeping in from the gulf toyed with the draperies and cooled her with its soft touch. She picked up the book of plays and seated herself near the french doors where the soft zephyr wafted through. After a while the book sank to her lap again, and her gaze rose and reached out to the sea. As she stared, a face formed in her mind, but it was not the one she expected. It belonged to the man in the portrait, and in her mind the countenance became animated, changing with different moods. Laughing, frowning, thoughtful, tender . . .

Lenore's brows came together sharply. Somewhere beyond the blank wall in her mind was a memory of him, and she thought she knew him well.

It was some time later when Malcolm returned on his black steed. The animal was in a heavy lather, having raced the whole distance from town, but the steed's exhaustion did not seem to disturb the man who prodded him forward again, away from the house, and to Ashton's tent. He made several passing circles in front of the courtyard before bringing the stallion to a halt there. Keeping the restless horse in check, he called out with a derisive chuckle, "Come on out of hiding, *Mister* Wingate. I want to talk with you."

Wondering what mischief the man was up to, Ashton stepped to the open flap of his tent, and Lenore came out to stand at the end of the porch, prodded by the same curiosity. She shaded her eyes against the spreading rays of the lowering sun and bit her lip worriedly as she watched Ashton move to the edge of the decking.

"What are you about today, Malcolm?" Ashton asked, peering up at the man with a cocked brow as he casually trimmed the end of a cheroot.

Malcolm ignored the question for a moment as he patted his horse's neck in a show of affection rarely displayed toward his animals. With no mind for how long they lasted, he rode and used them hard until they wore out; then, unconcerned, he found another steed to push through the same accelerated life span. "I've heard in town that you've been looking around for a horse to buy for a lady."

"That's right," Ashton admitted, speaking out of the side of his mouth as he lighted the thin cigar.

"Might I ask what lady?"

Puffing the tightly rolled leaves alight, Ashton squinted up at the man, and only when he was assured that the cheroot was lighted did he deign to take it from his mouth. "Lierin was quite a horsewoman at one time." He plucked a tiny piece of tobacco from his tongue and flicked it from his fingers. "I thought she might enjoy the gift."

Malcolm's eyes turned icy with the hostility he bore the other man; then he smirked. "Lenore is fairly talented herself, but if you think I'm going to let my wife accept a gift from another man, you've taken leave of your senses."

Ashton shrugged leisurely. "Oh, I wasn't going to let the horse be taken into your stable, Malcolm. I want better care given to it than that." Placidly he pointed with the end of the cheroot to the nervously prancing steed. "Treated like that, it would never last."

Malcolm made no excuses. "I get what I want from them." His large mouth twisted in a jeer. "The same is true with women."

The smokey eyes hardened as they met the man's taunting grin; then Ashton slowly stroked a thumb along his jaw. "I've seen some of the women you use . . . in Ruby's Tavern. They're about as sorry as that horse."

Malcolm stood in the saddle, tempted to launch himself from the mount, but common sense prevailed, and he relaxed again to lift his heavy shoulders in a shrug. "With some women at least we seem to share the same taste."

"It's not difficult to admire a woman like Lierin." Ashton tucked the cheroot into his mouth and reflectively savored its quality for a moment before removing it again. He clicked his tongue before he made comment. "What I'm wondering is what Lenore saw in you."

Malcolm's dark face went livid, and again he had to fight to control the violent urges. With an unappreciative sneer, he returned the gibe: "I've been curious about you, too, and I'm beginning to believe you pressured Lierin into marrying you. You've certainly made a pest of yourself around here."

A soft chuckle shook Ashton's shoulder. "A pest to you, maybe."

"It's needless to rant on about our lack of regard for each other," Malcolm stated coldly. "I don't believe either one of us is suffering from any illusions concerning our feelings."

"I don't think so," Ashton agreed. "The hatred seems mutual."

Malcolm smiled tightly. "Then you can understand why I'm not going to let Lenore accept your gift, so you might as well save your-self some expense."

"I wasn't concerned with getting your approval when I started searching, Malcolm," Ashton responded, unperturbed. "Expressing your feelings to me changes nothing. I've already found a mare for the lady. In fact, it should be delivered to me shortly."

"I won't let her accept it!" Malcolm shouted. "Can't you under-stand?"

Ashton lifted his shoulders in a lazy shrug. "The mare will be kept here for Lierin's pleasure. Hickory can see that the horse is made ready for her whenever she wants it."

Rather slack-jawed at the man's audacity, Malcolm slumped back into his saddle. "I don't believe you. I really don't believe a man can be as stubborn as you are. You make me wonder what you have for brains. If you think I'm going to let Lenore ride that horse, you have none! Absolutely none!"

"You'd like to keep her prisoner in that house, wouldn't you?" Ashton challenged. "You haven't let her go anywhere without you while I've been here. . . ."

"For the obvious reasons!" Malcolm barked. "Because you're here! I don't want the same thing to happen to her that happened to Mary! And that took place right after you arrived! Tell me, *Mister* Wingate, why was that? It was peaceful and quiet before you came!"

"Of course, it was," Ashton replied sardonically. "There was no one to challenge your little domain. And you know as well as I do that neither I nor any of my crew had anything to do with Mary's murder."

"I don't know anything of the kind!" Malcolm objected.

"I thought you were smarter than that," Ashton sneered. "Maybe I was wrong. But then, I understand why you'd want me to be accused of the murder. You'd like nothing better than to be free of me, so you can keep Lierin locked up in that damned house!" The anger came upon him at the idea, and he jabbed an arm out in the direction of the wooden structure as he delivered the accusation: "You're afraid to let her go free, because you're scared you'll lose her or whatever she has that you want."

"What are you suggesting?" Malcolm squawked.

The coldness came back in Ashton's eyes as he stared boldly into the other's face and made his reply: "Her father is getting on in years.

He's a drunk and therefore accident-prone. You could be a rich man one day if you just hang on and let nature take its course."

"I have wealth of my own!" the other man insisted.

"Where? Show me where!" Ashton demanded. "As far as I can tell, you have no holdings. You're not a planter. You have no land. You come and go like the sparrow, settling in to roost wherever you can find a warm, sheltered spot and leaving nothing behind but your droppings when you flit away."

"I've had enough of this," Malcolm said, savagely jerking the reins through his hand. The horse tossed his head as the bit tore into his mouth and sidled away from the wooden platform. Malcolm turned him around in a circle, delivering one last suggestion over his shoulder: "Forget the mare, Wingate, and save yourself some money. I'm not going to let Lenore ride her."

He kicked the horse into a full-out run, then barely a moment later brought him to a sliding halt before the house. Leaping off the stallion's back, he thrust the reins into the stable boy's hands and mounted the steps to the porch. His footsteps fell like thunder against the planks, bearing testimony to his rage as he strode to the end of the veranda where Lenore stood. He did not notice how she trembled when she faced him or the hesitancy in the green eyes. He was too intent upon laying down his ultimatum and having her submit to his authority.

"That buffoon who lives in the tent over there has purchased you a mare. . . ." He smirked in hateful derision as he detected her surprise. "You needn't be overwhelmed by his generosity just yet, my dear. I forbid you to accept her." His eyes hardened with a dark, glaring sheen as he added, "And you will obey me."

He left her and pushed his way into the house, making Lenore flinch as he slammed open the door. It seemed almost peaceful after his passage upstairs, and after a lengthy moment of quietness she breathed a sigh of relief, deciding Malcolm's temper tantrum was over for the present moment.

The news he had brought settled down upon Lenore and, glancing over her shoulder, she saw Ashton still on the decking. His feet were braced apart, and one arm was folded across his midsection, with the back of the hand supporting the elbow of the other arm as he held the cigar in front of his mouth. She could almost see him squinting through the smoke and rolling the cheroot between his thumb and fingers as he stared at her. Even with the space that separated them, she felt the weight of his steady regard. A light blush warmed her cheeks as she sensed what he was thinking, and it had naught to do with Malcolm.

The delivery of the mare came the next day, thankfully while Malcolm was gone. A man on horseback led her behind him at a leisurely walk, passing across the front lawn and bringing Lenore out of the house in breathless haste to watch the flashy mare parade past. The steed was a bay with long, flowing mane and tail that swept full and free. The tail flagged high as the mare arched her neck and progressed with small, mincing steps, seeming anxious to break into a showy jig. She was tall and incredibly fine-boned, and Lenore sensed with certainty that the delicate bones in her slender legs would break long before her spirit did.

Regardless of the two guards who strolled out onto the lawn to prevent closer passage, the horseman continued on his casual way until he neared the decking outside the tent. Ashton came out to greet him with a broad smile, and the stranger swung down, shook hands, and then nodded as Ashton spoke and motioned for him to take the mare to a spot closer to the house, threateningly close to the boundary that marked the division between his own claim and the one he had allowed Malcolm. As the fellow complied, the two guards exchanged worried comments and, gesturing to one another, hurried to where they might prevent any possible infraction. Lenore went to stand at the end of the porch as the stranger displayed the mare, but it was not nearly close enough. Lifting up her skirts, she ran back across the veranda, down the steps, and over to where the small group of men were gathered around the mare . . . the guards on one side of the line, Ashton, the stranger, and the horse on the other. One of the guards glanced over his shoulder and saw Lenore coming, then hastened to block her passage. Ready for a set-to, Ashton stepped around the steed, but Lenore looked up at the man with some determination of her own.

"You will kindly remove yourself from my path," she commanded in a low, threatening tone, "or I shall be forced to make an advance, through you, over you, or however you would have it. If you persist, you will have to bind me physically, because I shall be tempted to rake the skin from whatever portion of your hide is available, starting with the face. Do I make myself clear?"

Ashton hid a chuckle as the fellow looked in wide bemusement at his companion, seeking some help there and finding none. It was one thing to get into a brawl with a man, but quite another to enter into a fray with a woman, especially one that displayed so much fire. Mumbling in worry, he stepped back, allowing her to proceed.

"Oh, Ashton, she's beautiful!" Lenore declared as she made a slow tour around the horse, unmindful of the boundaries that kept the men apart. "What's her name?"

"Heart o'Mine," he replied with a grin of pleasure.

Lenore laughed and fondly stroked the mare's withers. "An appropriate name."

"I thought so," he agreed, peering at her from under his brows as he smiled with boyish charm. "She's something special, just like you. You'll look good on her."

Lenore sighed as Malcolm's order came back to mind. "But I can't accept her. It would cause too much trouble."

Ashton had been expecting the reply. "I'll keep her over here where she'll be safe. Whenever you'd like to admire her . . . or ride her . . . she'll be ready for you. At your convenience, madam."

Lenore was sorely tempted. "Perhaps if I just borrowed her from time to time, Malcolm would let me ride." She shook her head, rejecting the idea, then settled her hands on her hips with an exasperated sigh. "I'm getting so bored in the house, I need to get out, and what better way than to ride?" A sudden inquisitive smile replaced her frown. "Can you have her saddled for me . . . now?"

One of the guards stepped forward. "Mrs. Sinclair, I don't think you should . . ."

"Bah!" Lenore promptly silenced his unfinished suggestion. "I'll do what I want to, and if Malcolm doesn't like it . . . then, that's too bad."

Grinning, Ashton took the mare's reins and began to lead her to where Hickory stood waiting outside the smaller tent, while the lady went racing back to the house in a rather undignified manner, lifting her skirts well past her ankles.

"Meghan!" she called as she tore up the stairs. "Meghan, fetch me a habit. I'm going riding!"

In no time Lenore was back, dressed in a summer habit of pearl gray, with a white jabot tumbling in lace-trimmed layers from her throat. As she crossed the boundary line, she took note that Ashton's stallion was also saddled and stood a short distance away where Hickory held him in check. Ashton waved the stranger farewell and stepped to Heart o'Mine, lifting Lenore onto her back while the cabin boy stood at the horse's head.

"We'd better see how much you remember," Ashton advised as he gave her the reins. "The last thing I want is to see you hurt."

Lenore complied with his request and tested the mare's performance through a walk, trot, and canter, all within a wide circle between the house and tent. To her pleasure, both she and the mare seemed in capable order, and Ashton swung up onto his stallion, adding his approval. Much to the fretting concern of the two guards, she rode away from the house, leading Ashton down along the shore and away from their prying eyes.

Her spirits lifted to immeasurable heights as she enjoyed the outing, the mare, and the company of her escort. There were so many things she wanted to talk with Ashton about, and he seemed as anxious as she to discuss the details of her childbearing state, wanting to know when the babe was due and where the pregnancy might have begun.

"Before we left for New Orleans, I think," she murmured, casting a wistful gaze in his direction. "You and Meghan are the only ones who know."

"For heaven's sake, don't tell Malcolm," Ashton warned. "At least, not while he's in the house with you." He hated to think what the other man might do to her. "You'd make me feel better about everything if you'd let me send him and his two buffoons away. You could stay in the house with your father if you wanted to, and I wouldn't even ask you to allow me to move in . . . or press you to go home with me where you belong."

Lenore tossed him another glance and laughed. "You're already pressing me to do that."

In roweling frustration Ashton settled back in the saddle. "All right! I admit it! And I try because I care!"

"Thank you," she murmured with a gentle smile.

A muted groan came from him as her soft, grateful look went through him and stroked the strings of his heart. Was she aware of what she did to him when such loving tenderness was displayed in her face? "You turn me inside out, woman," he complained with a helpless chuckle. "I am putty in your hands."

Lenore shook her head negatively. "I don't think so." She glanced back over her shoulder, realizing they were now some distance from the house. "We'd better get back." She giggled, relenting to the humor that set in when she remembered the two guards chafing as they watched her ride away. "I'm afraid if Malcolm gets home first, he may shoot his men."

"Good riddance," Ashton replied promptly.

"Oh, Ashton, you don't mean that." As he raised his brow in sharp disagreement, she burst into laughter again. "Perhaps I'm wrong."

They had turned their mounts and were heading back when Ashton halted his horse by the edge of the water and swung down. Lenore reined in her mare and watched him in wonder as he strolled back along the wet sand where he had just passed. He paused and kicked the sand with his toe, then stooped quickly, grabbing up a tiny crustacean, which he brought back to her and presented in the palm of his hand.

"A flea crab," he informed her, gently nudging the coin-sized creature with a finger.

"It looks frightened," Lenore commented as the tiny thing clamped his legs close to his body.

"Aye, madam, that it is." Ashton bent and brushed it from his hand, letting it go free on the sand again. Dusting his hands, he straightened and glanced up at her, then stilled as he found something in her eyes that he understood only too well: the same sort of longing he had experienced himself much too often of late. Half afraid to move, he lowered a hand to her thigh and waited while she searched his face. Slowly, very slowly she leaned down to him and touched her lips to his. It was sweet bliss in the afternoon, a heady nectar that stirred his senses . . . and his heart, a soft reawakening of all his love and fondness for her.

"While the cat's away . . . !" The caustic shout came from behind them, and they hastily drew apart. Looking around, they saw Malcolm sneering at them from the back of his stallion a short distance away. He prodded the animal forward and, reining up, pushed it between Lenore's mount and Ashton, not caring how roughly the steed advanced upon the man. Ashton stumbled back, avoiding the heavy hooves of the nervously prancing horse. Coming to a halt, he faced the other, who had placed himself very protectively before

Lenore. The broad face was full of venomous hatred as he stared down at Ashton.

"I told you to forget about buying my wife a horse." Malcolm's eyes were sharply piercing as he bent a glare on Lenore, and his growl came through clenched teeth: "And I told you not to accept the gift."

"I haven't . . . yet!" she retorted tartly. "I'm just using the mare for a time."

"Well, you may use her no more," Malcolm snapped and flung out an arm toward the house. "Get home . . . now! I'll deal with you later."

"I'll go, but only because I was going in that direction anyway." Lifting her chin loftily, Lenore complied with his wishes and left at a leisurely canter.

Malcolm turned back upon Ashton with a raging glower. "I know you'd like to lay my wife down and have your pleasure with her, but if you ever do, I'll rip out your heart and feed it to the fish."

"You're welcome to try," Ashton returned crisply.

Malcolm sneered. "I'm sure my men will be anxious to help."

"Do they do everything you say?" Ashton probed.

"Of course," Malcolm boasted. "I've known them for some years now, and I have no question concerning their loyalty."

"Then I'd like to know what one of them was doing working on my steamer a couple or so years back."

Malcolm stared agape at the man on the ground. "When was that?"

Ashton raised a brow sharply. "I've been trying to remember the precise time, but I know without a doubt he was there at one time, working for me."

Malcolm sneered. "Obviously he didn't like you well enough to continue."

"Or else he had other motives in mind for quitting."

"Such as?"

Ashton shrugged. "I'm not quite sure yet. When I am, I'll let you know."

"Please do." Malcolm's smirk returned. "Until then, keep your damned horse and hands to yourself."

Ashton smiled lazily. "As I said, Malcolm, you can't keep her prisoner forever."

The larger man thrust a hand inside his coat and, whipping out a pistol, promptly cocked the hammer. Ashton stumbled back a step, realizing he was completely defenseless against such an attack. At any moment he expected to feel the burning heat of a shot boring its way through his chest or head, and he could do naught but wait. Any attempt to assault the other would bring about the firing of the pistol that much sooner.

Malcolm enjoyed his power and savored it long and to its fullest as he waved the sights threateningly in front of the other. The hazel eyes showed concern, but as yet had not lifted one pleading look to him, and that really would have made his day. To have the high and haughty *Mister* Wingate groveling for mercy was his fondest wish.

"Well?" Ashton barked sharply. "Are you going to shoot me or not?"

"I'd love to," Malcolm replied with a smug smile. "I really would love to." He chuckled, relishing the moment a bit longer, then heaved a heavy sigh and raised the sights of the weapon from his opponent. "But I must save the shot for the mare."

Chortling in glee, he spurred his horse forward and kicked him into a full-out run. Ashton ran to his stallion and, snatching up the dangling reins, leaped astride, then followed the other man in hot pursuit. It was a race, to be sure, and Malcolm knew how to get every last measure of speed from his horse. This was one thing he did well. Leaning forward, he slashed the crop against the stallion's side. He chuckled deviously to himself, already savoring the idea of the bay mare lying dead in a pool of blood at Ashton's feet. It would serve the man right for all that he had done.

Lost in his musings, Malcolm suffered a start when the thunderous pounding of hooves became louder, and he twisted, throwing a glance over his shoulder. He had been almost certain that it was his imagination, but he gaped in shock when he saw the Wingate man gaining on him . . . rapidly. With a savage curse, he slashed the crop repeatedly against his steed's flanks, flinging droplets of blood out wide as he whipped it into a frenzy. Still, the other stallion reached out with its long legs, eating up the distance between them until horse and man drew alongside. Malcolm turned his head briefly and saw the other animal stretching out, and it seemed as if the steed did so for the sheer pleasure of the race. No whip marred his side, but he raced on because the challenge was there, and his heart pushed him to win.

Lenore glanced back as she heard the thunderous approach, and she saw Ashton raise his arm and motion for her to ride beyond the house.

"Get to the tent!" he shouted. "Go! Get that horse out of sight!"

"Stop her!" Malcolm bellowed the order to his men. "Stop her and that horse!"

Lenore did not know what was happening, but she trusted Ashton enough to obey him without question. She set the bay mare to a swifter flight, weaving around one man, who ran in front of her waving his arms as he tried to halt her or spook the horse. Past him, she got a little angry and charged lickety-split toward the other, who ran out to block her path. Seeing the oncoming approach of the charging steed, the man staggered back in some fear of being trampled. His eyes widened even more as the horse continued on the same course, and he suddenly realized that the lady was not going to swerve aside to miss him. She was going to run him down if he did not remove himself *posthaste!*

The man dove for safety, eating a lot of grass as he slid on the lawn, first on his face and then on his belly, and in the process scraping a lot of skin. Hickory was dancing up and down near the tent, gesturing for her to come quickly, and she came, pulling the mare to a skidding halt before the open door of the tent. The black man lifted her down and, grabbing the reins, led the mare inside. Lenore was wondering if she should follow when Ashton came charging toward her on his stallion. Malcolm was behind him, and as the first man slowed, Malcolm dove from his horse, across the other's, and swept Ashton from the saddle. Lenore gasped and stumbled back as the pair fell to the ground at her feet. Malcolm landed on top and immediately used the advantage of his greater weight to pin Ashton down, clamping his thickly muscled legs over that one's arms. Wedging a forearm beneath Ashton's chin, Malcolm leaned hard on his throat as he slipped his other hand behind the dark head and began to apply a choking pressure, or one that would break his neck.

"Malcolm, stop!" Lenore cried and grabbed at his arm, trying to drag him off. With an angry growl Malcolm shoved her aside, sending her reeling to the open door of the tent. The man's movement was enough to allow Ashton to wiggle an arm free, and with it, he slammed a hard fist into the wide cheek, rolling the man off him and winning his release. Promptly he was on his feet and moving. Taking a step toward the one who was rising from his knees, Ashton brought his own knee up hard beneath the other's chin. Malcolm's head rocked back, but rage pushed him beyond pain. Not even waiting for his thoughts to clear, he lunged forward and clasped his arms tightly about the lean waist of the other. He desired to hear the melodious sound of ribs cracking and began to squeeze, unmindful of the chopping blows that struck his neck and shoulders. Ashton rolled his head backward as the painful vise intensified, and changed his tactics. His fingers came up and probed for the other's eyes, applying pressure that Malcolm could not bear. The younger man cried out and flung himself away, holding his hands tightly over his face. Ashton followed, raised a booted foot and kicked sideways, catching the man in the ribs. Malcolm sailed back and landed hard. As he blinked to clear his blurred vision, he saw his wife standing in the open door of the tent, looking distressed, and behind her, Hickory seemed equally disquieted. Beyond them both, he glimpsed the mare that had caused the confrontation, and the determination took hold of him to make sure the steed never caused another.

Forgetting the pain in his eyes, he searched about for the pistol that he had dropped when he first launched his attack. He saw the gleam of the smoothbore, and his hand stretched out, grabbing hold of the butt. He brought his arm up and across, pulling back the hammer, but a shadow fell across him, and another blow from a booted foot struck his arm and sent the pistol sailing. The weapon flipped through the air and, striking the ground, discharged with explosive force. Malcolm screamed in pain as the searing heat of the shot sliced across his arm, and he rolled in agony, holding a hand clasped over his wound.

"I'm shot!" he cried. "Someone help me!"

Ashton stepped forward and, kneeling on one knee, yanked down the sleeves of the man's coat and shirt, ripping them away from the armholes until he could see the blood welling from the deeply grooved flesh. He made a quick assessment of the injury as Lenore hurried to him.

"A flesh wound," he reported in sneering derision as she knelt beside him. "It's nothing. Hardly more than a scratch. He'll be all right in a day or two."

Malcolm reddened and pressed a handkerchief over the wound, preventing any further view of it. He tossed a glare at Ashton and accused, "I could be dying, and he'd say it was nothing."

"I was hoping it would be serious," Ashton quipped. He rose to his feet and, with a hand beneath Lenore's elbow, drew her up beside him. "Wash it, wrap it, and then let him sulk alone. I don't think he'll try killing the mare again, unless, of course"—he raised a brow sharply as he gave the man a meaningful stare—"he wants some trouble with the sheriff."

Malcolm struggled to his feet, ignoring Lenore's attempt to help him, and stalked off toward the house.

Ashton wandered over to the discarded pistol and, picking it up, smiled as he examined it. "What wisdom directs this weapon? With unerring skill it has found the fool in our midst."

– Chapter Fifteen –

Robert Somerton returned home with a house-guest, a man of like years and with a comparable penchant for drink. Samuel Evans was said to be an artist and indeed seemed talented with a quill, even the one Lenore had discarded as useless. It was his favor to doodle at the writing desk in the parlor, where he enjoyed the company of her father. From there, he expounded with rampant verbosity about the wide variety of adventures he had experienced in his life. Lenore raised a wondering brow at his penchant for raving on with boasts and embellishments, and it seemed the more he imbibed, the more he enlarged upon his exploits and the more fanciful the strokes of his quill became. He created extravagant flourishes and long sweeping lines that took on more of a look of an ornate or elongated script than any landscape or drawing. In the creation of the latter he appeared to be lacking, but he was capable of changing the scrivening to whatever fashion suited his whim. Lenore was fascinated with his abilities and watched from over his shoulder as he penned his name in several different styles.

"Here now!" Robert chortled. "I can do as well."

Samuel hooted in laughing disbelief. "Not likely, my good man! Ye can't even write yer own name so it's legible. How do ye expect ye can wield a quill to yer likin' when ye can't even do that?"

"I'll show you!" Chuckling, Robert dabbed the quill in the inkwell and, with a great show, swept it across the parchment. When finished, he studied the results, then proudly displayed them to his guest and daughter. "There! 'Robert Somerton!' 'Tis clear as the nose on your face."

Lenore accepted the sheet with an amused smile and, at first, saw nothing more than a wild tangle of sweeps and rolls; then she frowned in bemusement as another signature came to mind. Strangely, it was the one in her father's book of plays. Of course, that did not seem likely. To write another man's name in one's own book . . . Why would anyone want to?

Her eyes lifted, and she stared at the elder man in puzzling question. Lately she had sensed a softening in his heart for her, and though she was not aware of the reason, it had pleased her to be treated more like a daughter of worth than one of no account. Still, there were times when she had trouble feeling anything more for him than pity.

"Come, Lenore," he urged, offering her the quill. "Show this good fellow here what a beautiful hand you have." He chuckled, tossing a glance toward his guest, who eyed the pair of them. "Your name, girl. Write out your name for us."

Lenore accepted the stiff feather and bent forward to fulfill the request, but hesitated as a chilling draft wafted through her body. There was almost a gleam of anticipation in Samuel Evans's eyes as he waited for her to perform the simple task. Though she could not say why she might have cause, his manner made her apprehensive. To compare one's writing with another seemed a simple, inconsequential thing . . . almost nonsensical. At least, it should have been.

She returned the quill to the well, noticing his surprise as she did so, and moved to the french doors in a rush as she heard a horse whinny outside on the lawn. It was Heart o'Mine, being exercised by Hickory. He led the mare at the end of a rope, and she trotted with precise, lighthearted cadence before her audience of one.

"It's that new mare of Ashton's," Lenore announced over her shoulder, thankful for the timely excuse. If she was being foolish, she had no wish to offend the men, but if there was something more to it than what they told her, she would just as soon avoid gratifying their whims . . . unless of course they first explained their reasons. "She's beautiful, don't you think?"

Robert mumbled a noncommittal answer and went to replenish his glass. "I'm not much of a horseman."

Lenore glanced around in some surprise, struck by his statement. What had made her think her father loved horses and was himself an exceptional rider . . . or at least used to be? Her brow puckered in a tiny, perplexed frown as her mind flitted back to the name in the volume of plays. "I was wondering . . . sir"—calling him Father still came hard—"who Edward Gaitling might be."

Robert choked and spewed out a mouthful of whiskey. Being the recipient of the gushing fount, Samuel Evans jumped up and hurriedly wiped at the side of his face and sleeve as he shot a sharp glance at her father. That one had some trouble getting his breath and, after so doing, took a long time clearing his throat. Mopping his forehead with a handkerchief, he sank into a chair and looked at her hesitantly. "Why do you ask, girl?"

Lenore faced the porch again, and her eyes fondly followed the high-stepping mare as she flagged her tail and pranced past, barely seeming to touch the ground with her black hooves. Finally remembering that her father had made an inquiry, Lenore glanced back over her shoulder. "I just saw the name in your book of plays and was curious, that's all."

"Oh, he's just some actor I've known for some time. He . . . ah . . . signed the volume for me after performing in one of the plays."

"Oh." His answer only left her more puzzled. "I see." She frowned, haunted by what she had seen in her father's handwriting. Was she making too much ado about something that was nothing?

Robert stepped toward her with a brief chuckle. "Speaking of signing one's name, Lenore, you were going to . . ."

She stepped out onto the veranda, leaving the men and that particular issue behind her. From the porch, she strolled out across the lawn where Hickory was stroking Heart o'Mine's neck and praising her for the fine horse she was.

"Ain't she somepin, Miz Wingate?" the black asked with a large, white-toothed grin.

Lenore's eyebrows came up in surprise. "I'm Mrs. Sinclair now, Hickory."

"Oh, Ah knows what dey sayin', missus, but Ah still has trouble believin' a sweet lady like yose'f would marry a man like Mistah Sinclair." He shook his head sorrowfully. "Anybody'd try to kill a horse like dis gotta be mean clear through."

Lenore smiled wryly. "My father once said that one can always tell a man by the temperament of the horse he ke . . ." She paused in midword, clearly confused. Her father had just denied knowing anything about horses, so where had the thought come from?

Hickory drew back his lips to display his broad, white teeth in a wider grin. "Mr. Wingate, he's gots some mighty nice ones, missus."

She rubbed the steed's silky nose as she glanced at the black. "You like the Natchez man, don't you, Hickory?"

"Yas'm." The black gave a definite nod and patted the mare's neck. "Ah sho' do."

"I do, too," she sighed. "And therein lies the problem."

Hickory chuckled. "Ah kinda reckoned yo liked him, missus."

His comment made her wonder if her feelings were a secret to anyone. Her voice turned wistful. "I do believe my sister made the better choice in husbands."

A soft chuckle shook the man's shoulders. "Like Massa Ashton say, Miz Wingate, we jes' have to wait an' see 'bout dat."

The *River Witch* was pulled up close to the dock and bedecked with garlands and flowers, enough to cover the recent canvas and board additions along the rail and to fill the air with a fresh and fragrant essence as the guests came aboard. Men in formal attire and women in silk and satin gowns, with jewels twinkling at their throats and fingers, passed along the decks and entered the large gleaming halls, where in one an orchestra was playing or in another the cards were being shuffled and games of chance being waged.

Lenore entered the second on the arm of Malcolm, and heads turned to view the couple in wide curiosity. Those closely acquainted with the Natchez man had heard some of the rumors floating about and were anxious to see the lady who was causing such a stir. She was hardly a disappointment! Gowned in pearl pink satin with touches of ecru lace adorning the sleeves and narrow bodice, she looked as delectable as any confection that was available on the lavishly filled tables. Her auburn hair was swept up in a soft, elegant coiffure, and at each ear teardrops of pearl dangled prettily from clusters of diamond-wreathed rubies. Falling around the long, slender column at her throat were two carefully matched strands of the same opaque gems, brought together with a similar catch of ruby encircled with smaller diamonds. The jewels were a recent gift from Malcolm, who declared them a peace offering for the way he had lost his temper over Heart o'Mine. He was most anxious for her to know that he could be generous with her, too.

The décolletage bared her shoulders sublimely and dipped enticingly to reveal the higher curves of her creamy breasts. Malcolm seemed taken with the display of the jewels on such a beautiful setting, but eyed his gift far less than he did the tempting roundness that was pressed full and taut above her gown. There his gaze lingered with much admiration.

With her at his side, the tawny-haired man strutted like a proud peacock with his hen, except in this case the latter far outshone the male. His manner seemed tender and solicitous as he stroked his hand along her arm or squeezed her waist, bestowing his caresses most whenever others were around and she could not resist without drawing some notice. He seized upon this advantage when they stood at the gaming tables. There, under the guise of watching the fall of cards, he laid an arm about her shoulders and stroked her arm, now and then brushing his long fingers against her bosom. Lenore blushed beneath his careless caresses and cast a surreptitious glance about to see who might be watching. To her relief everyone seemed more interested in the game of cards and the high stakes that were being waged than in her; everyone, that is, but Marelda Rousse, who had come to stand beyond the players at the far side of the table. As always, Horace Titch was with her and seemed as nervous as ever as his eyes flitted about in search of the Natchez man, who had not yet made an appearance. Marelda was troubled by Malcolm's display of affection, but she was amused by the distress it caused the younger woman. Any form of misery that came upon that one was bliss to her soul. She smirked as the green eyes clouded darkly beneath a disturbed frown, then raised a mocking brow when they found her and widened in surprise. Marelda offered a condescending smile and a meager nod of greeting. More than that might have indicated some slight forgiveness in her heart, and there was none.

Lenore's evening took on a lighter, warmer sheen when Ashton stepped through the door. Unmindful of how Malcolm's features tensed as he glowered at the other man, she filled her own gaze with the much-welcomed sight. Ashton was looking no less than magnificent in midnight-blue dress coat and trousers, gray silk vest, and blue-and-gray striped silk cravat. The usual crisp, white shirt struck a stark contrast to the bronze skin that had taken on a deeper, richer hue since his venturing to Biloxi. As he paused in the doorway, his gaze wandered searchingly through the guests, and when it touched her, his questing perusal ended. The green-brown eyes swept her with a slow, unhurried regard, then, lifting to meet hers, communicated a compliment with a warmth that was clearly unmistakable. If love was a substance to be seen and felt, then it was what she saw in his eyes and felt at that very moment. He wrapped her within its tender tendrils, and for a small space in time she reveled in her spiraling senses. She loved him; she could no more deny that fact than she could dismiss what he conveyed to her now.

At her side Malcolm sneered: "I suppose the fool thinks he can whisk you off to his cabin while you're here aboard his ship. He'd like nothing better than to show you a lengthy view of the ceiling."

Lenore coughed as she choked on her wine, and she turned her face away, delicately clearing her throat as a flush of color crept into her cheeks. She could not bring herself to tell Malcolm that she had already savored that view. Not only once, but on several different occasions.

An amused chuckle drew Lenore's regard back to the man at her side. "Wingate has no doubt arranged this whole affair to bring about such an end, but I have no intention of letting that happen." The dark eyes dropped to her. "You will stay by my side throughout the evening, madam. I have not forgotten the sight of you favoring the man with a kiss on the shore, and I wouldn't want you to embarrass me by falling all over him here."

"I don't intend to fall all over *anyone*, Malcolm," she stated crisply.

"Ah, my dove, I see I've ruffled your feathers." He laughed without humor. "Well, 'twill be more than your feathers I'll ruffle if I ever catch you with him, and I will start by gelding the man . . . before your eyes."

Lenore stared at him in horror and dismay, dreading the day when she would have to tell him that she was carrying Ashton's child. She shivered as his hand lightly caressed her arm and carefully lowered her eyes to hide her distaste.

Ashton sipped his drink as he watched the broad hand glide fondly over the arm of the one he loved. Unable to see her face at the moment, he could not tell how she was accepting this freely bestowed attention, but envy prodded him with cruel spikes, for it was strong in his mind that he should have been the one standing there claiming her as his wife. He noted Marelda nearing the couple and distantly wondered what mischief she was brewing.

The dark-haired woman halted before the pair and extended her hand to Malcolm, who immediately affected a gracious mien as he accepted it.

"I don't think we've met, sir," she murmured warmly. "I am Marelda Rousse. . . ." She turned aside to indicate her escort of the evening: "And this is Mr. Horace Titch, a good friend of mine."

Gallantly Malcolm brushed his lips against the thin fingers. "Malcolm Sinclair, at your service, my lady," he vowed and, straightening, rested a hand on the small of Lenore's back, feeling her stiffen as he did so. "And this is my wife, Lenore Sinclair."

Marelda's eyes briefly touched Lenore, and her smile grew slightly mocking. "I had the pleasure of meeting your wife while she was at Belle Chêne. Except that then, everyone . . . that is, *almost* everyone . . . thought she was Ashton's wife." She nodded in a curt acknowledgment of Lenore. "Your jewels are lovely, my dear. They remind me of some I've seen before, except those were lost . . . or stolen. . . ." She tossed the subtle gibe down like a thrown gauntlet and, then dismissing Lenore, turned back to continue her conversation with Malcolm: "I, of course, realized at the time that it was impossible for a drowned woman to come back alive, but Ashton was clearly befuddled and insisted that she was his wife."

"He can be a difficult man," Malcolm replied, briefly directing a cool glance toward that one.

"I see that you've had some disagreement with him." At his brief nod Marelda laughed gayly and shrugged. "Haven't we all." She bestowed a tight smile on Lenore. "With the possible exception of your wife, of course. The two of them seemed quite cozy there for a time. It's a wonder that you and Ashton didn't end up in a duel."

Malcolm raised a wondering brow as he considered his wife. "I fear Mr. Wingate took unfair advantage while my wife was in his home, but she has quite clearly rejected all thoughts of being his wife now." The dark eyes met the hesitant glance of the green ones. "It's been enjoyable having her home where she belongs."

"I've heard that Ashton is still pressing the matter." Marelda glanced aside at Horace, who was eager to accept any attention she gave him. His dark, watery eyes glowed with warmth until she continued: "Someone should tell him he's not welcome here."

Horace opened his mouth to deny the possibility that he would be the bearer of such a declaration. He thought he would just as soon avoid any frontal clash with Ashton, but when Marelda's eyes hardened, Horace felt the sweat pop from his pores, and he groaned within himself. Hadn't he done enough for her already?

"I've tried." Malcolm put on an injured expression. "But the man is stubborn and refuses to listen, even to Lenore's father."

"I . . . ah . . . don't think he listens too well," Horace stated nervously.

"Then he should be shown," Marelda suggested. "A man who is blind must be led about by the hand."

"He doesn't lead too well either," Malcolm observed dryly.

"Come now," Marelda cajoled and turned a taunting smile upon Lenore, noting how the color had drained from her cheeks. She could not believe the little twit cared enough for Ashton to become physically upset by their discussion. "There must be a way to deal with a man like that."

"I . . . ah . . . think I'll go out for a breath of fresh air," Horace said and hurriedly excused himself. Wiping his heavily sweating brow, he hastened across the room. He would never object to Ashton Wingate getting his due. Indeed, he hoped it would fall upon him soon . . . but not from him personally.

As he stepped beyond a small grouping of people and came into a small open space, Horace raised his gaze and was startled to meet Ashton's mildly amused and inquisitive stare.

"Good evening, Mr. Titch." Ashton conveyed the greeting over the rim of his glass.

A chill coursed through Horace's veins, and ducking his head, he stumbled away with a lame excuse: "I've got to talk to a man outside about some business."

He charged out of the suddenly airless room and, gaining his escape, leaned against the outside wall to pant for breath. It seemed to be a growing fear of his that Ashton would one day take revenge for all he had done. A form moved in front of him, and not sure who it might be, he gasped in sudden fear.

"Mr. Titch?"

Horace sagged in relief. It was not the Natchez man, but the one he had consented to meet aboard the vessel.

Inside the hall Lenore fought her own discomfort as Malcolm's hand settled on her bare shoulder and pulled her to him, but her growing nausea roiled up like an ugly serpent. Marelda had turned the topic to the weather, engaging the man in conversation, and observed the play of his fingers on the naked skin while she discussed the past history of violent storms along the coast. One of similar intensity raged up within her as she witnessed his casual caresses. It set her on edge that he displayed such an eager interest in his wife. Ashton had been equally enamored with the wench, and yet, when she, Marelda, had offered him the untainted gift of her body, he had coldly rejected her, as if she might be something worthless in his eyes. It galled her unmercifully that both men lusted after the little tart. Yet as she continued conversing with Malcolm, Marelda began to detect a subtle leer in his smile and eyes that hinted of an interest in her. The idea of extending an invitation to the man tickled her fancy. She could then show his haughty wife what it was like to lose a man to another woman.

"Tell me, Mr. Sinclair . . ."

"Oh, please, there's no reason to be so formal," he objected with a smile. "Malcolm is my given name, and I freely give you leave to use it."

Marelda accepted the correction with a slight nod: "Malcolm, then."

"That sounds better," he replied. "Now, you were saying?"

"I was going to ask if you had ever toured the *River Witch*." Her dark eyes glowed above a sultry smile. "There are a number of rooms to see, all rather quaint and cozy . . . very private. Would you care to see them? I'd be more than happy to show you around . . . and, of course, Mrs. Sinclair. I'm sure Ashton wouldn't mind."

Malcolm glanced aside at his wife, putting the question to her in the form of a raised eyebrow, but Lenore had been standing tense and very still throughout their conversation, hoping against hope that her nausea would go away. It seemed evident to her that Marelda Rousse quite literally sickened her. "I'm sorry, Malcolm, but I'm really not feeling too well at the moment." She made the statement cautiously, hardly daring to breathe. The air in the room seemed stale and musty, and she had difficulty maintaining a calm demeanor while the heat pressed down upon her, and her stomach threatened to rebel against the strong wine. Even Malcolm could not mistake the pallor in her cheeks as she urged, "But please, go on without me."

Malcolm inclined his head, readily accepting her direction. He could clearly see that she was ill, and he doubted that even Ashton Wingate could become amorous with a woman who was threatening to heave up her stomach. As for himself, he was going to indulge himself for a few moments and possibly initiate an intimate friendship.

When the two left, Lenore walked slowly and carefully through the press of people. Her goal was the nearest door, whatever direction that might be, and she dared not turn her head to see where Ashton was as she made her exit, for any slight movement might prove her undoing. As the night air settled its warm breath upon her, she heard Marelda's distant laughter mingled with Malcolm's deep chuckle and turned stiltedly in the opposite direction.

Ashton dabbed his handkerchief in a glass of water and leisurely strolled across the room. He left by the same door and then paused on the deck to listen. He thought he saw Horace Titch stumble back into the shadows farther down the passageway, no doubt to avoid meeting him, but he caught no glimpse of the one he wanted to see. He strode along the deck, his eyes probing the darkness between the lanterns until, on the far side of the steamer, he detected the pale glow of Lenore's gown near the railing. He moved to where she leaned against a post and laid an arm about her shoulder, making her start and stare up at him in wide-eyed surprise.

"It's all right," he soothed in a whisper.

Lenore sagged against him in relief, feeling weak and completely drained. She marveled at his gentleness as he bathed her face, and beneath his tender ministering the waves of revulsion began to ebb.

"Feeling better?" he murmured after a moment.

She nodded lamely. "I think so."

"Do you want to lie down in my cabin?"

"Oh, no. Malcolm would be angry." She started to laugh, but gulped and waited until the twinge of sickness passed before she again attempted a smile. "I think Malcolm is afraid of the sights you'll show me in your cabin."

Ashton placed a gentle finger beneath her chin and lifted it until he could meet her gaze. The moon cast a multitude of starry lights in her eyes, and he lost himself in their tender warmth.

"You've been drinking," she observed. The smell of brandy on his breath was strong enough to make her heady. "More than your usual glass or two, I'd wager."

"Worry can drive a man to drink," he replied wryly.

"Worry?" She searched his face with the inquiry. "What are you worried about?"

Ashton chafed as he confessed, "Malcolm . . . and his hands on you . . . and you being up there in the house with him all the time . . . while I have to stand and watch you from afar."

Footsteps came along the deck toward them, and they looked around to see Malcolm approaching them with long, irate strides. His cravat was gone, and his shirt and vest were open down the front, showing his wide chest. Apparently he had been busy in the short time he had been gone.

"Something told me I'd find you making a pest of yourself!" Lunging forward, he caught Ashton's shoulder and shoved him back against a post. "Damn you! I want you to leave my wife alone!"

"And I want you to leave mine alone!" The retort snapped back as Ashton tossed away the offending hand. He was not long on temper tonight.

Malcolm shook a large fist before the other's nose threateningly. "She's mine!"

Ashton scoffed: "I say not, and if you care to, we can settle the matter tonight."

In a quick movement Malcolm slid his hand inside his coat and snatched forth a small derringer. Ignoring Lenore's startled gasp, he shoved it beneath Ashton's chin. "Don't think you can make her a widow so soon, my friend."

He had hoped to arouse at least the same show of concern he had seen in Ashton's face on the beach, but this time the tolerant smile remained. Distantly Malcolm wondered if the icy rivers of the North coursed through his adversary's veins. He craved to shake that unperturbed confidence just once and see the man grovel for mercy at his feet. He hated that unruffled composure almost as much as the man himself. "Go ahead. Move one muscle," he urged. "I'd like to blow your head off. It wouldn't distress me in the least to feed your carcass to the fish."

"You have a witness," Ashton calmly reminded him, "unless you intend to do away with her as well."

"I'm sure she'll be happy to be rid of you," the younger man sneered.

"Malcolm, stop it!" Lenore was not as casual about the threat as the one who was being menaced. "Please! Put that thing away before you hurt someone!" Her fear mounted as he ignored her request, and her panic drove her to be forceful. "Put it away, Malcolm, or by all that's holy, I'll go to Ashton's cabin and forget that I ever had anything to do with you!"

Ashton's brows rose in heightened interest, and he taunted the man with a lopsided grin: "Well, what should the lady do?"

"Ashton!" Lenore cried, aghast at his careless disregard of the danger he was in. "He will kill you!"

The tiny derringer prodded Ashton under the chin as Malcolm's fingers tightened convulsively on the ivory handle. He wanted so desperately to have the man out of his hair, but there was much he would lose, and he did not consider himself a fool when it came to what was important. Still, he trembled at the sheer temptation of what was at hand . . . until there was a loud *clatch* and something small and hard probed into his belly. Warily Malcolm's eyes descended and then widened as he saw the bore of a somewhat larger pistol pressed into his midsection.

"I've had enough of your threats; now I have one of my own to give."

Malcolm stared in rapt attention as Ashton's words thudded into him like fists pounding against his chest. Or was it his heart that thumped so hard against the inner cavity?

"I'm going to start counting," Ashton informed him, "and if you don't kill me before I reach three, you won't get another chance." He stretched out his free hand and pushed Lenore gently away, ignoring her frantic pleas for them both to be reasonable. "One . . ." His eyes glittered as he felt the pistol shake against his throat. "Two . . ."

The weapon was jerked away with an angry curse, and Malcolm ground his teeth as he met the mockery in those hazel eyes. As he stepped back, Ashton slid his own pistol beneath his coat and, in its stead, pulled out a long cheroot, which he leisurely puffed alight.

"I suggest you take care with your threats from now on, Malcolm," he said. "Someone might take offense and blow your fool head off."

Malcolm did not appreciate the advice. "We'll see what comes of all this, *Mister* Wingate." Taking Lenore's arm, he marched her along the deck, putting Ashton far behind him in a short amount of time.

Ashton followed at a slower pace, wishing he had Lierin's approval to dismiss Malcolm from her life. Until he had it, he could do naught but watch them from afar, and it was no easy or pleasant task.

Malcolm paused outside the gaming room to adjust his clothing and glared at his wife as he smoothed the lapels of his coat.

"Your cravat is gone," she reminded him calmly and asked offhandedly, "Did Marelda enjoy her view of the ceiling? Or could she see much in that short a time? Indeed, you must have just completed the swiftest seduction ever performed."

"*Youuuu!*" Malcolm growled. "Right when . . ." He searched about for the proper words and found none he could tell his wife. "Then it struck me, and all I could see was you . . . with him . . . having your fun with him!"

"Marelda was probably disappointed that you couldn't finish what you had started." Lenore lifted a brow to a lofty height as he pushed his face close and gnashed his teeth at her. "I'm truly sorry, Malcolm, that I disturbed your moment of conquest. If I see the matter correctly, you were only thwarted by your reluctance to have me do the same thing you were doing, and I find that rather amusing."

His hand caught her arm again, none too gently, and gritting out a smile, he entered the ballroom and swept her into a waltz. They moved with stilted motion, each annoyed with the other, each angry, and each aware of the attention they had gained. It vexed Malcolm that the dance lacked the fluid grace of another he had been witness to, and that was the one when the Wingate man had led her in a swirling motion around the pavilion. Absent, too, were the appreciative comments made by the guests.

"Have I told you how divine you look this evening, madam?" he asked, trying to break the ice that encased her and held her reserved from him. "You're the most beautiful woman here."

Lenore caught a glimpse of Marelda coming into the room, and by the woman's reddened countenance and the glare she tossed at Malcolm, Lenore decided the woman was none too pleased. "Marelda is back," she informed him coolly. "And she's looking slightly enraged. Don't you want to go to her and make your amends?"

"She doesn't matter to me," he scoffed. "She's only someone to relieve myself with until you yield to me."

Lenore stared at him in amazement. "How can you even think of me yielding myself when you act like a rutting tomcat? And certainly not after you've been with Marelda."

"Are you jealous?" He smiled, amused by the idea.

"Fear would better explain my reasons to avoid going to bed with you, Malcolm. I might catch something I don't want."

Malcolm's ego was seriously deflated. "You're a cold woman, Lenore Sinclair."

She averted her face, remembering a time when she had played chase with Ashton through the master suite at Belle Chêne. Giggling and dropping pieces of her clothing in his path, she had fled before him, and it had seemed at the time that he had purposely delayed catching her until the last garment had followed the descent of the others; then with a long arm he had reached out and brought her close to him. There in his embrace she had teased him with a wanton kiss, then had pulled away and danced against him in a manner that Salome had never dreamed of. Was she truly cold? Or just particular about the man she was with?

She stiffened as Malcolm's arm tightened about her narrow waist and brought her closer to him. He bent to drop a light kiss on the pale shoulder, now aware that Ashton had entered the room. He knew the other closely observed them, and his spirits soared as he thought how he could torment the man. His warm breath sighed close to her ear. "If your Mr. Wingate insists upon sniffing after you, my dear, then I think I should make him suffer."

"What do you mean?" Worry was evident in the lovely visage as Lenore lifted her gaze to him again.

Malcolm loosened his embrace, allowing her to move back a step. His expression was almost cocky as he led her around the floor. "It's obvious the scum wants to get into you, but since you belong to me, I shall remind him of that fact." His fingers dallied at the small of her back, and he gave her a warning glare when she turned a bit rigid. "Be careful, my love. If you do not allow me this moment, I'll make you pay dearly."

"Pay?" She repeated the word with growing trepidation. "What is it that you're trying to do?"

He tilted his head in Ashton's direction. "I want that buffoon to realize finally just whose wife you are, and I'm going to make him rue the day he contrived this little gambit. While we're here aboard the *River Witch*, you will allow me to touch you as much as I want to."

"Do I detect a threat in your plan?" she asked with rampant sarcasm.

Malcolm seemed as smug as a pampered cat as he replied, "You have kept me from your bed for some time now, madam, but I am growing impatient. The idea of separate bedrooms is becoming intolerable, and I think the time will soon come when I must reaffirm our married status . . . just in case you've forgotten how it was between us." His eyes dropped to devour the fullness above her gown. "Thus far I've been concerned for your welfare, but you seem fit enough to bear *his* attentions. So, why not mine? I *am* your husband."

Ashton's jaw tightened as he watched the lustful perusal sweeping the swelling bosom, and as the cabin boy passed with a tray, he reached for a liberally filled glass of brandy. He hated those probing gazes that were wont to linger there upon her breasts. He disliked the mouth that kissed her smooth skin and the hands that pressed her narrow waist. Perhaps he had made a mistake in creating interest among his friends for this occasion. At the moment it appeared that Malcolm was the only one enjoying the event.

Lenore stared up at Malcolm, aghast at what he proposed. "Are you saying that I must allow you to maul me in front of all these people?"

A corner of the large mouth drew up in a subtle sneer. "I don't care about the others, my dear. My only concern is that fool who persists in calling you Lierin."

Lenore nodded slowly in displeasure, beginning to understand his ploy. It was not passion for her that prompted him to be amorous as much as hatred and jealousy of the other man. "And if I don't cooperate, you will force your attentions on me anyway."

Malcolm shrugged indolently. "While you've kept to your chaste bed and denied me my husbandly rights, I've had to appease myself with harlots, but I'm getting tired of those bawdy butts twisting beneath me." He stared intently into the wide emerald eyes. "I crave fresher game to sport with."

"So either way I'm caught." She assessed her situation drearily.

"Choose which is worse, madam."

"I think you already know the answer to that."

His eyes flared with the insult of her light gibe; then he chuckled sneeringly. "You think *he* can pleasure you more than I can?" He flung up his head and snorted contemptuously. "You don't know very much about men if you believe that."

"I've forgotten a lot, that's true." Her tone was bland. "But I'm *re*learning swiftly, and I'm beginning to think that I was in a state of distress when I married you, or else I saw something in you that just wasn't there."

There was a stir in the room, and everyone turned as Sheriff Coty came through the doors, holding a struggling Horace Titch by the scruff of the neck. Everyone gaped and gathered around as the lawman halted beside Ashton.

"Here's one of your thieves, Mr. Wingate. I caught him red-handed, trying to sneak away with the rest of the pirates, but we caught some of 'em . . . and this one." He shook Horace as a dog shakes a rat, much to the outrage of that one.

"You fool!" Horace twisted around on the tips of his toes, which were the only part of his body that could reach the floor and allow him some leverage to resist this humiliating seizure by the lawman. "I tell you I was being robbed myself! And they made me go with them!"

"Certainly, Mr. Titch, and you just happened to have these jewels in your pocket." Sheriff Coty dipped a hand into his own pocket and pulled out a diamond pendant. "We found some of the guests locked in one of the forward cabins, and they had been robbed. They went out for a stroll on the deck, and that is when his men"—he nodded toward Horace—"caught them unawares and took what they had. It would have been only a matter of time before they came in here."

"But I was out on the deck," Lenore commented, clutching a hand to her throat.

"Then you were lucky, ma'am," Sheriff Coty observed politely. "Someone musta been watchin' over you."

"And I was out there," Marelda stated, pushing her way through the gathering.

"Marelda, tell them I didn't have anything to do with this," Horace pleaded.

"He a friend of yours, ma'am?" the lawman questioned.

"Yes," Marelda replied slowly, wondering what trouble she might be letting herself in for.

"Well, that's probably why you didn't get robbed, ma'am. Mr. Titch likely told the brigands not to hurt any of his friends."

"This whole thing is ridiculous!" Horace declared in outrage.

"That's what I thought, too, when Mr. Wingate asked me to watch over his steamer, just in case someone tried anything. You can imagine my surprise when me and my men started seeing them thieves poppin' out of hidin' and then flittin' across the dock to come on board. Looked like they planned it real good, except Mr. Wingate had a better plan."

"Has any of the guests been hurt?" Ashton asked in concern.

"Just a mite shaken, that's all," the lawman replied. He jerked his head toward Titch again. "I'm going to put this one behind bars and then ask him some important questions."

"Someone make him listen to me!" Horace pleaded as he held out his arms in desperate supplication. "I didn't take *anything!* I tell you, the thieves put that necklace into my pocket to make it seem like I did."

"That's fine and dandy, Mr. Titch, but one of them brigands also said you were one of them. He met with you here on board, and you paid him to do it."

Horace searched about for an answer. "I don't know who he was. I just met him in the tavern, and he asked to speak with me while I was here on the riverboat."

"What reason did he have?"

"None." Horace shrugged his shoulders. "I mean, he didn't give any. He just robbed me."

"Well, if he did, you came out better for it with that there necklace in your pocket . . . at least, you would have, had you not been caught."

– Chapter Sixteen –

"Lier . . . in. Lier . . . in."

Lenore frowned in her sleep and rolled her head on the pillow.

"Where are you? Lierin? Lierin? Come out. Come out, wherever you are. . . ."

She was hiding behind a carefully clipped shrub partially shaded by the manor looming in the background. A young red-haired girl crouched beside her, and they hid their giggles behind cupped hands as the stalking footsteps came closer . . . closer. . . .

"Lierin . . . Lenore . . . Come   out . . . Come   out . . . Wherever you are. . . ."

"Shhh," she warned her sister silently as that one threatened to burst into laughter and reveal their hiding place. "He'll hear you and find us both."

The tiny pebbles of the walk crunched beneath the hesitating footfalls that came ever nearer. Seeing a large manly shadow fall on the lawn nearby, they pressed against the shrub and waited, scarcely daring to breathe as the shadow advanced with slow, stealthy caution. It disappeared by degrees, falling onto the shrub that protected them as the man stepped closer; then quite unexpectedly a bee flitted past their noses, startling them both, and they scrambled away with cries of alarm.

"Aha!" The man's voice rang with a note of victory as he leaped past the shrub and pounced into view.

Torn from her dream, Lenore came upright with a gasp and stared about the dark room in wide-eyed panic. The face in the portrait! It was the one in her dream!

"Lierin . . . Lierin . . ."

A sudden chill shivered along her spine as she pressed back upon the pillows, trying to listen above the frantic beating of her heart. Had the voice come from her dreams to torment her?

"Lierin . . . Lierin . . ."

"Ashton!" The name flared through her brain as she realized that what she had heard was not part of any fantasy. It was Ashton! She threw herself from the bed and, flinging open the french doors, ran out onto the veranda. Reaching the balustrade, she searched frantically for the one she was sure was there. But where? Her eyes swept outward, anxiously skimming over the grounds and sweeping the shoreline; then a sound close by made her look down. There, right below her, the tall figure leaned against a post of the lower porch.

"Ashton!" she whispered as loud as she dared. "What are you doing down there?"

"Ah, my Lady Lierin! My queen!" he called up and, stumbling away from the house, swept her a gallant bow. "I have finally beckoned you from your chambers. My soul despaired at my lengthy failure, but now it doth quiver at the sound of your voice."

"Go home, Ashton," she beseeched him plaintively. She was afraid of what Malcolm would do if he caught him. "Go back to your tent, and go to bed."

"Nay, my lady." He shook his head and staggered unsteadily as he moved farther away from the house. "Not without your soft, sweet breast to lay my head upon."

"Malcolm is here!" she reminded him frantically.

"I know! 'Tis what torments me! I have maneuvered my knights as best I can, but he's still there, holding my queen."

"Malcolm will hear you! Please go away," she implored. "He'll kill you if he finds you here!"

Ashton reflected upon her statement a moment and leaned his head back with a chuckle. "He's welcome to try, my lady."

"He will! And you're in no condition to defend yourself," she chided.

"Ah, madam, I'm not concerned with defending myself. 'Tis you I've come to protect. I lay my sword at your feet, offering my services . . . my arm for your protection . . . and whatever portion of me you may have need of." He lurched forward a step. "I shall defeat the arrant foe who has captured you, and then I shall take you to yonder castle." Sweeping an arm about, he indicated the huge tent that had become his home. "Lo! It sits there awaiting your presence, my lady."

"I can't go with you!" she cried in a whisper. "Now go back . . . please. . . ."

"I shall not leave without my lady," he firmly declared, striking a stance of stubborn resolution for a brief second before he stumbled and fell spinning to his knees. There he collapsed like a limp rag doll with his long legs tucked beneath him and his hands braced upon the turf. Hanging his head between his shoulders, he moaned, "Lierin . . . Lierin . . . Come down to me."

The agonized plea wrenched her heart, and she felt a rush of tears at the misery she heard in his tone. Anxiety was there, too, filling her with dread as she hurried to the stairs, but her love beckoned. Her bare feet flew down the stairs, and ignoring the last step, she leaped to the lower level and raced out onto the front lawn. There, she paused in some confusion, for he was gone. Vanished! She glanced about, her eyes searching the moonlit yard for the manly form she knew only too well.

"Ashton?" she called in a whisper. Cautiously she moved toward a small grouping of trees on the east side. "Ashton, where are you?"

Suddenly she gasped as she was seized from behind, and an arm, slipping about her waist, swirled her around. Another gasp was startled from her as she was lifted from her feet and brought firmly against a long, hard body. Eager lips covered hers, and she was engulfed in the intoxicating essence of brandy. The kiss went through her, flicking awake her senses and making her stirringly aware of his manhood as her thighs slid against his.

"Ashton, behave," she pleaded breathlessly as his mouth sank to her throat. She closed her eyes and rolled her head away, trying to escape those burning kisses that branded her. Her world tilted crazily in a spinning orbit as his mouth dipped down and caressed her breast through her gown. She shivered as the moistness seeped through the light cloth, and the glowing coals of desire began to spill like a lava flow through her body. His hand was on her buttock, clasping her close, and at the bold, manly touch of him, a hunger grew in the softness of her.

"I want you, Lierin," he rasped in a whisper. "I can't go back without you."

The realization seeped down in her that the longer she resisted going back to his tent with him, the better his chances were of being shot. Get him back and leave him where he would be safe, she thought.

"Ashton, I'll go back with you," she whispered unsteadily as his lips moved to the opening of her gown. "Just put me down, and I'll take you back."

"I'll carry you." Setting her to her feet, he swept an arm down to lift her up again, but she laughed and placed a hand on his chest, halting him.

"We'll both go rolling if you do." Her fingers traced along his cheek as she gently chided, "You're too drunk, my darling."

"I've had a few," he admitted with a slightly injured air.

"A few!" With a soft chuckle she slid her hand down along the lithe muscles of his arm and settled it upon the waiting palm. The long, thin fingers entwined with hers in a loving grasp as she whispered, "You've had more than a few, my darling." She gently tugged at his arm, and they staggered side by side across the moonlit yard. He was wont to stop often and pull her into his embrace, but she urged him on with a sweet promise, "In the tent, my darling."

Reaching their destination, Ashton swept back the tent flap, allowing her to enter first. With eyes that were wide in amazement, Lenore roamed around. She had not expected such grandiose appointments and was rather awestruck. Several lamps illumined the interior, lighting her way around the furnishings and over the rich carpets. The gold silk hangings of the bed shimmered against the glow of the bedside lamp, and it was to this resting place she came to stand and stare. It was difficult to take in all the wealth at once.

Ashton watched her from beneath his brows with that sort of manly-boyish hesitation that was so much a part of his charm. How could she deny him anything when he looked at her like that? But she must . . . for his own good.

"I love you," she whispered with a tender smile, "and I'll stay for a while, but I need more time to clear my thoughts."

Ashton released a disappointed sigh in slow, halting breaths and gave a reluctant nod, turning away. The brown shoulders gleamed as he drew off his shirt, and Lenore stared at the dark expanse, remembering when she could freely stroke her hand over the wide breadth of his shoulders and along his lean, muscular ribs. Becoming aware that she was being affected by the sight, she averted her gaze and reddened profusely. If he only knew how she desired him . . . !

Staggering around, Ashton dropped into a nearby chair and tugged off his boots, then leaned his elbows on his knees and hung his head in mute dejection. The posture pierced Lenore's heart, but she curbed the feeling that grew in her, for it was a dangerous longing. Moving with whisper-soft tread, she drew back the bed hangings and folded down the luxurious coverlet. She followed in the same order with the sheets and smoothed the folds with her hands as she pulled them snug, then stood back with a hesitant glance in his direction.

"Come to bed, Ashton," she softly implored. He looked up with an unspoken inquiry, but she lowered her eyes before his probing gaze. "I'll sit with you for a while; then I must go back."

With a sigh Ashton raised himself from the chair and made his way unsteadily around the end of the bed and to the far side. There he turned his back to her and, dropping his trousers, sat down on the bed. He made no further attempt to comply with her wishes, and in curious wonder Lenore went around the bed and found his eyes closed beneath a harsh frown, as if a pain had started throbbing between his brows.

"Ashton?" Her voice was whisper-soft.

The lashes lifted abruptly, and he fixed her with a direct stare; then, releasing his breath, he slowly reclined upon the pillows. Lenore felt a warming in her cheeks and a quickening in her blood as her eyes skimmed over the manly length of him. She had often compared him to a gladiator of olden days, with his long lithe muscles rippling beneath his bronze skin. He was no less impressive lying naked upon the bed. It was not a new sight for her, but one that she realized she had missed viewing during the time they had been separated. In wifely compassion, she bent and, tugging the trousers off his feet, swung his long legs onto the bed. She pulled a sheet over his nakedness and tidied his clothes, wistfully caressing them with her hand as she hung them on his silent valet. Blowing out the lamps, she returned to the bedside across from where he slept, and sat cross-legged upon its softness. Her eyes wandered around the darkened interior, and she felt consumed by its blackness. Carefully she lay back upon the pillows, making a firm resolution not to sleep, and put her mind to the task of remembering. . . .

* * *

"Whither will I wander . . . Thither will I roam . . . 'Round the world, and back again, this way will I go. . . . Marching down the steep hill . . . Tramping up again . . . Ever will I ramble . . . 'Til I'm home again. . . ."

The sea breezes whipped the auburn hair with its breath, setting its softly curling length and the long ribbons adorning it into a wild, frenzied dance. Watching her sister frolicking far ahead of her on the beach, she giggled and slipped her small hand inside the much larger one that brushed her arm. The tall man reached down and lifted her high upon his shoulder, much to her squealing delight, and they chortled together as he pretended to be her steed and galloped after her sister. Her thin fingers curled in the mass of dark hair, seeking security at the lofty height, and she knew without looking down that his face was squarish . . . and his eyes were deep green. . . .

The woods were dense and darkly shaded as the two girls crept forward. Her sister, a young woman barely fifteen, gestured with a finger across the lips, and they stilled. She waited, searching with her eyes; then she saw the deer they had stalked lift its head in alert attention. His ears twitched to catch the sounds around him; then with a start he glanced behind him. His large eyes stared a moment into the shaded coppice, until a faint snap of a twig surprised him, and he bounded away in the opposite direction. Disappointed, the two girls moved together; then a familiar voice called from where the twig had snapped: "Lenore . . . Lierin . . ." A man clothed in a brown hunting suit and toting a long gun beneath his arm came tramping through the trees. "Lenore . . . Lierin . . . where are you?"

"Lierin?" the voice sighed against her ear before warm lips brushed her cheek. "Lierin . . . ?"

"Yes?" she sighed and, rolling onto her side, snuggled against the warm body.

"Let me love you, Lierin . . ."

The words seeped into her dreams, and she saw a distant figure, standing near the railing of a steamer.

"Let me love you, Lierin. . . ."

"Yes," she breathed.

Wandering through the depths of fantasy, she welcomed his

embrace and lay back. The roaming hand moved upward from her waist, and her eyes blinked as she heard the sound of rending cloth. Her heart took flight as the kisses came upon her breast, and she realized this was no illusion. This was reality at its boldest. She shook her head in a mute denial, but the movement was lost in darkness; then it seemed not to matter anymore. She was where she wanted to be . . . home!

She trembled beneath the warmth and fervor of his bold caresses, and her breath mingled with his as their lips touched and their tongues played a rousing game. They were two beings in love with one another, consumed by their emotions, driven by their desires. He pressed eager kisses upon her throat and savored the honeyed sweetness of her breasts, making her gasp at the scalding heat of his mouth. He freed her from the last shreds of her gown, and they rolled in leisured slowness upon the bed, turning as their mouths slanted and twisted in ravenous hunger. Her arms held him close, while her fingers kneaded the firm muscles of his back, slipping admiringly over his lean waist, then spreading over the taut buttocks. They tumbled again in languid motion, bound by the length of her hair, and she rose above him, arching backward as his mouth caressed her bosom. The slender limbs came astride him, and she shivered as her questing hand brought him home. The burning heat pulsed through her, flicking every fiber of her being awake. She leaned forward, raking her fingers through the crisp matting covering his chest, and teased him with a provocative kiss, touching her tongue to his. He taunted her with his body, and she luxuriated in the feelings he aroused in her. She gave in return, and the smooth strokes of her body made Ashton catch his breath. They played on, and time ceased to be as they slipped beyond the present into the heady world of bliss.

Afterward, she slept in his arms, her head resting on his sturdy shoulder and her auburn hair tumbling loose across his pillow. Ashton inhaled her sweet fragrance and dared not move lest he wake her, but his swelling heart seemed unable to contain the bountiful measure of his joy.

A raging snarl brought him fully awake three hours later. The sun had made an entry into the day, shining through the open flap of his tent, and his eyes came open as a large shadow blocked its light. The dark form bent slightly as it swept through the opening, and in two long strides Malcolm was beside the bed. His face contorted with dark fury as he stared down upon the beauty who slumbered peacefully in the arms of the other man; then he turned a glare upon that one who calmly watched him.

"You . . . bastard!" Malcolm's lips twisted in loathing contempt, and he stretched out a hand to whip away the sheet, but he promptly found his wrist seized by the iron grip of those long, lean fingers.

"My wife is not properly dressed to receive company at the moment, Malcolm," Ashton informed him curtly.

"*Your wife!*" Malcolm wrenched his arm away with a snarl, and his eyes burned as he met the bemused, sleepy gaze of the one he woke with his outburst. Fear came quickly to the lovely visage, and jeering, he gave her an insulting perusal, slowly sweeping the length of her. The muslin sheet covered her, but the dips and swells were very much apparent beneath the clinging cloth. The sheet seemed to taunt him with its display of her, and there was no denying that she was naked under its light covering. The evidence was there for him to take full note of, and he did, pausing on the soft peaks of her bosom, the narrow curve of her waist, and the shapely limb that was tucked beneath the other's. The intruding knee filled the sway in the sheet between her thighs, bespeaking the man's claim to her. Evaluating every last detail, Malcolm considered the results and thought he had never seen her looking more beautiful. It maddened him that it had been the other man who had so affected her, and his lip turned in a caustic sneer: "Did you sleep well, madam?"

Lenore found no reply to give him and averted her face, meeting the tender regard of the heavily lashed eyes above her own.

"Now that you've had your little fun, *Mister* Wingate, I want you to leave here," Malcolm declared with venom. "You've done enough harm to me. Now I'll have to live in hell until I see if anything sprouts from your seed."

A darkening scarlet stained Lenore's cheeks as she murmured a reply: "You might as well know, Malcolm. Come the winter I shall be giving birth to Ashton's child."

"*Nooooo!*" Malcolm leaped forward to seize her from the bed, making her cringe away in terror, but suddenly his eyes widened as he found himself staring into the muzzle of a large pistol, which was pointed directly toward his nose. He did not know where the weapon had come from, but it was there now, and the sweat popped out on his brow as Ashton pulled back the hammer with his thumb.

"I told you if you ever touched her, I'd kill you, and I mean it." Ashton allowed the threat to sink in before he waved the man away with the pistol. "Now back off."

"I've been cuckolded by the pair of you all this time!" Malcolm accused, stumbling back. He met the dubious smile that traced the other man's lips and watched him turn the pistol aside and release the hammer. "All this time you've been wallowing in your lusts and making me out a fool!"

"I thought he was my husband!" Lenore flared, clutching the sheet over her bosom as she came upright in the bed.

"She *is* my wife," Ashton stated and saw the rage his statement brought forth in the tanned visage.

"If she is *your* wife, then why in the hell did she marry me?" Malcolm demanded.

"That's what I would like to know," Ashton replied. "I really can't understand why Lenore married you."

Malcolm's arm slashed out toward the woman. "She *is* Lenore!"

"Lierin," Ashton casually corrected.

The younger man gnashed his teeth in frustration and searched about for the clever argument that would finally convince the man, but he found none. He whipped his arm around and, with the gesture, commanded her to leave the bed. "Get out of his bed now and come home where you belong."

"I think you'd better leave, Malcolm," she replied.

"What! Are you bashful in front of your own husband? Will you bid me go and let him stay and view all that you have?"

Lenore raised her gaze to his jeering countenance. "I mean, I think you'd better pack your clothes and leave the house . . . this morning."

Malcolm gaped and, stepping back, shook his head. "No! I have a right to be there!" He shot out his chin toward Ashton. "He's the one who has to go. Not me!"

"I don't want to take the risk of your staying here and doing some harm to us. I'd like to feel safe in my own house. I have a care for the baby I carry."

"What about him?" Malcolm's face reddened beneath that one's amused regard. "Where is he going to stay?"

"Wherever he likes," Lenore answered simply. "I intend to ask him to escort me back to England. I used to have a nanny, and I know she will recognize me, and she holds nothing against Ashton. She will put to rest any doubts about my identity."

"And if you find out that you are Lenore?" Malcolm smirked.

"I shall take a long time in thinking over my situation. To be married to you and give birth to another man's child is hardly acceptable."

"I'll agree to that!" Malcolm jeered.

Lenore ignored his sarcasm. "It would be too difficult living in the house with you after this morning. Therefore I must ask you to leave before I return."

"If I go now, I won't stay. I'll be back."

"There won't be any reason for you to come again, Malcolm. If I am truly Lenore, it is finished between us. I will obtain a decree of divorce. . . ."

"So you can marry *him?*" Malcolm cried. "That should give the gossips something to talk about."

"I can't help what they talk about, Malcolm," she replied. "I must think of the child."

"Yes, I suppose the little bastard will have to have a name."

Ashton's eyes fixed the man with a chilled stare. "You're as free with your insults as your threats, Malcolm, and I grow weary of both of them." He casually checked the pistol's priming. "I think it's about time you leave. I have matters to discuss with the lady."

The tawny-haired man glared at them for one last time and, unable to vent his frustration, took his departure. He stalked toward the house, mulling over several options in his mind. He was not finished yet with *Mister* Wingate.

Ashton rose to his feet and, wrapping a towel around his hips, went to peer out the tent flap. Flipping it closed, he came back to the bed. "As Malcolm said, he'll be back," he muttered. "He's not going to give up this easily."

"I don't see any reason for him to come back." Lenore searched his face as he sat on the bed beside her. "Why should he?"

"There are many reasons why he might be prompted to, and all of them center around you."

She smiled and her eyes shone with the combined glow of love and amusement as she laid a hand upon his bare thigh. "Lord help us if he's as persistent as you, *Mister* Wingate."

Ashton tossed her a grin. "I was fighting for something I desperately wanted, madam. My queen!"

A warm chuckle escaped her. "And now that you've won the game?"

The wide shoulders lifted in a casual shrug. "There are a few more maneuvers to be taken to seal my final victory; then it shall be complete."

"Are you still insisting that I am Lierin?"

He slid closer and, reaching across her, braced a hand on the bed as he lowered a kiss to her shoulder. "I can't believe there are two of you exactly alike."

Lenore laughed nervously and caught his arm to keep from falling as his encroaching presence threatened to press her back upon the bed. He murmured against her throat, and she rolled her head to the side as his lips moved upon her skin. His free hand wandered down her bare back, pressing her toward him, and she forgot the covering of the sheet. It tumbled to her hips as she slid her arms around his neck and met his passionate kiss with eagerly parting lips.

Ashton cast a glance toward the small clock that graced the interior of his tent, wondering how soon Lierin would return from town where she, Mr. Evans, and her father had ventured in the carriage. She had invited him to the house to share the midday meal when they came back from Biloxi and then had laughed when Ashton gallantly assured her that her presence was all the nourishment he needed to subsist.

Sarah had viewed the trio's departure from the doorway of the tent as she waited for him to bid the younger woman farewell, and then, in Lierin's absence, he had deigned to give his attention to the ledgers she had brought. The *River Witch* had not yet taken up its station offshore, but aboard the *Gray Eagle* there was increased activity as Captain Meyers and the crew began making preparations for her departure to the Caribbean. Sarah would be transferring her work to a cabin aboard the steamer, and Ashton spoke of his plans to send her back to Natchez on the steamer if things went well concerning Lierin. For the first time since he had made her acquaintance in the Under-the-Hill tavern, Sarah dared to ask him about the woman he was in love with and how Lierin, or Lenore, had come to be in her present situation. Ashton told her what he could and left her to make her own decision about the other redhead.

As he finished, Sarah sighed pensively. "It's horrible to be caught up in something that's as frightening as that, not knowing whether you're sane and just a victim of someone else's malice . . . or if you really are mad and you deserve to be kept away from . . . everything." She gazed down at her tightly clenched hands. "Sometimes I wonder about myself . . . if I've been affected by my own hatred and need for revenge." Lifting her head, she stared across the space of the tent, seeing naught that was within her view. "I glimpse a man's face . . . and then I think: I know him! He was one who helped make my life hell! He took my name and scribbled it across a sheet of paper! And then all that I owned became my husband's, to do with as he willed, while he cast me in hell. He had no reason to wait for my demise, and it amused him to keep me alive. And why not? He had everything, with but a flick of a pen. . . ." Her brows drew down harshly. "Someone else's pen. Not mine!" She rubbed a narrow hand over her arm and, blinking back tears, met the gently inquiring gaze of her employer. "I'm sorry, Mr. Wingate. I'm rambling on again."

"No need to apologize, Sarah," Ashton murmured compassionately. "It sounds as if you need someone to talk to."

"Aye, that I do, Mr. Wingate." She heaved a laborious sigh. "I watched my father ruined . . . possibly murdered, and then I found myself falsely . . . imprisoned." Her gaze flicked up briefly, uncertainly. "It was not the sort of prison you'd normally imagine, Mr. Wingate. It was a hellish place . . . with chains . . . and whips . . . and roaches crawling over the food. A man was hired to tend me, to make sure I did not escape . . . and then he was killed . . . and I know not the reason . . . except that he had begun to show some pity for me. And now, I see things that seem familiar . . . and I fear what might happen to another . . . if I don't speak out . . . and yet, I'm not sure about myself . . . or if I'm actually seeing what I think I'm seeing." She stared up at him, and the pleading was there in her eyes, desperately yearning for him to comprehend what she was trying to tell him. "Don't you understand, Mr. Wingate? I was in there too long. Much too long."

Ashton felt the hackles rise on his neck and could find no reply to make. Sarah made him anxious, but he could not quite pin down the reason. He watched her become flustered and embarrassed by her verbosity, and to ease her distress, he reached to pour her another cup of coffee. Lightening it with a meager dribble of cream and a lump of sugar, he handed it to her. Her gaze raised hesitantly, and his empathy for her welled up within him as he saw her gathering tears. As she reached out to receive the offering, he set aside the coffee and took her hand in both of his.

"It's all right, Sarah," he soothed her. "I have listened to all you've said . . . and I think I am beginning to understand."

Her gaze searched the bronze visage anxiously. "Do you, Mr. Wingate?"

"Aye, Sarah, I think I do."

The woman left, and a deepening anxiety set in. Ashton glanced often toward the clock, wishing Lierin would return, and nervously paced the floor. He spent several moments changing clothes, donning riding breeches, shirt, and tall boots. After all, he had promised Lierin to take her out riding that afternoon. He had even planned to take her beyond his camp in the late evening and introduce her to the delights of cavorting naked in the surf, perhaps even to end the interlude by making love to her there on the shore. The idea had tickled his imagination more than once since he had arrived, but right now, he would just be satisfied if she returned quickly . . . so he need not fear for her safety.

Restlessly he smoothed his hair with a brush and peered in the small mirror that hung above his washstand. Though a draping of cloth formed a wall behind the piece, providing a modicum of privacy while he dressed, the mirror was attached to a post, which lent its support to the tent. Within easy reach were his silent valet, the bathtub, and his chest wherein his clothes were kept.

He bent to retrieve his hat from the top of the trunk, and started as something large and gleaming flitted past his shoulder, missing him by no more than a hair's breadth. The silvered glass shattered, sending fine shards spraying outward, and his head snapped around to stare for barely a second at the shiny blade that now protruded from the cloth-covered post. Hearing the rapid, thudding approach of his would-be assailants behind him, he snatched his pistol from the top of the chest and whirled, whisking the weapon around, but before he could bring it into play, a pair of hefty bodies slammed into him, bearing him backward over the trunk. The privacy panel was ripped from its moorings and dropped beside him in a heap. He glimpsed the evil glint of another knife being drawn back to strike a death blow and caught his arm in the fabric, bringing it in front to use as a shield and let it take the thrust of the dagger. No more than a short second later a hard fist drove a painful blow to the side of his ribs, and he lashed out with the butt of the pistol, striking the man smartly alongside the temple. The brigand fell beside him, and though his collapse left him engaged with only one foe, Ashton was aware of two others entering his tent. Jamming the muzzle of the pistol into the tangle of cloth and knife, he levered back the hammer and discharged the piece, charring the front of his shirt with the muffled blast. The assassin jerked away and gaped down in surprise at the swiftly spreading red stain on his chest, and then he rolled back to the floor, dead.

Ashton dropped the now useless pistol and seized the blade from the cloth. Out of the corner of his eye, he saw one of his most recent visitors rushing at him with a thick-bladed knife. Coming two or three strides behind him was another assailant, and this one bore a short boarding pike. There appeared to be no question as to their intent. They were out of spill his blood before the sun reached its zenith.

As the first neared, Ashton swung his elbow upward, smashing the fellow across the bridge of the nose and causing him to stumble back in sudden pain as blood flowed from his nostrils. Seizing the advantage, Ashton reached out a foot to hook behind the man's heel and jerked, sending that one sprawling backward into his companion. The fellow gave vent to a single loud scream and stiffened, spreading his arms wide and dropping his weapon. Slowly he toppled forward, the pike blade firmly imbedded in his back while the weight of his falling body jerked the haft from his startled companion's grasp.

Now the odds appeared even, and Ashton faced the last man, who slipped a long, slim blade from the top of his boot and backed away. As he did so, his eyes flicked beyond Ashton and then gleamed with a new light. It was enough to warn the Natchez man and remind him that one of the first pair had only been knocked unconscious. He threw himself to one side just as the brigand launched himself at his back. Ashton swept the knife around, and the man squealed like a stuck pig as it caught him in the side. It delivered hardly more than a flesh wound, but the bleeding brigand did not pause as he stumbled toward the door and disappeared outside.

The last man attacked before Ashton could recover, but again the cloth panel deflected the blade. The fierce glaring eyes of the miscreant displayed his determination to force it through, but Ashton slammed the butt of his blade against the side of the frizzy head and, as the man recoiled, flung his arm aside. They crashed to the floor, and the tip of the stiletto was driven firmly into the carpeted floor. Ashton landed another hard blow against the sturdy jaw of his opponent, rolling him away, but the thick-fingered hand stretched out and grabbed at the hilt of the thin blade as the man tumbled. Scrambling to his feet, he found Ashton already on his and braced to meet his attack. The two men circled each other warily with their weapons at the ready. The barrel-chested cutthroat lunged forward with a slashing blow, but Ashton parried the attack handily, and the other backed away with a growing red stain on his upper sleeve. From that point on, there was to be no rest for him. Ashton advanced with the heavier knife, thrusting, feinting, ever testing the defense as the other fell back. The miscreant began to sweat and realized his end was but a mere mistake away. He tried to fend off the relentless attack with his thin knife, but once again Ashton feinted, luring the defending stiletto aside, then struck with all his strength. The large man grunted, dropped his knife, and wrapping his arms about his middle, staggered out into the sunlight and fell face downward upon the deck planking.

Ashton glanced around, for the first time aware that flames were beginning to creep up the side wall of his tent. The already thickening smoke choked off his breath, and the mounting crackle of the fire spurred him toward the door. Reaching it, he took a step through, then halted as he saw the threatening muzzle of a pistol directed toward him. Above it swam the leering face of the man he had flesh-wounded. Before he could draw back, the weapon exploded with an ear-deafening crack, and Ashton recoiled as the shot sliced a burning path along his ribs. The pain seared through him, and he clasped a hand to his side, feeling there the wet stickiness of his own blood. He choked as the smoke billowed toward him, and through stinging eyes he saw the chortling man brandishing a second pistol in his other hand.

"Come out and die, ye devil!" He shook the weapon at Ashton, and roared with laughter. "Or stay an' burn! One's as good as the other, jest so's ye *die!* 'At's what the man says!"

Coughing, Ashton fell back from the doorway and squinted tearing eyes against the sting of smoke as he glanced about for his own pistol. In the thickening cloud of black it was not within immediate view, and he ran to his chest, holding an arm across his face to shield it from the smoke and the growing heat of the flames. He liked neither of the choices the man presented him and meant to provide another. Lifting the heavy lid of the trunk, he seized his derringer and stumbled back to the doorway. He blinked to clear away the tears and peered out, but the brigand was nowhere to be seen. Cautiously he crept out onto the deck and, through a teary haze, saw Lierin's carriage pulling to a skidding halt in front of the house. In hardly a flash she was scrambling down and running toward him. He was relieved to see her, but knew the dangers of her coming close.

"Go back! Go back!" he cried, and then whirled as the mad chortling sounded behind him.

"So ye've come out," the brigand observed leeringly as he stepped from behind a nearby shrub. He aimed his pistol at Ashton's midsection and fondly stroked the barrel of it with his other hand. "The liedy's returned jest in time to see ye laid to rest." The pig eyes flicked down to the derringer, then returned a glare to Ashton's wary regard. "I figgered ye were after somethin' like at, but ye won't have time to use it."

Ashton heard an explosive roar and expected to feel the shot boring its way through his belly, but strangely the pain did not come. He stared at the crumpling man for one brief, incomprehensible second, then turned a startled gaze beyond him toward a large dark shape coming at a run. It was Hickory hurrying forward with a musket clasped in his hands. Reaching the dead man, the black stared down a moment and then lifted wide eyes to Ashton.

"He was gonna kill yo, massa," he said in some astonishment.

"Aye, that he was, Hickory," Ashton sighed in relief. "But you have saved the day."

Lenore's heart had stopped, but now it was beating again at a thunderous pace, and she was on the run, holding her skirts high as she raced across the lawn. She saw the bloodstained shirt of the one she loved, and fear burrowed down deep in her heart. Flickering images of a tall figure standing near the deck railing pierced her mind and mingled with countless other impressions, all of Ashton. Striding, sitting, standing, laughing, frowning, smiling, he was there with overwhelming intensity, filling every fiber of her brain. The illusions were vast in number and indistinguishable one from another. Then lastly came the intruding memory of her dream, when she had stood with Malcolm above his grave. . . .

"Oh, Ashton! Ashton!" she cried as she flew into his widespread and welcoming arms. He clasped her close as she sobbed out her fear, and she felt his lips brush her hair and his voice speaking to her in a soothing tone; then she gasped and stumbled away with him as the billowing tent burst into a roaring wealth of new flames.

"Get the horses out of the other tent!" Ashton shouted to Hickory, and leaped across the low shrubs to follow the black who had turned and was sprinting toward the smaller tent.

Lenore lifted her hand and stared down with fixed attention at the blood glistening on her palm, and her heart began thudding. Everything blurred and then went slowly dark around her. The impenetrable density of the black shroud closed in upon her until there was naught but utter darkness. *In the dead vast and middle of the night . . . the very witching time of night, When churchyards yawn and hell itself breathes out Contagion to this world . . .*

A dim spot of light growing!

A flame! A fire! A fireplace! A hearth with tools! A broad hand grasping a poker, lifting it, slashing it down on the head of a horrified man! Again and again, until the man slumps lifeless. The cloaked form of a man slowly whirling, raising the poker again, then a hot, sharp pain in her back.

Running down a dark hall! Heavy footsteps behind her! The cold breath of fear panting down her neck! A door slamming behind her and a bolt jamming home! Scrambling from a window and running! Running! No! Riding!

A narrow lane, trees flashing by . . . and then a fire! The asylum where the woman was kept a prisoner! No help here! A dark form looming behind her! The woods! Trees again! Faster! Faster! Jump! Swerve! Hang on! Don't fall now! He'll catch you!

An open field ahead! Escape! Jump! A thunder of hooves beside her! A charging team! Coming at her! *Oh, noooooo!!!*

Once again blackness . . . deep, dark, impenetrable . . .

– Chapter Seventeen –

Lenore's eyes fluttered open, and she stared into the worriedly frowning, soot-smeared face looming over her. A trace of a smile touched her lips as she lifted her hand, and Ashton seized it in an eager, but gentle, grasp before lowering a kiss upon the slender fingers. Her gaze moved slowly about the interior of her bedroom. She lay fully clothed upon the silken coverlet of her own tall four-poster. Meghan stood close to the head near Ashton and bathed her forehead with a cool, wet cloth. Robert Somerton had taken up a stance at the foot and appeared rather disconcerted as he clasped a hand about a bedpost. Some vague image seemed to obscure his countenance as she stared at her father, and she flicked her lashes to clear her vision, but when she fixed her attention once more on the white-haired man a diaphanous visage again blurred and distorted his features until his jaw became squarish, his hair dark, and his eyes green. A disturbed frown puckered her brow, and in deepening confusion she averted her face.

"What happened?" she asked in a hushed whisper.

Ashton's frown relaxed slightly as he replied. "I believe you fainted, madam."

"Aye, mum, that ye did," Meghan readily agreed.

"But how did I get here?" Lenore indicated the room with a brief sweep of her hand.

"Mr. Wingate carried ye, mum," the maid supplied the information.

Lenore tried to lift herself from the bed as a memory came back to her, but she closed her eyes again and quickly retreated to the pillows as the room swam dizzily around the bed. Ashton's hand dropped upon her shoulder in a silent urging for her to rest. Feeling his touch, she lifted silken lashes and conveyed her distress in anxious questions. "Your wound? Is it serious?"

"A flesh wound, madam, nothing more," he assured her. "Meghan has offered to bandage it for me."

Lenore breathed a trembling sigh of relief. "You frightened me."

"I'm sorry, my love," he murmured. " 'Twas not my intent."

"Not yours . . . but obviously someone else's! That man was out to kill you!"

"I do believe he was, madam," Ashton admitted. "And so were the others."

"Others?" She raked her brain and then recalled that she had seen another body sprawled on the decking. "There were two of them?"

"I believe I counted four," he calmly supplied the information.

"Four!" she gasped and braced up on an elbow. "How did you ever manage to escape?"

"Talent, madam." The hazel eyes gleamed at her. "I seem to have a certain aptitude for brawling."

Lenore dropped back into the feathery softness and groaned at his humor. "Oh, Ashton, you're making light of it all. Don't you know those men could have killed you?"

"I believe that came to me at the time, madam."

"What were the thieves after?"

"My heart, I gathered."

She looked at him with a quizzical frown as she framed the briefly worded inquiry, "Not thieves?"

"Assassins," he stated. "They were apparently sent here by a man."

"But who?" The suspicion came quickly. "Malcolm?"

Robert Somerton promptly entered the conversation and shook his head in a quick gesture of denial. "Now, girl, don't go blaming this mayhem on Malcolm. 'Twas that Titch fellow on the *River Witch* last night, that's who did it. Malcolm told me what happened. 'Twas him. He had lots of reasons to see Wingate dead."

"But Horace has been taken into custody by Sheriff Coty," she argued.

Robert spread his hands and shrugged. "So? He hired the thieves last night. Why could he not have hired the assassins for today's attempt?"

Ashton considered the man a lengthy moment. "Horace swears he's innocent. . . ."

"And you believe him?!" Robert laughed shortly. "Addlepated, that's what I'd call you if you think that."

"Just say that I haven't closed my mind yet to the possibilities," Ashton responded. He tilted his head thoughtfully. "What I'm wondering is why Marelda came rushing to Horace's defense and what venom she bore Malcolm when she claimed the jewels he had given Lierin were stolen from a friend of hers about a year or so ago. She said when she first saw them she wasn't sure they were the same, but after giving it more thought she became certain they were."

"Stolen?!" Lenore laid a hand where the necklace had been and looked to Meghan. "Fetch them for me. They must be taken to the sheriff, so he can look into Marelda's claims."

Meghan hurried across the room to the highboy and, unlocking a secret compartment, drew it open, then turned with mouth hanging slack. "They're not here, mum. They're gone!"

Bewildered, Lenore frowned and shook her head. "But I put them in there last night. . . ."

"Aye, mum, I saw ye," the maid affirmed, equally perplexed.

"Did you see anyone come into my room while I was gone?" Lenore asked the woman.

"Mr. Sinclair was in here early this morning an' found ye gone, but he took off again in a raging fit. He didn't stay too long, mum."

"And he didn't return?"

"Well, I'm not sure 'bout that, mum. When he came back from the tent, he sent me . . ." She glanced toward Somerton, as if reluctant to continue in his presence and cautiously proceeded. "Ye were needin' clothes, he told me, an' he was gone when I come back from takin' 'em ter ye."

"And the two guards?" Lenore pressed. "What of them?"

"They were sleepin' in the parlor when I come down at break o' day, mum, an' when Mr. Sinclair left, he took 'em with him. Besides the chore boy, the cook, an' meself, that left yer father an' Mr. Evans comin' an' goin' in the house 'til ye come back ter yer room. I'd say just about anyone could've taken 'em, mum."

"Heaven only knows who has them now. Malcolm has gone, but Mr. Evans will be back later tonight. . . ."

"You're not going to blame this thieving on my friend either,"

Robert declared. "If you ask me, someone else had a hand in this . . . and had plenty enough time to do the deed while we were in town." He bestowed a direct stare on Ashton for a short span of a moment, then under that one's dubious regard he lifted his shoulders. "Then again, Horace might have sent his men to do the handiwork while a few of the miscreants entertained Wingate here. You wore the jewels last night, and so he knew you had them. Whatever the case, 'tis apparent they're gone now, and not likely to be recovered."

Lenore carefully raised herself and, with Ashton's assistance, sat up on the edge of the bed, letting him smooth her skirts as she braced back on her hands and waited for the world to correct its orbit. She ignored the brow her father sharply elevated at this apparent intimacy, and braved a smile for Ashton.

"Are you feeling better now?" he asked in concern.

She gave a slow, cautious nod, thankful that her answer was for the most part true. "I'm much better . . . except . . . I'm terribly hungry."

Meghan chortled and hurried to the door. "I'll tell the cook ye be feelin' better now, mum. Ye an' the mister come down whenever ye like."

The maid departed, and Robert followed reluctantly to the portal. "I . . . ah . . . guess I'll be going down, too." He turned a questioning eye toward Ashton, seeming opposed to leaving the pair alone together. "Coming, Mr. Wingate?"

"In a moment," Ashton replied, pointedly waiting for the man to remove himself from the room and close the door behind him.

Robert vented a low, derisive snort. "Haven't you caused enough woe to come to this house without makin' a kept woman of my daughter?"

Ashton's head came up, and he gave the man a mildly disdaining stare. "Perhaps one of us should leave, Mr. Somerton. We don't seem to have much to say to each other."

Robert shot a glance toward his daughter. "Well, I know which of us she'll want to stay."

The portal slammed behind the elder, and Lenore watched Ashton as the sound of her father's angry stride drifted back to them. The twitching muscles in the lean cheeks clearly portrayed his ire, and with a tender smile she slid her arms about his neck and kissed his frowning brow.

"It doesn't matter what he says," she whispered. "Whether I am Lierin or Lenore, I still love you."

His questing mouth found hers, and for a long, pleasurable time they savored the hotly flaring passion that catapulted through them. Clasping her knees, he pulled her toward the edge of the bed and bent to lightly nibble at her ear. "You have too many clothes on."

A thought struck her, and she leaned back in his arms to probe the smoky eyes. "The tent . . . ?"

Ashton moved his shoulders in a slight, upward motion. "Gone, I fear."

"Oh." Her voice was small with disappointment. "It seemed so . . . nice out there."

A grin tugged at his mouth. "The tent is gone, madam . . . but we still have what made it nice." He placed a lightly provocative kiss upon her parted lips as he answered the unspoken question in her eyes. "Each other, my love. We need nothing more than that."

"I could use some nourishment," she teased.

He started to laugh, then grimaced and clasped a hand to his side. Smilingly he admonished, "Don't torture me with your humor, madam."

Gingerly Lenore pulled aside his bloodied shirt and examined the long gash in the flesh along the side of his ribs. "You need to be tended."

Ashton rubbed a hand through his hair and caught the whiff of smoke that drifted from it. "I need a bath!"

"That can be arranged, too. I'll tell Meghan to have one prepared for you right away." Brushing hard against him, she slid off the bed and, having no place else to put her feet, used the space on either side of his. Her downward movement left the bulk of her skirts wadded between them, and the ever-rutting rake grinned at the opportunities presented him. His hands slipped beneath her petticoats and roamed the delightfully rounded ending of her torso, bringing her warming gaze up to his. "Would you consider delaying that order a moment or two, madam?"

The softly glowing green eyes spoke her answer before she gave one in a barely breathed murmur. "I don't see where a few moments will matter one way or another."

Ashton lifted her back to the bed and leaned close against her loins as he plied his talent to unfastening the back of her gown. "I thought you were hungry."

"Who needs food when there are better things to do?" she asked with a smile flirting at her lips.

It was much later when a properly garbed and freshly bathed Lenore unlocked the hall door leading to the attic and climbed the steep stairs to that lofty area. A small force of men had come from the *Gray Eagle*, but with assurances that no one had been injured in the fire they had returned to the ship and were instructed to be wary of any curious activity around the house. Ashton was resting in Lenore's room, having been up most of the night, but she was feeling restless, as if something beyond the barrier wall that held her memory captive was beckoning to her. She now knew what had led to her collision with Ashton's coach, but there was still the matter of the man's murder to be dealt with . . . and the attempt on her own life. It was rather frightening to know that someone whose face she had once seen wanted her dead. If it was only because she had been a witness to a murder, the man was still out there somewhere, waiting for her . . . and she knew not who it was.

The contained heat in the attic immediately brought a fine dappling of moisture to her skin, but she did not plan to stay. She knew what she had come for. The portrait of the man who had haunted her when she looked at her father. Taking up the framed painting, she removed the cloth sheathing and stared at the square-jawed visage. It did not seem so stern now . . . for it had become an almost cherished sight in her dreams. She ran a trembling hand over the dried oil, stroking the area of his chin, and in flickering impressions she saw a tiny hand lovingly caress that strong jaw. The man lowered a kiss upon the small auburn head that nestled against his chest, and Lenore blinked back sudden tears as she experienced all the same warm feelings the girl had felt then.

"Robert Somerton?" she whispered the question and, with growing assurance, declared, "You are my father. You are Robert Somerton."

Her heart leapt for joy, and blinded by a rush of happy tears, she clasped the painting to her and took a step toward the trap door, only to stumble over something large and heavy blocking her path. She moved the portrait aside to see, and stared down with growing perplexity at the huge trunk she had tried to open on her last visit to the attic. She had all but forgotten it was here. Her slender fingers lightly traced the straps that bound it, seeming to call forth an illusion of servants loading the piece in the boot of a carriage as she stood with Malcolm at the door of this very house and bade farewell to departing guests. She was gowned in the pale blue organdy, and it seemed they were being congratulated on their recent nuptials. When the last couple was waved off, Malcolm took her in his arms, and they exchanged a lengthy kiss before they entered the hall, laughing. He strode into the parlor, and in her mind she could see the steps of the stairway before her as she ascended, then the door of her bedroom was being pushed closed. Through a murky haze, she stared at her own image reflected in the mirror of her dressing table. The eyes were slightly wistful, not quite happy, as if yearning for something that could not be. The jaw firmed, and a gleam of determination came into the green eyes. Straightening, she began to tidy her coiffure, then her heart started racing as her vision lifted to a tall form standing just beyond the open french doors. The face was not handsome, but she knew it well from her tormenting nightmares, except now he was not screaming, nor was he being bludgeoned to death by a poker iron. She felt the same scream building in her lungs which had threatened to burst forth then, but the haze cleared, and she saw the man step quickly forward with an anxious, almost pleading gesture for her to be silent. His eyes were fearful as he glanced nervously about . . . like a little ferret . . . then he moved to her dressing table and picked up the folded piece of parchment he had earlier passed to her. He opened it and gave it over into her hands, urging her to read. Lenore sensed the dismay she had experienced then, but she was ignorant of the cause. The man pressed other articles in her hands, and with each her distress deepened until once again her attention was on the man. Raising a hand, he moved backward, bidding her to come . . . bidding her to come . . . to come . . . to come. . . .

Lenore's eyelids fluttered as the impressions left her and her mind cleared. She glanced down at the trunk and knew with sudden certainty that she must see what was inside. A heavier tool had to be found to pry free the locked flap, and she determined to fetch one soon after removing the landscape from the parlor wall and placing her father's portrait in its stead.

Taking the painting with her, she made her way carefully down the narrow stairs and entered the lower front room. Once again she dragged a straight chair to the fireplace, took down the wooded scene, and hung the painting of the square-jawed man. She tucked the landscape out of sight and sat down in a wing-backed chair to wait for the one who called himself her sire. It was barely half an hour later when he strolled in with his nose in a book.

"It's a hot one today," he observed, loosening his cravat and moping his brow. "Why, the fish are fairly jumping from that big boiling pot out there."

He chortled at his own humor, but his laughter faded in swift degrees when he looked up and found himself beneath the weight of Lenore's stoical stare. He cleared his throat as he moved away and, pouring himself a libation, settled on the settee. Raising an arm above his head, he leaned backward, stretching himself, and then froze. His mouth slowly descended to convey his surprise, leaving him gaping at the portrait.

"Good heavens!" he gasped. Sitting forward in a rush, he shot a glance toward her, finding her expression unchanged. His features clouded as a deeply troubled frown creased his brow, and hurriedly he gulped down another unhealthy portion of whiskey before wiping a hand across his mouth.

"Can you tell me one thing?" she asked in a quiet voice.

He took another quick swallow before he asked, "What is it that you want to know, girl?"

"Who are you?"

He bounced in agitation on the seat. "What do you mean, daughter?"

"I . . . don't think I am . . ."

"Am what?" He appeared perplexed.

"Your daughter," Lenore stated simply.

He stared at her agog. "Why, of course you are!"

She replied with a slow, negative shake of her head. "No, I really don't think so."

"What is this? Another lapse of memory?" he questioned almost angrily and gave a short, scornful laugh. "We've been through this before, I believe."

"Yes," she agreed, "but I am beginning to see things clearly now." She lifted her hand, bringing his attention back to the portrait, but he quickly ducked his head, as if he felt some shame viewing it. "This is my father, isn't it?"

"Good lord, girl! You've lost your mind," he charged, blustering.

A lovely eyebrow arched queryingly. "Have I? Or am I just beginning to get it back?"

"I don't know what you mean!" He sprang to his feet and paced the floor restlessly. "What has taken hold of you? That damned Wingate fellow comes into this house and suddenly you cast away all who love you. . . ."

"The name in your book of plays . . . it's your name, isn't it? Edward Gaitling . . . Shakespearean actor."

The white-haired man moaned and twisted his hands in deep distress. "Why are you tormenting me like this, girl? Don't you know that I care for you?"

"Do you?" Her tone was doubting.

"Of course!" He flung a hand about in a wild, frenzied gesture. "I am your father! And I care for my daughter!"

Lenore sprang from the chair with an angry command. "Stop it! You are not my father! You are Edward Gaitling! There is no further reason for your pretense." She raised a hand to indicate the portrait once again. "This is my father. This . . . is . . . Robert Somerton! And I want to know who I am! If I *am* Lenore Sinclair, why was there need for all this chicanery?"

Edward Gaitling opened his eyes wide in surprise. "Oh, but you *are* Lenore . . . and Malcolm is *really* your husband."

She shook her head in painful confusion. She had desperately hoped that he would make a different announcement. "Then why all this pretense? Why have you played the part of my father?"

"Don't you see, girl?" He came toward her holding out a hand in pleading supplication. "With you being in Wingate's house and believing you were Lierin and his wife . . . and him strongly declaring it was so, you needed something more than Malcolm's word to sway the balance."

"But why couldn't my real father do that?"

"Because he is in England, girl, and Malcolm was afraid of what would happen between you and Wingate. By the time your father could have been summoned and traveled here . . . good heavens! . . . you could have almost borne the man a child!"

His exaggeration made her cringe inwardly, and she was the one now who twisted her hands in dismay. "So Malcolm hired you to perform for me."

Edward Gaitling seemed unable to manage more than a brief, hesitant glance in her direction. "I guess . . . that's the way it happened."

"You seem particularly loyal to Malcolm," she observed distantly. "How long have you known him?"

Edward tossed down another swallow, and as he lowered his glass, he gripped it between both hands. "I've known him for a long time, I guess."

"Before we were married?"

"I . . . ah . . . I've been away . . . for a long time," he answered lamely.

"Then you weren't informed of the wedding?"

"No . . . I wasn't . . . I can't tell you anything about that."

"I remember . . . part of it," she said.

Edward's head snapped up. "Oh? But I thought you couldn't . . . remember very well."

A wry smile touched her lips. "I told you . . . it's beginning to come back."

A worried frown flitted across his brow before he hurriedly dropped his gaze. "Malcolm will be happy to hear that."

"I really don't see why."

"Eh?" He peered at her in confusion.

"Even if I were to regain all my memory, it would not change things between us. I don't know exactly why I married him . . . but whatever was there between us is there no longer."

Edward's shoulders sagged, and he heaved a laborious sigh. "Poor Malcolm. He does love you, you know."

"I'm not at all sure about that, but it doesn't matter. I've made up my mind."

"Will you be going back to Natchez with that Wingate fellow?"

"I don't see why you need to know my plans." Lenore released her breath haltingly. "I'd like you to leave the house as soon as you can. There's no further reason for you to stay."

Edward Gaitling looked at her in surprise, then his wonder ebbed into a disconcerted frown. Giving a reluctant nod, he set down his glass and moved to the door. He paused another long space to gaze back at her, then slowly made his way from the room. Lenore could hear his footsteps on the stairs, ascending at the same lagging pace, and in the still house, she heard the closing of his door a few, short moments later.

The house grew quiet and still, and in the loneliness of the parlor Lenore lifted her gaze to the portrait, wondering about the man who was really her father. If she could correctly discern anything from the glimpses she had of him in her memory, he was a man who really loved his daughters. Ashton would be like that, she thought with a wistful smile. He would be a good father. He loved so well. Indeed, she wondered why her sister had not somehow fought to live and claim the happiness he could have given her.

Lenore shook her head, trying to reject the thoughts that came to plague her, but they persisted, and she had to yield her mind to their presence. Had she a right to take her sister's place? To seize upon Ashton's devotion for another and selfishly claim it for herself? He had assured her that he would love her whether she was Lierin or Lenore, but was it true? With his dream swept away by tragedy, had he been too eager to grasp at whatever facsimile became available? And was she taking advantage of his love for her sister to fill an emptiness within herself?

She groaned inwardly as a weighty guilt came down upon her. Edward Gaitling had put a name to her. A kept woman! The mistress of her sister's husband! Adulteress!

A depressing coldness clamped its clammy hands upon her as the heavy lump in the pit of her stomach grew weightier. She had begun to sense that the white-haired man was not her father, and with the suspicion, a hope that she might not be Lenore had begun to form. Still, if she had recognized the facts as being what they were, she would have accepted the fleeting memories of her marriage to Malcolm as truth. The blue gown ... the wedding guests ... the trunk ...

Lenore lifted her head, feeling a burning need to see what the chest contained. She set herself to finding a chisel and hammer and, accomplishing that feat, retrieved the landscape and climbed once more to the attic room. Now in the late afternoon the heat in the closed space was nearly unbearable, but she worked at the lock with a fierce purposefulness, disregarding the mugginess and the gown that began to cling cloyingly close to her dampened skin. Finally, the flap broke free, and she quickly lifted the top. An empty tray met her gaze, and a quick flash of a memory filled it with neatly arranged possessions. In her mind she could visualize her gowns packed beneath the wooden compartment. Almost eagerly she lifted the tray and set it aside. There the images halted . . . abruptly. Nothing but large stones filled the bottom. She stared down at them, suddenly unsure of herself and more than slightly puzzled. She bent to move one aside, then a strange, sickly sweet odor touched her nostrils, reminding her of something spoiled. Warily she turned her head, and her eyes slowly widened as they settled on the dark reddish brown stains smeared across the inner lining.

With a gasp Lenore stumbled back, hitting her head sharply on a low rafter, and was brought up short by the confining timbers. Her stomach heaved, and she covered her mouth with a shaking hand. Averting her face to deny any chance glimpse of what she had just seen, she pressed her brow against the slanting wooden brace. A strange creepiness made her skin crawl, and while her heart quivered, a frosty chill shivered up her spine. Her mind began to tumble in a dizzying gyre, and she squeezed her eyes tightly shut to forbid any intrusion of the nightmare that threatened.

"No, no," she moaned miserably as once more the poker was lifted and brought down with murderous intent. She cowered, wanting to see nothing more of it, but the horror was relentless and seeped into her brain until all she saw was . . . blood! Her mind screamed at the terror she had witnessed, and then the tall, broadshouldered form came slowly around with a dark cloak swirling about it. The face was enraged, the eyes flaring, the mouth snarling, and the visage was one she knew!

"Malcolm!" she gasped, flinging her eyes wide.

"You bitch!" his voice barked from the stairwell, and though she whirled to flee, he was there immediately behind her, grabbing her arm in a cruel, unrelenting vise and ensnaring the heavy chignon at her nape. He shook her head until her vision blurred, and then he twisted her head around until she thought her neck would snap. A sharp pain shot through her head at his abuse, but she stiffened her jaw, refusing to whine or mewl for mercy.

"You killed him!" she accused through gritted teeth. "You murdered him! And you stuffed his body in my trunk so you could get rid of it."

"You shouldn't have left here with him," he snarled close to her ear. "You should never have listened to him! I was waiting for you downstairs . . . and I waited . . . and waited. It was time for us to go aboard the ship. We were to sail to Europe and abroad, but still you didn't come down. Then the coachman came running in and said the carriage had been stolen by someone who had hit him over the head, and when I ran upstairs, I couldn't find you."

"But how did you know where I had gone?"

Malcolm laughed without humor. "The note the bastard wrote to you . . . you left it on your dressing table. Then I knew who had been here and where he had taken you . . . to Natchez to see his sister . . . to provide you proof of what he said . . . and to secure her release with your testimony." His short, snorting chuckle came in derision. "Sarah! Another bitch! She didn't trust me either . . . but she loved me. *You* lust after that devil, Wingate."

"Bigamist!" The tendons in her throat tensed into tight cords as she tried to pull her hair free from his grasp, but he yanked her head back upon his shoulder and, slipping an arm about her throat, applied pressure until she was forced to cease her struggles or be choked to death. Her outrage was not so easily subdued. "Murderer!"

Forcing her face around with his wrist, Malcolm stared down into the blazing emerald eyes and smirked. "You needn't be jealous, my pet. I took care of her. She's naught but ashes now."

"You set fire to the madhouse?!" Lenore questioned, horrified at the extent he would go to achieve his own ends.

"I'm very good at building fires, my dear," he boasted. "I take great pleasure in doing it well. Whenever I've paid others to do a like service, they have failed me. Wingate's warehouses, for instance. A clever ploy to get him away from Belle Chêne so you could be pressed to do the honorable thing, but those sheds were supposed to burn . . . all of them, and the blame was to be cast on Horace Titch."

The wall was slowly crumbling, and the horror was beginning to spill through the widening fissures. "You had Sarah committed after we met, while her brother was still abroad and I was in England. I don't know what evil quirk of your mind made you choose Natchez . . . or why you didn't kill her."

"I had gained the sympathy of the family attorneys with all the distress I had to go through having to commit her. It would have been foolish to arouse their suspicions, especially when any investigation into the accident that killed her father would have implicated me. Since the lawyers were willing to believe her brother would never return, they let me have everything I needed. It was disappointing to learn how quickly the family's wealth could be exhausted. I had just seized upon another outlet when her brother came . . . and took you away."

"We had only arrived in Natchez and were making plans to visit Sarah the next day. How did you manage to arrange everything so quickly?"

"You made the mistake of traveling by carriage across land, my dear. I left immediately by boat and went up the Mississippi by steamer. You had to allow rest for the horses and a night's lodgings; nothing delayed me." Malcolm loosened his grip on her arm and caressed it as he murmured against her ear. "You should never have come to his room when you did . . ."

"I heard arguing. . . ."

"Aye, and your curiosity nearly bought you a grave, my love. I could not let a witness to one of my murders live, no matter how fond of her I was." His stroking hand came upon her breast and sent a shiver through her. "It would have been so easy if you'd have allowed me to remove the man's body in secret. Then you'd have thought he had disappeared and was only playing you for a dupe. You certainly would not have been able to make inquiries at the madhouse after I torched it and secured the silence of those who knew me."

"I really don't understand the workings of your mind, Malcolm," she said in some amazement. "Can you honestly believe you can continue in your evil ways?"

"I'm very ambitious, my dear . . . and I have the intelligence to bring into being all that I desire."

"If you think you're so intelligent, tell me why you filled my trunk with stones and left it here to be discovered. Why didn't you just dump it in the river?"

"Oh, but I couldn't. At least, not while that coachman I hired watched me so closely. He helped me carry it out of the inn and kept insisting he'd handle the baggage . . . even when we got here. I didn't want the servants to open it, so I had him help me bring it up here. It seemed safe enough behind a locked door."

"But the body . . . when did you get rid of it?"

"The first night we stopped on the road . . . I had to sneak out of the inn and carry it into the woods . . . then I filled the chest with stones so the coachman wouldn't get suspicious. You just don't know how much I regretted that you went off without our driver."

"A man you hired!" she scoffed. "Even if he had consented to take us, he'd have left a trail so wide, you couldn't have missed it."

Malcolm gloated. "I have been blessed immeasurably by the loyalty of my men."

"Cutthroats! Thieves! Rapists!"

He chuckled at her rising ire. "I have to allow them a few pleasures now and then."

"Why didn't you let them take me? Why did you make such a pretense of saving me from them?"

"Ahh, my dear," he sighed. "There are some pleasures a man wants to preserve for himself."

"You could have forced yourself on me then. Why did you insist on courting me and pressing for my hand?"

"I was not content with mere tidbits. I wanted it all. The first time I saw you, I was intrigued by your beauty. When I made inquiries, you became even more desirable to me. I thought I had lost you . . . and then to my joy I found that my men had taken you prisoner. They had made plans to ransom you, but first they agreed to pass you around among themselves. . . ."

"That's when you fought them off."

"I had to make it look good, you understand. When I delivered you safe and sound to your father . . . I became a hero." Malcolm's brows drew downward into a sudden scowl. "But even then you denied me . . . and it seemed that I had failed. I was turned away, but my hopes rose again when you came to Biloxi to live." His fingers tightened as they came upon her arm, and he was pleased by her pained grimace. "You still did not make it easy for me. You were too set on mourning your husband."

"Aye! And I should never have let you wear down my resistance. I would have saved myself a lot of misery." She resisted the prodding prongs of fear when his hand lifted to caress her throat, as if he seriously contemplated her extinction. "If you're going to kill me, Malcolm, get it over with," she gritted. "There's nothing to stop you now."

"Ahh, but there is, my dear." He chuckled with more amusement. " 'Twas the reason I married you. Your vast fortune could do great wonders for me. I have all the documents I need to prove that we are married. They'll give me title to everything that is yours. There's even a will. . . ."

"I'll never sign anything like that!"

"You needn't, my dear. Samuel Evans is quite adept at his work. He wrote out the documents and made them look legal. He can just as easily sign your name to them. Why, no one even noticed how he touched up our marriage document. I could not let that devil Wingate know just when we exchanged vows."

"For all of your planning and scheming, Malcolm, you'll still get nothing. If I die, what I have . . . except for this house . . . reverts back to my father. It's *his* wealth, and *his* it shall remain."

Malcolm regarded her with heavily hooded eyes that gleamed above a smug smile. "I've already taken care of that matter. By now, the man I sent to perform the task has no doubt carried through, and your father's demise will soon be announced."

"Nooo!" she moaned, falling limp against him.

"There, there, my dear. No need to mourn. With your father in England and you here, you can almost make believe he still exists. I only await the word of his death to begin collecting, since it is the law that I inherit all that he leaves you, but if you have the imagination for it you're quite free to think of him as still alive."

Wearily she rolled her head upon his chest. "What do you plan to do with me?"

"Oh, I'll keep you around for a while, just to make sure there are no surprises concerning your father's inheritance. I don't want Wingate intruding into this. I know a little madhouse along the river where you will be safe . . . until you are of no more use to me."

"And then? Will you set fire to that, too?" Her inquiry was sharp with sarcasm.

"Oh, I might. It makes things simpler that way."

"And it doesn't matter how many you kill in your effort to destroy one?"

"Those miserable souls, they're better off dead."

"Not everyone would agree with you, Malcolm," she flung over her shoulder.

"I know. Sarah's guard found me out and tried to stop me. I killed him in the cookhouse, and then dragged his body into the house to be burned. Of course, his death was something I had arranged anyway, so it was hardly a loss."

"You're evil, Malcolm," she accused. "Evil. A spawn of Satan."

Growing tired of the discussion, Malcolm pulled her with him as he turned. "Come along now. I want to see where your lover is."

"Lover?!" Her temper flared anew.

"Never mind that now. I want to see Wingate's face when I threaten to blow your head off. . . ."

She fought him in sudden desperation, for the moment ignoring his ruthess grasp, but it was difficult to disregard the derringer that he pressed beneath her chin.

"If you think I won't use this, you're wrong. Samuel Evans has worked for me for some time now, so he'll do whatever I ask . . . even penning a note that would explain why you took your own life."

He dragged her to the stairs and, slipping an arm about her narrow waist, lifted her off her feet and started his descent. She dared not struggle, for he held her out over the edge of the stairs, and he seemed to delight in taunting her over the open space. His sudden dips snatched her breath and inspired his low chuckles.

At the lower door Malcolm paused and leaned close to her ear. "Where is your lover?"

Her heart trembled inside her chest. "I think I'd be a fool to tell you."

"No matter." He was unaffected by her lack of cooperation. "My father will tell me."

"Your father?" She tried to see his face, but could not. "Who might that be?"

"The sot," he sneered.

"Edward Gaitling . . . is your father?" Her astonishment was complete.

"Not one I'm proud of, but the only one I can claim."

"And does he know all about your activities?" she queried in wonder.

"Many of them, I suppose. Some he doesn't approve of, but he has much to make up for. He deserted my mother when I was but a young lad . . . and it was only after she died . . . and I was a man full grown that he came pleading for my forgiveness. He's been trying to make up for his sins ever since."

"By committing more?" Her short laugh revealed her contempt. "No wonder he drinks so much. It takes a lot to dull his conscience."

"Bah! He's squeamish. He turns his back so he can tell himself he's not aware of what's going on. He plays ignorant. He's still wondering about Mary, but he knows she overheard us talking. I just accepted the fact that I had to get rid of her, but I made it pleasurable for her until the end."

His captive shuddered in revulsion. She had never known a man as evil or as depraved as he. If anyone deserved to be imprisoned in a madhouse, it was he, but his crimes reached far beyond the maladies of those poor souls.

Malcolm opened the door and stepped into the hall, toting her as he would a doll. Hurrying footsteps sounded in the lower corridor, and Meghan's voice drifted up in a wordless melody. Malcolm growled a low warning and tightened his arm around the slender waist, making his hostage writhe in pain. Her fingers clawed at his coatsleeve, trying to pry his arm free, for it seemed doubtful that her bones could stand the strain.

"I'll find out anyway," he whispered. "So you might as well tell me where Wingate is."

"In my bedroom," she gasped in agony.

"How convenient for you to keep your lover abed until you are ready for him."

She refused to answer and give credit to his remark. He loosened his arm enough to allow her to breathe, but the pistol nudged her jaw again, warning her to silence while he carefully crept down the hall toward her chambers. The door was closed, and he set her to her feet at the portal, then imprisoned her there with his own body.

"I'll be right behind you," Malcolm breathed against her ear. "If you make any forward move to get away from me, I'll get either you or him with this shot. Do you understand?" He waited until she replied with a hesitant nod of her head. "Now open the door . . . very carefully."

Her hand trembled as it closed around the knob, then complying to every word of his command, she turned it until the latch clicked free. With wildly thumping heart she pushed it inward, moving cautiously forward as she did so. Ashton was lying on his side facing the door and had been sleeping, but as she entered, his eyelids came slowly open. He smiled sleepily as he saw her, but then his eyes lifted, caught the glint of the derringer beside her shoulder and the large shape behind her. Not waiting for an explanation he dove toward the bench at the foot of the bed where he had left his own derringer beneath his clothes, not caring at the moment that he flattened the sheet which had covered him under his naked form.

"I'll kill her!" Malcolm barked and shoved the bore of the small pistol into her throat. "So help me, I will!" He let the other man digest his threat a moment, then he directed, "Now carefully . . . take whatever weapon you're after . . . and place it on the floor in front of the bed and slide it very slowly over here to me. If you make one quick, unnecessary movement, she will be the one to pay for it. And if you think I don't have it in me to kill her, then you'd better ask her how many I've already done away with."

Ashton's gaze met his lady's, and reading the troubled disquiet in the green depths, he knew they were both dealing with a dangerous man. As instructed, he removed the pistol from beneath his clothing and, coming to his feet, laid it on the rug and pushed it out toward them, then gave it a light shove, sending it sliding slowly across the floor.

Malcolm took the slender wrist that was close at hand and prodded his captive again with the pistol. "Pick it up by the cylinder and hand it to me butt first." He smirked in pleasure as his orders were obeyed and, slipping the extra derringer into his coat pocket, chuckled at his power. "Strange how the pair of you have come to respect me. Perhaps you are finally learning." Laying his arm around his hostage's shoulders, he waved the pistol toward Ashton. "I'll allow you to get your trousers on now. Though my wife may prefer your present state, I'm sure Meghan will be unduly shocked if you go downstairs wearing only that patch on your ribs. My men would have saved me considerable trouble if they had taken care of you as they should have . . . especially if they had done so at the very beginning."

"Just what are you planning?" Ashton asked sharply as he shoved a leg into his trousers.

"If you must know, Wingate, I'm going to take you downstairs and wait for the rest of my men to come. I've told them to use caution coming to the house. I don't want to make anyone on your ship suspicious of our activities here."

"And once your men get here?" Ashton thrust his other leg into the pair of pants and began fastening them.

"Then, of course, there will be enough of us to deal with you as I would like. I promised Lenore if I ever caught the pair of you together, I'd see you gelded. . . ."

"*Noooo!*" The cry came out in a frightened wail, and once again the woman fought the restraining arm that held her.

"I know how you must treasure that part of him, my dear, but you should never have betrayed me with him."

"Betrayed you!" She twisted in rage at his accusation, and though his arm slipped down and tightened agonizingly about her ribs again, she would not be stilled. Ashton stepped forward with a low growl, but the gleaming bore of the derringer swung around, bringing him to a sudden halt. A frightened cry broke from the woman, and she quickly submitted herself to Malcolm's will, pleading, "Don't! Don't hurt him. I'll do anything you want. Just don't hurt him. . . . Please."

"Your concern for him is touching, my dear." Malcolm's disdain seeped into his tone. "You might have bestowed some of that on me when you had the chance and saved yourself some grief now."

"Did you show concern for me with your lies and deceptions?" she inquired snidely.

"'Twas only a small matter of bigamy," Malcolm casually excused. "Sarah is dead now, and we'll deal with the other problem shortly."

The tearing green eyes lifted to Ashton's wondering stare, and she wept as she told him, "Malcolm was already married when he spoke the vows with me. He had put his wife in the madhouse, and then he set a torch to it just to get rid of her."

The dark brows raised in surprise. "Then you are Sarah's husband," Ashton mused aloud. "What she was seeing here was not her imagination."

Malcolm frowned as he peered at the other man closely. "How do you know Sarah?"

The broad, bare shoulders lifted indolently. "You were not successful in killing her. She works for me now."

"The little bitch!" Malcolm showed his teeth in a snarl. "She always did give me trouble."

"If she ever gets her hands on you, Malcolm, your trouble up until then will have been minor," Ashton remarked laconically. "She did not exactly appreciate being locked away in an asylum."

The full lips twisted sardonically. "Neither will this one."

Ashton returned his attention to the one he loved. He read her trepidations in her troubled gaze, but at the moment he could neither say nor do anything to console her.

"When you go downstairs, Wingate, walk far ahead of us," Malcolm instructed. "You can guess what will happen to your mistress if you disappear out of my sight or make any sudden moves."

"You can't expect to hold us hostage while her father and the rest of the servants look on."

"Ashton, the man is not my father." She brushed at the tears that spilled down her cheeks and sniffed. "He's Malcolm's father."

"Aye," Malcolm agreed. "And by now he should have the rest of the servants locked safely away." Moving carefully across the room with his burden, he motioned Ashton to the door with the gun. "Let's go now. And be careful if you have a care for this redhead."

Ashton strode leisurely ahead of the man, glancing back now and then to see how Lierin was faring. As before, Malcolm carried her in one arm and kept the weapon ready to use in his other hand. When the pair reached the lower hall, Ashton was already at the settee. He halted at the younger man's command and turned to face the doorway as Malcolm stepped through.

"Hurry it up," the tawny-haired man flung over his shoulder as Edward Gaitling came rushing from the back of the house with a long length of cord. "Get Wingate tied . . . and be quick about it. No mistakes now."

Ashton looked directly into the reddened gray eyes as the actor came forward, but Edward dropped his gaze in sudden haste and, stepping behind the taller man, drew Ashton's arms behind his back and secured the wrists with several tight loops of the rope and a trio of firm knots.

"Tie his ankles, too," Malcolm ordered. "I don't want the bloody bastard kicking me."

Edward pushed Ashton back onto the settee and warned, "You know of course that it won't do you any good to attack me."

Malcolm sneered at his father's feeble attempts to subdue the man by logic. "Wingate knows if he tries anything Lenore will die, now do what I told you."

Lumbering footsteps came from the back of the house, and everyone in the room paused to listen, Malcolm with bated breath. Two brawny shapes stepped to the parlor door, and when he spied them, a long sigh of relief slipped from his lips. One man had frizzy red hair and bore a pair of pistols in his belt. The other carried a long gaming gun, and a knife was tucked in a leather sheath at his waist. A mass of black hair brushed his shoulders.

Ashton's hackles rose as he recognized the brigand, and he bent a sharp, questioning stare upon Malcolm. "Are these some more of your men?"

The younger man directed the pair to take up their positions, one beside the hall entry, while the other was motioned to a place near the french doors. Finally deigning to acknowledge Ashton's inquiry, Malcolm turned a smirk over his shoulder. "What if they are?"

Ashton jerked his head toward the small giant. "That one came aboard my steamer during a pirate's attack. He's the one who shot me after Lierin fell overboard."

Malcolm laughed shortly. "He'll get that chance again soon enough."

"And your other man . . . who guarded the house," Ashton pressed. "He worked in the engine room about that same time. No doubt he sabotaged the engine when the pirate's barge came into view."

"Well, aren't you the smart one, *Mister* Wingate," Malcolm sneered.

"If they're your men, then you must be the leader of the band of pirates who've been making raids on the riverboats . . . and who attacked mine."

Malcolm presented a question to the red-haired man. "How soon will the others be coming, Tappy?"

"Some should be comin' in shortly," the miscreant answered. "A few more'll be comin' later on. The rest are gettin' the ship readied for when you get there."

"We won't be able to leave here until after dark," Malcolm replied. "I don't want Wingate's men coming after us."

"Ye've called out a small army ter deal with one man," Tappy observed. "An' he looks like he's wounded, at that."

"Wingate killed four of our men this morning and that's all he got! A mere scratch!" Malcolm snapped. "I'm not taking any more chances with him. Robert Somerton was a very rich man, and I don't want anything to spoil my inheritance."

"What be ye goin' ter do with the man here?" the black, straggly-haired one asked with a leering grin.

The pirate leader laughed in amusement as he detected the eagerness of his cohort. "Why, Barnaby, I thought you might enjoy cutting Wingate up a mite, then the lady can really have his heart to carry around with her while she's in the madhouse."

A sudden shriek of rage rent the air, and Malcolm stumbled back as a sharp heel scraped rudely down his shin. In the next instant he found himself set upon by a clawing, biting, hissing she-cat. He yelped in pain as her long nails raked across his cheek, drawing blood, and with a back-handed slap he sent her reeling to the floor. In the very next moment he had to swing the pistol around and halt Ashton as that one came rushing toward him with a snarl. It was most apparent that Edward Gaitling had forgotten the bonds for his ankles.

"Go ahead and use it," Ashton challenged. "I'm dead one way or another, but if you shoot me, you will be taking the chance that my men will hear and come to investigate. They know there's trouble in the wind, so why don't you go ahead and shoot me? Tell them you're here."

Barnaby stepped between the two men and, with a broad hand on Ashton's chest, shoved him back upon the settee. "Now don't ye go ruinin' me fun. I likes the idea o' carvin' ye up a mite, an' I wants ye ter stay safe 'til then, so's ye don't get wore out none 'fore I gets ter ye. I wants ye ter be able ter scream real good."

Holding a handkerchief to his bloodied cheek, Malcolm glared down at the woman whose eyes fairly snapped with green fire, then he whirled upon his father in a savage temper. "You sot! I thought I told you to tie Wingate's ankles. Can't you do anything right?"

"I'm sorry, Marcus," Edward apologized, shriveling in shame. "I'm not used to all of this."

"Marcus?" Ashton made the single name a query.

"Aye! Marcus Gaitling," Malcolm tossed at his adversary. "But I changed my name, and it's now Malcolm Sinclair. 'Twas my mother's name, Sinclair." He delivered a sneer to his father as he added, "And I prefer it."

A trio of men broadcast their presence as they stomped through the hall from the back and sauntered through the door of the parlor. Malcolm glanced at them briefly, then caught Edward's arm as the elder bent to attend to Ashton's bonds.

"Go fetch Meghan and tell her to get upstairs and start packing some baggage for her mistress. I'm sending a couple of these men up with Lenore. They can guard outside the doors while she changes into suitable traveling attire. If we're going through Biloxi in a carriage, I want everything to look normal."

As Edward hurried from the room, Malcolm yanked his second wife to her feet and snarled in her face. "I'm going to send you upstairs, and if you give me any more trouble, Barnaby will have my permission to start carving. Do you understand?"

She nodded briefly and, with a worried glance at Ashton, left the room with her two escorts. The two men set themselves to guard the exits of her bedroom, one in the hall and the other on the porch, and by the time Meghan arrived, her mistress had already formed a plan. She took the derringer Ashton had given her aboard the steamer and checked its loading as she laid out the details to the maid.

"Tell the guard on the porch that I've fainted, and when he bends over me, hit him with this." Quelling a shiver of revulsion, the younger woman pressed the poker iron into the other's hand. "It's the only thing we have in the room that can accomplish what we want, and that is to see him laid out unconscious without the other guard being aware of it." She had to force her mind away from the horror she had witnessed and set it to winning Ashton's release, but was trembling so much she could hardly speak. "Meghan, are you up to it?"

Meghan's grit was not hindered by a nightmarish memory. "Mum, if it means me life, an' I have every reason to believe it does, I'll be doin' it with zeal."

The maid caught the iron, and her mistress subdued the temptation to tell her to be gentle. She was not sure how well she was going to bear an actual recurrence of an attack made with a poker iron, but when Ashton's life was at stake, she was ready to subject herself to the test. No other object would prove as effective in subduing the man. A glass lamp or vase might have shattered and alerted the man in the hall, and neither she nor Meghan had the strength to make a club from a chair leg. The iron was their only safe option.

The younger woman curled face-downward on the floor and gave Meghan a nod when she was set. "Now call him in . . . and be careful."

Meghan flung open the doors and, in a frantic mein that Edward might have envied, beckoned to the knave who loitered on the porch. "Hurry! Me mistress has fallen an' struck her head. Come lift her onto the bed."

Tappy came running in and, seeing the feminine form lying crumpled on the floor, tucked his pistol in his belt and bent down to pick her up. In the next moment a piercing pain filled his head, then came darkness, and he tumbled unconscious alongside the redhead. That one had braced herself to still her panic as the poker thudded into his head, and she dared a cautious peek to assure herself the man was still breathing. He was, and that posed a problem which had to be taken care of before she could feel secure in leaving him.

"We'll have to tie and gag him, or else he'll alert the others," she whispered to Meghan. "After we do so, I want you to slip out and go for help. If they haven't taken Hickory, perhaps you can reach him. The sheriff must come here with as many men as he can lay hold of. We're dealing with an unworthy lot of pirates and murderers."

Meghan's worry increased as she watched her mistress remove the pistol from the miscreant's belt. "But, mum, what will ye be doin'? Where will ye be goin'?"

"Downstairs. They threatened to start cutting on Mr. Wingate if I tried anything, so hopefully I can stop their bloodletting and deliver a surprise they're not expectin'."

"Ye're goin' back into that devil's den?" the maid questioned in astonishment. "Ye'll not likely come out alive."

A wistful smile curved the younger woman's lips as an image of a tall man gripping a wooden railing came to mind, and she knew from experience that life without Ashton would hardly be worth living.

The sun dipped lower in the west, and Ashton distantly mused that it was like the sand that sifted through the narrow waist of an hourglass marking the dwindling hours of his life. With so many guards holding their weapons upon him, he was beginning to despair that he would find an opening to launch an attack. His hopes rallied briefly when a team of horses brought a carriage rattling up the drive. The presence of the conveyance gave his adversaries a start until Malcolm noticed a pair of his own men sitting in the driver's seat. The miscreants relaxed, and a moment later a burly man stepped to the parlor door and, reaching back, pulled a struggling woman into view.

"Look who I found in Biloxi." The man chortled as he swung his captive around to face the occupants of the parlor. Her face was red and enraged, and the green eyes blazed in outrage. Malcolm gaped in stunned silence, while gasps of astonishment came from his companions. Edward Gaitling slowly sank to the settee, perhaps more confused than anyone.

Ashton came to his feet and stepped forward for a better look. "Li . . . er . . . ?" he began, and then halted. The features were similar, but not as refined. With sudden certainty he shook his head. "You're not Lierin."

"Of course not. I'm her sister, Lenore. And who might you be, sir?" she asked crisply. "Are you part of these ruffians who kidnapped us as we were leaving the boat?"

Ashton began to smile and then to chuckle with real, heart-felt humor. "I do believe someone has made a mistake and sent me the wrong portrait." He sobered slightly as he cocked a querying brow. "Mrs. Livingston?"

"Yes," she answered warily. "And you?"

"I am your brother-in-law, Ashton Wingate," he replied.

"Ashton?!" Her eyes widened in dubious wonder. "But he's dead."

"No," the Natchez man grinned broadly as he replied. "I'm very much alive."

"But Lierin was sure that Ashton was dead," Lenore insisted. "She saw him die . . . and Malcolm showed her the grave."

Ashton raised a brow as he cast a glance toward the other man who had finally managed to close his mouth. "My grave? And where might that have been . . . and just when precisely did he show it to her?"

"Lierin said Ashton was buried near the place where the pirates attacked the *River Witch*. Malcolm showed her the grave shortly after he rescued her."

"I fear Malcolm has deceived us all . . . or at least tried to." Ashton faced the lady with a vow. "I swear to you that I am very much alive and the bearer of the name, Ashton Wingate. I believe your sister will attest to that."

"Where is she? Where is Lierin?" Lenore demanded. "I want to see her."

Ashton almost smirked as he turned to Malcolm. "Would you mind having one of your men fetch *my* wife?"

Malcolm returned a glower to the challenging hazel eyes, then with a gesture of a hand sent one of his men on the errand. "Get her down here . . . and make sure her maid comes with her." As the other left the room, Malcolm bent a curious stare upon the woman who was jerking off her gloves and his eyes narrowed slightly as he inquired, "What are you doing here?"

"We came here to see Lierin, Malcolm. An attempt was made on my father's life, and he grew anxious about Lierin's safety. He sailed from England, came by the islands, and bade me to journey with him the rest of the way."

"Your father is here?" Malcolm inquired in amazement. "But where?"

"He's in the carriage. He didn't like the way that buffoon was treating us and set upon him. The pair of bullies knocked him unconscious, and he hasn't come around yet."

Malcolm faced the fellow who had brought her in and flung out an arm toward the front porch. "Get out there, you idiot! I don't care if you have to carry Somerton, get him in here. He's too dangerous to leave out there alone!"

Lenore displayed some wonder as she watched the man scamper out, then she lifted a confused stare to Malcolm. "Am I wrong in assuming you're the leader of this band of misfits?"

Ashton was in amazing good spirits as he seized the moment to introduce the man and his companions. "You are correct in your assumptions, madam, and if perchance you do not know his real name, this is Marcus Gaitling, son of . . ." He twisted slightly, indicating the actor, who raised bleary eyes to the young woman. "Edward Gaitling, Shakespearean actor." Ashton nodded toward the other men who stood about the room. "These are some more of Malcolm's associates . . . and I would do the honors for them, except," he shrugged, "Malcolm hasn't told me all their names."

"It doesn't matter," the pirate leader snapped.

"Temper, temper," Ashton chided.

Malcolm swung around on him in a fit of rage. "You needn't gloat, *Mister* Wingate. She may be your wife, but it will do you little good . . . nor will it benefit her or the child she carries. You'll be dead shortly . . . and she'll be confined to a madhouse."

Lenore gasped and laid a trembling hand to her throat. "You wouldn't."

"I regret to say, madam, that Malcolm will do anything to see his purposes served," Ashton stated wryly. "What I'm wondering now is how he plans to get rid of you and your father. . . ."

Malcolm smirked. "That will be taken care of easily enou—"

"Unhand me, you brigand!"

The shouted command made Malcolm jump and glance around in sudden dismay as stumbling footsteps ended in a loud crash against the outside wall of the house.

"I'll make my own way, damn you! Now where is my daughter?! Where is Lierin?!"

Thundering footfalls came into the front hall, rattling the glass in the door as Malcolm had never thought of doing with his awesome entries. The pirates glanced at each other in worried confusion, but they had no time to obey Malcolm's angry gesture to get into the hall and seize the man. He came striding in on his own.

Ashton had once given up the thought that he would ever meet Robert Somerton face to face, but he knew as soon as he laid eyes on the graying dark head and blazing green eyes, that this was indeed the sire of Lierin Wingate. One of the brigands bolted forward to grab the older man's arm, but he was slammed carelessly aside, and as he struck the wall and slithered senseless to the floor, Robert came around with another thunderous demand.

"Fetch me my daughter!"

The pirate who had been sent after Lierin sidled past the man and entered the room, carefully avoiding the raging intruder as he did so. Hurrying to Malcolm's side, he made a whispered announcement. "She's not to be found, sir. She and that maid of hers . . . they knocked Tappy out . . . and left him all bound up."

"Find her!" Malcolm shouted. "Don't let that bitch leave here!"

Ashton glanced over his shoulder as he glimpsed a movement on the veranda, and he saw the tail of a skirt flick past the open french doors. Casting a wary gaze around, he found the miscreants occupied with Malcolm, who was angrily giving them orders. Straightening his stance, Ashton moved cautiously backward until he stood on the threshold of the double doors. He held his bound hands outward, away from him, and waited as unseen fingers plucked at the cords. It was nearly dark and they did not have much time left to secure their freedom. His brows lifted slightly in surprise as a large pistol was placed in his grasp. The time was not appropriate to thank the hidden angel for her gift, but he would strive to bestow the full measure of his gratitude at a later moment . . . when their victory was firmly in hand.

Behind his back, he tucked the pistol into the top of his trousers and then cleared his throat for attention. "Maybe Lierin has gone up to the attic to hide. She has been up there before."

Malcolm came around at Ashton's suggestion and, seeing how close the other man was to the french doors, yelled another command to his companions, "Get him back in . . . !"

"I'm coming!" Ashton barked and leisurely sauntered toward the settee, keeping his hands folded behind his back.

"I promised that bloody bitch I'd see you cut," Malcolm growled. "I think it's about time I let Barnaby have his fun."

"Really, Malcolm. You have become such a boor lately," Lierin chided as she swept through the french doors. She fervently hoped that she appeared more serene than she felt. The dam had broken completely away from her memory, and it was flooding back with vivid detail. With her entry she won the gawking stares of the band of thieves who cast befuddled glances between the twins, but Lierin hardly noticed as she continued to berate her second husband who had made a bigamist of her. "All you can do lately is threaten people. You haven't been successful in killing anyone since Mary. . . ." She heard the startled gasp of Edward Gaitling and wondered if something his son had done had finally shocked the actor. "If you're not careful, we'll stop taking you seriously."

"You bitch," he growled. "I thought you were an angel when I first saw you with Wingate aboard the *River Witch*. I told my men to kill him so I could have you, but you have meant nothing but misery for me."

"Tsk, tsk," she shamed and, shrugging her shoulders innocently, crossed the room with a shawl draped over one hand. She moved to her father who was being held to his position by the menacing bore of a gaming gun. Robert Somerton's eyes glowed with pleasure as he gave his daughter a casual inspection, and with a laugh that trembled slightly, Lierin came into his wide-spread arms. As she did so, she dropped the small derringer she carried into his pocket and breathed close to his ear. "The one without a shirt is a friend of ours, Papa. The rest can go to Hades."

Robert Somerton pressed a kiss upon her brow, then setting her aside, stepped toward Malcolm with a demand. "I want to know what the bloody devil is going on here. When you brought Lierin to England, we were under the impression that you had saved her from the pirates who had killed her husband in an attack upon his steamer, but here you are, looking very much like the villain in this game."

"He is," Edward Gaitling slurred from the settee. He tipped the crystal decanter that he held and poured an ample draught into his glass. "My son has seized the moment in hand and made his own bed . . . may he rot in hell."

Malcolm's eyes flared as he glanced at the white-haired man, then his lips curled as he faced Somerton. "Your daughter would have drowned but for my men. They caught her by the hair as she was swept near the barge and going under. They pulled her aboard and saved her life. You ought to be grateful—"

"Grateful!" Lierin cried. "Why, you buffoon! It was their attack on the steamer that nearly killed me! They shot my husband, and for all I knew he was dead. Then you came into their camp to receive the spoils, few that they were, and you pretended to rescue me. Oh, how gallant you were to brave so many. You won my release, and then took a grieving widow to see her husband's grave which bore a tombstone that you had purchased. An empty grave!"

"I could have filled it!" he retorted. "Would that have made you happier?"

"You tried!" she accused. "You paid your cutthroats to kill him, but he was too much of a man for the lot of them."

Barnaby chuckled. "We'll see how much of a man he is when I start slicing."

Lierin whirled to face the shaggy-haired man. "You bloodthirsty lout! I'll see you sent to hell before I'm finished with you!"

"Oooh, a right fiery bitch, she is," the unkempt bloke taunted with a leer. "I've gots me a bit o' Indian blood runnin' in me veins, an' ye knows what Indians like best?" His eyes twinkled at her. "Scalps! That's right, an' yours would make a fine one, I'd say."

Lierin dismissed his threat with a scoffing jeer and turned back to Malcolm. "When you took me to my grandfather's house, we saw something there that confused us both. Lenore's portrait was gone, and when we arrived in England, neither my father nor Lenore knew where it was. But you knew, didn't you! Or rather, you guessed. You were aware that Ashton was still alive, and you realized he was sent the wrong portrait by mistake. When you returned there, you knew where it was. There was no need for you to search for it, but you were looking for more evidence to convince me that I was Lenore . . . and I think you were still there when Ashton and I came."

"Aye," Malcolm sneered. "I saw the pair of you there, and it only made me more anxious in my quest to separate you again. Your memory loss was my good fortune, and I meant to make the most of it. Wingate had supposed you dead, and all I had to do was make him believe you were Lenore. I even had Samuel Evans change the name on the marriage document to read Lenore instead of Lierin Wingate."

"But Ashton wasn't so easily persuaded, was he?" Lierin derided. "From the very beginning he has thwarted your manuevers and turned your gambits to his favor. . . ."

"The prize is within my hands now, my pet," Malcolm responded with a caustic laugh. He was elated at the thought of the other man's demise, but when he turned a superior smile to Ashton, he saw the mockery gleaming in those smoky depths. The glowing eyes rattled his confidence and made him wonder if there was anything that would move the Natchez man to fear. Once again he tried. "Weill will be left here for dead, and Horace will be blamed again. Poor Mr. Titch, he has been a valuable asset in my game. I'll miss him."

"The sheriff might not be so gullible," Ashton replied. "I warned him last night that it seemed too easy and the thieves might be using Horace as a scapegoat."

"You set a trap for my men," Malcolm jeered. "And you caught a little rabbit in the snare, and once the foxes are released, he'll be the only one who's left."

"You also took back the jewels you had given Lierin," Ashton said.

Malcolm shrugged and smiled. "She kicked me out. Why not?"

A badly slurred voice came from the settee. "Marcus told me she was really Lenore. . . ."

" 'Twould seem you have played us all for fools," Somerton accused. "Even your father. You have gone to great lengths to make my daughter your wife."

"Lierin had something I wanted." The full lips smiled slightly.

"Wealth. She was my best hope to gain it. I courted her relentlessly and finally she agreed to marry me." He frowned sharply. "But on our wedding night she left me . . . to seek out proof that I was already married. She couldn't even allow a benefit of a doubt. She believed the man."

"He showed me evidence!" Lierin exclaimed, striding forward. "Your marriage license, a small miniature of you and Sarah . . . and a letter sent to her brother from the attendant whom you hired to guard her . . . except he began to care about her . . . and didn't like what you were doing to her. Her brother went searching for you . . . and found you making plans to wed me . . . and on the afternoon the ceremony was performed, he tried to warn me and even pressed a note into my hand, but I was busy and didn't read it . . . until later. . . ."

"And you left me on our wedding night!" Malcolm shouted.

"Aye!" Lierin cried. "And you don't know how happy I am that I never went to bed with you!"

It was Ashton's turn to gape in astonishment. He stared at the two who glared at each other and began to chuckle. The sound was infectious. Robert Somerton started to chortle and Lenore hid a giggle behind her hand. Lierin's laughter tinkled brightly in the room, but it was Ashton's amusement that sorely beset Malcolm.

Gnashing his teeth, he lunged toward the other man and seized him by the throat. His fingers sought to close, but suddenly, surprisingly he heard a familiar click and felt something hard prod him in the belly. Cautiously he lowered his gaze, and his breath halted as he saw the dull gleam of a large pistol. He lifted his gaze to Ashton, and felt his own vitals begin to roil with dread.

"Call off your villains, or you're a dead man," Ashton warned softly.

Malcolm made a futile attempt to shake his head, but the negative gesture would not come. He caught the sound of another hammer being drawn back and almost sighed in relief until Barnaby squealed, "How'd the bloke get that pistol? Someone! Get him!"

It seemed a miracle, but suddenly there were men with guns rushing through the french doors and Sheriff Coty was leading the pack. The miscreants bolted for the hall door in their attempt to escape, but other lawmen came through the front door while others ran in from the back.

"Meghan!" Lierin cried through a rush of joyful tears. "Bless her dear heart! She made it through and saved us!"

Sheriff Coty seized Malcolm's arm. "You've been causing a lot of trouble, I hear. I'm sure Titch will be relieved to see you arrested for the crimes he has been accused of."

Robert Somerton came forward as the lawman dragged Malcolm away and extended a hand in friendship to Ashton. "I don't know who you are, young man, but my daughter says you're a friend."

Lierin laughed gayly and slipped her arm through Ashton's. "Something more than a friend, Papa." Her eyes danced as she won her father's attention. "This is my husband . . ." She saw his eyebrows raise in surprise. ". . . Ashton Wingate . . . the man I love with all my heart."

Robert Somerton stared at the couple for a long moment as tears gathered in his eyes, then he laid his other hand over the two that were already joined. "It's good to meet you, son, and a very good pleasure to welcome you into the family."

Lierin caressed her husband's bare arm as she murmured, "I'm glad you approve, Papa. Now perhaps your grandchild will have a name and a father to be proud of . . . just as I am proud of you."